Penthouse
Uncensored IV

Penthouse Uncensored IV

By the Editors of *Penthouse* Magazine

GRAND CENTRAL
PUBLISHING

NEW YORK   BOSTON

Grand Central Publishing
Hachette Book Group
237 Park Avenue
New York, NY 10017

www.HachetteBookGroup.com

Printed in the United States of America

First Compilation Edition: August 2004
10 9 8 7 6 5

Grand Central Publishing is a division of Hachette Book Group, Inc.
The Grand Central Publishing name and logo is a trademark of Hachette Book Group, Inc.

Library of Congress Control Number: 2004101807
ISBN 978-0-446-69243-4

Cover design by Susan Newman
Cover photo by Spencer Rowell / Getty Images
Book design by Charles A. Sutherland

CONTENTS

PART ONE

PART TWO

CONTENTS   vii

Part One

Part One

HIGHWAY, MY WAY

*M*y wife and I have now been married for twenty years. Betty is in her forties and I've just passed my fiftieth birthday.

Our adventure began on a hot Saturday afternoon in the summer. We had been working in the yard and were hot and tired. Around half past four, we went indoors and I mixed us a couple of gin and tonics. As we relaxed with our drinks and talked, Betty suddenly remarked that she did not know why, but she was getting horny. She asked what I could suggest to ease her longing. I told her to get into something sexy and we would go to a nice restaurant for dinner. She thought that was a great idea, so we showered and got dressed. She wore a tight, sheer blouse with no bra. Her breasts are not truly big, but they are a nice handful, with nice nipples, and they looked very interesting under her blouse. She also wore a full skirt with no panties or slip. I gave her a big kiss and rubbed her titties a bit. I could tell she was getting very excited about the evening ahead.

While we drove to the restaurant I rubbed the insides of her legs so she wouldn't forget we were out for fun. Arriving at our destination, we were told there would be a half-hour wait for a table, so we went into the lounge and sat at the bar. As the bartender took our order, his eyes almost popped upon seeing Betty's breasts pressed against her tight blouse. When he finally went to get our drinks, the other bartender came over with water and napkins so he could get a good look, too. Betty was getting hot from knowing that both guys were turned on by the sight of her.

The bar was not solid in front. It was latticed, with holes about a foot square. Apparently, whenever a sexy female sat at the bar, these guys took advantage of the situation. With my wife there, they kept ducking down behind the bar, as if to look for something. But what they really were doing was looking up her dress. When Betty realized this, she put her feet up on the rung of her stool and pulled her skirt above her knees. When one of the fellows ducked down, she slowly spread her legs apart. Since she wasn't wearing panties, the sight must have been most stimulating.

Deciding to join her game, I reached over and ran my hand slowly up the inside of her thigh to her pussy, which was pretty wet. I slipped one finger, then a second one, into her cunt and soon was having fun frigging her. Then I noticed that one of the bartenders had reached through the bar and had his hand on her leg. I moved mine away and he slid his up all the way to Betty's pussy and slipped two fingers in as I had done.

I don't know if Betty was aware of who was finger-fucking her, but she certainly did enjoy it, getting hotter with every passing moment. Soon she was moving with the motion of his fingers and I knew she would climax shortly. Her breathing became faster and her complexion reddened. All of a sudden she covered her face with her hands. "No," she murmured. "Oh no." And then she came, with just enough fuss for the couples on either side of us to realize what was happening. Fortunately, the hostess came over and told us that our table was ready. As we left the bar, Betty's face was still flushed with excitement.

After dinner, since it was still hot outdoors, I rolled down the car windows so there would be plenty of fresh air. Before starting the engine to drive home, I slid over close to Betty, put my arm around her and gave her a big kiss. I started to play with her titties, too, and I could tell this pleased her greatly. I unbuttoned her blouse and pulled each side of it around her back, where I tucked the tails into the waistband of her skirt. Now the whole front of her torso was naked. I played with her breasts, massaging them and gently squeezing the nipples. Then, with my left hand, I pushed her skirt up above her waist. Her pussy was exposed. I slid my hand up her thigh. She opened her legs wider and then put her right foot up on the seat. This caused her pussy to be pulled wide open. I put two fingers inside and slid them in and out and around her hole. With my right hand I was still feeling her titties and nipples.

She was so passionate by now that I thought someone else ought to enjoy watching her. We drove from the parking lot and headed toward home. The road, a four-lane highway with a center divider, was not crowded. I drove in the left lane so that the other cars would be on my right and, at stoplights, the people in them could get a good look at Betty, who had pulled down her skirt to where it belonged but left her blouse wide open and her breasts fully exposed.

At the first red light we encountered, a small van stopped alongside us. The driver, a nice-looking young man, was watching as I rubbed Betty's breasts. His eyes opened wide. Betty just looked at him and smiled.

The light changed to green and I started for the next one, about four blocks ahead. I was lucky because it changed to red just as I drew up to it. Again I put my right arm around Betty and played with her titties and nipples, but I also put my left hand between her legs and slid it up to her cunt, raising the skirt as I did so. The van had stayed with us and pulled up alongside. Since his seat was a bit higher than ours, the driver had a clear view of Betty being played with. His girlfriend, whom I hadn't seen before, was sitting next to him, enjoying the sight of everything I was doing to Betty.

The light turned green and off we went again, with the van right beside us. The next stop was a long one, because there was a four-road intersection. As we slowed to a halt, Betty turned to face the window and put her right leg up on the seat. When I'd stopped the car, I pulled her skirt up above her waist, so both her pussy and her titties were now completely in view of the couple in the van. I knew I would have more than three minutes at this light, so I began more leisurely to finger Betty's pussy with my left hand and rub her titties with my right. In the meantime, the girl in the van pulled her sweater up to expose a beautiful pair of breasts, which her boyfriend was busy feeling.

By now I had Betty so hot that she couldn't sit still. The pace of my finger-fucking was getting faster and faster and she was doing her best to engulf my fingers in her cunt. With words of encouragement from the couple in the van, Betty moved against my fingers as if they were my cock. Then, suddenly, she excitedly cried out and came right there in front of us all. I continued working my fingers in her and she kept having orgasms for a while longer. The couple in the van applauded—and then the driver suggested that we all park off the road ahead so he could get closer to what he had been watching me play with.

When the light turned green, I pulled ahead and parked at the curb. The van stopped right behind us. The couple got out, walked up to the door on Betty's side and opened it. Betty, meanwhile, had not changed position, so she sat facing the door with her crotch and titties exposed. The couple, after introducing themselves as Harvey and Lucy, just gaped for a few moments at Betty's naked parts. Harvey then began playing with her breasts with one hand while reaching with the other for her cunt. He soon had a couple of his fingers inside her hole. Lucy figured that looked like fun, so she reached over and slipped one of her fingers into Betty's pussy, fondling her tits with her other hand.

By this time, Betty was writhing on the seat. She was being simultaneously finger-fucked by Harvey and Lucy. In a few minutes she started bucking against their fingers, faster and faster, and then—bang!—she came in a wild orgasm. It lasted almost a minute, and then, I would guess, she had a series of three or four smaller orgasms before calming down. Harvey and Lucy rubbed her cunt and titties a little while longer and then said they wanted to show us something.

Harvey pushed Lucy up close to me and then sat on the other

side of her. Lucy reached over, unbuckled his pants and, as Harvey arched his back to help her along, pulled them down to his ankles, along with his shorts. Grabbing his prick, she rubbed it vigorously until it was hard as a rock. Then she slowly engulfed his cock, sliding it inch by inch into her mouth. Her pace quickened as her lips slid up and down the length of his cock until it was glistening with saliva. She poised herself over his erection, facing forward, and pulled her skirt up and her panties down. She leaned forward, giving all of us a good view of her pussy. Harvey played with her pussy awhile, and then she slid down onto his rigid cock. Up and down she went, getting wilder with every second. Harvey helped by pushing his cock into her each time she slid down.

I was so excited that I reached over and pulled Lucy's sweater up to her neck. Betty and I both played with Lucy's titties while she was being screwed, and Betty put one hand around Harvey's prick as it went in and out of Lucy's cunt. Finally, Lucy climaxed and Harvey came immediately afterward.

We all then rested awhile. When we got our breath back, our new friends drove off and Betty and I drove home to a fantastic lovemaking session. Needless to say, it was one night that neither of us will ever forget.

NEVER TOO OLD

I am a senior citizen who lives a few miles from the center of Baltimore. On the day in question, I was driving down to visit friends near Annapolis, a beautiful old colonial town some forty miles away. Along the way, I pulled into a shopping center to get a sandwich and a soda. I parked next to a compact car and noticed a very attractive woman standing in front of it with her hands on her hips. When I got out of my car, she looked at me and shook her head. "Trouble?" I asked.

"I've done some dumb things in my time," she replied, "but locking my keys in the car has to be the dumbest."

I noticed that she had a nice ass and good-looking legs, but her frilly blouse and her jacket kept me from seeing her tits. I guessed she was probably about fifty years of age.

I said, "Well, let's see if I can help you."

About two weeks earlier, I'd found a large ball peen hammer on a road and thrown it into the trunk of my car. Now I opened the trunk, picked up the hammer and jokingly said, "Does it make any difference which window I break?"

"Oh, no," she said. "Don't do that. I'll get a cab and go home to get my other set of . . ." She stopped talking for a moment, then said, "No, I can't do that because all my other keys are in my purse—and that's locked in the car, too."

I laughed and put the hammer back in the trunk. Picking up a Slim Jim, I said, "I'll take care of it."

She looked at the tool in my hand and said, "You mean you are going to break one of the windows with that?"

"Stand in back of the car, look the other way, put your hands over your ears," I told her. "I'll let you know when you can look. I'll give you my wallet to hold, just so you'll know I won't steal your car." I tried the door on the driver's side a few times, but with no success. I then went around to the passenger's side and, on my second try, I sprang the lock, opened the door, removed the keys from the ignition and said in my most gallant tone, "Here are your keys, madam. I'll take my wallet back now, thank you. It has some secret telephone numbers in it that I wouldn't want you to see." I said it with the most friendly smile I could muster.

She couldn't get over how quickly I'd opened the door, so I showed her how a Slim Jim works. She was ever so grateful and offered to pay me for being "such a wonderful locksmith." When I refused to accept her money, she asked where I was headed. I told her that I was driving down to Annapolis to see friends. "That's not very far," she said. "Please, let me buy you lunch before you continue your trip." She told me that the restaurant in the shopping mall served a terrific bacon, lettuce and tomato sandwich. I accepted her invitation and we walked to the restaurant, where the waitress knew her. Besides a BLT for each of us, she ordered a bottle of wine. My new friend and I engaged in a lot of small talk, during which I mentioned that I like to go crabbing on the Eastern Shore in the summertime. She told me that she knew where to catch really big blue crabs near the mouth of the Chesapeake Bay.

Then she told me that she was the caretaker of a large shore home that was situated only about three miles south of the shopping center. She also told me that her employer did a lot of crabbing. "If you like," she said, "I'll show you the place."

She was a very good-looking woman with a winning personality. When I asked if I might encounter a jealous husband, she replied, "Hardly. I've been a widow for over six years."

When we got to the place, I saw a spacious bungalow. The grounds were large and well-kept. In the two-car garage sat a pretty, two-tone Cadillac. She told me that her employer used the Caddy only for things like business meetings and special occasions.

At the rear of the house, the grounds sloped down to a shaped pier that extended about sixty feet from shore, and she pointed out the swimming area to me. About thirty feet to the left was another pier. An adjoining boathouse contained a twenty-eight-foot cabin cruiser that was out of the water, suspended by slings. The boat had recently been painted and was ready for the summer, still three months away. My hostess showed me how the boat could be lowered and raised on the slings, and when she closed the winch controls and turned around, we were standing face-to-face. Without a word she put her arms around me, and we were locked in an embrace. We kissed passionately, and then she said, "I decided during lunch that I wanted to do that. I hope I don't have to apologize for being so forward." My answer was to lean forward for another kiss, and I noticed that her lips were parted to receive my eager tongue. As she Frenched me, I let my right hand drop lower and lower, until I was holding the left cheek of her ass—and it felt great! She apparently was enjoying it every bit as much as I was. Next I went to work on the interior of her mouth with my tongue. She began moaning and groaning. She moved her groin against mine and her breathing became irregular. I really think that she had at least one orgasm just from these preliminary activities.

We finally let up, and she said, "Come on. I'll show you the rest of the place." Beyond the boathouse was another building that housed two rowboats, a couple of outboard-powered vessels, and a whole lot of tackle and gear for crabbing, fishing, waterskiing and various other water sports, all of it neatly stowed in its proper place.

The house itself was spotless. The basement contained a utility room for washing clothes, a bathroom, a Ping-Pong table and a standard-size pool table. She mentioned that the owner liked to shoot pool and was a pretty good shot. I said that I'd like to challenge him to a game someday, to which she smiled enigmatically and said that such a match was a very distinct possibility.

The ground floor of the house included a beautiful kitchen-dinette, living room, bathroom and one large and one medium bedroom. Everything was clean and attractive. In the large bedroom I noticed a picture of a handsome man on the bureau. A few minutes later, while I was examining an old print of a sailing ship, I saw her put the picture of the man into a bureau drawer.

We got into another clinch, but not before she had removed her jacket and I'd seen that her tits were small. That was entirely okay with me, however, because I prefer small boobs. During lovemaking, I like to be able to fit a whole breast in my mouth.

She was really getting excited as I French-kissed her and played with her tits. When we finally broke, she said, "My bust isn't very big, but it sure is sensitive. In fact, it's one of my weak spots." I assured her that her breasts were just right for me, which seemed to make her very happy. As we moved toward the bed and lay across it, I continued kissing her and removed her frilly blouse and bra. Her firm tits had beautiful rose-colored nipples that were getting harder by the second. I kissed her forehead, her eyes, her neck and then one of her tits, causing her to moan and her body to tremble. I know that she had another orgasm then.

I started kissing her from her tits down across her stomach to her sweet-smelling mound. When I got there, she covered her pussy with one hand and pushed my head away with the other, so I worked my way back up to her tits and started all over again. The same thing happened again when I got down near her cunt. The next time, as I was kissing her belly all over and she was moaning with pleasure, I put my hand into her panties and, with her cooperation, slid them off. I think she must have thought I was going to fuck her then and there, because she raised her legs high in the air. But I quickly put my middle finger into her pussy, simultaneously kissing her pearly love button. At that, she lifted her ass at least a foot off the bed and screamed, "Oh! Oh! Oh!"

I worked on her clit and cunt hole with my fingers, causing her to have orgasm after orgasm. She held me there so firmly that I couldn't have pulled away gracefully even if I had wanted to. When I finally let up, she put her hands on my face and said, "What you just did to me was wonderful. I enjoyed every moment of it, but we'd better stop." She told me that she had been celibate since her husband passed away six years ago. She added that she sure didn't want to get pregnant at this age. Rubbing my hard-on against her leg, I told her not to worry, that I'd go out to my car and get a rubber. She said she would wash up while I was gone, and I ran out to my car as fast as I could.

She was still in the bathroom when I returned. After another fifteen minutes or so, she emerged in a pretty negligee. (I think she had taken a douche.) We promptly got into it again and it wasn't long before her negligee was off. I started kissing her pussy again, and she didn't deny me this time. After I tongued her awhile, she lifted her ass again. I kept running my tongue from her clit to her absolutely delicious cunt hole, sending wave after wave of excitement through her body. She kept moaning and pressing her crotch against my busy mouth until she must have come three or four times.

Finally, I put the rubber on, coated it with K-Y jelly and started to enter her, inch by inch. I was surprised at how tight she was, considering her age and the fact that she was so wet. So I took my time, and it felt exquisite. After I got all the way in, I stopped to let her cunt adjust to my size, but then she took over and started humping me hard. She kept it up, using everything she had, and I started to pound into her, too. She locked her legs around my back and went right along with me, never missing a stroke.

Finally, when she started pumping faster and let out a hell of a scream, I knew she was peaking. I kept pumping away. When she screamed again, I let go of my wad.

Afterward, I just lay there for a few minutes to regain my composure. She did the same. Her eyes were closed and she was breathing heavily. For a moment, I thought she had passed out, but then she opened her eyes and looked at me. She pulled my head down and gave me a long kiss. My flaccid cock was still in her. "You have made me do something that I haven't done in an awfully long time," she said. "I enjoyed every second of it. In fact, it was fantastic. I'd never had sex like that before." She said she had no idea of how many times she had come, since she hadn't bothered to count. When I pulled out of her, she moaned a soft sound of disapproval. I lay there, cuddling her and talking, and I found it hard to believe when she told me she was sixty-three years old. She told me that her late husband would kiss and hug her awhile, rub her titties, run a hand around her crotch a little and then put on a rubber and screw her. He'd been okay in bed, she said, because be nearly always gave her an orgasm. But he had rarely kissed her on the mouth, the titties or anywhere else. Certainly he would never have done what I had just done.

I began kissing her and playing with her tits again, and it was obvious that she was getting aroused. She asked if I had another rubber. When I said yes, she said, "Why don't you take a quick shower in the basement while I shower here—then we can continue our discussion?"

That's just what we did, and, when we reconvened, she had on an even sexier negligee, but I took that off pretty quickly. Again I started at her forehead and kissed my way down her body. Before I even got to her nipples, she was squirming and moaning and groaning with passion. When I got to her clit, I kept pulling on it with my lips, which really set her on fire. Her clitoris was almost an inch long. As I mouthed it, I couldn't believe the jumping and bouncing she was doing on that bed— the sheet was soaking wet from the juices that flowed from her cunt.

I had some difficulty getting another full erection. Even so, although I was only about half hard, I told her to get on her hands and knees. She was reluctant at first. But when I promised not to hurt her, she did get down—and I entered her pussy slowly, doggie-style, and only then did I get a full erection. I must have pumped in and out of her for more than twenty minutes while playing with her clit and titties. It was unbelievable how she kept having orgasms. When it appeared that she was about to collapse on the bed, I held her up by her hips until I unleashed my jism, filling the entire reservoir at the tip of the rubber.

After we'd rested awhile and gotten dressed, she told me she could not believe that she'd ever have another sexual experience to match this one, but she looked forward to doing it again in the near future. She reminded me that the crabbing season was still a good ways off, but that was no reason for me not to pay her a lot of visits. I took her phone number and promised to keep in touch so she could let me know when the owner was away again. "I am the owner," she confessed. "I didn't lie to you. All I said was that the owner was away, which was true." She told me that her husband had owned a trucking company that he'd built up from scratch and it now belonged to her. She had a fleet of eighteen dump trucks. Her brother ran the business. He and his wife resided next door to her. He'd often suggested that she should go out with some nice fellow once in a while and enjoy herself, but she hadn't followed his advice. She had gone out with one guy, but he came on too strong, trying to run his hand up her dress before they even sat down to dinner. She just wasn't ready for anything like that so soon after her husband had passed away.

As I was getting into my car, her brother arrived and she introduced me to him. He was a good-looking, well-built man who gave me a firm handshake. He said he had seen my car in the driveway and thought he'd better check it out. She told him that I would be coming back to go crabbing when the season began. I think he suspected that his sister and I had been intimate that afternoon. When he left, he seemed to wink at me.

As soon as her brother was out of sight, she gave me another big hug and kiss. She said she hoped I wouldn't forget her too soon. I assured her that I would be back real soon. I could never forget a wonderful woman like her.

Oh, one more thing. She never asked me if I was married, which I am.

RAINY DAY PLAY

$\mathcal{T}$he October afternoon was warm, the sky cloudless and blue—an ideal Indian summer day. I was on vacation and headed for what we in Wisconsin refer to as "up north," a mythical land of pristine wilderness that exists primarily in people's imaginations. Still, it is possible to find pockets of solitude there during this time of year. I was headed for one now, a small national-forest campground that is seldom used after the summer tourist season.

Anticipating a leisurely week of fishing, canoeing and hiking, I drove unhurriedly, stopping often to enjoy the weather and fall foliage that was now at its prime. Crimson maples, golden birches, terra-cotta oaks, all glowing in a final blaze of glory before the snows of winter fall to lock the land in mystery and frigid silence.

It was dark by the time I reached my destination. I was disappointed to find that a single tent was pitched in the otherwise vacant campground, a two-person mountain tent set up next to a Toyota that bore a canoe on its roof. Probably a couple or two guys out for some fall fishing, I thought. My favorite spot was unoccupied and well away from the other tent, so my good spirits returned as I pitched camp by the light of my gas lantern. I erected my four-man tent and stowed my gear inside. I hung a tarp over my small picnic table. The food and cooking gear remained in the back of my car as a precaution against furry things that go bump in the night. Then I hauled my canoe to the lake, leaving it on the shore. Finally, I visited the rustic facilities and retired to my tent to grab a few Z's before dawn.

The beautiful dawn I expected didn't come. The sky was dark, dirty and gray when I awoke. A steady downpour beat against the tent. The campsite was awash in rain. Donning damp clothes and a rainsuit, I visited the facilities before squishing along the muddy trail to the lakeshore. Angry black clouds scudded low over the lake out of the northwest. White-caps churned across the steel-gray waters. The slanting rain obscured the opposite shore. I thought about yesterday's sun and warmth as I returned glumly to my tent to catch more sleep. Soon I was snug and warm in my downy cocoon, dozing contentedly. The rain was thrumming a monotonous staccato against the tent.

"Hello in the tent!"

I abruptly became fully awake. Did I hear a voice just now? I wondered. A woman's voice? I was dreaming, I supposed.

"Please, can I come in? It's cold out here and I'm soaked to the skin."

A voice indeed. "Sure, come on in!" I replied.

The tent flap flew open and a soggy figure in jeans, flannel shirt and untied hiking boots appeared. The tent flap was quickly closed and zipped up.

"Thanks," said the soggy visitor in a husky, unmistakably feminine voice. "My tent is flooded, everything is soaked, and I'm really freezing my ass off! Have you got a catalytic heater or something?"

She was tall, about five feet seven, and in her mid-twenties. Pretty face. Long, wavy, raven-black hair. The part of her encased in wet jeans looked very nice, but it was hard to tell about the part in the flannel shirt.

"No catalytic heater, but I've got the 'or something,'" I replied.

She stood, shivering and shaking. I reached into my clothes box, took out a beach towel and tossed it to her.

"Get out of those wet clothes and dry off," I ordered.

She hesitated for an instant, then stripped to the buff and dried herself vigorously with the fluffy towel. She looked very nice where the flannel shirt had been, too. Jiggling invitingly as she toweled herself, her firm, upturned breasts, tipped with bing-cherry nipples, looked delicious. Her stomach was flat and well-toned. Curving from her narrow waist, her rounded hips led my appreciative gaze down to her long, shapely legs. Milk-white bikini marks contrasted boldly against her deep tan. Her naked body radiated an unmistakable aura of femininity coupled with uncommon physical strength. To me she was the personification of Diana, Roman goddess of the moon and of the forest.

While she dried herself off, I unzipped my down-lined sleeping bag and formed it into a blanket. I also unrolled my other, synthetic-filled bag, unzipped that and then quickly spread it on top of the foam sleeping pads that I'd placed on the tent floor. She stood naked and dry now, but was still shaking and covered with goose bumps.

"You look like you're on the edge of hypothermia," I said. "Lie down next to me under my sleeping bag."

I lifted the edge of the cover to reveal the potential warmth that awaited her. She burrowed beneath the covers without hesitation, eager for some heat. Her teeth chattered with cold. I turned on my side to face away from her. "Press yourself against my back and absorb my body heat," I suggested.

She snuggled against me, and I flinched at the shock of her frigid body against my warm flesh. It was like cuddling with an ice block. Gradually, though, she began to thaw. Her shivering ceased, her goose bumps vanished, her body warmed and relaxed. Her breathing grew gentler, rhythmic, and she fell asleep. The rain hissed through the trees and drummed on the tent. I, too, was soon sleeping.

Later, though—I couldn't say how much later—something awoke me. Hard rain was still pelting the tent. The light level was about that of a candlelit restaurant. Gradually I became aware of my guest's fingertips brushing softly up and down my side, the pressure of her pliant breasts against my back.

"Good morning," I said. "I trust that you're fully warmed up now?"

"Mmm, like a piece of toast. Thanks for the use of the heater," she replied.

"Anytime at all. Stay and use it for as long as you like. And by the way, my name is Carl."

"And I'm Sandy. Pleased to meet you."

Except for the sound of the rain, there was a moment of silence. Her hand continued to stray up and down my side.

"So, what would you suggest a couple of campers do on a rainy day like this?" I asked lamely. "Got any board games in your pocket?"

"I'm fresh out of pockets right now," she said while feigning a search for them. "Hmm, doesn't appear you've got any at the moment either." She lifted the sleeping bag to peer underneath. "Nope, no pockets, but I do like the colors you wear. I'd venture to say that a man who wears red-striped black underwear is probably not boring and that he can manage quite well without any 'bored' games."

We laughed as she molded herself to the contours of my back

again. Her hand started caressing my side again. Her feathery pubic mound now began undulating slowly against my rump.

"I think I know what we can do," she breathed into my ear. "Good way to generate more heat."

This Diana is no virgin, I thought. "Great way to pass a dreary day, too," I said.

Sandy's stroking fingers now began to explore farther afield. Down my side to the top of my briefs they went, there to move teasingly back and forth above my pubic hair as they probed beneath my waistband. My member twitched with anticipation as her curious hand came closer and closer to it. But then her hand retreated to my navel and up to my chest to massage and stroke my pectorals. My throbbing cock hardened and grew nevertheless, until the swollen glans peeked above the top of my briefs.

"Nice body," Sandy purred. "Hard and soft, all at the same time."

Her hand then drifted down to my waistband again. Her index finger circled lightly around the apex of my pulsating erection. The first drops of love-lotion oozed from the hole there.

"My, what a friendly fellow," Sandy whispered. "It feels to me like he's really anxious to come out and play."

Getting to her knees in a single, graceful movement, she threw off the sleeping-bag cover and straddled my legs as I rolled over on my back. She peeled off my briefs like the skin of a banana. My seven-inch phallus stood tall and proud. Sandy bent and cradled it in both hands as if it were a bird or a helpless kitten. The index finger of her right hand rubbed the red glans until a few more droplets of my pre-come fluid emerged. She massaged the slick secretion into the head and the thick shaft. Electric sensations radiated through every nerve in my body. More cock cream dripped from my excited nozzle. Sandy collected it in her cupped hands, raised it to her lips and lapped it up.

"Finger-lickin' good," she said, smacking her lips. And she bent again, teasing my cock lightly with her lovely mouth. Her long hair tumbled down to brush my belly. She looked up coyly and flung her hair back over her shoulders. "You'll enjoy it more if you can watch the action," she explained. "Now spread your legs."

When I did as I was told, Sandy lay down between them. She brushed her rosy nipples across my cockhead several times before lowering herself to smother my overjoyed phallus in the cleavage of her satin-soft breasts. After several minutes of tit-fucking me, she slid down farther and took the root of my slippery shaft in her right hand. Then she began licking it from base to tip as if it were a Popsicle. I sighed in ecstasy when her sweet lips encircled the cap while her tongue continued its sweet titillation. Her head finally went down on my seven-incher, which gradually disappeared into the depths of her velvet mouth. She played my flesh flute like a virtuoso, building and heightening the intensity of pleasure that surged through my being, bringing me to the very brink of a climactic explosion—and then she stopped what she was doing!

"There." She grinned. "So much for the appetizer." Sandy got on her knees again, straddled my hips and brushed her hedge over my erect probe. She moved forward, rubbing her pussy against my stomach and chest. She stopped when her soft heather was right above my face.

"Eat it," she said hotly.

"My pleasure," I replied.

I licked her inner thighs, tantalizing but not yet touching her labial lips. I worked up and around her downy mound to her navel, which I attacked vigorously with my tongue. Then, running my mouth over her taut stomach, I began a meandering return to her impatient cunt. Sandy leaned back, raised her hips, grabbed her ankles and braced herself in this position. The entrance to her pleasure purse opened slightly, revealing a bright pink interior that glistened with love-honey. I grabbed her taut haunches with both hands and plunged my tongue deep inside her, determined to lick and suck her dry.

"Oh God! That's it!" Sandy exulted. She raised herself up,

took hold of my head, pressed my face hard against her flaming womanhood and started rocking to the rhythm of my oral probing. I licked her engorged love-bud, explored the depths of her passion pit, drank deeply of her flowing nectar. When I sensed that she was close to coming, I reluctantly withdrew from her sweet honey-pot, not wanting to bring her to climax just yet. Sandy released her grip. She sat limply astride my legs. Her eyes remained closed and a dreamy smile played across her flushed face. Droplets arisen from sexual arousal clung to her pubic fur like sparkling dew. Sliding my fingers within, I collected a handful of her warm juices and rubbed them well into her heaving breasts. Twice more I did this, until her tits and nipples glistened with her own lotions. I fondled her slippery globes and lovingly pinched the hard, brown bullets at the tips.

Sandy growled with sensual satisfaction. She loved it. She leaned forward to press both her fleshy mounds against my rotating palms. Sometimes she'd put her hands over mine and guide me to the places she wanted me to pet. Soon I took her by the shoulders and brought her down on top of me. Our lips met and locked. I tasted my own pre-come as our tongues dueled wildly.

After several dizzying minutes, I broke off the kiss and moved my lips to her chin, her neck, her pussy-lotion-drenched breasts. I licked and sucked her nipples, and buried my face in the valley of her cleavage. The taste and smell of her, the feel of those firm mounds, drove me to a frenzy of desire. My joystick pulsed and quivered. I wanted to shove it all the way into her tight, wet cunt!

Sandy was hot, too. She slid down along my body until she sat astride my thighs again. She took my erection in her hands, raised herself to her knees and poised her dripping cunt over my trembling cock. Slowly she impaled herself on my flaming dagger, taking it to the hilt within her moist, satin sheath.

"Time for the entrée," she whispered.

Sandy's vaginal muscles caressed my rod while she herself sat motionless. Then she began to rotate her hips while still flexing her vaginal muscles. My organ's throbbing became more pronounced. Sandy closed her eyes and started to rub her tits and knead her nipples with both hands. Her internal muscles began squeezing harder. She was soon humping up and down and round and round. I began to moan with pleasure.

Sandy's right hand moved down between her legs to finger her clit. Her left continued working over her breasts. Faster and faster she pumped my cock with her pussy. I grabbed her tight buns and thrust up to meet her every bump and grind. The tension grew. Sandy's gasps and moans told me that her pleasure was waxing as well. Finally my pulsing probe couldn't stand it any longer. It spewed its milky load in a violent series of eruptions. Every contraction of my cock sent waves of delight leaping across the synapses of my nerves.

At the same time, Sandy was trembling in the throes of her own convulsive climax. Her body arched and stiffened. She cried out in ecstasy. Her proud breasts bounced with the rhythm of her humping, which was controlled in turn by the sensual spasms of her multiple orgasms.

Our chests heaving from our exertions, we wound down from our shared sexual high, experiencing the waning tingles of the afterglow. My wearied cock shrunk and slid out of her. Sandy collapsed happily into my arms. I pulled the sleeping bag over our exhausted bodies to preserve the warmth we had generated. Sandy nuzzled her cheek against my neck. Her hair cascaded over my arm and shoulder.

"I'm glad my tent flooded," she whispered in my ear.

"Hope it stays flooded," I replied.

"Oh, I think it'll probably be too wet to use for the rest of the week," she countered with a sly grin.

Outside, the rain pattered insistently against the roof of the tent.

TALES FROM THE DARK SIDE

*R*ecently my wife Jenny began taking exercise classes at the local health spa, though she did not really need to. Her 36-23-34 figure needs no improvement, but she said that she was alone too much and bored because I work six days a week.

One afternoon I happened to finish work early and decided to meet my wife at the club. Since my waistline was getting out of hand, I wanted to see if it was worth my becoming a club member, too. When I arrived I found a couple of men there, working out on the machines. I asked if they had seen a redheaded young woman, to which they replied that I might find her in the Jacuzzi.

Sure enough, as I approached the hot tub I heard my wife's tinkling laughter. Then I heard the deep tones of a man's voice. She and he were both laughing as I peered around the corner. Jenny was sitting on the edge of the Jacuzzi in a new bathing suit, a gauzy one-piece, cut high on the sides and dipping deep in the front and back. The suit surprised me, since Jenny had never before bought anything that revealed such an amount of skin. This was the first time I had seen her in the suit, and I was really surprised at its lack of cover. The high-cut sides emphasized Jenny's long, lithe legs. The low scoop in front reached below her swelling breasts, exposing at least half of each snowy orb.

After gaping at my wife, I turned my attention to the man who was with her. He was a perfect male specimen, with broad shoulders and a hard, flat stomach. His thighs were like tree trunks and every part of his body was muscled. All he had on was orange bikini briefs. Perhaps the most amazing thing about his appearance was the deep ebony tone of his skin. He was the darkest black man I have ever seen. His hair was short and a thin growth of hair adorned his chest.

Then my wife said, "Thomas, this is ridiculous. What would happen if someone were to come in right now?"

"Babe, don't worry," he replied. "I told the boys outside to steer

everyone clear of this Jacuzzi until they hear otherwise from me."
Thomas then leaned over and took my wife in his massive arms.

Talk about being stunned! My wife comes from a southern
Baptist family that espoused hatred for blacks. In fact, I know her
father was a member of the Klan. This knowledge—together with
the fact that Jenny was a virgin when we met, and stayed that
way until our wedding night—caused me to stand there with my
mouth wide open. As far as I knew, her pussy had known no other
cock but mine.

So I just stood and watched as Jenny brought her full, red lips
to meet Thomas's lips. He caressed her shoulders as their tongues
played a cat-and-mouse game. They continued to kiss as his
hands moved from her shoulders to her neck. He then began to
trace a finger down her cleavage and cupped her right breast.
Thomas's black hand began to slowly knead my wife's full round
tit. He seemed content just to squeeze the fleshy mound through
the thin material of her suit. As the nipple grew stiff under his
massaging, he began to pinch it.

"Baby, you have to have the greatest tits I have ever seen,"
Thomas commented as he continued toying with Jenny's nipple.
Her only reply was to take hold of his head and urge him on as he
kissed his way down her neck. With one hand still on her breast,
Thomas placed his other hand on Jenny's thigh. I watched this
invader begin a slow journey to the junction of her legs until it
made contact with her nylon-covered cunt.

Thomas then ran a finger lightly along the thin strip of fabric,
eliciting a deep sigh from my wife. He began to massage her pussy
through her suit. Jenny was in seventh heaven as her breasts and
her pussy were expertly rubbed by this black Adonis. I didn't
know what to do, whether to rush in and break it up or just to
stay and continue watching (I know I had the biggest hard-on
ever).

Suddenly Thomas went for broke and inserted a finger under
the nylon that covered Jenny's cunt. I watched in fascination the
finger-fucking that she was getting. Soon his other hand deftly

pulled the crotch of her bathing suit to one side, exposing her glistening cunt. Thomas's fat finger, diving repeatedly in and out of my wife's pussy, became coated with her love juices. Her bright red cunt hairs made the darkness of his finger stand out as it dug itself deeper in Jenny's cunt.

The finger-fucking continued for a few minutes. Then, between the kisses he was planting on my wife's breasts (which he had now removed from their covering), Thomas said, "Jenny, sweetheart, feel me. See how hard I am." Jenny slid her hand down to the crotch of his suit. It looked like a bulging orange tent and her hand looked tiny as it gently stroked his huge cock through the swimsuit. "Come on, honey. You know you've been dying to see ol' Henry since you first started coming here, huh?" (That solved the mystery of whether or not they had done this before.) "How about letting my love-stick have a little air?" he added.

Jenny pulled the drawstring of his bikini and, like a jack-in-the-box, Thomas's cock sprang up. It was at least ten inches long, with a shaft as thick as a Pepsi bottle. I was amazed at the sparseness of pubic hair surrounding this monster. The gargantuan size of his balls defied description.

Jenny seemed to be fascinated by this totem of manhood, and some time passed before she could move her hand to touch it. Thomas leaned back on his elbows and watched my wife play with his dick.

"I know you're just dyin' to taste my cock, aren't you?" Thomas said to her. I knew he was asking too much. Jenny had always detested sucking cock, and told me so in no uncertain terms on our wedding night. Imagine my surprise, therefore, when my wife leaned over and almost touched the tip of his cock with her lips. I stood transfixed as she looked up and smiled at Thomas and then ran her tongue up and down his mighty shaft. She maintained eye contact with him as she swirled her tongue all over the helmet of his cock. When she began to swallow the black monster, I couldn't believe what I was seeing. First, the huge head disappeared in her mouth—then, inch by inch, she took nearly half of his cock in her mouth. It glistened with Jenny's saliva as she let it slide slowly out of her mouth. Just as slowly, she then let it sink back between her lips.

"God, you do that good!" Thomas said. "I bet you don't suck your ol' man this way, do you, honey? (Boy, was he right!) I love watchin' my cock sink between your lips. That's it! Take more! Try to get more into your gorgeous mouth, baby."

Thomas gripped Jenny's head and began to fuck her mouth. His rod pistoned relentlessly between her lips, and she grabbed his hips, trying to shove more of that cock into her mouth. "Baby," he said, "there ain't no way you're going to make me fill your white mouth with my seed. Ol' Henry has a date with a red-head."

With that, Thomas extracted his cock from my wife's mouth. He had her lie down on the bare white tiles. When he stood up in the water, he towered over her. I watched with wide eyes as he lowered his trunks and leaned over Jenny's body. Pulling the crotch of her swimsuit to one side he pressed the tip of his massive black cock against the pink lips of my wife's cunt. "Baby, are you ready for ol' Henry?" he asked teasingly.

"Yes! Put your penis in me now," Jenny begged between low moans.

"Penis, baby? This here is ol' Henry, king of pussies, about to conquer again." With that, Thomas parted Jenny's pussy lips and pushed a couple of inches of his meat between them. A low animal groan escaped from her throat as inch after inch slipped into her eager snatch. I figured there was no way she could take in all of Thomas's rod, for she had always had problems with my seven inches. Jenny writhed upon the wet tiles as Thomas sank more and more of his cock into her. I could only stare dumbfounded when the last few inches finally disappeared into her. Only his gigantic balls and a thatch of intermeshed red and black pubic hair remained visible as Thomas, his great cock buried entirely in my wife, began humping his body in unison with hers.

Jenny held Thomas's taut ass as she pushed her cunt against his pounding cock. Thomas increased the tempo of his pumping, placing his hand under my wife's ass. Like a jackhammer, he kept ramming his thick cock deep into her cunt, grabbing and squeezing her supple buns, pulling her harder against him. Jenny could only grunt with each stroke as her black lover thrust the instrument of his passion into her, again and again. "Yeah, baby! Fuck me like you never fucked before!" Thomas chanted.

In response, Jenny somehow raised her hips from the tiles and, with Thomas's hand supporting her, she arched her back to engulf even more of that rampaging cock. Thomas began to grunt louder as he increased the power and pace of the fucking he was giving my wife's pussy. With a final groan, he began coming—and it seemed to me that he continued coming for an eternity. But, finally, he slowed his strokes and a rivulet of pearly white jism seeped between his cock and Jenny's pussy. He finally stopped humping but continued holding on to her ass, keeping her suspended above the tiles, impaled on his manhood. "Well, how'd I do?" he asked as he withdrew his now-shrinking member.

My wife didn't answer. As she lay back on the tiles, Thomas scooped up a gob of his come and laughingly placed it on Jenny's face. She hungrily lapped it up. "Honey," said Thomas, "it looks like you could use some more loving, but ol' Henry is only good for one performance at a time. If you'll meet me tonight at Sam's Place, though, I'll introduce you to some other boys, okay?"

Instead of answering him, Jenny just scooped up more of his semen and kept feeding herself. Thomas simply laughed, pulled up his suit and turned to leave the room. I ducked into a closet and waited until he'd left. Then I made for the side exit and headed home to wait for Jenny.

When she finally got home, about an hour later, I said nothing of what I'd seen at the spa. I just asked how her workout had gone. She smiled and said it had gone fine. I asked if she wanted to go out that night. Jenny nodded yes and went up to take a bath. While she was in the bathroom, I asked her where she wanted to go. After a few seconds of hesitation, she said, "How about Sam's Place?"

"You mean the strip joint?" I asked. "Okay, that'll be fine." That was all I could blurt out as my mind screamed "Bingo!" When she began dressing, I could only stare. Jenny was putting on my favorite of her outfits. It was an aqua-blue dress that didn't quite reach her knees. It was cut low enough in front to show just a hint of cleavage (her most daring dress).

"Special night, tonight?" I asked.

She hesitated before answering. "Not really," she said. "I just wanted to look nice for you, honey."

I laid my plans as I drove our van to Sam's. My intention was to see just how far my newly brazen hussy would go. To my surprise, I was looking forward to my wife's making it with another guy.

When we got to Sam's, I parked and escorted Jenny inside. It was a singles hangout. Several women were dancing around the room in various stages of undress. The rest of the room was dark and full of small tables. When we sat down, I saw a sign that said Amateur Night and wondered what it meant. After waiting vainly for someone to take our order, I got up to get drinks at the bar. As I walked across the room, I looked around for Thomas and his friends. After getting the drinks and turning to go back to the booth, I saw Thomas appear as if out of thin air. He was sitting next to my Jenny with two of his friends. I moved to one side and worked my way across the crowded dance floor until I was behind the booth.

"So why did you come, if not to see me and my friends, Jenny, babe?" I overheard him say.

"But my husband's here with me," Jenny protested. "I can't let him see us together."

"That wimp!" Thomas croaked. "I can take care of him."

"Do that," Jenny warned, "and you'll never see me again. Got it, sweetheart?"

"Sure, babe. Anything you say. But what are you doing here if you didn't come to see ol' Henry and company?"

"I don't really know right now, okay?"

"Sure, but we'll only wait a little while for you to make up your mind."

With that, Thomas and his friends left the booth. I waited a couple of minutes before rejoining Jenny, who had composed herself by then. As we sipped our drinks and talked, I noticed that she kept glancing at the bar, where Thomas sat with his friends. After a few drinks, Jenny loosened up and began to laugh and giggle. We danced a few dances, during which she sort of dry-humped me. I was really beginning to get amused by this, but then the club manager announced that the amateur-night competition was about to begin. This evening, he explained, it would be a striptease contest, and he proceeded to pick women from the audience. A few, with encouragement from their mates, accepted the challenge. When he asked Jenny to perform, my heart skipped a beat. Although she could dance like a pro, I was surprised when she coyly accepted the offer.

The manager and five contestants went backstage and, a few minutes later, the competition began. I awaited Jenny's turn nervously. She was last to perform (the first four contestants were average at best). Dancing to Ravel's "Boléro," she was in fine form, twirling her skirt so that, every now and then, you could see her perfectly formed thighs and a flash of her panties. As the tempo of the music increased, it really got Jenny going. She reached back and slowly unzipped her dress. With a sensuous shrug of her shoulders, the dress slid to the floor—and my wife was standing there in only a matching bra-and-panties set I had given her. The bra was barely large enough to enclose her full breasts. You could tell how excited she was from the size and hardness of her nipples, plainly visible through the filmy silk. Her tiny panties were also of silk, with lace inserts.

Jenny continued to prance about the small stage and then climbed on the bar. Still swaying to the music, she now began to give a show to those seated at her feet, including Thomas. Some guys reached out to caress her long legs, and several began waving money at her.

Jenny danced over to one and stooped so he could insert a bill in the waistband of her panties. This really got the crowd going (none of the other dancers had been so bold). Encouraged by the crowd's applause and shouts of approval, Jenny moved close to Thomas, who obviously was enjoying the show in a big way. Jenny smiled and began to dance especially for him.

Thomas took a bill from his wallet and waved it at her. She squatted to allow him to put the bill in her waistband. As the crowd chanted "Lower! Lower!" Thomas reached out and hooked a finger under Jenny's waistband. Instead of inserting any money, he proceeded to pull down her panties until her whole cunt was showing. Jenny's eyes were closed as she continued swaying her hips, apparently unconcerned that her pussy was in full view. Thomas then cupped my wife's red muff in his hand. I watched as he inserted a finger into her cleft. The crowd was screaming now as my wife rotated on Thomas's finger. After a few moments, she raised herself slightly and hesitated as he stuffed his money between her cunt lips.

The rest of the act was anticlimactic. Needless to say, Jenny won the competition hands down (or, you could say, pants down). Flushed and clutching her dress to her chest, she rushed back to our booth, followed by loud cheers. The luster in her eyes told me how much she had enjoyed her show.

She asked to go out to the van to straighten herself up, and I told her to go ahead. I glanced over to where Thomas was sitting and did not see him. After a few minutes' wait, I went out to the van. The parking lot was dimly lit, but that didn't prevent me from seeing Jenny and Thomas in a deep embrace. They were standing behind the van, and both of its back doors were open. I watched as he raised Jenny's dress over her head. With his big paws, he began to grab and squeeze my wife's tits and pussy through her bra and panties.

"I knew you were one hot honey," he told her. "Your pussy is really dripping, and now you're gonna get it good!"

I saw him stuff his whole hand down into her panties. Jenny leaned against the van as Thomas continued to feel her up. He started to finger-fuck her, causing her to shake and buck. Thomas's two friends then came around the van. One, a tall, skinny guy, reached out and squeezed Jenny's melons. "You were right about this here bitch. She sure is fine," he said as he fondled my Jenny and put his hand down her panties. Tom's was already there, and two hands proved too much for the delicate fabric to contain. It ripped apart and I could see both black hands massaging Jenny's pussy.

"Mama, I bet you want to taste some of my long cock, don't you?" the tall, skinny man said as he snaked his tongue down her neck and shoulders to lick Jenny's nipples through her bra.

Thomas removed his hand from her crotch, gently pushed Jenny into the back of the van and climbed in with his two friends. I went over and peered through the side window as Thomas was removing the remnants of Jenny's clothes. He positioned himself between her raised knees and drove his huge cock into her gaping cunt. Jenny's body was lifted off the van's soft carpeting from the impact of Thomas's driving monster. Meanwhile, the tall, skinny guy went over to Jenny's head. His was one of the longest, slenderest cocks I have ever seen, and he inserted it in her waiting mouth. She devoured this new intruder as it slid back and forth between her lips.

The third black man was grossly fat. When he tired of waiting on the sidelines, he pushed the skinny fellow away and dropped to his knees beside Jenny's head, unzipping his huge trousers as he did so. A large, fat cock popped into view below his great gut. I watched as he draped his limp member across my wife's lips. Automatically she opened her mouth and sucked it in. I stared as it started to grow and harden. Jenny opened her mouth wider than I thought possible to keep the fat black sausage in her mouth, sucking it passionately.

The skinny man squatted over my wife's chest, placing his cock in the valley of her cleavage. Using both hands to mash his meat between her fleshy mounds, he received the tit-fucking of his life.

Jenny was totally abandoned to her lust. She was bucking, squealing, writhing, grunting and groaning uncontrollably from the incredible pleasure of her threeway with these men. Thomas's huge cock continued to piston in her cunt, its blackness contrasting starkly with Jenny's creamy white skin.

About this time I felt a tap on my shoulder and turned to find a policeman aiming his flashlight in my face. I kept silent as he ordered me to leave the parking lot immediately. Not wanting to compromise myself, I simply walked away. When I turned for one last look, I saw the policeman entering the rear of the van!

Unsure of my emotions and needing time to think, I caught a cab and went directly home. I knocked and our son's babysitter opened the door. Karen, a college freshman, who baby-sat to help finance her education, asked how the evening went and where Jenny was. I told her that Jenny was visiting friends and that I didn't care when she came home. Karen sensed that something was wrong. She sat down with me to talk. I had always liked her and felt that she liked me. We always talked about what she was going to do after college. Sitting with her on the couch now, I asked if I could get her something to drink. When she said yes, I went and got us each a cold beer.

As we talked, I began to appreciate Karen's charms. She was wearing a flowery summer dress, and I could make out the faint scent of her perfume. Our conversation became more and more open. Every once in a while she would touch me on my knee as if to make a point. I continued to admire her lithe form. Karen had occasionally swum in our pool, so I knew she had a lovely body. I especially liked her long, slim legs, which were tanned to golden brown. She seemed so innocent—yet so sexy.

Karen finally placed her hand on my knee and didn't remove it. I gazed into her eyes as she talked on about her projected nursing career—only to fall silent and smile a meaningful smile. A tacit understanding arose between us. I took her hand in mine and kissed the tips of her fingers.

I took her in my arms as she raised her lips to mine. Karen whispered of how she had always wanted to make love to me. I could only smile and hold her closer as she told me of her longing for me and how much she'd envied Jenny. My arms wandered over her back as we kissed. Soon Karen's hand began to explore the growing bulge in my trousers. I unbuttoned her dress and Karen stood up to let it fall off. My excitement grew as I stared at her body, which was now in white panties and bra. Karen returned to my arms and our lips touched again. I felt her nipples grow rigid as she rubbed them against my chest. I began to massage her cunt right there in the living room. It wasn't long before we were both naked and she was lying expectantly on the couch. I positioned myself above her and poked my engorged member deep into her, causing her to grunt loudly. I began pounding into her, and she began bucking in a frenzy of lustful desire. Planting her feet on the couch for support, she lifted her pelvis to match me, thrust for thrust. Her ass was at least a foot above the couch.

When I couldn't bold back any longer, I came inside her with a loud grunt. After another moment, she came wildly. We rested awhile with my soft cock still in her, then I slowly withdrew it. Karen kissed me on the cheek, got up, dressed and left without another word—as if nothing had happened. I went upstairs and fell into a deep, if not contented, sleep.

BALLING ALI

I was a virgin when I married at eighteen, and so was my husband. After twenty-two years as a wife and mother I had settled into a comfortable, if unexciting, rut. I am an outgoing woman and have been told I am attractive, but as far as anything wild happening—well, it seemed that sort of thing was for other people, but not for me. I knew that I had many hidden fantasies, although there was no hope of my husband unlocking these desires. He is a very nice man, but "passion" is not his middle name, if you know what I mean. His idea of being naughty consists of thumbing through the *Sports Illustrated* swim-suit issue when he thinks I'm not looking. When we're in bed (and that's the only place he'll do it—in bed) he likes to get his rocks off without much foreplay or fuss, and then quickly floats off to sleep.

One of my favorite pastimes is bowling. My husband doesn't care for the sport, so we never bowl together. But he had no objection to me joining a league on my own, which I did a couple of years ago. I was a little nervous, as I don't usually go out by myself, but everyone in the league seemed friendly. Plus, it was fun bowling once a week, and fun, too, looking at the men, some of whom were quite handsome.

The first week of bowling, I didn't flirt the way some of the other women did, but concentrated mainly on getting my average up and silently admiring the attractive guys from afar. But the second week of bowling, a good-looking, younger man with short, dark hair caught my eye. Although we didn't talk that night, I found out that his name was Dean and that, like me, he was married.

By the third week everyone was a bit closer, and our team bowled on the lanes next to Dean's team. By now there was a lot of flirting going on, mostly by the men, but it was the same old crap—a lot of desperate double entendres about "picking up a split" and aiming for "the middle pin." Some of these guys were so hard-up I felt sorry for them, but what can you do?

That night, after the matches were over, I joined a lot of the other bowlers for drinks in the alley bar. It was good to be away from my home and family and let loose for a couple of hours. Dean was there, and after a while—and several strong drinks—I got up my courage and went over to talk with him. "I'm Ali," I said, not sure if he knew my name.

"Yes, I know," he said. "You're famous. A lot of the guys in the league call you 'Bowling Ali.'" I cringed at that, afraid that I was in for another round of bad jokes from another married man who just wanted to get laid. But I was happy to find that Dean was actually very funny and not at all like the other men. Yes, he was also a bit of a flirt, but at least his jokes weren't as stupid as some of the others. We talked for a long time after everyone else left, and I felt something I hadn't felt in years: sexy! Dean and I had much in common, and I loved his brown eyes and youthful looks. But it was getting toward midnight and I worried what my husband would say if I stayed out too late. As I was leaving, Dean gave me a kiss that just about knocked my socks off. I lay awake for hours that night, wondering what it would be like to have sex with him. When I finally did fall asleep, I had the most erotic dream.

In it, Dean and I were in my house, naked and fooling around on the living-room couch. He was talking to me in a way no man ever had, telling me how hard his cock was and how much he wanted to stick it inside my hot, hungry pussy. He made his point by pressing both thumbs into my cunt, working them in and out of the dripping hole one at a time, like a set of pistons. I was crying out, begging him to go faster, and he did. When I climaxed in the dream, my body seemed to rise up off the couch.

When I floated down again, Dean was on top of me, fucking me with strong, feverish thrusts. Each time his cock slammed all the way inside me I lifted my hips to meet him halfway. He was grunting and gasping and saying, over and over again, "I'm fucking you. Fucking you hard. Fucking you the way you want to be fucked."

At this point in the dream, my husband walked into the room. He didn't say a word and neither did I. In fact, instead of being embarrassed I looked at him and said, "Watch me. Watch me get fucked." I took Dean's cock from every position imaginable as my husband stood by calmly and watched. It felt good to have him see me being so thoroughly pleased by another man. My legs were high above Dean's shoulders, my feet pressing against the sides of his face. I rubbed his cheeks with the soles, telling him to sink his cock into me as hard and fast as he could.

The dream was most intense when Dean was screwing me from behind. He didn't ram his prick in and out of me when we were in this position, but ground it into me very slowly. I could feel every thick, throbbing inch of his meat as he pulled out, then sank back in again. I begged him to fuck me faster, to shoot me full of come, but he continued to fuck me with exquisite slowness. Finally, it was I who came, my body shuddering and practically exploding with an orgasm so powerful, so real, that it woke me from my sleep. Two fingers were buried deep inside my cunt, and a third was pressed tightly against my clit. My legs were soaked, the juices from my pussy pooled on the sheet beneath me.

The next day I was shocked to receive a lovely bouquet of flowers at work. Everyone thought they were from my husband, but when I read the card I realized that Dean had sent them. For the rest of the eight weeks of leagues, we snuck off to a quiet bar or diner after bowling and talked. We were dying to go to bed together, but I was too uptight about cheating on my husband. But when I read about an out-of-town couples' tournament, I decided to take the plunge and asked Dean to be my partner.

It was tricky, because we didn't want our spouses to know what we were up to, but it was also fun planning it—we were like a couple of kids sneaking off to fool around someplace their parents wouldn't find them. We arrived at our hotel in separate cars and checked into separate rooms. Until I met Dean I'd never considered making love to another man besides my husband. But when Dean walked into my room, all I could think of was getting into bed with him.

I was wearing a short terry robe over my panties and was feeling hot and horny. As soon as Dean closed the door behind him I pulled him to the bed and tore off his clothes. I was on fire, tingling from head to toe, and took his hard cock into my mouth. The taste of his pre-come on my tongue made my head spin. I sucked his balls and licked his long shaft. I was surprised at how different his cock was from my husband's in taste, look and feel. These differences were, in themselves, very exciting for me, and made me work at Dean's prick with every ounce of imagination and energy I had.

I pumped his cock fast while tonguing the soft head and rolling my palm against his balls. He warned me that he was going to come. I pulled away at first, uneasy about taking another man's semen in my mouth. But as he began to shoot his load I could not control myself any longer. I locked my mouth back down around the hard thickness of his dick and swallowed as five or six thick jets of come exploded onto my tongue. Then I rubbed some of the warm come on my lips, savoring the taste and sticky texture.

Dean pulled me to him in a passionate kiss. I anxiously sucked his tongue as he played with my nipples. He pulled on them with his fingers, making them grow hard as diamonds. He ran a hand up my smooth thigh and fondled my pussy for a moment before moving up to my tummy. He rubbed the hot flesh and played with my navel, poking his fingertip into the little hole and even giving it a few licks with the tip of his tongue. Then he slowly slid his fingers back inside my panties. As he reached my clit, I opened my legs wide to give him access to my cunt. I pulled his mouth to my breasts, which were dying for attention. He sucked my tits while finger-fucking me, driving me crazy with lust.

Soon Dean knelt over me and lowered his tongue to my pussy. He kissed my neatly trimmed pubes and licked the swollen lips, prying them apart with his fingers and stroking them lovingly with his skilled tongue. Then he went to work on my clitoris, flicking his fantastic tongue back and forth against it so briskly it felt as though I had a vibrator pressed up against the bud.

I could stand it no longer. I pulled him to his feet and covered his smooth chest with kisses. I remembered the dream I'd had about him and how, in it, I'd told him exactly what I wanted him to do to me. I was overcome with the desire to talk as candidly with him now, and so I began to whisper in his ear. "I want to feel your cock inside me," I said hotly. "Put it in me. Put it in my pussy." Dean grabbed hold of his cock and rubbed it up and down and side-to-side against my pussy lips. I opened my legs in anticipation of what I knew would be powerful thrusts. Slowly, he pushed the head inside. I gasped as it stretched the walls of my cunt. Lifting my legs high in the air, I reached around to grab his ass and draw him deeper inside me.

"Put it in all the way," I said. "It feels so good in there. I want you to fuck me a long time."

He worked his big tool in and out of my cunt, pushing so deep that I could not believe it. I played with his balls, and my clit, as he fucked me. The sensation of this new and wonderful cock inside me, after having slept only with my husband, was enough to send chills up and down my spine. But the fucking Dean was giving me was incredible. He varied his speed from time to time so that for a few minutes he'd be balling me nice and slow with deep, steady strokes, and at other times would be cranking so fast we looked like some kind of cartoon fucking machine.

Twenty minutes of this drove me over the edge, and my body shook in a mind-blowing orgasm. I pulled Dean's mouth to mine, running my tongue through his lips as another wave of climax swept up from my pussy and through my entire body.

To my surprise I heard myself saying, "Fuck me again. My cunt is on fire. I want your cock. All of it, all of that good, thick cock." I'd never talked dirty to my husband in my life, but being with a new man was a liberating experience. I took his cock in my hand and felt it pulsing. It was hot, almost burning up, and I guided it to my cunt once again.

I grabbed Dean's ass with both hands and pulled him deeper into me. The room was filled with our grunts and groans. We were fucking all over the bed. The sheets were in a ball at our feet and the bed was squeaking like a hungry pig. I lifted my hips and bucked hard against Dean. I simply could not get enough of his great fucking. It wasn't until we fell asleep, his cock still inside me, that we got any rest.

After our match the next day (we placed second), we met back at my hotel room. Dean was in an adventurous mood. "Tell me what you want me to do," he said. "Let's have some fun."

I thought about it a moment, then got an idea. "You strip for me while I watch," I said. Sitting on the couch, I looked on as Dean took off his shirt, pants, shoes and socks. Standing there in his briefs, he was a most attractive man. I licked my lips in approval and his cock responded by poking its head out the top of his underwear.

"Put on something sexy," he said to me.

I excused myself and changed into a see-through teddy I'd bought just for the occasion. If my husband knew what I was wearing, or what I was doing, his head would've spun. But I didn't care. It had been years since I'd felt so wonderful or sexy.

I returned to my place on the couch, this time in my sheer nightie. Reaching for my breasts, I began to play with them. I pulled the fabric aside so that first one nipple, then the other, could be seen. Then I bent my head and licked my tits. I had never even thought of doing anything like that before. It was as though I were a different woman—and I loved it.

Dean pulled his briefs off, letting his cock spring free. He walked over to me and pressed his cock to my lips. I took it into my mouth, running my tongue over the swollen head. I then rubbed his prick on each of my nipples, which made me shiver with lust.

Dean then lifted me onto the table, unfastening the crotch button of my teddy so that by the time I was on my back, my cunt was fully exposed. "Don't undress me," I said. "I don't want to wait another second. Just put your cock in me and fuck."

Dean leaned forward and ran his tongue over my clit and pussy lips. It felt wonderful, but I begged him to fuck me. It wasn't a soft, wet tongue I wanted in me, but inch after hard inch of solid dick. "Please put it in me now," I begged. "I love to feel your mouth on my cunt, but I need to feel that big cock inside me."

He rubbed his prick on my pussy lips and then plunged it in. The feeling was even more exciting than the night before, because now I was getting familiar with the feel of Dean's body, the shape of his muscles and the taste of his flesh. I put my feet on the edge of the table and lifted my hips so that my pussy was at a perfect angle to take his thrusts. Dean put his hands on my thighs, pulling me against his cock as hard as he could. He didn't move at all, but simply drew me to him again and again. I had never been taken so powerfully or surely, and it was less than a minute before the first of what was to be many orgasms screamed through me.

The juices from my cunt were dripping down my leg. Dean worked his cock in and out of me faster and faster. "Suck my nipples while you fuck me. Make me hotter," I begged. He pulled my teddy aside to expose both breasts and sucked at them. I was delirious and urged him on. "Fuck me harder. Oh yes, yes! Your cock is stretching my pussy and I love it. Fuck me with all of it. Fuck me!"

Amazingly, Dean came but went right on fucking. I didn't feel him soften for even a moment. "Tell me what you want now," he said while pumping into me.

"All I know is that I need more of your cock," I said. Dean disengaged from me for a second, took a couch cushion and put it on the floor. I got on my hands and knees on the cushion and took his beautiful cock in my mouth again. I worked on it with my tongue and hands until it pulsed against the insides of my cheeks. "Fuck me again, Dean," I urged. "From behind."

Dean got behind me and slipped his cock into my box. He reached for my tits and gently rubbed and pulled the nipples. He continued playing with my breasts while he pleasured my pussy with his magnificent tool. I was on fire and wanted Dean to know how hot I was. "You turned me on the second I first saw you at the bowling alley," I said. "I wanted you to suck my tits even then. I wanted to know what your cock looked and tasted like. I wanted to know how it would feel inside me. Now I know, and it's better than I could've ever hoped." With that, we both came again.

It's been two years since that tournament, and our relationship, as well as our bowling averages, has continued to get better. It may not be right to cheat on my husband, but I'll never be sorry and will always be grateful for meeting Dean.

SERMON ON THE MOUND

I am twenty-six years old and blessed with a tight little body and long legs that seem to get more than their share of attention. One of the things that really turns my husband on is the thought of me being a tease in public. Although I don't indulge him too often, I must admit to occasionally giving in to the temptation. Gerry and I don't always get to spend a lot of time together during the week, so when we go out on weekends, even if it's just for an hour or so, I enjoy wearing clothes I know will really get him—and everyone else—hard. I have quite a collection of miniskirts and sexy tops that always do the trick.

While showering and getting ready to go out for breakfast with him one Sunday morning, I decided to tantalize Gerry with an outfit I knew would make him a walking hard-on all day long. I selected a short, rather snug little denim skirt that stopped just above the middle of my thigh—covering only enough of my crotch and ass to satisfy the laws governing indecent exposure. I added to this a red knit top and a pair of red, super-sexy high-heel pumps that I knew accentuated my well-developed legs. Driving to the restaurant with me by his side, Gerry could barely keep his eyes on the road.

When we got there, he opened the car door for me. Sliding off the seat, I gave him a clear view of my crotch. When he saw that I had on nothing more than a teeny little G-string underneath, I thought his incredibly hard cock would rip through the seam of his jeans. Besides being totally sheer, the G-string just barely hid the lips of my baby-smooth, clean-shaven sex. I couldn't remember when I'd ever seen him so excited.

We were seated in a comfortable booth in the corner. Not long after we sat down, three men were seated in the booth directly across the aisle from us. They looked as though they'd just gotten out of a Sunday service of some sort, as they were carrying prayer books and had little gold crucifixes pinned to their lapels. All three were conservatively dressed, and had that vacant look common to people who spend too much of their time in church. When the waitress delivered their menus and one of them responded with "Jesus loves you," Gerry and I looked at each other and rolled our eyes.

Although our booth was quite private, the section where we were sitting was elevated a bit. As a result, these men had a bird's-eye view of the area directly under our table. While Gerry and I looked over our menus, I occasionally glanced in their direction and couldn't help but notice that all of them were sneaking peeks under our table, trying to get a look at my crotch. It was quite amusing the way the three had inched their way to the center of their booth, positioning themselves to get the clearest view possible of my nearly exposed pussy.

I guess I was caught a little off-guard by this. I know I'm the type of woman men can't help staring at, but these three were, from all outward appearances, religious fanatics. Now, suddenly, they'd become world-class voyeurs. Well, as they say, the flesh is weak. But these Bible-thumpers were soon to find out just how weak!

Gerry had also noticed them staring. He was getting quite a kick out of it. I didn't have to ask him what he was thinking; I knew he was dying to see me tease these guys silly. If I had ever relished the thought of being an exhibitionist, this situation certainly was too tempting to resist. Being dressed as I was, with every inch of my deliciously prepared frame exuding sex, I couldn't have planned it any better. I was aware that my miniskirt—dangerously short to begin with—had slid well up my thighs, leaving little to the imagination. Our friends at the next table weren't making much of an effort to control themselves either. They were all staring at me now, making little comments (which they didn't think I heard) about the "glorious creation" in their midst. When they suddenly let loose with a rousing cry of "Praise the Lord!" I decided to give them something for which they could really thank God!

Moving slightly in my seat, I positioned myself to what I knew would be their best advantage. Now they all could have a fantastic view straight up my skirt to where the folds of my womanhood were concealed. With my face hidden by my menu, I parted my legs slightly. Then, placing my hand on my lap, I began slowly stroking my fingers up and down the inner surface of my thigh. I acted as though I wasn't really aware of what I was doing, although nothing could have been further from the truth. While slowly letting my fingers crawl higher up my thigh, I gradually spread my legs wider and wider apart. Peeking over the top of my menu, I could see three horny men looking right up my skirt—mesmerized by some force they couldn't control. I knew that if their eyes could eat, I would definitely be on the menu.

A wild and erotic thought entered my mind. It was so nasty I wondered, Do I dare even consider it? Admittedly enjoying the attention of their hungry eyes, and feeling my inhibitions rapidly disappear, I thought, Why not? As soon as the waitress had taken our order, I excused myself to go to the ladies' room. I didn't reveal my plan to my husband, but just told him I'd be back in a minute.

In the rest room I combed my hair, checked my makeup and, without giving myself a chance to change my mind, unzipped my skirt. With a naughty giggle I slipped my G-string down my legs, stepped out of it and stuffed it into my purse. Finding that my G-string was soaked with my sticky juices made me suddenly aware of how really turned on I was. Then I quickly zipped up my skirt and headed back to our booth.

The thought of being totally naked under my skirt made my pulse race. Sitting down, I kissed Gerry. I was careful to keep my legs together, intent on making the most of my little surprise. My husband didn't suspect what I was up to, even though there was no hiding the lump of erect cockmeat in his pants. I ran my fingers along its hard length and gave it a squeeze. It was solid as a rock! I wanted to bring him off right there, and it took every bit of self-control within me to keep from jerking him off under the table. But I did do the next best thing. Opening my purse so he could look inside, I let him see my G-string rolled into a ball. The biggest grin came across his face. He could hardly believe that his favorite fantasy was about to take on a new dimension. I have to say that, for a moment, I had trouble believing it myself. But the cunt smell wafting up from my purse left no doubt that this would be one memorable breakfast.

The waitress brought our food. I could see that the three Holy Rollers across from us were still looking at me, anxious for more of whatever I was willing to show. I could hardly wait to see the looks on their faces when they saw that my little trip to the ladies' room was for their benefit as well as ours. Without prolonging the moment of truth any longer, I slowly spread my legs and "absentmindedly" placed my hand on my thigh as I'd done a few minutes earlier. As my fingers roamed cuntward, I spread my thighs as far apart as I could. The men seemed to be having a great deal of trouble eating their breakfast. One of them dropped his fork on the floor. It may have been out of shock, but I believe it was a ploy to bend down and get an even closer look at my cunt, because when the waitress picked it up and gave him a new one, he seemed gravely disappointed.

With my pulse already racing, the touch of my fingers on my sensitive skin was beginning to make my temperature rise. I found myself dying to satisfy the growing itch between my legs.

Knowing their eyes were following my every move, I let my fingers travel the remaining distance to my throbbing clit. I almost gasped when my hot, aching bud was touched by my index finger. With three sets of eyes glued to my naked crotch, I started slowly sliding the tips of my fingers up and down my pussy lips and in and out of my slippery hole. The squishy sound got my husband's attention. I could practically hear the rapid beating of his heart.

I finger-fucked myself while pressing a thumb against my exposed, swollen clit. I knew I was driving them crazy, and as for Gerry, he was about to cream his jeans. I was trying to nonchalantly eat my breakfast while jerking off, so it was up to my husband to inform me that two of the men were rubbing their own cocks under the table! Hearing this, I picked up the pace and briskly pumped my finger in and out of my pussy.

It was no secret anymore that I knew they were watching me play with myself, so I was able to dispense with the pretense of eating and get down to the business of making myself come. My entire body was rocking. My legs were opening and closing and the entire booth shook. The sound of the table rattling as my legs banged against it filled our little corner of the restaurant. We were starting to draw the attention of other customers, in addition to our religious friends, when I climaxed. My entire body seemed to explode as the heat of orgasm surged through me.

Having finished what I'd set out to do, I took a few deep breaths and went back to my omelet. My husband, who was beside himself and hornier than a soldier on leave, took my cunt-drenched fingers into his mouth and sucked them lovingly. The three men, having long forgotten their breakfast, silently motioned for their check. When it arrived, they picked up their prayer books and coats and speechlessly made their way out of the booth. Gerry and I couldn't stifle our laughter as we watched one trying to hide the large wet spot on the front of his pants, and the other two attempting to conceal the enormous, protruding bulges in front of theirs.

Gerry and I were about as horny as could be. We weren't able, or willing, to keep our hands off each other for the rest of the day, and enjoyed some of the best lovemaking we'd ever had.

OTHER PEOPLE'S HUSBANDS

*F*rom the beginning, there was never any question as to whether my beautiful wife, Dana, would take other men to her bed. Over the past five years, Dana has had affairs with many different married men, including a number of my friends. Don't get me wrong—Dana's not overly promiscuous. In fact, she's quite selective in choosing her lovers, preferring to get involved in long, passionate affairs rather than one-night stands.

I'm quite comfortable with Dana's infidelity and, to be honest, I find nothing more thrilling than watching her get ready for a date.

My wife, at thirty-one, is more attractive than many women ten years her junior. She works out constantly, keeping her body firm and trim. Dana is about five feet tall. Her shapely ass and firm tits support the saying that good things come in small packages. With her long red hair and pretty face, she has little trouble attracting men.

Late one Friday night, after a wonderful dinner at home, Dana announced that she wanted to go dancing at a local club. She had me call one of my friends, whom she'd recently seduced, but unfortunately he wasn't home. "Oh, well, I guess it's just going to be me and you tonight," she sighed, obviously disappointed.

Dana intended to attract quite a bit of attention. She chose one of her sexiest outfits. She emerged from the bedroom wearing a red spandex miniskirt, black thigh-high stockings and red pumps with four-inch spiked heels. Her skirt was so tight that it was readily apparent she wasn't wearing panties.

It took fifteen minutes to reach the club. Dana and I soon

found ourselves seated at the bar. I had just finished paying for our drinks when a handsome young blond guy asked her to dance. Dana looked over at me with a sexy smile as she accepted his invitation. The two of them were soon gyrating to the loud music.

For the next hour, I continued to sip my drink as I watched my wife dance with one man after another. Dana's provocative attire and sensuous movements attracted quite a bit of attention. Suddenly I felt someone tap me on the shoulder. When I looked around, I saw my boss, Dave. "Your wife seems to be having a good time, huh?" he asked. He watched my wife's dance partner run his hands over her smooth, round ass while giving her a wet French kiss. I didn't know what to say. I tried vainly to think of some way to get rid of him.

Dave is very athletic and, with his brawny physique and handsome features, I didn't trust my wife around him. I really didn't want my relationship to become the talk of the office, so I stammered something about having to leave soon. Just then the song ended and Dana came bouncing over to our place at the bar to retrieve her drink. "Hi, Dave," she said as she took her seat at the bar. "What are you doing here?"

"Well, my wife is visiting her mother tonight, and I thought I'd check out all the sexy young ladies at the club," responded Dave, giving Dana a sexy smile. "Gary here says you two have to leave soon. Is that right?"

"No way. I'm not leaving. Gary, you can leave if you want, but I'm just getting started," she said. And with that, she grabbed Dave's hand and led him onto the dance floor.

Dana was her usual flirtatious self. As the evening wore on, I noticed that Dave was becoming increasingly aggressive. They had just finished a particularly steamy dance when I saw my wife lean over and whisper something into Dave's ear. Immediately, Dave grabbed her by the wrist and led her toward the exit without saying a word to me.

As I sat there sipping my drink I began to get an incredible erection as I pictured my wife and boss together. After about five minutes of deliberation, I decided to sneak out into the parking lot. I knew Dana would be very angry if she caught me spying on her, so I remained absolutely quiet as I made my way out toward our car.

Fortunately, there was a low concrete wall near the edge of the parking lot, and I was able to crawl right up next to the car without being discovered. As a matter of fact, with all the noise the two of them were making, I doubt they would've noticed an audience of thirty people. When I finally reached the section of wall nearest the car, I raised my head up to find that the back door nearest the wall was open so that I could see directly into the backseat of the car. It was a sight I'll never forget for the rest of my life.

My wife had removed her dress and was leaning over to suck Dave's huge cock. I had heard rumors in the office about how well-hung my boss supposedly was. I have to admit, his cock made mine look quite small in comparison. "That's it, baby. Suck it. You like that big cock, don't you?" he moaned as Dana bobbed up and down. Dave had one hand on the back of my wife's head, and with the other hand he was busy playing with her juicy pussy. My cock was near the bursting point. I unzipped my pants and pulled out my throbbing tool. I had just begun to jerk off when Dave suddenly pulled his prick away from Dana's red lips and said, "Come on sweetheart. I want you to really *suck* my cock!"

She smiled up at Dave, then began sucking his cock like mad. She really got into it, when Dave abruptly sat up and instructed her to lay back on the seat. "Oh God," she cried, "stick it in me. I want your big cock in me."

"You are one horny little bitch," Dave groaned, burying his massive prick to the hilt inside my wife's pussy.

I continued to quietly massage my swollen rod while Dave fucked my wife to one orgasm after another. Dave's broad shoulders completely blocked my view of Dana's face. I would have given anything to see my wife's facial expressions. It was obvious she was having the time of her life.

Watching the ease with which Dave made my wife climax, I really came to appreciate Dana's obsession for sex with other men. In contrast to my wife's rather halfhearted responses to my lovemaking, Dana was delighted in his every movement and was, in fact, more excited than I had ever seen her before. She was moaning, "Oh yes, I love your big cock! Fuck me harder! That's it! Yes!" She ran her hands over the taut muscles of Dave's ass and bucked her hips, engulfing every last inch of his prick. It was quite a sight.

Suddenly, Dave threw back his head in triumph and growled, "Oh, baby! Yes! I'm coming!" At the same time Dana cried, "Oh, yeah! That's it! Come in my pussy!" From my vantage point, I could see Dave's muscular buttocks clenching together as he exploded in orgasm, spurting torrents of semen into my wife's welcoming hole.

The excitement of watching my boss and my wife in simultaneous orgasm prompted my own climax. I began shooting gobs of creamy sperm all over the concrete wall.

When I had regained my senses, I peeked over the wall. Dave and my wife were passionately kissing. His cock was still buried balls-deep in my wife. I knew from experience that she was flexing her pussy walls, milking his cock of every drop of warm come.

By this time I figured I had better head back into the club to await my wife's return. I tucked my spent cock back into my pants and made my way back to the bar. I waited another fifteen minutes before Dave and Dana walked in. Dave had his arm around my wife's waist, and Dana had that delicious "just fucked" look written all over her face.

"Where were you two?" I asked, pretending I wasn't aware of the events that had just taken place.

"Cut the crap, Gary. You know where we were," Dave sneered. "We were out screwing in your car, that's where." He ran his hand over Dana's shapely ass. Dave was quite proud of the fact that he had just fucked my wife, and he wanted to gloat a little. "Go ahead, Dana," he casually remarked. "Tell him how good it was."

Dana was positively glowing. She cooed, "Oh Gary, it was the greatest. I've never come so much before. He really fucked me good."

"You know, Gary," Dave said. "I don't think you've been keeping your wife satisfied. You wouldn't mind if I stop by now and then to fuck her, would you?" He kissed her on the cheek.

"I guess not," I replied.

"It'll be great, Gary," my wife went on. "Dave says he'll be able to stop by a couple of days a week on his way home from work. You'll have to wait until later to come home, but just think—by the time you get home, I'll already have my pussy filled with Dave's hot come. You'll get to enjoy sloppy seconds all the time!"

Dave finally said he had to leave; his wife would get suspicious. He gave Dana a lusty kiss goodbye and left the club. My wife and I left soon after him. As we walked to the car, I slipped my arm around my sexy wife's waist. There was no way I could keep secret the fact that I had watched Dana and Dave, so as soon as I had closed the car door, I confessed that I had watched their frenzied coupling. As I got to the part about spilling my load on the concrete wall, Dana giggled, "I know I should be angry with you, but I guess it is kind of cute that you wanted to watch Dave and me. Can you believe how big his cock is? Now that's what I call a real man."

"I just hope you don't get spoiled," I responded.

"Oh, come on, Gary, don't worry," she sighed. "You know I love you. I've told you before that I like sex better with bigger guys. You saw how horny I was with Dave. You've never brought me off like that. Have you?"

"Yeah. That's true. I suppose I shouldn't be so selfish. So long as Dave can fuck you better than I can, I guess I can't complain."

"That's more like it," she said. "Hey, let's jump in the back and you can be the second guy tonight to do me in the backseat of our car!"

With that, Dana pulled her dress over her head and climbed over the seat. Well, I didn't have to be asked twice. The head of my cock was soon nudging her wet pussy open. With one motion, I buried myself deep. I was soon thrusting in and out of her soaked pussy. I've always enjoyed fucking my wife after another man has had her, but this was the best ever. The remnants of Dana and Dave's copious juices, coupled with the fact that my wife's pussy was still loose from Dave's big cock, had me trembling with desire.

Dana urged me to come, saying, "That's it, Gary. Just remember how sexy I looked with Dave between my legs. My pussy is filled with his cream. You like that, don't you?" Dana's dirty talk soon had me groaning, "Yes! Yes!" as I reached my second climax of the evening, blasting my sperm deep inside her.

I have to admit that since her affair with Dave began, Dana couldn't be happier. My only regret is that I didn't encourage her to seduce him sooner.

POOL PARTY

I had an experience this past summer that I will never forget. It happened just after I arrived home from my first year in college.

I am the youngest of four children and I have three older sisters. Since my parents divorced when I was very young, my father did not live with us while I was growing up, and it was sometimes lonely to be the only male in a house full of females. I spent my adolescent years surrounded by my sisters and their girlfriends. I was always considered the "little brother," and though they never seemed to notice me, I certainly paid a lot of attention to them. Starting when my hormones were just beginning to surge, I would frequently watch my sisters and their friends sunbathe around our pool in their scanty bikinis.

The pool behind our house is surrounded by a high fence and trees, providing total privacy for sunbathing. When my mother and I were not home, my sisters and their friends had the house and pool to themselves. They would sunbathe and lounge around the pool for hours. Many times I would come home unnoticed while they were sunbathing. I could see them from my bathroom window, which is situated in the back of the house, and would often enjoy the view without their knowledge.

Two summers ago, when I turned eighteen, I developed a strong lust for Amy, one of my sister's friends. Amy had the most incredible body and wore the skimpiest bikinis. She was the continual subject of my sexual fantasies. Even during the winter, while I was away at school, I fantasized about Amy's body as I pumped away on my dick.

This past summer I had just come back home after my freshman year of college. Though I had been relatively small while in high school, I had grown a lot during the past year. I had also been lifting weights in the campus gym, so I was looking trim and muscular. Though I had dated at school and was told I was really cute, I left my first year of college still a virgin.

No one was in the house when I arrived home, but a note indicated that everyone would be back sometime in the late afternoon. I realized I had the whole house to myself. It was a very hot day, and after surviving finals at school I was looking forward to having nothing to do. Since no one else was home, and I felt like being a little wild and crazy, I took off all my clothes and jumped into the pool naked.

The water was rather cold, but this was the first opportunity I had ever had to skinny-dip, since normally at least one of my sisters was around and I am basically a modest guy. It felt really great to swim totally nude. After paddling around for a while I got out of the pool and stretched out naked on a lounge chair. I figured I'd get some sun and catch a short nap. I quickly dozed off in the warm sun.

I woke with a start—I thought I had heard a strange noise. As I opened my eyes, I wasn't sure if I was still dreaming. There in front of me, less than five feet away, stood my sister's friend, Amy.

She had come over to sunbathe and assumed one of my sisters would be around. She had on a really sexy bikini and was even more beautiful than I remembered. She didn't say a word as I fully woke up. She was staring right at my dick. While I was asleep I must have been having some kind of sexual dream, because my dick was semi-hard. I guess I had been holding on to my dick while I was sleeping, because as she stood there I could feel it growing bigger in my hand. I was speechless as she stared at me. Soon I was holding the hardest and largest erection I have ever had.

Amy said that I wasn't the little boy she remembered. She had a big grin on her face while her eyes were locked on my pulsing dick. She said I had really grown since she last saw me. I knew she was horny, too, when she told me that looking at my lean, naked body and pulsating penis really turned her on. She came over and sat next to me on my lounge chair. I could see her nipples pushing against her bikini top. She said that seeing me holding my hard penis excited her. She also said that she had always been curious about how guys masturbated and wondered if I would mind teaching her the finer points of jerking off, since I already had my dick in my hand.

Stretched out in front of her, totally naked, with my hard-on in my hand, I decided that this was one opportunity I simply could not refuse! Amy said she wanted me to show her exactly how a guy masturbates and tell her what it feels like. I finally spoke for the first time, saying I would be happy to show her if she would take off her bikini top and put some suntan lotion on her tits. I admitted that I had often admired them from the vantage point of my bathroom window. She quickly agreed and took off her top. Then, with a sly smile on her face, she slathered lotion on her naked breasts, paying special attention to her erect nipples. She knew the sight excited me even more.

I started stroking my dick and explaining the finer details of how I stimulated my penis. She watched as my hand quickly slid up and down the length of my dick. I told her that as my excitement grew I increased the rate of my strokes. I admitted that I was really turned on by her breasts and asked if the growing wet spot on her bikini bottom meant she was as turned on as I was. She responded by taking off her bikini bottom, exposing the beautiful bush I had always fantasized about. Needless to say, my strokes became even more rapid and my balls felt as if they were going to explode from all the excitement.

Amy started to rub her wet cunt with her fingers and said that watching me jerk off really excited her. I told her that seeing her tits had gotten me so excited that I was about to come. She asked me to stop and hold off my orgasm. Though I was almost at the brink, I reluctantly stopped. Then she reached over and grabbed my frustrated hard-on. She told me she wanted to stroke my dick and see what it felt like to hold a guy's penis as he came. I couldn't believe it! Here was the girl of my dreams fulfilling my number-one fantasy!

After I calmed down a little, I took her hand and showed her how I liked to move the skin on the shaft over the head of my dick on each stroke. As she started to stroke with one hand, with the other she took my hand, placed it on her wet mound and told me to rub her cunt. I said that I was seconds from shooting my wad and would not last long. She asked me to tell her to stop just before I reached the point of no return. As I was rubbing her cunt she languidly stroked my dick, keeping me in a frenzy, on the brink of orgasm. She started and stopped several times before I finally told her that I couldn't stand it anymore.

She was moaning by now as I continued to finger her lovebox. I could feel her excitement grow, and she suddenly started to quiver. I asked her to pump the hell out of my cock. I burst into the most intense orgasm of my life as she pounded my dick, and my come pulsed out onto her hand and my chest. She was so turned on that her body quaked as I drove my fingers even deeper into her wet box.

Though my dick was softening as I was recovering from my intense orgasm, she was really hot and ready for more. She said she wanted to sit on my manhood and feel me inside her. Though I thought it would take a while for my now limp penis to respond, it became as hard as steel as soon as she grabbed it. I certainly wasn't going to refuse a chance to lose my virginity with the girl of my fantasies!

She was quivering with excitement as she climbed on top of me. She reached down to guide my rock-hard member into her waiting cunt. As my dick slipped into her warm pussy, I realized this was going to be better than anything I had ever fantasized about while masturbating. In order to avoid shooting my wad on the spot, I used all of the self-control I could muster to just stay still. Amy must have sensed that I wanted to sustain the pleasure, because she leaned forward while my dick was fully implanted inside her and started kissing me. Without moving my pulsating dick, I reached up and started to rub the oil-covered tits I had fantasized about for years. After some intense groping I felt my member was ready for another round of stimulation, so as we kissed each other I slowly started thrusting. Her warm cunt gripped my six-inch virgin dick as I slammed it in as far as it would go. As my hands explored her body, my strokes quickened. Though she said she wanted to go slowly and make it last, she was slamming her hips against mine to meet each of my thrusts. She must have decided to go for it, because all of a sudden she went crazy and pounded her body into my groin. Though I wanted this to last, I felt her cunt tightly grip my penis. When she started to moan really loud, I knew I could not last any longer.

I told her I was coming as I rammed my dick into her as hard as I could. This orgasm was even wilder and lasted even longer than my earlier one. I felt my come pulse inside her as I continued to pound away. After several more of my spasmodic thrusts she, too, shook violently in orgasm. After recovering from our major workout, it occurred to me that I had just had the time of my life.

Unfortunately, we did not have a chance to repeat our workout again during the summer, though I did get a chance to ogle the girls during several sunbathing sessions. I did notice that while they were sunbathing Amy would often opt to go topless and would periodically look up at my bathroom window and smile. I'm sure she knew I was often up there, watching her.

I am now back at school and vividly recalling my summer experience. I do not think I am fantasizing when I say that I expect this school year will provide many more sexual firsts.

HOT FOR TEACHER

*A*fter about a week of rising at eight in the morning for my math class, I decided to stop going. My friend told me when tests and quizzes were going to take place. I went only on those days.

My professor is a five-foot-eight blonde who is thirty-three years old. She has long legs and is very pretty. One morning I decided to drop by and see what was going on in class.

Mrs. Drake went through the day's lecture, then gave out the homework assignment. Just as I got to the door, she said, "Phil, I would like to speak with you."

Busted.

"My records show that you have missed seven weeks of class," she told me. "I think you owe me some make-up time." I'd never heard of make-up time, but I was only a freshman and hadn't heard of a lot of things. She handed me a sheet of paper and told me to meet her at her home promptly at six-thirty that night.

I arrived at her door at six-twenty, eager to get my make-up time over with. Mrs. Drake answered the door wearing a pair of cut-off jeans and a black T-shirt. She moaned something about my being early and turned around. I followed her inside. She led me into the kitchen and said that I could start making up time by doing the dishes.

As I washed, she stood behind me and told me that her husband had taken their son to see his grandmother for the weekend and had left the house a mess.

After I finished the dishes I vacuumed the whole house, then cleaned her son's room and the bathrooms. Mrs. Drake caught me staring at her quite a few times. I couldn't help it. Her clothes weren't tight or anything, but she looked incredible. After I put a set of clean silk sheets on her bed, I looked up and caught her staring at the bulge in my shorts. She played it off by saying, "I think it's time for a break."

She poured two glasses of champagne and led me into her living room. I fell into the easy chair, and she sat directly across from me on the couch. We talked for at least an hour, and soon the bottle was empty. (She drank most of it.) Then, quite out of the blue, she said, "Phil, I didn't really have you come here for make-up time. Shit, there's no such thing as make-up time. If anyone found out that you were here cleaning my house, I could lose my job, as well as my marriage."

Her hand slipped up her shirt to fondle her breasts. "I've had my eye on you since the first day of class. I was very upset when you began cutting." She stood up and pulled off her shorts and T-shirt.

There before me stood my professor—drunk, naked and giving me an incredible hard-on! She was very skinny, her tits sagged ever so slightly, and her pussy was neatly trimmed. She sat back down on the couch and buried her middle finger inside her cunt. "I haven't been fucked in four years. I need a good fuck. My husband just doesn't cut it."

She walked over to me. I said, "Mrs. Drake, I'd love to but . . ."

She placed her hand over my mouth. The aroma of her pussy flowed into my nose. Without a word, she got on her knees and pulled out my fully erect cock. She ran her tongue around the tip a few times, then sucked it into her mouth, taking in only half of my length. I put my hands on her head and ran my fingers through her hair while she slurped away.

Then she pulled my cock out of her mouth and said, "Please

shoot your load in my mouth. It's been so long since I've tasted a man's come."

She went back to work on my manhood, sucking and slurping more intensely than before. In a few seconds I felt that familiar itch in my balls. I pushed her head into my groin and shot my load deep into her loving mouth.

She rose with a smile, wiped her mouth and said, "You taste so good. I forgot how much I love the taste of come." I stood up and gave her a deep kiss, tasting my own come in her mouth. I pulled my shirt off and sat her down on the couch. Our lips met again, then I ran my tongue down to her tits. I spent a long time sucking her hard nipples, alternating from one to the other. Then I slowly ran my tongue down her body to her bush. I kissed her inner thighs and all around her gash, enjoying the sounds of her moans.

I looked up and watched her pinching her nipples. I sucked her clit and she came instantly, her screams filling the house. "Oh, oh, oh, God, yes, oh, yes!" When her body stopped shuddering, she said, "Fuck me now, Phil! I want to feel you inside me!"

We hurried into the bedroom. She got up on the bed on her hands and knees, sticking her lovely ass into the air. I got behind her and slid my prick into her juicy quim. She passionately moaned and tossed her head. Her body started to shiver. I felt her cunt tighten. Her loud moans and the sensation of her grip on my pole were too much for me. I bucked wildly as my hot load poured into her.

When I had emptied my balls, I lay down next to her. She took my limp dick into her mouth and began sucking like a madwoman. In about five minutes she had me harder than steel. She squatted over me and inserted my shaft into her love-hole. Slowly she went up and down on my cock. She rubbed and pinched her nipples as her pace increased. She moaned, "It feels so good to be filled with cock!"

By now she was riding me as if she were possessed by demons! I felt her cunt grip me tightly as another intense orgasm overtook her. Then she collapsed on top of me and shoved her tongue deeply into my mouth. I flipped her over and started ramming my cock into her as hard and fast as I could. She wrapped her legs around my back and raised her hips to meet my thrusts.

She said, "I love you, Phil," between grunts. I felt the tension increase in my balls so I pulled out of her, not wanting to come yet.

"Why don't you put that tongue of yours to some good use?" she asked. I know how to take a hint. I licked and sucked her twat, occasionally licking her clit. She rode my face, crying, "Eat me! Make me come again! I want to come!"

As I lapped her juices, she slipped into a 69 position. She sucked me so hard, I immediately came in her mouth. When my jism stopped flowing, she got off of me and gave me a long, deep kiss, letting me again taste my salty seed. When she broke the kiss, she laid her head on my chest, whispered, "I love you, Phil" and then gently fell asleep.

When I awoke in the morning, Mrs. Drake was sitting on the side of the bed. She was wearing a black camisole and looked amazing. "Good morning," she said. She told me to take a shower while she cooked breakfast.

We spent the day talking, making love and watching television.

When it got dark outside, she told me that her all-time fantasy was to make love under the stars. She grabbed my hand and led me into her backyard. She laid me down on the soft grass, knelt between my legs and took my limp prick into her mouth. When I was rock solid, she told me to fuck her from behind again. She got down on her hands and knees. I knelt behind her and slipped my rod into her dripping snatch. I fucked her for all I was worth.

When her orgasm hit, she let out an ear-piercing yell. I was afraid someone would hear her, but apparently she didn't care. We continued to fuck. When her neighbor's light came on we ran into the house, giggling like children. We went up to her bedroom to finish what we had started.

Mrs. Drake lay on her back when we reached the bed. I put her legs up over my shoulders and pumped her bush with all the strength I could muster. She yelled, "Fuck me harder! I want everything you've got!" A blazing orgasm overcame her.

She told me to come in her mouth, so I sat on her chest and put my cock between her lips. I told her to relax so she could take my entire length. I fucked her mouth, savoring the delicious feeling of my rod going down her throat. In no time at all I shot my load and collapsed next to her, completely spent. We fell asleep in each other's arms.

In the morning I heard her in the shower. I hopped in with her. She went down to her knees, without a word, and blew me as the hot water rained down on us. I pushed her away and lathered her body with soap. Then I held her against the tile wall and fucked her brains out.

We decided to continue on dry ground. We hopped out of the shower, dried ourselves with a towel and ran back into the bedroom, hopping onto the mattress. I licked and sucked her nipples until she was almost crying with pleasure. Then I moved my face down to her crotch and used my tongue and lips to bring her off. She barely had time to catch her breath before I leaped on top of her, slid my cock in and gave her the humping of her life.

Before I left her that afternoon, she made a deal with me: She would allow me to visit her on Fridays. Since her house was off limits, she said we would use her van. Then she made me promise not to tell anyone about our relationship. I agreed.

Now I need some sleep. I don't want to be late for class tomorrow!

NAVY BOY

I am a military man. I'm in the navy and being in this branch of the armed forces allows a man to see and experience many things. I have been halfway around the world three times. However, of all the exotic sights, sounds and sensations that I've had the pleasure to witness and experience, nothing tops the pleasure I enjoyed with one supremely sensual lover.

I was in the Philippines (for the fourteenth time) when I met the woman I'll call Myra. I was on leave and I had gone with a buddy of mine to a place just outside of Olongapo on a wet, rainy Friday afternoon.

The only things on my mind were drying off and having a good meal and some drinks with friends. Little did I suspect the delights that fate held in store for me that evening.

After having a satisfying meal at a little eatery, the two of us moved on to a bar. My buddy and I had been in this establishment for a couple of hours when I first saw her.

I was drinking, playing pool, flirting with the local girls and generally taking it easy when she came in. I noticed her right away.

Myra was short, about five foot one. Dressed as she was, in a baseball jacket and blue jeans ripped strategically along the front and back, she looked like a Philippine version of the American rock 'n' roller, Joan Jett.

I watched her for a while, admiring her dark, searing eyes and sensual face. Then she looked up and noticed me.

Our eyes met. Her eyes seemed to pierce through me to some secret, inner place. It was a look I'll never forget. I had to meet her, but her beauty had me spellbound.

For what seemed like hours, I just sat there, dazed. I finally got my nerve up and approached her. I felt as if I was being drawn by an unseen force, and I didn't want to fight it.

I introduced myself and we chatted for some minutes, making

small talk about what had happened in the Philippines since my last visit. After a while she mentioned that she had to go to another bar and asked if I would like to go along. Being no fool, I said yes.

I soon found myself with her in another establishment down the road. We had been at this new place for only a half an hour when she said she was tired and hinted suggestively that she wanted to go home.

She shyly asked if I would accompany her. Would I? I wanted nothing more. I took the bait like a salmon during breeding season and swam with it.

About fifteen minutes later, after a short walk down a deserted side street, we came to the house where she lived. Once inside her apartment, she went straight to her bedroom, with me right behind her. In her bedroom, she locked the door behind us, turning and looking at me with a stare that felt as if it was peeling the clothes right off my body.

We stood frozen in place just a few feet from each other. I was looking her up and down and aching for a taste. Finally I broke the stillness and pulled her toward me. Her body felt small and delicate in my arms.

As she drew near to me, we slowly kissed, her hot tongue probing my entire mouth. Without saying a word she slowly undressed me, kissing me as she moved down my torso toward my pants. As she undid my belt and unzipped my fly, she looked up to me with those powerful brown eyes and slowly removed my pants.

Now it was my turn—only I didn't stop at her panties. I took her small frame in my hands and peeled off her clothes as slowly as I could, paying close attention to her nipples as I removed her top and bra.

If you have never been with a Philippine girl, you've missed one of the most beautiful sights a man can behold. The women of the Philippines are blessed with unbelievably gorgeous nipples. As I took each beautiful, rosy nipple in my mouth, the little things grew instantly until they reached about three-quarters to one inch long.

Finally, I slowly removed her pants and panties, kissing and caressing the entire length of her body. Her pussy, framed with sparse black hair, was as beautiful as the rest of her.

Now I took her and gently lowered her to the bed, caressing her continually. I moved to her pussy and eventually to her clitoris. I was rubbing her pussy for only a few short moments when she let loose a quiet little coo. That was the first sound either of us had made since we'd entered the room, and it seemed to spear the silence. Her pussy was drenched with her love juice and emitted a lovely, musky odor that intoxicated me.

She got up and stripped the last pieces of clothing from my body. My whole nervous system was alive and tingling. With me on my back, she spread my legs. Caressing my manhood, she gave me that look again. She slowly licked her full, luscious lips and moved down to the head of my cock.

Her mouth felt heavenly, gradually engulfing me while her hand busily caressed the shaft of my throbbing member. She worked slowly, up and down my cock. Every time she neared the head, she would let it pop out of her mouth. Then she would open wide and swirl her tongue around the head, paying particular attention to the underside of my member.

This unbelievably pleasurable treatment of my cock went on for what seemed like an eternity until she sensed my urgency. Then she sped up her motions until she was slobbering all over my hot, tingling rod.

Her saliva oozed down my shaft, giving me an unforgettable sensation. It oozed all the way down, down my balls and finally down the crack of my ass. At that point, she stopped her movement. She no longer had to move—I was furiously fucking that wonderful mouth of hers.

I lasted no more than another five strokes when I exploded more powerfully than I ever had before. I thought I might black out, it was that intense. My whole body went numb from the excitement of my climax. Then we rested, showered and smoked a couple of cigarettes.

Soon we returned to our nest. Now I intended to really take my time. Placing her on the bed, I again caressed her lovely vagina, slowly sliding my fingers in and out, paying close attention to her clit until I could sense the approach of her climax. Unlike her first orgasm, which had been almost lady-like, when her orgasm hit this time, she writhed and bucked on the bed. The heat of the night was evident by the pool of sweat at her cleavage.

I slowly spread open her legs. Looking into her hungry eyes, I teasingly slid my cock into her. She was tight. Her pussy fit like a vise and held me there. I knew I was in for the ride of my life. I started slowly, not wanting to explode too fast.

We fucked in perfect unison, like lovers who'd known each other for years, taking our time. I was picking up my tempo when she wrapped her legs around me and grabbed my back to pull me closer. I felt her pussy tighten suddenly on my cock. God, I thought, I must be in heaven and she must be an angel. Now I was bucking like a wild horse. We were both moving frantically. I was pounding my cock into her and I could hear my balls slapping against her soft brown ass.

As we continued, her ankles and heels pressed into my ass as if to spur me on. I was fucking her so hard I thought we would both explode.

She clutched my back tightly with her fingers. She threw her head back and emitted a loud scream of ecstasy. That cry of pleasure was all it took to push me over the edge.

Feverishly pounding into her, I came in burst after burst. I arched my back and growled loudly. Myra's neighbors probably thought I had turned into a werewolf, but at this point I wouldn't have cared if we were in a department store window. I bent down, my sweat dripping onto her skin, and pressed my open mouth against her neck, tasting the sweaty saltiness of her hot flesh. I could feel both our hearts pounding madly.

Then I rolled onto my back and lay there as spent as if I had worked all day doing manual labor in the humidity of the summer sun.

She rose gracefully, smiling at me with those soft, sensual lips. She slowly looked down my body. Finally her gaze stopped at my flaccid member, which was covered with our juices. She moved her head down to my cock. Engulfing it with her mouth, she licked and sucked me clean.

Eventually we got up and took another shower. Soon after, I was forced to reluctantly leave my Philippine princess because I was due back at the base.

I was able to see Myra two more times before I shipped out to where I am now, but it wasn't nearly enough. I don't know if I'll ever see her again, but I thank her for the time we had together. I cherish my memories of her and know that I'll never forget my Philippine girl.

BIRTHDAY PRESENT

I'm walking through my apartment fondling my balls and pulling on my stiffening schlong as I relive the most unforgettable experience of my life.

I run a small women's goods business and work with some of the finest foxes you could imagine. For my thirtieth birthday I had decided to treat myself to a new Mercedes. When I went to pick up the car I was accompanied by Lorrie, a full-bodied redhead who serves as my executive secretary.

I had planned to share the occasion (and my cock) with Lorrie later that evening, but as we left the Mercedes dealership she asked me to drop her off at her place. She claimed she needed a few hours to freshen up and get herself ready for the evening's festivities. Lorrie gave me a delicious kiss as we arranged to meet later. Then, almost as an afterthought, she said, "By the way, the girls all got together to get you a special birthday present. You'll find it when you get home. We think you'll like it." I had no idea what was in store for me.

I arrived shortly thereafter at my apartment. When I opened the door, I found a pair of high heels in the living room. A few feet beyond, nylon stockings. It didn't take any ingenuity to figure out just what kind of "present" awaited me. "Oh ho ho," I softly chuckled. A golden silk dress lay at the entrance to the hallway that joined my bedroom. My coat and suit jacket dropped to the floor as I followed this enticing trail.

As I entered my bedroom, I discovered a lacy bra and sheer panties on the floor. Elayne, my receptionist, was spread across my champagne-colored satin sheets. "Happy birthday," she softly purred. "Have I dressed suitably for the celebration?"

"Oh my goodness," I sighed. I felt myself rapidly losing control. My cock sprang to life, threatening to rip right through my pants. I couldn't get naked fast enough!

I sank under the spell of this sultry goddess. Elayne is a vision from heaven. She has shoulder-length blond hair with traces of light brown, and hypnotic blue-gray eyes. Her lips were full with sexual arousal yet pursed with nervous anticipation. My eyes, the guidance system for my heat-seeking missile, locked on to her fantastic brown pussy.

Elayne lay propped up on her elbows, her lovely legs slightly raised back and spread enticingly. Her light skin, golden-tan from a recent Caribbean vacation, glistened with love oils. Her rosebud nipples perked up from her well-formed breasts as her hands traveled down her belly toward her creaming crevice. As she grabbed her left ankle to raise her leg, lifting her ass-cheek slightly off the bed, Elayne massaged oil into her soft, smooth behind.

Her heavenly hole puckered open in invitation. An oily index finger traced its way from Elayne's tight little asshole straight along the length of her glowing pink slit, tickling her engorged clitoris. She let out a little squeal and wiggled her hips in plea-sure. I was on my knees, moving across the bed with my blood-engorged lance straining to sex-crazed proportions.

"Spread them back, Elayne," I commanded as my steaming, dripping missile approached its entry tube. Her eyes transfixed to mine, and then to my steely shaft as it penetrated its target. My cock instantly plunged to the depths of her cunt, sliding sweetly through her abundant flow of cream. The sensation of her well-lubricated, snug-fitting fuck-hole was maddening. I paused mo-mentarily to maintain my control. Elayne was still raised against the pillows. She stared into my eyes with the confidence that she was about to fuck my brains out.

I turned my attention to the gorgeous brown mink framed be-tween her lovely thighs. I slowly slid my dick out until just the head was inside her, loving the look of her glistening juices on my pole. Then I pumped it back in to the hilt.

My nymphomaniac receptionist was grinding herself against me like a wild woman. Elayne screamed, "Oh yes, fuck me, fuck me, oh Christ, fuck me, fuck me, yes, yes, fuck my cunt, yes!" I vocalized my ecstasy with equal enthusiasm. I was thrusting furi-ously, banging in and out forcefully, giving this horny bitch a royal whomping! It was beautiful watching my throbbing dick disappearing inside the furry love-basket of my golden goddess!

Elayne lost control. Her legs clamped around my waist to pull us closer. Her hands grabbed my ass, then my balls, trying to stuff me inside her. She pulled my mouth to hers, fusing our tongues with hot, sticky saliva. Elayne shrieked in orgasm, using her legs to pull me closer still. I followed with a gut-wrenching orgasm, blasting a hero's load of spunk deep into her cunt. I must have fired about twenty rounds of love into her heavenly snatch.

When I withdrew, my cock was purple and red and dripping with goo. Elayne's vagina was a deep, glowing pink. Come and cream flowed generously down her crack, dripping from her ass, wetting the sheets. We took turns tasting and feeding each other the love potion we had concocted.

Elayne told me I had to recover quickly because the celebration was still young. Even though I was spent, I was mildly intoxicated from the afterplay. I was tempted to suck the honey from her pussy, but she stopped me, informing me that I had an assistant for that job. Elayne took me by the hand to the guest room.

Lorrie and April, my girl Friday, were locked in a passionate embrace. I was asked to lie on one bed while April placed a liplock on my limp tool, still spent from Elayne. Her tongue playfully tickled my cock. I almost couldn't handle it. The sight of Elayne and Lorrie in the next bed soon helped get my prick throbbing again. And April was an expert cocksucker!

Elayne lay sprawled on her back, eyes closed and legs spread. Lorrie pulled back her long, black hair and clamped onto Elayne's hips as she feasted on her sweet pussy. She began to lick and suck the cream of our lovemaking from Elayne's dripping cunt. She was so beautiful that I wanted to fuck that precision set of pubes again! Then Lorrie stood up, her mouth dripping with cream. Elayne concentrated on pleasing herself.

Lorrie walked over to me, swirling her tongue until her full lips were completely slick with jism. She planted her soaking mouth on mine, letting the slick juices slip between our tongues while rubbing the overflow all over my face.

Meanwhile, April had my dick engulfed in her warm, wet, delicious mouth, bathing it with her hot saliva. She stood up momentarily to drop the lacy white gown that was still hanging on her elbows. On her upper thigh I noticed a small tattoo of a butterfly, the witness to many an alert pecker as they passed through her trim, coarse cunt hairs to the wet wonders beyond. Her curly brown hair hung down to her full pair of tits. A thin pearl necklace was now the only item she wore. She flashed a sexy smile and brushed her lips against the tip of my rigid cock.

Lorrie straddled my face, grasping her labia and pulling them apart as she eased her vagina onto my nose. My tongue flickered gently up and down the crack of her ass. Her scent was intoxicating! In seconds she was rocking, moaning, and babbling. I raised my head back for air and sucked on her clit, licking furiously as her juices ran down her legs.

Lorrie moaned and cried with pleasure. I continued to devour her juicy cunt even as my jaw began to ache. "Oh, yes! I'm coming!" she moaned, crushing my face between her snatch and her thighs while almost pulling the hair out of my head. She collapsed against the headboard, while I lay trapped beneath her steaming ass.

April had been sucking me like a pro, her cheeks drawing in for maximum suction, her tongue licking the underside of my cock. It was a blowjob I'd never forget. She used her lips, tongue, mouth, teeth and throat to explore my cock, balls and ass. Fortunately my cock was long in endurance after Elayne had drained me.

Then I felt April impale herself on my shaft. Her sex-hole felt like warm honey and butter as she melted on top of me. I humped her slowly, gently, and deeply, holding my wad. Lorrie was kissing and caressing my torso. Elayne joined her. Soon they were alternating between sucking April's tits and licking my slippery dick and her quivering cunt while we fucked. Then they climbed onto the other bed to engage in their own erotic duet.

As April squirmed on top of me we both slowed down to appreciate the spectacle that was unfolding on the other mattress. Elayne gradually, quietly began to explore between Lorrie's thighs, massaging her clit while sliding two fingers in and out of her soaking pussy. Slowly she licked Lorrie's body, kissing her belly and making her way up the torso. As Elayne sucked a big, brown nipple into her mouth, Lorrie groaned with pleasure.

Lorrie reached around and grabbed Elayne's ass, pulling her up so that their lips met. Every part of their bodies seemed to fuse together—lips to lips, breasts to breasts, cunt to cunt. Elayne and Lorrie were like one unified mass of womanly pleasure.

April's sticky cunt pulsed around my embedded prick. Her hips gyrated in passion. I watched her wispy, hungry beaver eagerly munch on my log. After she had come three times, she pulled off. A sweet, squishy, sucking sound came from her soaking pussy as our fusion was broken. My dick stood eight inches high, bathed in her honey. April resumed her suction lock and I pumped in synchronization. My dick was throbbing and pulsing in anticipation. My balls and asshole contracted as my second thick load of the evening erupted into April's mouth.

She licked me clean and crawled up to kiss me, the taste of my come and her honey still in her mouth. We drifted off to a brief sleep, but the birthday festivities continued throughout the night and into the next morning. My three blue-eyed party girls were a most enjoyable feast.

GOING DOWN UNDER

Six months ago I took an island vacation to one of those adult resorts where everything is included: waterskiing, sailing, snorkeling and other activities. This was the kind of place where all the employees are beautiful, tan, perfect young things. I had gone on this type of vacation in the past, so I knew the routine. I usually focus my energies on tanning, drinking, flirting and showing off my body to as many men as I please. This time, however, I decided to partake in a scuba program which was highly recommended.

At the beginning of the first lesson, I questioned my decision. Did I really want to take so much time away from my other activities? It wasn't until Derrick, our instructor, introduced himself that I knew I had made the right decision. His body was well-defined and firm. I was immediately turned on by the tight, rippling muscles which I gazed upon, slowly moving my eyes down his chest, to his stomach, to his waist, to whatever lay beneath the sexy sarong he had loosely wrapped around his hips.

We had to commit to four days of lessons just to learn how to properly use the equipment. Then we went on to learn correct breathing and hand signals before we could actually dive. This gave me the opportunity to make my attraction apparent to Derrick. I'd play little tricks to get him near me. For example, when I was putting on the tank and diving jacket (it's very heavy and awkward equipment), I'd call over to Derrick and ask him to help me clip the front of the jacket shut—I just couldn't seem to get it to work. He'd take both hands and grab the clips, which would conveniently place his hands directly on my hard little nipples. I'd almost orgasm right there. Another day I complained that the combination of the heavy tank, my sunburn and my tight bikini top hurt too much, so I changed into a T-shirt. When I came out of the water, my round, perfect little breasts were barely covered by the soaking wet cotton shirt. My nipples were looking Derrick straight in the face. I knew I was teasing the hell out of the poor guy, but it is his job to maintain decorum—after all, there were six other people in my class, so he had to behave professionally.

The only other woman in the class was a beautiful French woman. She had thick, long, dark-brown hair, larger breasts than I, but an equally tight, rounded, lovely ass. I knew she had the hots for Derrick too—in fact, we both continually bombarded him with challenging sexual jokes which often disrupted the class.

Finally, on the fifth day, we were scheduled to take our very first open-water dive. We boarded the boat at six-thirty in the morning. It was a beautiful sunny day. I wasn't as enthusiastic as I could have been—I was very hung over, probably still a little drunk from the previous night's fun. Nevertheless, we finally arrived at our site. We all suited up for the first dive of the morning: tanks, jackets, flippers and masks. Then we clumsily waddled to the back of the boat and went down into the most beautiful, serene, colorful, sensuous world I'd ever encountered. It was an incredible experience. The coral, the fish, the feeling of weightlessness—I felt like I was in another world. All of it was so physically and mentally exciting, I didn't know what to do with myself!

At the end of the dive, our group was the last to congregate at the sand bar, which is suspended fifteen feet or so beneath the boat. One at a time Derrick pointed to each diver, directing the flow to the surface and back to the boat. Since I was the last diver, I began to surface when it looked clear, but I was stopped by Derrick's hand. He pulled me back down to the sand bar and, with one hand, he reached for the top clip of my jacket and opened it. I was so excited—my head was rushing and my breasts were aching to be touched. He reached in, pulled down my bikini top and began to fondle the sensitive tips of my nipples. I was getting dizzier, consumed by a fantasy that was wildly turning into reality! He removed the regulator from his mouth and began sucking my tits. The bubbles were slightly distracting, but then his hand traveled up from my knee, slowly toward my hot, slippery, throbbing pussy. He pushed aside the suit and began to masterfully bring me toward climax. I was madly turned on. I wanted his hard cock in me deep, hard and fast.

I reached for him but he intercepted my hand, looked me in the eyes and signaled for me to surface. Cruel, I thought. But when I got back on the boat I was quite happy to have had the experience at all.

We lifted anchor and powered to the next dive site. Derrick and I were finding it difficult to hide our smiles. Marcelle, my French girlfriend, had an idea about what might have gone on down there, but she could only guess and tease me about my secretiveness. I'm sure Derrick saw our interaction, because the second dive was even better than the first.

We all descended eighty feet or so, this time for what seemed to be only ten minutes. After this short dive, we returned to the sand bar and Derrick began the elimination process once again. This time, however, he left both Marcelle and me for last. Marcelle was floating between Derrick and me. He looked at me, winked and proceeded to begin his little game with Marcelle as I watched. He pointed with his finger first to his mouthpiece, and then to Marcelle's breasts. To my surprise she shook her head, no, and began to return her own signals. She pointed her finger and lowered it slowly to her mouth, and then ever so slowly she trailed her finger down the side of his face, down his neck, over his chest to his cock, which was by now obviously growing very hard under his wet suit.

Derrick's eyes almost popped out of his mask. He was, however, more than happy to oblige. Keeping his regulator in his mouth, he began the very awkward task of stripping off his tank and wet suit. First he unclipped the jacket and tank, and secured them to the bar we were hanging from. Then he unzipped the wet suit, revealing his muscular arms, chest and stomach, and finally a sexy little green, nylon bikini which was stretched to the limits. His cockhead was reaching out of its confines, reaching out to be sucked by Marcelle's mouth. She fondled him, reaching back behind his balls, and then brought her hand over the balls, up the shaft to the head. I was very hot and jealous at this point.

I watched her hand going up and down the hard shaft of his cock and I couldn't help but reach into my own suit, only to find the hottest and wettest pussy I have ever had. My clit was hard and sensitive. I was wildly turned on to what was happening, so I fondled myself madly. Then I decided to make a bold move. Marcelle and Derrick watched me closely as I proceeded to take off my bikini bottoms. I pushed them into my jacket pocket so that they wouldn't float away. Then I spread my pussy lips as wide as possible and signaled to Derrick that he should watch closely.

Marcelle continued to stroke Derrick's cock slowly but firmly. He was taking deep breaths from his regulator more frequently as he watched me. I stroked my fingers deep inside my cunt, back and forth, until I was shaking. I was surprised at how slick I still felt under the water. I kept moving my fingers until it seemed that Derrick was going to explode. Then I stopped and quickly moved my hand to my breasts. As I pulled and twisted on my sensitive nipples, I watched Derrick's cock throb in Marcelle's hand. His expression said he couldn't take much more.

Marcelle drew a few deep breaths through her mouthpiece, and finally got down to the challenge at hand. On the third breath she removed her regulator and plunged his cock into her mouth. It seemed to go deeper into her mouth with every stroke. I was wondering how easy it could be to suck and not choke under so much water, and I was eager to try it. She lasted a pretty long time before she had to put the regulator back in her mouth. Still, I thought I could last longer.

After Marcelle regained her stamina, they both turned to me and signaled it was my turn. I was unbelievably ready for this. I love to give head as it is, but to be given the opportunity to suck that gorgeous cock in front of another woman, while scuba diving, was too much! I literally dove toward Derrick. After taking my preparatory three breaths, I plugged his cock into my mouth. That sweet taste of pre-come in the back of my throat made me suck harder and faster. To my amazement, the need for air wasn't hitting me. I just wrapped my hands around his tight ass and, sucking him hard, brought his cock deeper and deeper into my throat—deeper than I ever thought possible. By this time I was starting to need air, but I was determined. I was sucking even faster and harder when all of a sudden he pushed me off of him. I pulled myself together, got my regulator and reached for his shaft. I began to stroke it hard, up and down. Then I squeezed and stroked some more. After I jacked him off for a while, I began to feel the telltale, slow rumble deep within his cock. Then I squeezed.

He exploded in a matter of seconds. His semen came, not in spurts, but in a long, white stream that just seemed to grow as a natural extension from the end of his cock. We were all in absolute shock. But the intensity was broken when a school of brightly colored small fish swarmed in and began wildly feasting on his juices. It was an amazing sight. I couldn't help thinking what lucky fish they were.

Marcelle and I surfaced. Everyone on the boat was suspicious—after all, we'd been down for a long time. We tried to hide our smiles, but we blew up laughing when Derrick, our wonderful instructor, surfaced triumphantly with jacket and tank in one hand, and his wet suit in the other. Everyone was hootin' and hollerin' at Derrick, making lewd comments—most of which were validated when Derrick looked at me and shouted, "What the hell do you dive with a tank for?" I guess I really know how to hold my breath!

I have been home for five months now. I am in the process of getting my diving certification. I think I'll become a teacher.

THE PRINCESS BRIDE

I'm very lucky to have a wife of twenty years who's sexier now than when we first met. She's five-foot-seven with dark hair and a great face. She's thinner now than when we married, and her soft skin and 34C breasts haven't changed; her great ass and legs still drive me crazy. What's really improved is her sensuality and her experience—she knows how to please me in a hundred ways and is ready to try new things to give me pleasure. I'd like to describe the relatively tame but very satisfying experience we had last night.

I called home during the day and found that our daughter was going to sleep over at a friend's house. In my mind, I immediately went into sexual fantasyland to imagine how we could take advantage of the rare privacy this assured Regina and me. Before ending the call I told Regina that I'd love to spend the evening with a princess. She knew that I was telling her how to dress for me, since her wardrobe for our private times includes a wide range of lingerie and outer clothing from the demure to the outrageous—some items that are meant only to be worn in the privacy of our home. Tonight I wanted her to wear soft, sensuous garments that could be worn in public.

I told Regina I'd make dinner reservations at a posh area restaurant and that I trusted she could be dressed in some of her nicest demure clothing by seven o'clock, when I'd pick her up for a very special date. I told her that after a leisurely dinner in an elegant and romantic setting, I'd like to bring her home and enjoy her body. She asked if I had anything specific in mind and I told her that I'd be thinking about it all afternoon. I said she had to agree in advance that once we arrived home I could do anything I wanted. She readily agreed.

I intentionally arrived home before seven o'clock to find my date still getting ready. This allowed me a peek at her lingerie before it was covered. I knew this would enhance my mental images during dinner. She was wearing an entire ensemble of black silk. Her legs and ass looked fantastic in silk stockings, a black garter belt and a bikini bottom. Her ample breasts were seductively covered in a black silk bra with lace trim (she had sewn push-up pads in the bra when I bought it for her, which created some delicious cleavage for my eyes to feast on). A black silk slip soon covered all of these areas but, by adding its own sensual softness and mystery, it actually added to my wife's overall sex appeal. I wanted to grab her on the spot, but was firmly told to leave the room while she finished getting ready to go out.

Regina finished dressing in a few minutes. She was wearing a very proper but sexy, dark dress in a silky fabric. Her best perfume and jewelry completed her ensemble. Her makeup was subdued but nicely done. Her overall appearance was that of a very good-looking, sophisticated lady. Only I knew how truly sexy she looked underneath her dress. She looked great—exactly in the style that I had requested.

We had a very nice dinner. Looking around the restaurant, I couldn't help but compare my wife to the other women in the room. I concluded that she was definitely the sexiest. Even in her nonrevealing clothing she has an aura of sex appeal most women don't have. I told Regina this and she blushed.

I whispered to Regina across the table that I kept visualizing her without her top layer of clothing and that I wanted to grab her and bury my face between her breasts right then. Being in a public place obviously made this impossible, but the formality of the restaurant made the imagery all the more appealing. I got a hard-on from thinking about Regina sitting there in her sexy bra and slip, and softly told her how she had worked her magic on my cock from across the table without doing anything. She smiled suggestively and said it sounded like I didn't want to be with a princess anymore. I assured her that there was nothing inconsistent with my mental images since the princess I had in mind was a horny princess who loved sex.

In a few minutes, Regina told me in a throaty whisper that as she had dressed she felt that her breasts were somewhat swollen from their normal state. She said she had cradled them in her hands to get a better idea of their size. Regina said that while this started as a clinical gesture, as she had her breasts cupped in her hands she thought of me and how excited I'd get if I could see her hands almost unconsciously begin to fondle herself. This didn't continue for more than a minute or so, she said, but she thought I would enjoy hearing about the incident. My dick twitched and I smiled. As Regina spoke, her fingers reached for an imaginary piece of lint on the front of her dress. She allowed her fingers to linger suggestively near her right breast, knowing that, combined with her speaking about her breasts, her hand movements would tease me like crazy. They did.

Our dinner ended with the valet getting our car and me attempting to subtly brush up against Regina's body as we waited. The drive home was spent with my hand on Regina's thighs, pushing her dress up and enjoying her legs through her stockings.

As we neared our home I reminded Regina that once we were inside she had promised we would do whatever I requested. In keeping with the spirit of our evening so far, I wanted to make love to her in a special way which I thought would give her great pleasure. She agreed.

The house was dark as we entered it. I told Regina to stop and wait. I lit two candlesticks I had placed near the door, gave her one to carry and took her other hand in mine so I could lead her where I wanted.

We found our way by candlelight to an open area in our bedroom. I placed the candles on a nearby dresser. In the candlelight the room was no longer a familiar part of our home. In fact, to add to this illusion, I had placed a straight back chair in the room and covered it with a dark burgundy sheet. When Regina saw this I'm sure she wondered what I had in mind, but she said nothing.

I told Regina that I had loved being teased by her sensuality all evening. As I spoke, Regina and I were standing facing each other, so I reached out and caressed her soft face. I allowed my hands to trail down her arms to her hips. She felt great and seemed to enjoy my touch. Pulling her to me, we kissed in a passionate and romantic way. As it began, at least, our kiss had more love embodied in it than sex; on the other hand I'm sure Regina could feel my noticeably hard cock and was intentionally pressing up against it. My hands roamed over Regina's shoulders and back and found their way to her hips and ass more than once.

When the kiss finally ended we were both quite aroused. I told Regina that she had seduced me completely. She was beautiful and I loved her. I was now going to make love to her entire body. She moaned at the thought.

I told Regina that I felt compelled to gradually strip away her clothing—tenderly kissing and caressing her soft skin—not for my pleasure but for hers. Her only role was to relax and enjoy my worshiping her. As I spoke I began to slowly unzip her dress. My mouth soon found her neck and shoulders and I kissed each area as it became exposed. Seeing and feeling her body in her silk lingerie was intoxicating. My hands skimmed over her ass and hips, the silk slip minimizing the friction and accentuating Regina's soft curves. I moved behind her and ran my hands over her chest and down to the front of her thighs. Feeling Regina was exciting to me, and I could tell that she was enjoying my hands on her.

Regina stood quietly as I stripped her, alternately watching me or closing her eyes. Her body language told me she felt my love and was deriving great pleasure from my tender approach.

I eased the straps of her slip off Regina's shoulders and pushed the neckline down. This gave me access to the luscious mounds of her breasts, which peeked through her lacy bra. I gently ran my fingers over these exposed areas of flesh and kissed them, exercising tremendous restraint so as to be gentle and loving. I've always found Regina's breasts very exciting. Obviously their beautiful, sexy presentation to me in silk did nothing to lessen the thrill.

When I finally removed Regina's bra her hard nipples begged for attention, but I was determined to take my time and give Regina pleasure through loving touches rather than direct contact with her erogenous zones. My hands and mouth both paid homage to her breasts but brushed her nipples only lightly. Similarly, when I removed her bikini, I was restrained in my caresses of her Venus mound but made enough contact to give us both some pleasure. My hands and mouth concentrated more on her hips and buttocks. They felt wonderful with and without the bikini.

Removing Regina's clothes must have taken more than fifteen minutes as each garment prompted me to fondle and caress a new part of my lovely wife's body before, during and after the item was removed. Long kisses further prolonged the endeavor and added to our ever-increasing passion.

When Regina's ensemble was reduced to a silk garter belt, stockings and heels, she had reached one of my favorite levels of dress. Regina's legs are long and very well shaped; displaying them in stockings and heels emphasizes their sexuality and is a huge turn-on for me. Similarly, exposing the fair skin on Regina's upper body while leaving her hips and legs clothed in dark colors really calls attention to her breasts and invites me to make love to them.

I told Regina again how beautiful she looked and how I wanted to give her extreme pleasure as a sign of my love, then I hurriedly stripped off my own clothes down to my shorts.

I escorted Regina to the burgundy-covered chair, sat down and had her sit on my lap facing me with her legs on either side of mine. Her feet were on the floor, which gave her balance and allowed her to relax. This position gave me total freedom to use both hands over almost her whole body and placed her beautiful breasts directly in front of my face. Her perfume filled my nostrils as my eyes drank in every detail of her breasts and, in particular, her very erect nipples. I again wanted to bury one of those delicious nipples in my mouth, but held back.

My one hand enjoyed Regina's stockinged leg while the other caressed her breasts. My hands switched positions a few times and both glided over Regina's ass as I enjoyed fondling every part of her. Regina's body was totally accessible to me and we both loved it. Her eyes were closed and she made soft sounds evidencing the pleasure she was receiving from my wandering touch.

As I got more and more excited my hand seemed to move faster and more forcefully. Instead of softly caressing, I was now rubbing Regina's thighs and grabbing her ass. My hands no longer just brushed her nipples and fondled her breasts lightly; now I was beginning to hold each breast, kneading it firmly while feeling Regina's erect nipple rub on the palm of my hand.

After resisting the temptation for several minutes, my mouth finally descended on Regina's breasts as my hands cupped them and held them captive. She groaned as she felt the wetness of my tongue on her nipple for the first time and her body seemed to reach a new level of sexual tension. She was no longer passively enjoying being touched; she was sexually on fire! In turn, Regina's response to my mouth excited me tremendously and encouraged me to lavish much more attention on her nipples.

Both hands cradled and fondled Regina's breasts as my tongue explored every bump and ridge surrounding first one and then the other areola and, of course, the nipples themselves. My teeth carefully teased each nipple as my tongue pushed each of them in succession against my teeth and lips and I sucked lightly on each one. After switching back and forth, my mouth began to concentrate on Regina's left breast. My hand fondled her right one and my fingers soon focused on her right nipple. It was rock hard and about one-quarter inch long.

After enjoying the sensation of rolling this sensuous nub in my fingers, my thumb and forefinger maneuvered to find a secure grip and I began to squeeze Regina's nipple more forcefully. My fingers no longer moved—they simply applied continuous pressure to the very sensitive but firm flesh. Regina's arousal doubled in seconds. I could feel her entire body tense up, and the breast in my mouth was pushed harder against my face. I instinctively sucked harder and my tongue flicked over the sensitive nipple. Regina's thighs began to squeeze mine and her body almost rose up above my lap. My free arm encircled Regina's back to make sure her breast stayed planted firmly in my mouth.

Regina's breath now came in gasps and her body became incredibly tense. Finally she groaned loudly as a huge orgasm swept through her body, causing it to first jump and then relax. I maintained my grip with my hand and mouth on her breasts for another minute or so until Regina's noises and flailing arms made it clear her nerves couldn't take it anymore. She collapsed against my body and I hugged her as spasms continued to run through her for several minutes.

When the spasms seemed to have passed, I directed Regina to stand. I removed my shorts, turned her around and had her back up so her legs were straddling my knees. I guided her body downward to sit on my lap again. This time, however, her velvety wet pussy was destined for my rock-hard cock.

I slipped in easily as she was so well lubricated that her legs had begun to get wet; I soon felt her sensuous wetness on my balls.

My hands held Regina's hips as I rotated her ass on my cock

and thrust my pelvis upward to get in as deeply as possible. I murmured that I had a very great need to bury myself deeply within her; Regina moaned at the thought and seemed to be enjoying the sensation of my cock straining to reach new depths. I kept one hand on Regina's hip to maintain my penetration, but enjoyed fondling her breasts from behind with my other hand. She felt great!

I became aware that Regina was spreading her legs wider and soon felt her hand reach down between her legs for my balls. She cupped her hand under them and lifted them up, forcing me even deeper inside of her pussy. Her hands seemed to be lifting me and fondling me with exquisitely light touches from her long fingernails. It was fantastic! Her hand became an extension of her pussy. It was exactly what I wanted. I've never felt myself deeper inside of her nor more welcome. The wetness on my balls was also a constant reminder of the pleasure I had just given Regina. It was an unbelievably great feeling.

Feeling as if my cock and balls had been swallowed up by Regina's dripping pussy was more than my aching balls could stand for long. Even though I couldn't move much in this position, Regina's handling of my balls was more than enough stimulation. I soon began to feel the pressure of my long-awaited climax well up at the base of my cock and move slowly up its length. I pushed Regina's hips down on my cock to gain every possible millimeter of penetration. It almost burned as my come exploded from the tip and countless muscles in my body seemed to have involuntary contractions. I pulled Regina tightly against me and told her again how much I loved her.

A LOOSE WIRE

*I*t was a hot, sticky, summer day—the last day of classes—and I had just walked my girlfriend to her car. We embraced in a nice, long, passionate kiss and she was on her way home. As she turned onto the main highway I waved goodbye and heard the shrill horn of her Volkswagen as she sped away.

Even though I lived near the lake, where there was sure to be a refreshing breeze, I didn't relish the prospect of going back to my apartment alone. Denise had lived with me all semester, and I didn't know if I could face our empty bed—a bed that had seen a lot more slamming than our desks had seen cramming. I decided to take a walk.

I was casually strolling toward the lake when I noticed a beautiful pair of legs sticking out from under the hood of a Toyota. My curiosity got the best of me and I proceeded in the direction of the gams. And what a set they were! Probably the most beautifully formed legs I had ever seen. As I approached, I got a full view. The suntanned legs were long and lean, and the tight little white shorts the woman wore not only emphasized the length of her legs but also gave me a sneak preview of her creamy, untanned ass.

She had on a tight, white, sleeveless T-shirt that snugly caressed two of the firmest and largest breasts I'd ever seen. What's more, it was obvious that she did not have a bra on. The T-shirt was flimsy enough to allow the sides of her breasts to spill out through the armholes, and as I drew nearer I could see the darkness of her nipples, which stood firmly erect. Mesmerized, I felt a warmth in my groin. My prick was getting hard as a rock, and I casually put my hand in my pocket to quiet it a bit.

As I neared the car, I was becoming intoxicated by the scent that exuded from her body. Her face and hair were stunning. Only in my fantasies had I seen a more perfectly shaped woman. Long, soft, brown curls neatly framed her classic good looks. Her mouth was soft and sensuous. The fullness of it enticed me further. Her eyes were soft and dreamy, and her pert little nose gave her an impish appearance. Her lashes were dark and long. The sight was so unbelievable that I nearly pinched myself to make sure that she was not a Penthouse Pet I had fashioned in my imagination.

Her beauty was paralyzing. I found myself choking on my words as I approached her. Damn, I thought, could I get my rocks off with a dish like that!

She appeared relaxed when I asked her what the problem was and offered my assistance. She told me she was having some difficulty starting her Toyota. I offered to take a look. Even though it was getting dusky now, I could see the loose wire dangling, and I immediately and very deftly reconnected it. Then I jumped into the car and started it up. My goddess in distress was beside herself with gratitude. I told her to think nothing of it.

When I was in the car, I had inhaled the sweet fragrance of some expensive perfume. I was getting hotter and hotter by the second. When I got out of the car and proceeded to pull down the hood, the girl nonchalantly pressed her beautiful tits against my back. I did not back off. I turned around and stared at her and her devilish grin. I had a feeling I was in for some heavy action when she lovingly licked her lips.

I asked her whether there was anything else I could do for her. She asked if I could tell her where she could find a phone; she had to call her friends and tell them that she'd be late. I suggested she use mine at home since it was only a block away. When she asked if it was any trouble, I answered emphatically, "No, it isn't."

When we got up to the third floor, I fumbled with the lock. Up to this time, I had been so cool. Again, she pressed her tits on my back. I did not resist. Once inside, I led her to the kitchen, showed her where the telephone was and offered her a glass of beer. While I was reaching into the fridge, she took out her checkbook and offered to pay me for my services. As far as I was concerned, I was interested in only one payoff—and money had nothing to do with it!

She walked back into the living room and I followed a few minutes later. When I saw her sitting on the sofa, I nearly dropped the frosted mugs of beer. She had thrown her shirt on the floor and those firm, enormous breasts were begging to be sucked and caressed. As I moved in for the kill, she sat up and slid her little shorts down to around her ankles. She had the most delicately curled bush of brown hair I have ever seen. She sat back on the sofa and gently tugged on her pussy hairs. Every so often she would spread her lips and tease her clit. She slowly lifted up her eyes to meet mine and silently begged me to come to her. I felt sensations like I had never felt before, and my prick was so swollen that I thought it would pop out of my pants.

When I stood in front of her, she immediately undid my belt, pulled down my zipper and reached in for my cock. I could not in my wildest fantasies believe that this was happening to me. I had never been so horny in my life. She first caressed my cock with her massive tits and then tenderly put it in her mouth. Her tongue was doing all sorts of contortions on my dick, and they felt terrific. I let her continue with the blowjob while I grabbed at her tits, rubbing their ample contours.

By this time my dick was trying to touch my navel, and I had to get it inside her somehow. I pulled her to the carpet and turned her onto her stomach. She had the tightest little ass I had ever seen. I put my hand on her clit and began to rub. She let out moans of pleasure. Laying my chest against her back like a blanket, I placed my dick on the lips of her pussy, letting it do its work. Feeling that musky warmth so near, the head started to throb, gently working its way into her hole of its own accord. The beauty below me let out a gasp as my cock sprang up inside her. Reaching under her, I grabbed the massive tits, pulled the girl up and went at her with wild abandon. I could feel her playing with her clit while I reamed her from behind, and when I felt her pussy tighten and shower my dick with her steaming come, I shot my load deep inside her.

We lay quietly for a few minutes, and then she urged me to eat her out. Her pussy smelled like clover. I pulled at her hair and proceeded to suck each pussy lip one at a time. I opened her legs wider, and then I spread her puffed-out lips, exposing her clit. It was a juicy little fella. I started out slowly, sucking and then gently nibbling on it. She loved everything I did and pressed my head further down. I licked her hole for a while, and then concentrated on her clit. Her moans started to get louder and suddenly she arched her back, pressing her mound into my face. I felt shivers going through her body and just kept working on that clit. Her ass was in the air by now, and soon a gigantic convulsion took hold of her. Within seconds she was fingering herself, and then she squeezed her thighs together, filling my mouth with come.

When I looked up, all I saw were her heaving and sweaty breasts as she fought to regain her breath. I blew on her torso to cool her down and her nipples shot up like two rockets. I began to suck her tits one at a time. She was enjoying every minute of it. In my state of euphoria, I did not hear the door to my apartment open. There, standing above us, was my girlfriend. I was dumbfounded. Before I could explain, she had proceeded to take all her clothes off and join us in a ménage à trois. My girlfriend is usually as conventional as I am, and I'd never have dreamed that she would have joined in. But she jumped on my anonymous friend with the same enthusiasm that she usually brings to our heterosexual encounters. She started licking the stranger's hole like a woman possessed. Her ass was sticking up in the air and I moved in for the kill. It was such a strange situation that I felt like I was fucking Denise for the first time ever. We changed positions for the next hour or so before we all fell asleep in exhaustion.

Next morning, when I woke up, only my girl and I were in bed. On the dresser, however, there was a note. "Dear Friend: I never thought that a loose wire could bring so much erotic bliss. Thanks for everything—Erica." Well, I finally found out her name, although it really didn't matter—I never saw Erica again.

AEROBISEX

I am a successful professional woman—marketing vice-president for a small but rapidly growing construction firm in a major city on the East Coast. My husband never fails to compliment me on my looks. Personally I think he exaggerates my beauty, but my long, auburn hair and firm ass do turn many a head.

One recent Friday afternoon I left work early to go home and change for my aerobics class. Standing before the full-length mirror in my bedroom, I unbuttoned my blouse under which my nipples, covered by a white, silk camisole (no bra), began to harden in the cool of our air-conditioned apartment. I unwrapped my skirt, stepped out of my lacy slip and inspected myself in the mirror. I noticed that my commitment to exercise was paying off: my smooth stomach had lost its slight swell and was almost flat. As I turned sideways my long, athletic legs and tightly rounded butt were highlighted by my high-heel pumps and silk stockings. During these warm summer months I rarely wear panties, and the contrast of the tight straps of my garter belt and my soft, pale ass is a sight that my husband appreciates. As my hands slowly drifted up to lightly brush my breasts through the material of the camisole, it occurred to me that I was still a bit randy from the wonderful fucking my husband had given me that morning. I hoped that the impending workout would take my mind off my libido.

I arrived at class just in time. During our warm-up I looked around to see who was there. As I scoped out the crowd of about forty or so, my eyes met those of a new girl whom I had not seen before. She smiled at me and then looked away. During the work-out, I occasionally managed to check her out in the mirror. She was obviously curious about me as well, because we locked re-flected glances several times, upon which we would both quickly look down, slightly embarrassed. The girl was lovely in an earthy sort of way. Her hips were a bit wide, but not unattractive. Her shoulder-length, blond hair bounced freely as she danced.

After class, while I was gathering my things and catching my breath, I looked up to see her standing there. "Hi," she said, "my name is Maria. What's yours?" I stammered for a minute, then told her. I fumbled for something to say as my eyes trailed down the V of sweat that made her top cling to the front of her body. Her sparkling blue eyes bespoke a kind, perhaps vulnerable, inte-rior. Soon we were yakking away like old friends. Having both re-cently moved to the area from almost the same part of my home state, we found that we had much in common. Suddenly I re-membered that I had an extra guest pass to my club, so I suggested that we both cleanse our pores in the sauna. She also had a change of clothes with her and was more than willing to soothe her exhausted muscles with me in the whirlpool.

The club is just a couple of doors down from the dance studio, so we soon had keys and found our lockers, which happened to be right next to each other. As we peeled out of our sweaty gar-ments, I tried to see (without being too obvious) what treasure her outfit had been concealing. In fact, I caught her looking me up and down in what can only be described as an amorous man-ner! She looked guilty as hell, so I defused the situation with a laugh and a smile, and we headed for the girls-only sauna with just our towels wrapped around us.

The locker room had been deserted except for us, and the sauna was no different. Maria sat on the higher level of wooden slats and I sat one level below her. We quickly fell to talking about men, jobs and sex. At one point she unabashedly swung one of her legs up on the slats. I felt my face flush as I tried not to examine her exposed genitals. She seemed not to care that she was showing all. Neither of us spoke for a minute, and I gave in to temptation and drank with my eyes the exquisite beauty between her legs. Her blond hair was neatly groomed and her pussy lips shaved like mine. Her pink, inner lips protruded from her swollen vulva like the symmetrical petals of some fleshy rose. Her rounded ass was flattened against the wood of the sauna bench, and I found myself thinking what it would be like to tongue her twat while grabbing her sweet butt with both hands.

I leaned back against the wall and unwrapped my towel, parting my legs and seductively stroking the insides of my thighs. By this time I was genuinely horny and suggested we try out the whirlpool.

Dropping our towels, we eased ourselves into the warm, roiling water. I closed my eyes and let the jets buffet my aching muscles. From previous experience I knew that if I positioned myself just right, I could enjoy the bursts of bubbles on my clit. Maria at once remarked how "really great" it felt, and I realized that she had also discovered my technique. I also realized that she had moved much closer to me than would appear appropriate to anyone entering the room. Under the water her hand found mine and squeezed it tightly. She smiled, said that she was very glad to have met me and was looking forward to being my friend. Feeling audacious, I pulled her hand to my leg. I could hardly believe what I was doing. I spread my legs as she took the initiative and moved her eager fingers to the heart of my desire. She knew exactly how to tantalize. She brought me to the edge several times and then, much to my dismay, two fat ladies walked in. We quickly moved apart and tried to disguise our guilt.

Later, as I showered, I struggled with my conscience. The same old worries: What if I'm gay? Still, it *had* been exhilarating, and I found myself wishing we could continue in more private surroundings. We quickly dressed sans underwear and headed for her place.

I called my husband from Maria's apartment and told him that I was going to be out late. Having taken care of that, I looked around Maria's apartment. It was tastefully decorated—feminine, but not girlish. Her book collection tended toward the avant-garde. Ayn Rand and Solzhenitsyn were typical of the authors on her shelves.

Maria entered the room with two Mai Tais. They were perfect. As we settled into her plush, overstuffed couch, she tactfully broached the subject of getting high. I, of course, jumped at the opportunity. She deftly rolled a fat joint and we smoked. She turned down the lights a bit and put on some light jazz music. She pulled me up to dance. Though I protested that we had suffered enough exercise for one day, I found myself drawn into the rhythm. We passed the joint back and forth as we undulated in synchronization.

Still, I contemplated leaving before things went too far, but the more I looked at her, dancing slowly with her eyes closed, the more I wanted to stay. Just then she opened her eyes. A silent agreement was reached and we moved close to one another. We embraced and kissed. Our lips met, at first tentatively, then with growing passion.

She suddenly pulled back and, taking me by the hand, led me toward the bedroom. Her lair, I thought.

She lit a candle on each side of the bed and sat on the edge. Sitting next to her, I took the lead by sliding my fingers into her soft, golden hair and pulling her head back. Her slender neck exposed, I kissed and nibbled my way from her shoulders to her ears and back again. She sighed and murmured how "nice, very nice" it was. Moving again to her face, I sought her mouth, which beckoned me silently. Her sweet kisses aroused my senses with an electricity that made my cunt drip with anticipation. I wanted to taste all of her and for her to make love to me.

I became conscious of her hands moving up under my shirt to my breasts. Thus emboldened, I did the same to her and soon we had each other's shirt off, both of us reveling in our newfound toys. I never dreamed a woman's breast could feel so wonderful. I had certainly caressed my own many times while masturbating,

but this was totally incomparable. As I rolled her hard nipples between my fingers, she gently pushed my head down. Lifting her
heavy tit to my lips, I sucked her pink bud into my mouth. I
greedily tried to fit her entire breast into my mouth, much to her
delight. I was content, however, to swirl my tongue around and
around her areola.

She then dutifully paid at least as good attention to my tits as
I had to hers, taking special care to lightly brush the undersides
(just the way I like it). Again we kissed with our breasts rubbing
together. She was warm. She was soft. I was in heaven.

I moved my hands to her jean-encased legs as her kissing became move frantic. The aroma that emanated from her crotch
was amazing! This girl's cunt must be on fire, I thought. As I unbuckled her belt she groaned her appreciation for me finally getting down to business. Her tight pants snapped open as I undid
the button at the top, easing the zipper down.

I lightly touched her soft belly before toying with her small
patch of hair. I pushed her back on the bed and lay on one elbow
as I explored further. Her pussy was soft as a kitten, fantastically
slippery between her lips. I couldn't resist plunging my middle
finger into her well-lubricated hole. She whimpered with lust as
I stroked in and out. I removed my hand from its wet haven and
brought my fingers to my face, deeply inhaling her aroma. I tentatively raised my extended finger to my lips and had my first
taste of a woman. Maria's mouth joined mine and we both savored her sweet juices.

This was too much. I frantically removed her shoes and socks
and wrestled her pants down from her full hips. I stood to take off
the rest of my clothes. Then I lay on top of her with my leg between hers and one of hers between mine. We kissed more and
ground our eager pussies against each other. I began to kiss my
way down her body. I passed by her pussy to kiss the soles of her
feet and lick her toes. As I took her big toe in my mouth and
began to "blow" it as I would a cock, she reached down to rub her
pussy. "You just wait," I said, pushing her hand away. I didn't want

to torture her too much longer, so I kissed my way back to her treasure trove, alternating legs on the way up.

In the flickering candlelight I could see she was dripping with anticipation. Her tiny, pink clit had swollen to where it was conspicuously protruding at the top of her slit. I slid my arms underneath and around her legs and pressed my face to her sex. I pushed the hood of her clitoris back with my upper lip and stiffened my tongue to mercilessly lash at her exposed clit with a diversity of motions. To say she was enjoying herself would be an incredible understatement. Never in my life have I seen someone so wild! She jumped around and undulated her hips like some sort of rodeo bull or something. She forcefully used her hands to urge me to press even more tightly against her. Within seconds I could see the insides of her thighs begin to quiver. Her hands left my head and, as they began to clutch at the sheets, she ceased bucking and began a sort of a howl/moan/screech that must have begun deep in her belly. As she arched her back and let go, I continued licking her quickly disappearing love-button for all I was worth. What a racket! I was sure someone was going to call the police, but her screams, which came in waves along with the convulsions of her body, made me feel triumphant and powerful. In the back of my mind, I always knew I would be good at this.

I slid up next to her. Her trembling body glistened with sweat. Though I was content just to relax, she obviously had caught her second wind and began to kiss me with the gratitude of someone who has been exquisitely satisfied after a long period of deprivation. "You're gorgeous and that was the best I've *ever* had," she said. "Now I will try to make you feel as pretty as you have just made me feel." True to her word, she began to kiss me hotly all over my body. She rolled me over and began to massage my shoulders and back. I was in ecstasy. Tenderly kneading my legs and ass, her fingers slid to my pussy. I parted my legs to give her better access. I felt her kiss my behind, and for a second I felt embarrassed that a woman was examining my most private areas up close. Her insistent, probing tongue soon overcame my resistance, though, and I let her have her way.

She worked her way down to my eager pussy and quickly found the perfect spot. I brought my knees underneath me and lifted my ass to allow her to work her magic. She pressed her face against my snatch. I don't know how she could breathe, but she didn't seem to mind. She licked and sucked my cunt and clit like a woman possessed. She brought me to the edge again and again, just as she had done in the hot tub, but she wouldn't let me come. Desperate, I begged her to let me finish. "All in good time, my dear," she replied. She allowed me to roll over onto my back and get more comfortable.

Barely missing a beat, she resumed her delicious torture. She moved around until her knees were beside my head, then lifted one leg over me and brought her soft (and still quite wet) pussy down to my face. I eagerly pulled her ass to me and again began to suck and tantalize her cunt as she did the same to mine. It felt as though a continuous current of pleasure were cycling through us.

Closing my eyes, I surrendered to her shaking head and lashing tongue. This time she didn't hold back. An orgasm began to build within me that felt as though it began at my toes and fingertips and worked its way toward the center. Suddenly it happened! I have never before and never since experienced anything like it. I lost all track of time. It seemed to last for five minutes as the waves of uncontrollable release swept over me. I vaguely remember biting her leg, for which I apologized later. Exhausted, we fell asleep in each other's arms.

THE NATURAL

$\mathcal{F}$or years I have lusted after my wife's best friend, a luscious, leggy blonde named Paula. I always thought it would be just a favorite fantasy, but a conversation with my wife, Sue, and a great opportunity made my dream come true. Several months ago, my wife began telling me about the intimate confessions that Paula shared with her. Sue knew it turned me on to hear about Paula's sexy thoughts. Paula, still a virgin, has been getting increasingly hot for a hard cock.

About a month ago, Sue told me about a really cock-hardening conversation she'd had with Paula. It seems Paula had decided the only way she could manage to keep a boyfriend *and* her virginity was to learn how to give head. I teasingly suggested that we should let Paula watch while Sue gave me one of her cock-spurting blowjobs. I even offered to let Paula practice on my stiff joint. My wife dismissed both suggestions as being utterly outrageous.

But for an exhibitionist like me, the thought of Paula watching Sue lovingly sucking my rod was too much to forget. Many times during solo sessions, the thought of Paula joining my wife on her knees for cocksucking lessons was what brought me off. Those wad-blowing visions were still in my head when Paula came over to the house recently to get ready for a Christmas party. My wife is good with makeup and Paula wanted her to make up her face.

Paula brought various party dresses along, and girls being girls, they both began trying on different dresses in the bedroom. Then they would call me in to ask my opinion. Well, to say my cock was getting harder by the minute would be the understatement of the decade. Finally, I got the opportunity I had been looking for. Paula had on high heels and an incredibly sexy, short, backless black dress that showed off her legs encased in sheer black stockings. My wife, on the other hand, was between changes, wearing only her panties and holding a towel across her bare tits.

I profusely complimented Paula as I moved over behind my wife. Pressing my hard cock against her panty-covered ass, I slipped my hands up under the towel and began rubbing my wife's great 38-inch breasts.

"Bill, stop that," Sue exclaimed. "Not in front of Paula." Paula's mouth flew open in surprise at my brazen act.

"We're married, dear, and Paula doesn't mind, do you, Paula?" I cajoled.

Paula, still speechless, shook her head to indicate that she didn't mind.

"I guess we really can't blame him," Sue said, her ass rubbing against my straining cock. "We have tortured him with our modeling, I suppose."

Paula couldn't take her eyes off the towel covering the movements of my hands on Sue's massive jugs. Paula has an athletic body with small tits, and I suspected that she wanted to see me massage Sue's big tits. So, as I kissed my wife's neck, I eased the towel down until it fell to the floor. Then I gave Paula a good show as I gently squeezed Sue's ample tits until her nipples got hard.

By this time, Sue was squirming and moaning, so I took things a step further.

"Sue, why don't you show Paula how to suck cock?" I said. "Why shouldn't she learn from the best?" Sue turned around, gave me a long French kiss and dropped to her knees. My dreams were about to come true.

She unbuckled my belt, pulled my pants down around my ankles and slowly edged my bikini underwear down my hips and over my bulging cock. Paula moved closer to watch, her breathing ragged.

As I gently placed my right hand behind my beautiful wife's dark curls, Sue parted her lips and touched her tongue to the rock-hard tip of my prick. She licked lightly around the crown, then slowly, sensually, eased inch after inch of my cock into her mouth. Finally, after working about half of my thick tool into her hot oral cavity, she began bobbing her head up and down on my joystick. The motion of her head, the friction of her lips and the hot wetness of her mouth made my balls boil.

Paula, watching intently, was mesmerized. After several minutes of this hot action, Paula had stripped off her green lace panties and was fingering herself. As my wife went down on me, I couldn't take my eyes off Paula as she gently rubbed her clit with her index finger, while closing her eyes and moaning. After a few moments, her little red tongue darted out of her mouth and swabbed her lips, making them shiny. Soon she had worked two fingers inside of her hot box, and she was thrusting them in and out. She seemed to have forgotten all about Sue giving me head, she was so caught up in her own ecstasy.

It was difficult to keep from coming, with the attention my cock was getting and the show Paula was putting on, but I managed to hold back. I had to feel Paula's tongue on my shaft and balls before I came. I *had* to.

I knew that the time was right to get Paula involved in the action.

"Sue, why don't we let Paula practice on a real cock before I shoot my load?" I said.

Sue was hot as hell by now. She was making loud slurping sounds and pulling hard for my come. But she backed off, turned to Paula and reached for her hand.

"Come on," she said with a big smile. "You don't want to miss this. There's nothing so sweet as a dick ready to give up its nectar."

Paula just groaned and dropped to her knees. Now I had a gorgeous blond angel on one side of my cock and my raven-haired wife on the other side.

"Just lick it," Sue said, as she worked her tongue up and down the length of my shaft. Paula cautiously stuck out her small pink tongue and touched my rod. After several minutes of licking,

Paula moved to the head of my cock and slowly sucked the knob into her mouth, licking the head.

My wife's instructions helped Paula get more and more of me into her mouth. Paula gagged a few times when my cock touched the back of her throat, but the girl had a natural talent for sucking man-meat. Before long, she too had worked up a smooth, hot motion as her lips almost left the tip of my prick, then plunged down the shaft. I knew I would have to come soon. But I also knew Paula wasn't ready to take a load of cream down her throat. My wife loves the taste of my come, and I wanted to reward her for the wonderful job of training she'd done by shooting into her mouth.

"Baby," I said, "why don't you show Paula how to take a hot load of come?"

Paula surrendered the cock to my wife's eager mouth, but kept her head near. Knowing I was close to coming, my wife's head bobbed furiously up and down my meat. My balls tightened, my cock jerked and the nut juice rushed from my balls like an express train. The first thick squirt shot straight down her throat and into her hungry belly. But then she jerked the rod from her mouth and the second spurt landed squarely on her red tongue.

Sue offered my slippery, slick cock to Paula, who eagerly licked my cock clean, getting her first taste of come. She said she loved the sticky, salty taste as the cream slid down her virgin throat.

Impulsively, Sue and Paula touched their come-coated lips together in a kiss and then smiled at each other. I see another adventure coming real soon.

SEA OF LOVE

A couple of months ago my girlfriend and I had the chance to go on a wonderful vacation to Ixtapa, Mexico. We stayed in a great hotel about six miles from town. On our second day there we discovered the hotel's Jacuzzi. It was big enough for twenty people and was situated on a floor which overlooked the mountains and the sea. It was also in an isolated alcove.

We couldn't wait to inspect this Jacuzzi. I was eager to see my girlfriend stretch out and relax in it. My girlfriend has gorgeous legs. She is slim, full of curves and incredibly sexy. I am also fairly attractive, tall and muscular.

After making sure that no one was around, we sat down and dangled our legs in the warm water. I immediately started cupping my girlfriend's mound from outside her string bikini, making the crotch slide into her almost hairless crack. Then I slid a couple of fingers up her already wet pussy and started massaging her back and forth. Just when things were getting good and hard we heard some footsteps and I froze.

Hurriedly, I took my fingers out of her pussy and we sank deeper into the water. A few seconds later a couple walked into the room. Being the exhibitionist that she is, my girlfriend sat by my side and started caressing my hard prick from under the bubbling water.

From the surface of the water we appeared to be sitting back, relaxing and enjoying a couple of beers. But below the surface my whole prick was out of my bathing trunks. Thankfully, the couple simply walked around the room and left. So we resumed our love-play. This time I had my girlfriend recline with her back toward me, facing the sea, so I could pull her bikini bottom out of the way and slide my prick into her.

It was great. I slid my seven and a half inches into her and found her hotter than the water around us. She was boiling! As she sucked my prick into her hot pussy. I slid one finger up and down her clit, something I know just drives her wild. Things were going great and we had just about established a rhythm when we heard some more footsteps. I had no time to put on my trunks, so with my prick almost bursting, I sank to the deeper end of the Jacuzzi. This time three young women came into the room.

They were looking for one of their friends. We told them that we hadn't seen anyone, so they turned to leave. At the very last minute, however, one of them, a good-looking, slim, blond girl, came back—right to the edge of the Jacuzzi. I could not hide my hard prick. The combination of two interrupted fucks had me hard as steel. Once again, my girlfriend began to slowly, deliciously stroke me back and forth, running her fingers over the sensitive head, around the hole, silently daring me to come.

The girl came over, leaning right over the edge of the water. There was no way she could not see my hard prick. She started saying something about delivering a message to her friend—they were going to the pool—but all the while she could not take her eyes off my cock, or my girlfriend's hand, which was covering and uncovering it.

Slowly, the girl put her hand into the water and grabbed my prick from the base, taking part of my tight balls and part of the shaft. She also started massaging me up and down, asking in a really low voice whether we had been fucking as they came in. When we told her it was true, she asked us whether we minded if she stayed behind and watched us. She was dying to observe something like this.

We encouraged her to stay. My girlfriend continued running her fingers up and down my shaft, down my balls, across my ass and back again. I couldn't take too much more of this and told them both so.

The girl waved her friends away and, in her running shorts and T-shirt, joined us in the Jacuzzi. She wasn't wearing any underwear, so when she hit the water, we could clearly see her pink, pert nipples and blond pussy through her skimpy jogging clothes. My girlfriend was as turned on as I was and she decided to remove her bikini bottom. I had neglected her for too long. With renewed gusto I started caressing her shaved pussy until my thumb, on her clit, made her buck wildly. My index finger was inside her boiling pussy and my other hand cupped and caressed her ass.

By now, Carla, my girlfriend, couldn't care if the whole hotel was watching. She just wanted to get off. Tawny, our young friend, held my solidly throbbing prick with one hand, and with her other hand she opened Carla's pussy wide, guiding my cock-head right to the opening. Carla's pussy almost sucked me in. I couldn't hold back any longer, so I started giving it to her hard, adding my own bubbles to the frothing water. Meanwhle, Tawny had pressed herself to my back and was caressing my balls from behind. That did it. With one last stroke, I came like I had never come before. I was pumping quarts of cream. Carla was bucking to meet my thrusts, practically making her pussy-crack merge with my balls, and Tawny was holding my balls tight from behind, whispering, "I love it!"

Afterward, as we were sitting around relaxing, Tawny said she was very glad she had stayed because she had never seen anyone fuck like that. She sat on the edge of the tub with her blond pussy showing through those sexy shorts. I started caressing her, first through the shorts, but as she began to get more excited she opened her legs wider and wider. Then I stuck a finger through the side of the shorts right into her sweet, young pussy. She was so turned on that, even as I parted her slick folds, I could feel her shudder in orgasm.

We all went to the showers together and Carla and I undressed Tawny. We didn't speak, we simply enjoyed the sensuality of the moment. Carla started feeling Tawny's small tits from behind while kissing her neck. Slowly, Tawny reclined back into Carla while I started kissing her from the knees up. I worked my way to her lovely young pussy, which was dripping from the water and her own musk. I could feel her trembling from excitement as I reached her tight pussy with my tongue and began licking her. Tawny raised her pussy to meet my tongue and I began licking her clit up and down.

By this time, I was hard again—something I thought would never happen so soon after my last orgasm. I began feeling Tawny's cunt with my fingers and opening her up in preparation for a glorious fuck. I opened her up further and further while sticking my tongue up as far as it could go. Finally, she came, rubbing her whole pussy against my face.

The Jacuzzi and my previous fuck had left me dead tired, so all I could do was stick my rock-hard cock in her. I could barely move. Carla started pumping me up and down with her hand while I was in Tawny's cunt. With a final shudder, I came. My knees were shaking. I could barely stand up, but I managed. I stuffed my now soft prick into my trunks and got dressed. Carla wrapped a towel around her shapely ass and went up to our room. Before leaving, Tawny kissed us both tenderly, got dressed and thanked us for a truly wonderful experience.

Thank God the next day was Sunday, though I needed to attend to some business with a client who ran a nearby hotel. This was supposed to be a working vacation. When I came back, around midafternoon, I found a note from Carla telling me to meet her down at the beach which was at the bottom of the cliff. That was the beginning of my second adventure.

Since the hotel faces a harbor and a cliff, with the beach running below about half a mile, we never bothered to dress while in our suite. As a matter of fact, because the balconies were separated by thick bunches of plants, we never even bothered to dress while going outside. This day I walked outside, fully refreshed after a nice shower and, as always, naked. As I was standing against the railing overlooking the cliff, I heard a young, definitely Mexican female voice wish me a good morning. I turned around fast, looking for something to cover myself with. I found a little cocktail napkin, which I put in front of my prick. Not enough.

The maid, who had been doing the next room, was a young woman whom we had often nodded to in the corridors. As a matter of fact, we had met her coming from the Jacuzzi the night before, but had not thought anything of it.

"You know," she said, "you have a big one even when it's soft. I could see it in your swimming trunks last night." She told me not to worry about the napkin and, since half my prick was peeking out of one end anyway, I let it drop.

"I saw you last night," she continued, "and I was so turned on that I came while watching all of you. When you came out of the Jacuzzi with your friends you looked really big. Even now it is beginning to grow, and it looks delicious. Your wife must be lucky." I explained that Carla was my girlfriend and made some remark about the impropriety of standing on balconies with a hard-on talking to beautiful girls.

"Don't worry, it's natural," she said, "and I like to see it get hard. Yours is beautiful. I did not know they could be so thick." She then described in great detail how much she liked the veins, the head at the end and the pre-come that was already oozing from it and dropping to the tile on the floor. Then she excused herself and quickly went inside.

When I entered the room again, after my coffee, she was there, smiling, sitting on the bed. She told me she had been thinking about it, had gotten more and more excited and decided to come in and at least touch it. I walked over to the bed, my erection so hard it throbbed, and positioned myself in front of her. Still dressed, she grabbed my hard cock and started touching it, running her hands softly over the head, down the shaft and down to my balls. After a couple of minutes she lowered her head to it and gave it a light kiss.

My prick shook. She ran her teeth lightly around the end of the head and, with her tongue, captured a drop of pre-come. While she kept it in her mouth, swirling it with her tongue, she used both hands to fondle my balls, playing them against each other and sending shudders up my spine. She continued sucking, moving her fingers from my balls to my ass and, stroking me there lightly, I told her to slow down a bit or I would come. At this she started running her hands from my ass to my balls, sucking harder and using her tongue against my peehole. I came. Gallons. She swallowed it all and, when I was finished, licked the head and the hole clean.

I just lay in bed, tired, wondering what was next, when she stood up and began to undress. She took off her uniform, bra and panties in one single motion. She was gorgeous. She was slim with small breasts, lovely dark skin, hard nipples and big pussy lips. The lips were easily one inch long. I pulled her close to me, then laid her down on the bed and lifted her legs over my head, making sure that she kept her legs wide apart. When my mouth was right next to those wonderful, long pussy lips I extended my tongue out to lick them. I licked up and down until she was trembling uncontrollably. At the same time, I reached to pinch her erect nipples. Her nipples became even harder and she began moaning loudly.

She told me to settle back down on the bed and started licking my balls, nibbling my shaft and running her tongue all over me until I was steel-hard again. This time, she climbed on top of me. I opened up her lips, which were wet and dripping, and inserted my cock. She almost couldn't take it. She had a tough time accommodating the knob, but when it did finally go through, the rest sailed in.

Inside, she was silky and oily at the same time. My cock felt as if it had been trapped in some soft but pulsating glove. She just held me there, pumping me with her cunt. She leaned on top of me so I could kiss her tits, and I took advantage of her position to reach behind her and open her ass-cheeks. She started moaning hard when she was open.

It was like jump-starting her. She clamped down on my cock, almost pulling my balls into her. I couldn't stand it. My prick was throbbing and I wanted to come so bad! She was frantic, rubbing herself with one hand, biting onto the other hand. She came like a rocket. I also came like a rocket.

The wet spot we left on the bed was unbelievable. She had come gallons from the look of it. She started getting dressed, leaving her panties and bra off. From now on, she told me, she would be absolutely naked underneath her clothes and, whenever

I saw her, I should feel free to stick my cock up her dress. Naturally, I left her a big tip for cleaning the room.

I took another shower, put on my bathing trunks and went down to the beach to meet my girlfriend, who was sitting with another girl admiring the sea. I tried to imagine what could possibly happen next.

THIS IS YOUR WIFE

*I*t all started as a joke.

I have been the breadwinner in the family since my wife and I married ten years ago, but women's lib has had its effects. Practically from the day we got back from our honeymoon, Doreen started complaining about how she always gets stuck doing the housework. After ten years of listening to this, I finally got tired of hearing it.

I told her to take a day off from her housework to go and do whatever she wanted to do. "I'll be the wife for a change," I said. We decided to put my plan into effect the very next day.

After sleeping in till almost noon, she had breakfast in bed, which I provided. Then she went off to go get her hair done, and see an afternoon movie. Meanwhile, I thought I'd have a little fun. As soon as she left the house I decided to get into some of her clothes. I put on a pair of her panties, a slip and one of her bras, which I stuffed with tissue paper to give myself some tits. I even shaved my legs, which was more fun than I'd expected. Doreen keeps a few boxes of her old shoes in the basement, and I found a stretched-out pair of high-heel pumps that fit me perfectly.

Once I was completely dressed, I got to work. The way I'd planned it, when she got back to the house I'd be swabbing the floor and bitching about how awful it was to be the woman of the house.

Now I'll tell you something weird. While I was doing all of this I was getting turned on! I don't know what did it; maybe it was the feel of those silk panties against my balls or something, but I really started getting off, walking around the house in a dress, lingerie and high heels. The strangest thing of all was that I couldn't get over how good I looked, and every time I passed by the living-room mirror I'd stand there, lift up my skirt and parade back and forth.

The hours passed and my wife still wasn't back, so I jerked myself off while looking into the mirror. Soon afterward, while I finished up the housework and got ready to cook dinner, I got another huge erection. There I was in the kitchen, making salad dressing from scratch, with this crazy hard-on pounding between my newly shaved legs. I was rubbing them together to feel the smoothness, when all of a sudden I heard Doreen's voice behind me.

"Well, well! What's all this?"

I figured my joke was going to be a hit—but when I looked up, there was Doreen with her best friend Jana, standing in the doorway and staring at me in disbelief! I was trapped. I didn't have anywhere to run.

"Doreen," Jana said, "you never told me!"

"This is my . . . husband," Doreen said. "I believe you've met."

"You mean your wife, don't you?" Jana replied.

I started to explain to them that it was all just a joke, but they wouldn't even let me finish. Instead, they continued to rib me about how I looked. I knew it'd be worse if I left the room, so I stood there with a hand on my hip and said, "Ha, ha, ha, very funny."

Doreen ran her hands over my "breasts" and said, "Nice tits." Then Jana picked up the edge of my skirt and looked underneath.

"She's even got panties and a slip on," Jana said.

"Cute," Doreen teased. "Very, very cute."

"Okay, that's enough," I said. I tried to push the dress down, but Jana's hands were too quick. "She's got a hard-on, Doreen," she said. "If we don't watch out she's going to come right inside her panties!"

"No," my wife said. "Really?"

Jana held the dress up again to show her. I was so embarrassed I didn't even try to fight them. Now they really started to go with it and began calling me Mindy.

"Mindy, would you make me a sandwich?" my wife asked.

Jana chimed in. "Mindy, would you bring me a beer?"

I decided the best way to handle this was just to go along with it. And you know what? I was still really turned on, being in Doreen's clothes and having her and her friend looking at me. I don't know what that outfit brought out in me, but it was sure bringing it out good.

Doreen and Jana sat there at the table, drinking beer and having me play maid for them, and I went along by curtsying and bending over so they could fondle my ass or stroke my tits. We were all having a good time! And I had always thought Jana was a pretty sexy woman, so having her feel me up like that right in front of my wife was turning me on in a big way.

The more beer they drank, the wilder they got, and finally my wife said, "Mindy, are you turned on again? Let's take another look inside your panties. Hold up your dress and show us."

"Yeah, show us, Mindy," Jana said in agreement. So, I stood there and held up the dress so they could see my bulging, erect cock, throbbing inside the satin panties.

"What should we do about that, Jana?" my wife asked.

Jana, who was pretty loose by then, said, "I don't know, but I think we'd better do something!" She reached her hand into my panties and slowly started stroking my rock-hard cock. I was going nuts!

"Take your panties down," she said. As I did, my cock popped out into view. Before I knew it—and I couldn't believe it—my wife's best friend was on her knees in our kitchen, sucking me off.

Jana had an expert tongue and a very hot, very wet mouth. She focused a lot of attention on the base of my cock, especially the sensitive area next to my balls. She worked fast, never taking her mouth off my tool, sucking it faster and faster as Doreen cheered her on.

The only time Jana stopped was to say to my wife, "Come on, girl. There's enough here for both of us!"

In no time, my wife was also on her knees, mouthing my prick. What an incredible feeling, getting a blowjob from two women at once! Jana stayed low, sucking my balls into her mouth, while Doreen feasted on the purple and swollen head of my cock. I was in heaven, as both women licked madly up and down the sides of my shaft until I couldn't hold it in any longer. When I shouted that I was going to come, Doreen planted her lips firmly around my prick and caught the first jets of sperm. Then she quickly pushed my rod into her friend's mouth, and Jana hungrily swallowed the rest of my come.

Both women took turns swabbing me clean. When the last of my juice had been licked off of my cock, my wife said, "That was great, but I think what I really want to do now is fuck the maid."

I was ready to comply and started taking off my clothes, when she added, "But first, Mindy, pull up your panties and fix us a drink."

And that was the beginning of some very interesting evenings with Jana and Doreen.

SOMETHING WILD AT THE CASINO

*W*e call it the "night of fantasy." After years of enjoying the letters in your magazine, my wife and I decided that such sexual delights would probably occur only in our fantasies and never be a part of our actual experience. All of this changed on a magic

night in Las Vegas when Lady Luck turned for us in the final moments of a weekend trip.

Our gambling stake, which had seemed like so much money on
Saturday morning, had dwindled to only one hundred and fifty
dollars by Sunday afternoon. My wife stashed twenty dollars for
cab fare, gave me the last hundred-dollar bill and said she was
going to try Keno, since the thirty dollars we had left could last
the longest time at that game. For the first time on our entire trip
a player got on a roll at the craps table, and I quickly won five
hundred dollars. The next shooter, an attractive blond woman,
kept the dice for forty-five minutes, leaving us ahead for the trip
by fifty-nine hundred dollars. I stayed for one more roll, and
caught another hot shooter who increased our stake to fourteen
thousand dollars. Just as I was trying to decide whether to stay or
make a run for the hotel room, I heard wild screams of joy from
the Keno area. My wife had hit a Keno ticket for twenty-five
thousand dollars. Even though taxes were withheld from her
miraculous ten-out-of-ten ticket, the payoff, in cash, was nearly
twenty thousand dollars. We had been on the ropes only two
hours earlier, but now we were suddenly holding over thirty-three
thousand dollars in hundred-dollar bills and were as excited as we
had ever been. Little did we know that the real excitement was
yet to come.

We went to the hotel bar to celebrate. Casino executives came
by with gracious offers: "Whatever you want—a suite, a dinner in
the gourmet dining room, *anything*." It was the proposal of "anything" that got my wife going. "Let's do something wild," she proposed, still flushed with excitement, "something really wild." I
thought she was talking about making another big bet, or flying
to Hawaii for a week, or something like that. She quickly cor-
rected that misconception. "Let's have a threesome," she whispered. It took me a moment to realize what she meant, and
several more moments to recover from the shock. "Are you serious?" I asked. "I've never been more serious," she said. "You set it
up. Hurry! I'm so horny thinking about it that I can't stand it."

It took me about ten minutes to work up the nerve to ask a casino executive about the "anything" offer. "Sorry, can't do that," he said quickly. I was a little embarrassed when I headed back to the hotel bar, both for what I had asked and for failing to find what my wife wanted. The idea was a big turn-on for me too, and I had looked forward to what might happen. I wondered who else I could ask.

Before I could tell my wife the disappointing news, a young man appeared at the table. He introduced himself as Frank, and said he had heard we were looking for a threesome. "Well," I said, looking at my wife for her reaction. When she hesitated, Frank plunged ahead. "Do you want a man or a woman for the third?" he asked.

"I—I don't know," my wife said. She was already breathing hard. I hadn't considered the option of a man in this party, but if it was what my wife wanted . . . "I know who you want," Frank said after a moment. "You want Fantasy. She is the greatest in all of Las Vegas, but she is expensive."

"How much?" I asked.

"Twenty-five hundred dollars for an evening. A bargain for what you get," Frank replied.

"How much for the second greatest?" I asked. Twenty-five hundred dollars was about ten times what I had expected to pay.

"You want Fantasy," Frank said firmly. "You will not be disappointed."

"You decide," my wife said, but her eyes begged me to say yes.

"I'll send her to your room in ten minutes. Here's the room key. A new suite for you, on the house." Frank left quickly.

It took us about fifteen minutes to find the new room, and for a few minutes we worried that we had missed our opportunity. While my wife showered, I paced the room, wondering what I had gotten myself into. Then came the knock on the door. I opened it to find a tall, slender, blond girl who looked no more than fifteen years old. She was incredibly beautiful. She smiled and said, "Hi, I'm Fantasy, and I'm really twenty years old. Everyone asks." She swept confidently into the room, set down her purse, and asked for a drink. While I fumbled with the ice, my wife came out of the bathroom, dressed in a robe. Fantasy greeted her with a kiss at my wife's cleavage, lowered the robe to her waist, and began kissing her breasts. "Your breasts are beautiful," Fantasy breathed huskily, "so much better than mine." My wife moaned in appreciation of the compliment and the expert attention her nipples were getting. I was instantly erect, watching in fascination.

Fantasy then lowered my wife's robe to the floor and led her, naked, to the bed. She removed her own clothing except for her tight blue silk pants. She fondled her own firm breasts for a moment, then whispered in my wife's ear. My wife returned the whisper, and Fantasy quickly rolled her on her stomach and began kissing her at the nape of her neck, then down her back, and finally, slowly, worked her way to the crack of my wife's ass. Fantasy's tongue lingered there, teasing. She licked up and down, and then she sucked the plump flesh of my wife's ass-cheeks, bringing a shudder from both of them. Fantasy's mouth remained there for several minutes, sucking deeply, then slurping back and forth. My wife's moans were soft, her mouth open and her eyes closed in ecstasy.

I could watch no longer, and I quickly removed my clothes to join the party. I went unnoticed for a few moments, then I guided my wife's hands to my raging erection. She quickly began sucking my penis, taking it deep. Her head moved quickly, almost frantically, up and down my length. Suddenly her moans became loud, startling me for a moment until I realized that Fantasy had moved her expert mouth to my wife's clit. Fantasy was there for only a moment, or so it seemed, before my wife was brought to a shuddering orgasm. Her usual quiet climax was replaced by a muffled, intense "Yes, yes, yes!" as she got off. Fantasy quickly moved up to my wife's mouth, kissed her, and whispered again. My wife's whispered answer once again left me in the dark, but only momentarily. Fantasy rolled her over and began kissing her breasts once again, while making it clear that I was to move to my wife's cunt. "Fuck me hard," my wife said in a voice that I hardly recognized as her own. I inserted my penis quickly and began fucking as hard as I could, hoping the moment would last for hours but knowing that I was only moments from coming.

"I want to feel your balls slap my ass," my wife hissed as I continued, watching Fantasy's beautiful head move on my wife's breasts. "Bite my nipples hard," she screamed to Fantasy as I finally came, feeling an orgasm so intense as to defy description. For several minutes my wife said nothing, then caught her breath and said, "My God, that was terrific! That was wonderful!" Once again, Fantasy whispered in her ear, and my wife asked, "What do you mean?" "The fantasy has only begun," Fantasy said. "Let me show you." Fantasy then got off the bed and began removing her tight silk slacks. She turned her back to us, showing us firm, tanned buttocks and muscular legs. When she turned around my wife let out a gasp. Her mouth fell open as Fantasy's enormous penis danced into view. For a long moment Fantasy let us drink in "her" body, then she began stroking the huge penis in her hands. The gigantic tube of flesh was quickly erect. Fantasy looked at my wife, smiled, and purred, "Fourteen rock-hard inches, all for you."

Fantasy walked to the side of the bed and grabbed my wife's head. "Tell me how much you want to suck it," Fantasy said. My wife reached hungrily for the mammoth member. Ever since seeing her first John Holmes movie she had fantasized many times about tasting and feeling an enormous prick. Her entire body was flushed as she took the penis into her mouth, grasping it with both hands. Her moans were even more intense now, and she ran her tongue up and down the massive length, to the balls, and underneath to the asshole. "Fuck me with it. Fuck me with it now," my wife pleaded.

This unexpected, incredible spectacle had aroused me once again, and I stroked my own penis as I watched Fantasy enter her cunt. Cries of erotic intensity came from my wife's lips as the giant penis began its long slide into her depths. She was moaning over and over. I had never heard her sound so turned on. Fantasy then turned to me and said, "Feel my balls." Fantasy's ass was as perfect as any woman's had ever been. I struggled momentarily with sexual ambiguity, then decided to go ahead. The heat of the moment overrode all inhibitions. My wife stopped me with her words. "No, no," my wife said, "fuck my mouth. I want you in my mouth and Fantasy in my cunt." Fantasy quickly lay down on her back and my wife mounted the oversize organ. I then got on top, entering my wife's hot mouth that was even wetter after the superb tongue lubing she'd given Fantasy. I thought my hard, excited thrusts had to be hurting her, but the only sounds were those of pure pleasure. I could see Fantasy's whopper cock sliding in and out of my wife's cunt. While my wife repeated "Oh God, oh God, oh God" over and over, Fantasy and I fucked the respective holes with total enthusiasm.

"Is there a giant cock in my cunt? Are you enjoying fucking my mouth?" My wife's words were heard through a blur of lust, passion and untold excitement. "Come in my mouth. I want to feel you come in my mouth." My second orgasm was even better than the first, and I collapsed on the bed to watch the rest of the action. My wife's explosive orgasm followed almost immediately. She shuddered, paused, and shuddered once again. Fantasy's quick, hard, extremely deep thrusts continued until my wife finally exclaimed, "No more! Please, God, no more."

My wife lay on the bed beside me, breathing deeply, as Fantasy began to lick her body all over, tonguing off the beads of sweat. Fantasy then took her penis and placed it between my wife's large breasts, pulled them together, and began titty-fucking them. On the upstroke, my wife's tongue would stick out to caress the tip of the tool. After a dozen more sensuous strokes, Fantasy shot several thick streams of come in my wife's mouth and on her neck. Fantasy's soft kisses continued all over my wife's body as my wife licked every drop she could find from her own fingers. Then she reached up to give Fantasy a kiss. I enjoyed watching them together so much that I merely sat there, smiling. I still could barely believe that my wife and I were experiencing such a fantastic night.

"I heard you were the best, and I heard right," my wife told Fantasy. Fantasy smiled and said, "You were the best for me too. I have to go now. I hope I see you again." Fantasy rose from the bed, dressed quickly, and I paid her. "Give him a big tip for his big cock," my wife said from the bed. Him? I thought it was funny at the time. That is the tale of our night of fantasy, but it is not the end of the story. On our next trip to the casino, it *really* got wild. But I'd better save that story for next time.

THE BEST MAN

I've always been excited by the idea of my wife getting it on with another man. Recently, an old friend presented me with the opportunity to turn my fantasy into reality during a week-end trip to the city.

An old friend of mine, Bob, had come to visit me and my wife Gina. He had served as best man at our wedding, and we've shared many good times with him.

This week was no exception. We partied it away consuming vast quantities of liquor and quality smoke. Gina, a thirty-five-year-old honey-blond aerobics addict, was definitely excited by the idea of another man in the house. In the evenings, after we adjourned to our respective bedrooms, I'd tease her about poor Bob, alone in his room with no one to play with. "A good hostess should take care of all her guest's needs," I said. "He's probably in there right now with his cock out, thinking of you getting fucked. Why don't you go help him out?" She didn't say anything but slid around on the bed and slipped my cock into her mouth. As she sucked, I reached over and played with her pussy lips, squeezing and separating them as she got creamier and began to squirm around the bed. "Pretend you're sucking Bob. Show me how you'd handle his cock. Make that big head come in your mouth."

The more I talked the hotter she got until I had three fingers pumping her pussy, and she was soon coming all over my hand. I couldn't hold back any longer and I shot my load into her mouth. She let it dribble out over my cock and balls, a sight I had always found extremely erotic. "How'd Bob like that one?" she asked with a smile. I just looked at her and said, "Babe, you're so hot I know he'd love you. Just leave it to me."

We decided to end our time together with a weekend trip to New York City to see a show and do some big city bar-hopping. We got lucky and ended up with front-row center seats at an off-Broadway play starring a gorgeous actress. The skimpy costume she wore left her tits barely covered, and I looked over at Bob to see his reaction. He was staring at her and smiling as though he hadn't seen a woman in a week. He had his hand on Gina's thigh near her knee.

After the show we stopped at a pub and ordered some tequila shooters and beers. Bob sent a drink over to a cute girl in a T-shirt. Her obviously braless breasts had gotten his attention. "New York must be the nipple capital of the world," he whispered. Gina looked at both of us and excused herself to go to the ladies' room. I wasn't sure if she was angry or jealous. I got my answer when she returned a few minutes later. She had obviously removed her bra, because we could now see two of the longest, hardest nipples in town poking through the thin fabric of her blouse.

I should probably tell you now about my wife. As I said, she's a workout fanatic and her efforts have resulted in a body that could pass for twenty-five. She measures 36-25-37 with a C cup hiding her elongated nipples. Her pussy is hidden behind a light covering of red hair, and when she gets hot, her lips swell up and open to reveal a two-inch clit.

I could tell by her face and those gorgeous nipples that she was more than a little warm already. After a few more rounds of tequila and good times at an assortment of clubs, we ended up past the point of pretense, and Gina had begun to flirt with anything in pants. I decided it was time to head out and told Bob to round up Gina while I grabbed a cab.

We all piled into the backseat. As the cab took off, Gina leaned over and gave me a deep, wet kiss. "Be a good hostess," I said. With that, she leaned over to Bob and kissed him. Then Bob and I proceeded to take turns with those soft lips. It began to get awful hot in that cab. Bob ran his hands over her smooth legs, and I pinched those dark, meaty nipples of hers. She was really panting by now and, sitting up with her back to the driver, began to unbutton her jeans. I thought the show had gone far enough and told her to wait just a minute and we'd be home. Gina just moaned a bit and fell back to kissing Bob.

At the apartment I had some trouble opening the lock, and when I finally got it open, I turned to find Bob with his arm around my smiling wife, who had her left hand pressed closely to his crotch. We stumbled into the darkened room. By the time I got the light on, Gina was already stripping her clothes off. Bob wasn't quite sure how far this was all going to go, and he stood quietly to the side and stared at the overheated woman in front of him.

I knew what she wanted and quickly got out of my clothes and presented her with seven inches of thick, oozing cock. As she lay on her back, I rubbed my cock over her tits and smeared her nipples with the sticky juice. She grabbed it and pulled it into her mouth, pumping the shaft with her hand while I fucked her face. It wasn't long before I felt a huge load of come welling up in my balls, and with a grunt, I unloaded in her mouth. She lay there panting, gobs of semen on her lips.

I turned to see Bob removing the last of his clothes. Bob was a rancher and had a lean, strong body to show for it—a throwback to his days as a collegiate swimmer. Those features, combined with his typical California-blond hair and easy disposition, made him a sure bet with women. As if that wasn't enough, the man was hung like a horse. His cock was a good eight inches and very thick, with a large swollen head. His balls were incredible! Two huge eggs in a bulging sac that hung down at least four inches.

He stood next to the bed stroking his shaft and staring at my nude and very aroused wife. "Be a good hostess," I said. Never taking her eyes off his pulsing cock, she spread her legs wide in invitation, but Bob took charge and pulled her to her knees in front of him. Her mouth opened wide and for the first time I saw her suck another man's cock. It was incredibly exciting as I watched her wrap her hands around his ass while he slowly fucked between her lips. I had always fantasized about watching my wife with another man, but the reality was far better than my imagination ever created. She could only get about half of him in, but the combination of her lips and tongue had Bob on his way to heaven.

Pulling my eyes away from the sight of his cock pumping between her open lips, I watched Gina's hips move in rhythm to his thrusts. Her pussy was wide open and wet, and I couldn't resist the urge to join in. I knelt down behind her and began to slap her pussy with my cock. She twitched and quivered with every slap, and it wasn't long before she began to moan around Bob's big dick. At that, I slowly thrust forward into her and watched as her juicy lips spread wide around my thick shaft.

Gina is not usually very noisy in bed, but tonight, with two cocks pumping in her, she was grunting and moaning in heat. "How do you like your two cocks, babe? Suck on his big head, make him come," I said, punctuating my words with hard strokes in her pussy. She responded by frantically pulling on his cock while her whole body trembled. Her actions and the excitement of the moment proved too much for Bob as he stiffened and groaned in orgasm. I saw him spasm at least three times as he pumped into her face, and when he backed away, Gina fell forward and rolled over. Her tits were shiny with juice, and I slid up her chest and began to slide my cock all over her slippery nipples.

Bob stood over her with his cock at half-mast, the huge shaft hanging halfway down his leg. Gina looked up at him with glazed eyes and said, "Don't stop now." I moved to the side as Bob slid between her legs and began to lick and nibble her pussy. He spread her lips with his fingers and licked her clit with short, teasing little strokes as she writhed and moaned with pleasure. After the workout we'd already given her pussy, she needed more than a teasing tongue to get off. I could tell she was on the verge of coming and told Bob to slip his finger inside her. He stuck two long ones inside her and pumped in time with his tongue on her clit. That put Gina over the edge. She came with a loud moan and a series of spasms like I had never seen before. Bob continued to slowly lick her until she begged him to stop, at which point we all lay back on the bed to catch our breath.

I guess we were all a little bit stunned by what had happened, and for a moment there was silence. Bob and I looked at Gina and smiled. We were all buzzed, happy and a little unsure of what was to come until Gina began to slowly transfer Bob's come from her mouth to her hard nipples, pulling and twisting them as she looked at each of us in turn. "Look's like there's one for each of us," Bob said. We bent toward her chest and each slipped a nipple into our mouths. The sensation of four lips on her tits must have been intense, because Gina just moaned and said, "You guys. . . ." I reached down to her pussy but found Bob's hand there ahead of mine. He was stroking her lips and probing inside her wet hole. I decided to lie back and enjoy the show.

The novelty of another man had Gina more aroused than I had ever seen her. Bob had that "slow hand" and seemed to be a virtuoso at getting her off. His fingers continued to stroke and probe in and out, alternately stretching then pinching her swollen lips. He then spread her legs and slowly slid his cock inside her. She had never taken such a big cock before. I slid down next to them and watched as his big cock pounded into my wife.

I have felt her wetness many times, but I had never seen so much juice drip out of her as it did while Bob was fucking her. Gina began to grunt in time to his thrusts. Then I saw Bob stiffen and a new flow of his come began to pour from between her lips. She continued to buck as he rolled off her. I quickly took his place.

My cock slid easily into her soaked pussy. I reveled in the feel of her body and the moment we were sharing. Gina was out of it by now, totally absorbed with the sex and the prospect of more. As I pumped into her, Bob moved up near her head and offered her his cock. She sucked it up in an instant, her hands massaging his balls as she tried to make him come again. Our endurance was extraordinary by now. We commenced to give her a serious fucking as she moaned and spasmed beneath us. Finally I pulled out and came on her tits as Bob succumbed to the feel of her mouth.

By now I was tired and lay down for a rest. Bob had been deprived too long and took Gina to his bed across the room. I couldn't see them in the dim light, but my ears made up for what my eyes were missing. "Does that feel good?" I heard Bob ask. Her answer was a contented "Mmmm. . . ." which was the last word I heard for a while, the only sounds being wet sucking and the unmistakable liquid slurps of a cock pumping between two fat pussy lips. I must have fallen asleep for a bit, because the next thing I knew, Gina was crawling in bed next to me and licking my chest and sucking my nipples. I reached down to her pussy and she was absolutely soaked. I could only guess at what games they had played. I stroked her back for a while as she went to sleep.

The next morning we all got up around nine. Our brains had the tequila tingles, and we were all more than a bit fogged from the late night and our three hours of wild sex. Gina was aware that we had partied, but she claimed that she couldn't remember anything after the clubs. I smiled at her and told her to go ask Bob. He was in the shower. When she returned about ten minutes later, her face was flushed and her eyes were wide and shiny.

After a deli breakfast we rode around town until it was time for Bob's bus to the airport. When we dropped him off, I was genuinely sad that we wouldn't be seeing him for quite a while due to the distances that would be involved. He kissed Gina and shook my hand. Then he left.

On the way home I asked Gina what she remembered about last night. She told me that she didn't remember much, and that when she had asked Bob about it earlier, they really "hadn't gotten around to discussing it." I began to recount the evening in detail, especially the parts where she was sucking and fucking Bob. She got so hot listening to the tale that we stopped in the parking lot of a shopping mall and fucked right there on the front seat, amid bewildered passersby.

It was a perfect weekend, the most exciting sex of my life.

I eagerly look forward to the day when circumstance and opportunity once again result in that blissful expression I remember on my wife's face as she took on two men.

WHO'S THE BOSS?

*N*ot long ago, my wife and I were reading an issue of *Penthouse Letters*. Jan noticed how aroused I got each time we read about a man who watched in secret while his wife made it with someone else. "Don't tell me you're one of *those* husbands!" she said to me. I admitted that the thought of her making it with someone else excited me. The conversation ended there, but when we made love that night I fantasized that I was off in some dark corner, looking on as Jan rode the prick of another man. In fact for the next few nights, each time we had sex I imagined it was someone else's cock, not mine, slamming into Jan's hot cunt.

About a month later, after we'd just made passionate love, Jan asked, "Would you really like it if I let some stud bury his big cock in my juicy little hole?"

"Yes," I said. "But remember, I get to watch."

The next afternoon, Jan called me from work. She told me her boss had been flirting with her for several months, making passes and trying to feel her up. At first she'd been annoyed. But our conversation of the night before had convinced her to make a bold decision.

"I'm going to fuck him this afternoon," she said, adding that I'd better hurry home and hide in the closet if I wanted to see the show. "After all," she teased, "it is your fantasy."

I made up some silly excuse at my office and raced home, wondering how I'd actually react to watching Jan fuck her boss. I'd met Steve before. He's about my age and quite good-looking. I could just picture him trying to sneak a quick feel of Jan's smooth ass, or finding some flimsy excuse to "accidentally" brush up against her tits. Jan has a sensational body. Who could blame Steve for wanting to taste it himself? The thought of all this office activity heated me up quickly as I drove home. More than once I had to adjust my seat belt to accommodate my hardening cock.

When I got to the house I stripped down to my underwear, took a stiff drink and headed up to our bedroom to watch for their cars from the window. In about twenty minutes they arrived. I stepped into the walk-in closet and pulled the door closed, leaving it open just wide enough for me to peek out.

It was Steve who got the ball rolling, so to speak. He ran his hands up and down Jan's body, nibbling her breasts through her blouse and cupping her ass in his big palms. As he undressed my wife, he kept complimenting her on how beautiful her body was. I'd seen Jan naked a thousand times. Yet seeing her this way with another man had my heart and cock throbbing double-time.

Jan was now naked, and Steve in only his briefs. Jan ran a finger along the outer lips of her cunt, then held it up to Steve's tongue. He tried to lick it but she pulled it away with a teasing giggle, spinning around in a playful dance, flaunting her tits and ass.

The tremendous bulge in Steve's briefs lured Jan to her knees.

With her head at Steve's crotch, she quickly pulled down his shorts. Steve's prick was already hard. It must have been at least eight inches long and as big around as her wrist. A massive tool! I rolled down my briefs, freeing my own significantly smaller rod, and watched Jan go to work on her boss' monster cock.

He moaned with pleasure and encouraged her on. Taking her head in his hands, he rubbed his stiffened limb back and forth across her face. Jan begged for his meat. She pulled it. Kissed it. Stuck out her tongue and lavishly licked it. It was all I could do to remain quiet as she bathed Steve's pole with her mouth, her head a blur as she feverishly sucked the mighty shaft.

I hid in the closet for two hours, long enough for Steve to come three times, twice in Jan's cunt and once in her mouth. I counted six orgasms for Jan, split evenly between the ministrations of Steve's huge dick and his limber tongue. His stamina was incredible. Each time he came, he stayed hard and just kept right on fucking.

He also had a terrific imagination, maneuvering Jan into what seemed to be an infinite number of positions. Every so often, she would smile over at me and give me a wink. At one point, while she was on all fours and Steve was diddling her clitoris and fucking her from behind, she blew me a kiss. I came twice myself— once without even touching my cock—just witnessing this variety show.

Steve got dressed to leave at about five o'clock. As he attempted to pull up his pants, Jan dropped to her knees, unzipped them, and took his soft cock in her hands, saying that she wanted to say good-bye to her "favorite friend" one last time. She tried to squeeze one more erection out of it, but that was too much to ask, even for Steve. She finally walked him to the door, not even bothering to put her clothes back on. They talked about the work they had to do the next day, then kissed good-bye.

I met Jan on her way back to the bedroom. Exhausted, but with a smile on her face, she hugged me. "I hope you liked watching your wife come on to the boss," she whispered in my ear.

"You were incredible. Did you like it as much as you seemed to?" I asked.

"Yes," she said, "but I'm worn out."

My cock hardened as I watched her walk slowly to the bed. I undressed, lay next to her, and sank my fingers into her cunt. She kissed me and said, "Honey, I'm really wet down there. It would be really nice if you'd wash me clean. With your tongue."

"You want me to lap up Steve's come with my tongue?" I asked.

"Well, honey," she answered, "it was your idea to have him fuck me. Look, your pecker is getting hard just from the thought of tasting my boss' come."

So it was.

"Go ahead, lick my cunt dry," Jan urged. She raised her knees and spread her legs. Steve's come was still oozing out of her pussy and down her thighs. I gave her a thorough cleansing. The taste of another man's come mixed in with my wife's sweet juice wasn't bad at all. Thanks to my tongue work, Jan had another orgasm, after which we both rolled over and took a well-deserved nap.

I don't know where this episode will take us, although it's clear we both enjoyed it. Jan had such a good time fucking and sucking her boss, I suspect it won't be the last time they take their work home from the office.

WEEKEND PASS

*E*ven though I enjoy an active, satisfying sex life, I've waited years to have the kind of memorable experience I believe is worthy of sharing with *Penthouse Letters* readers. I am a former soldier recently discharged from the regular army. During my stint in uniform I was stationed in West Germany. The incidents I'm about to relate happened during beerfest season, which is one of the greatest times of the year anywhere. It brings out the women in full force, and this time was no exception.

My story begins right after the last formation of the week. Dennis, Bill, Brian and I all had weekend passes and we'd planned to meet at a large beer tent later that night. Excited about what might happen over the next forty-eight hours, we showered, changed into our civvies and headed for the fest. By the time we arrived, most of our unit was already there with beers in hand, enjoying the band. As we joined them, my attention was immediately drawn to a beautiful woman, a brunette who was sitting near the stage. Our eyes met and we exchanged smiles.

"Hey, that one up front gave us the once-over too," someone said as we sat down. We joked about which of us should make the first move on this woman. After a few big mugs of German brew had loosened us up some, Gordo, a fellow soldier, elected himself the lucky point man. He went over and sat down to talk with her. Ten minutes later he returned with a big grin on his face.

She'd proposed that the both of them leave the fest and go out barhopping. But as a married man with damn near his whole unit watching, Gordo decided it wouldn't be a good idea for him to pursue the matter. Instead, he said to me, "Why don't you go for it? She sounds like she's looking for some dick tonight." I thought it over and agreed to give it my best shot. By this time, my buddy Dennis had noticed the brunette's friend, a redhead as voluptuous as she was. They were both drinking and laughing and looking over at us. We sensed a party up ahead.

Dennis and I finished our beers and beckoned the waitress. Just then, the brunette stood and called over to us, "Will you please order us each a shot of tequila?" The opportunity we'd hoped for had arrived. We ordered two shots of tequila for them, and two more for ourselves.

When the drinks arrived, I told the waitress to deliver two of the shots to the lovely women across from us. We toasted each other from a distance, the four of us doing the traditional lemon, salt, tequila three-step. Then we all exchanged smiles and waited to see what happened next.

About half an hour later, the brunette wanted to return the favor and asked, "Will you join us for another shot?" Dennis and I wasted no time going over to them. Their English was excellent. We spent about an hour exchanging life stories and getting to know each other.

The brunette's name was Maryann, and the redhead was Ellen. As we talked, Maryann nonchalantly rubbed her hand up and down my leg. Each time her slender fingers approached my thigh, my cock stiffened a little more. Once she'd noticed my excited state, she started to toy with my pants button. I leaned across the table and kissed her. Her tongue did a German folk dance in my mouth.

Then she licked and sucked on my earlobe, nibbling it playfully. The crowd around us started to cheer. It wasn't till we saw that the band wasn't even playing anymore that we realized we had become the main attraction.

Maryann got embarrassed and said she wanted to leave. I knew the fireworks display was about to begin, so I asked, "How would you like to watch the fireworks?" She grabbed my hand and led me outside. As the first burst of colors lighted the sky, I placed my arms around her waist. We started to kiss, our tongues exploring each other's mouths as our hands explored each other's bodies. Delighted that she wasn't wearing a bra, I cupped her warm breasts in my hands, circling the areolae with my fingers and teasing the nipples to hardness. A soft, deep moan escaped her lips. "Yes," she whispered, "play with my tits."

Now, a little tit was all right, but I had something a bit juicier in mind. Slowly moving my hands down the contours of her body, I worked my way to her snatch. As I unzipped her pants she said, "Here, let me help you." She undid the snap and allowed my hand to slip beneath the elastic waistband of her panties. She was already quite wet, and moaned as I found her clit. When, without warning, I eased my finger into her pussy, she loudly cried out a German word I'd never heard before. This got the attention of several people around us, who simply smiled knowingly and continued to watch the fireworks.

Maryann had long since made her way into my own pants. She was jerking me off, playing with my nuts and stroking my cock with her long fingers. We kissed nonstop for about five minutes, our tongues wrestling sloppily, and continued to give each other mutual handjobs. The slurping sound of me finger-fucking her could be heard ever-so-slightly between fireworks explosions. I hope no one recognizes me out here, I thought. Then again, I really didn't give a damn. Here I was in Germany, feeling up and about to fuck a woman I'd met less than two hours ago. I laughed to myself at all the guys I'd known who'd been afraid to join the army.

I discharged a bit of pre-come, which Maryann promptly rubbed all over the head of my cock. She had two orgasms just from the finger-fucking. After the fireworks ended we quickly buttoned our pants and, without saying a word, headed back to the beer tent.

At closing time, Maryann and Ellen asked Dennis and me, "How would you two like to go barhopping with us?" I gave my answer silently by playfully squeezing Maryann's firm ass. Dennis apologized and said he couldn't go. He had twenty-four-hour guard duty coming up, and must've figured he needed his rest. I had a feeling that before the night was over, I'd be the one who would need some sleep.

We said good-bye to Dennis and piled into Ellen's car. Maryann and I climbed into the backseat. Before Ellen had even put the key in the ignition, our hands and mouths were once again all over each other. We were quiet at first, but as Ellen drove, Maryann let out another one of her loud moans. The sudden sound made Ellen swerve, and we nearly hit a parked car.

Ellen watched us in the rearview mirror, and even she was breathing heavily. Maryann unbuttoned my pants and began pumping my muscle back to hardness. As it rose to life, she licked and sucked every inch of it clear down to my balls. Once in a while she would take a nut into her mouth and swirl it around on her tongue. It didn't take her long to deep-throat all of my seven-incher. The quickened throbbing of my cock tipped her off that I was about to come. She stopped and waited for me to cool down, but I couldn't hold it any longer. I pumped a river of hot jam into her mouth, which she swallowed with gusto.

As I tucked my limp penis back into my shorts, I realized the car was parked. Ellen was stretched out on the front seat, finger-ing herself to the little show we'd been putting on in back. She dipped her fingers into her pussy and offered them to me. I gladly sucked the tangy juice off of each digit. After all, I didn't want her to feel left out.

We all caught our breath, then walked to a club down the street. Once inside, we found a small booth and ordered some drinks to help us cool down from all the sexual heat that was passing between us. I led Maryann to the dance floor, where we danced to a few slow, sexy numbers. After a while Ellen suggested we go to another club, a place she worked at, where we could drink free. As we headed back to the car, I readied myself for an-other backseat blitz.

This time it was my turn to give. I pulled off Maryann's pants and ate her pussy to the tune of twin orgasms. As good as I am at going down on a woman, I must admit my own technique was en-hanced by the fact that we were riding over a very bumpy road.

When we pulled up to Ellen's club, Maryann reluctantly put her panties back on and we all went inside. This place was much smaller than the last, but very crowded. Right away, I eyed a tall, sultry blonde who was dancing with a middle-aged man. He was openly rubbing her tits (which were almost falling out of her top) and stroking her ass. She looked as though she wasn't enjoying his paws on her at all. Maryann asked if I was attracted to her, and when I answered yes, she asked the woman to join us.

With Maryann on my left, the blonde sat to my right. The two of them conversed in German for a few minutes. Maryann introduced her as Lise. I politely shook her hand, realizing only after a few moments that I was staring straight at her prodigious breasts. We both grinned sheepishly. Finally, Maryann gave out a big laugh that broke the silence. They talked some more in German, all the while looking at me and giggling like schoolgirls. I have to admit it felt strange not knowing exactly what they were saying, but I sensed we were all communicating in something pretty close to a universal language anyway.

Maryann explained that Lise was from out of town and was down that weekend for the beerfest. She had no place to stay and wanted to know if she could come home with us.

"Of course she can," I said.

"That's good," Lise said, adding, "I go both ways, you know." As she said this she gave my balls a gentle squeeze and kissed Maryann on the cheek.

We got to know each other a little more over a bottle of champagne. Finally, as it was getting late, Maryann suggested we go to Ellen's for a nightcap. By this time, Ellen had picked up someone and was also eager to go home and get down to some serious fucking.

And so once again it was back to the car, this time headed for Ellen's apartment. With Maryann and Lise sharing the backseat with me, I now had two pussies to play with. I got both women hot and bothered, but would always pull my fingers away just when they were about to come. When they'd had enough of this, I pulled my pants down and offered my cock to them. They enthusiastically took turns stroking, then sucking it, asking me which one of them gave the best deep-throat. Decisions, decisions. What's a soldier to do?

I told them it was a tie.

When we got to the apartment, Ellen and her date quickly disappeared into a back room. Lise and I started for the living room. "Hey, that's the wrong way," Maryann said as she stood in the bedroom doorway, playfully dangling a shoe from her finger. We immediately changed direction and joined her. The lights were dimmed and I quickly found myself sandwiched between these two German beauties. They were rubbing their crotches against my body, undressing me slowly and methodically. Lise removed my pants and commented on what good shape I was in. Their hands were all over me, rubbing, stroking, exploring. My cock was hardening for what must have been the twelfth time that night. By the time I was completely naked, it was stiff and ready for some more attention. I sighed in relief as they asked for help undressing.

I assisted Maryann first, kissing and licking her as I removed each article of clothing. Lise was not to be left out of the fun. She licked and probed Maryann's back, working her way down to swab her new friend's creamy ass cheeks with broad strokes of her tongue. We had Maryann moaning in no time, quivering and shaking and rocking with orgasm. Then it was Lise's turn. Maryann and I took our time disrobing her. As we peeled off her stockings, skirt and panties, we stroked the entire length of her body. It was all too much for her to take, and soon she was prying open her vagina with her own fingers. I licked and sucked her clit expertly as Maryann tongued her from behind. Lise started breathing deeply, and soon my mouth was flooded with her love-liquid. I pulled Maryann over and shared Lise's pussy juice with her as we kissed.

Maryann began to flirt with us, begging for more attention. So Lise and I positioned her between us on the bed. I licked my way up her thighs, her spine, around her shoulders, then slowly worked my way back down to her ass. I parted her cheeks and darted my tongue in and out of her box, giving her a first-class tongue-fucking from the rear. Lise was doing the same from the front, and our tongues met as we both fed on this beautiful, hot cunt. Maryann's familiar, high-volume moaning filled the room until finally Lise said, "I think she's ready to be fucked." It was one of the few things she'd said in English all night, and she couldn't have chosen a more appropriate phrase.

I immediately straddled Maryann, first teasing her by pushing only the head of my prick in and then withdrawing, then slowly rubbing my rod up and down the length of her pussy. I wanted her to feel the head sliding against her cunt-lips and clit. When I was sure she was ready for the fucking of her life, I entered her with one mighty thrust. This elicited an especially loud moan, even by Maryann's standards. Her pussy was well lubricated by this time, and so I gave it everything I had. Ramming my missile in to the hilt, I pumped faster and faster until a sucking sound came between us. A couple of times Maryann tightened her legs and called out my name. Lise was licking and kissing my ass-cheeks as I fucked Maryann.

In no time I felt that familiar unrest in my balls and told them I was going to come. I pulled out and pumped stream after stream of hot, white come onto Maryann's tits. The women swirled their fingers in the icing and licked them clean. When there was nothing of me left on her fingers, Lise sucked my cock, milking out the last sweet drops of cream.

I lay on my back and motioned for Lise to sit on my face. My tongue had a field day as it first probed her clit, then darted in and out of her hairy pussy with short, sure strokes. Her breathing came faster and her body spasmed each time I touched her sensitive bud. She arched her back and squeezed my head with her thighs and quaked with a powerful orgasm. I lapped up the juice from her red-hot well as quickly as I could.

"Now it's my turn to give you a spin," Lise said bawdily. As Maryann squatted down to meet my lips, Lise lowered herself onto my cock. I quickly bucked up to meet her thrusts, but soon leaned back, content to watch her dance on my dick while I continued to feed on Maryann's patch. Lise quickened the pace until I could stand it no longer. I expelled a magnificent load into her pussy just as Maryann flooded my mouth with an orgasm of her own. I'd long since lost track of how much pussy juice I'd swallowed since my weekend pass had taken effect just a few short hours before. I lay back exhausted, catching my breath and cooling down. Spent and satisfied, we all slept cuddled together until the late morning.

I was barely awake before the party began anew. It was as wild as the night before, with the bonus of each of us now knowing exactly what turned the others on. Ellen, our "hostess," was nowhere in sight. I never did see her again that weekend. For all I know she was still in the other room, fucking her brains out. Her apartment seemed to encourage such behavior. As for Maryann, Lise and me, we only stopped long enough for a little food, a little sleep, and a few walks in the park. But we were all too hot for each other to care to spend much time away from our little fuck nest. For the most part, the sex-a-thon didn't end until it was time for me to return to the base.

We exchanged addresses and phone numbers and made plans to meet again soon. All three of us piled into Ellen's car and headed for my base. Once we reached the main gate, I kissed them both good-bye and headed for the barracks with a big smile on my face. Our little adventures were to continue, but that's a story for another time.

Now that I'm home again, I have only to look at their pictures to take me back in memory to the weekend when I first began my tour of duty with those two beautiful, Bavarian babes.

SQUEEZE PLAY

I'm a buxom blond graduate student, age twenty-four, with great gams and a tiny waist. I don't know why studying makes me so horny, but it does. About twenty minutes after I start, I get that sweet, itchy, I-need-sex feeling between my legs. My unique predilection has led to some very interesting situations, as I spend quite a lot of time studying in the main library.

I remember once—it was at the end of the spring semester, and the library was pretty crowded—I was studying at a long table with a lot of other students. I was wearing pretty tight jeans, so tight I had trouble peeling them down to go to the bathroom. The seam in the crotch was pressed hard against my clit. It got more and more turgid, making me hotter and hotter as the hours wore on. This was one of my weaker subjects and I had to finish studying, but I was getting hornier by the minute. Pretty soon, without my really intending to do so, I found that my lush ass was starting to wiggle around. I was masturbating right there in the library!

Luckily, I'm experienced enough to not have to use my hands when I masturbate. I have terrific thigh muscles, and if I cross my legs just so, my thick, fringed pussy lips get caught in the crack between my thighs. And if I'm really turned on, I'll keep squeezing and pulling on my pussy lips with my thigh muscles. Pretty soon my vagina warms up and expands, my whole insides start pumping and I just go careening off the top in a sweet little orgasm.

So there I was in the library, feeling myself starting to get all revved up but trying to be as subtle about it as I could. I took a quick peek around. The table was pretty wide, and there was nobody directly next to me or across from me. No one else seemed close enough to notice. Besides, while my orgasms are intense, the movement of my body is hardly noticeable.

The first time I came pretty quickly with a few strong pumps of my thigh muscles and a few quick thrusts of my ass up from the library chair. I let my breath go—I tend to hold it when I'm coming—and relaxed.

Looking around, I noticed a guy sitting across the table to my right looking at me funny. I noticed how cute he was—dark hair with intense, Mel Gibson–like blue eyes—but quickly looked away. I was so anxious to appear cool and not betray my throbbing clit, racing pulse and the sure knowledge that I was going to come spectacularly again. I'm sure I had a little extra color in my cheeks, and my breath was coming a little fast. I could feel him scrutinizing me intently now, so I gave him a cool stare and turned a page. He quickly dropped his eyes and went back to his book.

Meanwhile, my legs were still crossed and my pussy was swollen and engorged. I started to get off imagining how red my cunt was, how much bigger and moister it was than when I wasn't hot with lust. I couldn't help myself. My jeans were tight and getting tighter by the second. My labia filled them full, pressing against the material. Without my being aware of moving, that irresistible rhythm started again. I sat up real straight and erect so I could bring full pressure to bear on the hard seat. I could feel my hot cream gushing into the crotch of my panties. It felt like it had soaked right through the denim. I hoped I wouldn't leave a wet mark on the seat when I got up.

This time, swaying a little in my chair, I felt my breasts hardening and swelling as I approached climax. I took a deep breath, held it and started squeezing my desperate little clit—although it wasn't so little now. I could just imagine how erect and throbbing it was! My thighs were working overtime. I felt the cushiony cheeks of my ass lift clear off the hard seat. I had a fleeting thought that I was rocking the table and should stop, but suddenly I felt the sweet explosion of a powerful orgasm churning inside me. It felt like it was literally shooting up from my fiery, overheated pussy, and I didn't care if the table fell over.

I came down slowly and regained my composure, hoping that what I was doing didn't show too much. I didn't dare look up at the Mel Gibson type across the library table, because I didn't want to stop. But I did manage to complete a whole chapter this time before slowly starting to rock my heated little parts again in the cradle of my thighs. I looked down at myself and noticed my huge tits, the nipples standing up big and proud. They were thrusting stiffly out of the silk fabric of my blouse like those big erasers you stick on the ends of pencils. I was sort of embarrassed and hoped nobody had noticed, especially not Mel.

I read some more. But soon my ass started to wiggle kind of urgently again in my seat. People were moving around me, looking for books, shuffling papers, and nobody seemed to be paying any attention to me. A good thing, too, because this next one was going to be a big one. I could feel it building. My pussy lips, my cunt and my lustful, insatiable clit must have been purple by now and more swollen than ever, hot as a potbelly stove. The need, the desire to come and come and come again was flooding me, heating my whole body. I hitched forward in the chair, my belly glued up against the table's edge, and smashed my frantic vulva down hard on the seat of the chair, pretending it was a man's pubis. I rubbed and rubbed myself against it, lifting my ass up and down as fast as I could. I slid forward in the chair a little so I could get a better grip on my clit. I had it going real good now, but God, how I wanted something between my legs, something fat, thick and thrusting! Then, ka-boom! I came in a hot, thick spurt, a gusher of lust and delight blossoming up from my loins.

I think that a whimper or two must have escaped from my lips, and I'd long before stopped pretending to read. A delicious throbbing in my whole crotch area from the orgasmic aftershocks distracted me for an instant, but I suddenly became aware that my bare feet, clad only in sandals, were wet. And getting wetter. I don't know what told me to do so, but I looked across the table at the cute brunet and saw an expression of agony on his face.

Then I immediately flashed on what was happening. He'd been watching me all along, started masturbating and was now shooting a hot load of come from his throbbing, erect penis all over my feet and legs! I dropped a pencil and, bending down to retrieve it, looked under the table and saw that he was aiming his rod straight at me with one hand. His other hand held his book open and his eyes remained studiously glued to it. And all the while, his dick was spurting and spurting like a fire hose! I thought it'd never end, but finally it stopped spurting.

Slowly I raised my eyes from this fascinating sight to his face. Our eyes met, and we grinned. Still grinning, we both then got up, packed up our books and left the library. Then, well, suffice it to say that that was the beginning of a delightful relationship. Sometimes we even go back to the library to jack ourselves off!

LIBRARY OF CONGRESS

Once in a great while, I will see a woman of such extraordinary beauty that she will leave me staring in openmouthed appreciation. Usually these incredible creatures continue on their way without noticing yet another awestruck male left lurching in their wake. The exception was "Marian."

I was in the county library where I was doing some preliminary research on my master's thesis. I was looking for a particular reference book when I noticed a movement out of the corner of my eye. Glancing to my right I saw an astounding example of feminine pulchritude striding toward me. For the briefest moment our eyes locked, leaving me reeling with sexual vertigo.

Trying to describe Marian's looks would be like attempting to explain the brilliance of Mozart. She was, quite simply, the most beautiful woman I had ever seen. But for those who must have a word picture, Marian was about five-feet-seven, one hundred ten pounds, with wavy blond hair surrounding an oval face that featured large blue eyes, a perfectly shaped nose, full lips and very white teeth. Her body set a standard by which all other females could be judged. High, full breasts, a flat, firm stomach, a hard, jutting ass and long, lean legs. She had a peaches-and-cream complexion topped with a golden tan that made her look like the ultimate California girl.

I, of course, couldn't have given you any of this description as I stood in a daze in the library. I probably didn't even notice the color of her hair. All I knew was that she was so beautiful it almost hurt to look at her. And it hurt even more to know that I'd never hold this fabulous creature in my arms. She was the type of woman reserved for millionaires, quarterbacks and movie producers. A married graduate student like me had a better chance of being elected Pope than having an affair with the likes of Marian.

My personal situation didn't keep me from enjoying the visual pleasure of watching Marian work in the library where she had the somewhat humble job of returning library books to their proper places upon the shelves. She was, I surmised, about eighteen or nineteen years old and a student herself at the local junior college.

Weeks passed into months until I knew exactly what days and hours Marian worked at the library. I knew what type of car she drove. I knew her wardrobe and especially appreciated certain tight-fitting T-shirts. I knew where to sit to best watch her reach and stretch her beautiful body as she replaced the books upon the shelves. But I didn't know her name, and I never even considered saying a word to her. And after that first day, our eyes never again met.

Although my thesis lagged because of my voyeuristic interest in Marian, my sex life with my wife improved. Our normally listless relationship heated up for a few months as my testosterone level was always higher after spending an afternoon watching Marian the librarian.

I also had numerous fantasies about Marian, which were generally composed of all sorts of idealized views of this gorgeous young woman. I saw her as bright and literate because she was always around books. I saw her as articulate and cultured for the same reason. And I saw her in bed with me because it was my fantasy.

One afternoon Marian didn't arrive at the library as scheduled and a mousy little girl took her place. I figured that Marian had taken the day off, but she didn't show up for the rest of the week. I was near panic as I realized that I might never see Marian again. I had no idea where she lived or anything else about her. I didn't want to lose her, but I didn't really have any right to go looking for her, either.

A month or more passed without a sign of Marian. I became reconciled to never seeing her again in much the same way that I was reconciled to living a life of quiet mediocrity. As strongly as I was attracted to Marian, I felt no right to allow my private fantasies to interfere with her life. I would just have to be content with seeing her picture in the paper when she married her millionaire, her quarterback, or her movie producer.

One day, weeks after my last visit to the county library, I was sitting at a table in a local coffeehouse, reading. I sensed someone at my table and looked up to see Marian. She looked straight at me and asked, "Can I sit down?"

I nodded my head dumbly and stared greedily as Marian sat opposite me. She wore an outfit that I'd never seen before—tight white shorts and a spaghetti-strap T-shirt that clung to her breasts like a second skin.

"You're one of the library peepers," she said.

I felt my face growing red and I couldn't think of anything to say. I was, after all, one of the library peepers.

"I knew all you guys," she continued. "I liked having you there. It makes it more fun to do something so fucking boring as working in the library to have a bunch of horny guys staring at your ass. But you guys were so nerdy that you would never hit on me. That's one of the weird things about the library."

"If you think I'm such a nerd," I said, "why did you ask to sit with me?"

"I need you to score me some pot and buy me some booze. I'm only eighteen so I can't get anything in the liquor store. And the cops in town all know me and they'll know if I try to score any pot. But they'll never suspect someone like you."

Obviously, I was insulted by Marian's proposition, but I wasn't so insulted that I was about to tell her to go away.

"I can get you a six-pack or something, but I'm not going to buy you any drugs," I said.

"Fuck the six-pack," she said coarsely. "Get me a bottle of peppermint schnapps and if you're a good boy I'll let you drink it with me. Get me some weed and I'll let you smoke it with me. And then, if you're really good, maybe you'll get a reward."

Marian gave me a licentious look that I'd never imagined from my cultured fantasy girl.

The mingling of lust and disgust left me momentarily at a loss for words. Marian apparently took this as a rejection and leaned closer across the table and said, "If you don't want to do it, I'll find some other asshole. . . ."

I could smell the stale reek of alcohol on her breath as she spoke. Feeling that she would only fall into worse hands if I refused, I nodded my head and said, "Let's start with the schnapps."

I left a dollar on the table to pay for my coffee and walked with Marian from the coffeehouse. She fiddled with the radio in my VW as I drove to a nearby liquor store. She replaced my classical station with a station featuring heavy metal/brain damage sound.

When I returned to the car with the schnapps, I found Marian going through my glove compartment.

"What are you looking for?" I asked.

"Drugs. Money. Whatever."

I rolled my eyes and said, "Where do you want to go?"

"Your house," she said.

"That's not possible."

"You got an old lady?"

"My house is not a possibility," I repeated.

"So you've got an old lady. Let's go to the beach."

"That's twenty miles from here," I said.

"I'll make it worth the drive."

I tried talking to Marian during the drive to the beach, but I learned little except that she was an extremely angry and alienated young woman. I had a difficult time reconciling her great beauty with her incredible anger. How could she be so bitter about life when she'd been given the kind of looks that most women could only dream about?

When we were close to the beach, Marian said, "I bet you used to think about me and jerk off."

"That's right. Except I imagined that you were a little more refined."

"You probably didn't imagine how fucked up my life has been," she said. "I mean every fucking guy in the world wants to lay me because I'm so fucking beautiful and all that shit, but once word gets out that I've been around a little bit people act like I'm a whore or something. Other girls sleep around and nobody talks about them. But it's like I'm on display, or I'm a trophy or something. Guys don't just talk about me and brag, they even make things up that I've never done. If you believed everything those assholes said, you'd think that I'd fucked every single guy in my high school and half the teachers."

"Is that why you drink?" I asked.

"I've just been drinking for a while. It kind of numbs things out. I mean it's like I don't have any real friends because the girls are all jealous of my looks and now no nice boys will ask me out because of all the lies they've heard about me. The guys that will go out with me try to get in my pants as soon as they get alone with me. And lately I've been letting them."

Marian took another nip from the bottle of schnapps and began to quietly cry.

After drying her eyes, she said, "I don't know why I'm telling you all this shit. I mean I don't even know your name or anything."

I told her my name and she told me hers. (It wasn't Marian, of course.)

When we arrived at the beach, Marian told me to drive past the main parking lot to a side street where I parked the car. She led me by the hand over the sand dunes to an isolated location where we found a spot out of sight and out of the afternoon wind. We didn't have bathing suits or a towel.

Marian took a swig of the schnapps and then leaned back against the sand dune. She pulled her skimpy T-shirt over her head, exposing her incredible, perfect breasts, which were even larger and fuller than I'd imagined.

I stared at Marian's breasts as she leaned her head back onto the sand dune and closed her eyes. Her small reddish nipples looked like tiny islands on the oceans of her breasts. The rest of her upper body was almost dainty in comparison—small shoulders, a flat stomach and a tiny waist.

The great blessing of Marian's fabulous face and body had somehow turned into a horrible burden. But at the same time as I wanted to help her, I also wanted to fuck her. Only a saint, a homosexual or a eunuch would have been able to resist her carnal charms.

Marian opened her eyes and saw me staring at her breasts. She looked from my eyes to my crotch and then asked, "Like what you see?"

"You're the most beautiful woman I've ever laid eyes on."

"I've heard that before," she said, while spreading her knees apart.

"You've got the kind of looks that will open doors anywhere in the world. You don't have to be stuck in some provincial town where a bunch of ignorant locals have branded you as some sort of modern scarlet woman. You're not stuck here. There's a whole world out there waiting for you."

She took another drink of schnapps and then said, "Yeah, waiting to lay me and then brag about it."

I looked closely at beautiful Marian, who was now beginning to rub her hand along the inside of her leg, and then I said, "If you get so upset about getting laid and having guys brag about it, why are you allowing yourself to be so easy? I mean, you don't even know me and you've done everything but rape me."

Her hand slipped into her white shorts and she began to rub her pussy. With her eyes now closed, Marian said, "There's only two things in life I love doing—getting high and getting it on. I just happen to be a very horny woman. I need sex every day. I'm like a nympho or something. I can't help myself."

I suppose I could have given Marian some psychological explanations for her fixations on sex, helped her see that there wasn't anything wrong with her, but I was too busy unzipping my pants. At some point, a man must be true to his biological instincts.

Marian opened her eyes and watched me undress. As I approached her, she took my penis in her hand and said, "Nice cock." She rubbed her hands on my balls and brought my staff toward her mouth. She licked the pre-come off my dick and then inspected it at close range.

"Why is it that nerdy guys like you always have these wonderful cocks?" she asked. "This thing must be eight inches long."

"I've always been kind of embarrassed by it," I said. "Back in high school the guys in gym class used to call me 'horse' and now my wife always complains that it's so big that it hurts her."

"The only way you're going to hurt me with this beautiful thing is if I try to deep-throat you. I can take most guys all the way, but I'd have to be a sword swallower to get all of you in my mouth. But you'll make my cunt happy."

She pulled down her pants, exposing a dark blond bush, and she said, "Lie on your back and don't get any sand on your prick."

I followed her orders and she crouched above me and carefully allowed my rigid cock to penetrate deep into her wet pussy. Sliding slowly up and down on my thick shaft while playing with her clitoris, Marian brought herself to shivering orgasm within a very few minutes.

She slumped onto my stomach, pressing her breasts against my chest, and said, "God, what a relief. Now what would you like?"

"I'd like to fuck your brains out," I said.

"You don't have to," Marian said. "I only come once. After that it's just a wasted effort. But fuck me if you want. Or I'll try to suck on that monster."

Marian now became a challenge of another sort, as I refused to believe that she could have only one orgasm. Getting her back in position straddling me, I got her to repeat her thrusts, while I used both of my hands to cup one of her breasts and bring its nipple to my mouth. Sucking, I felt Marian's nipple harden and enlarge. Stroking and squeezing her bouncing breasts in one hand, I moved my other hand down to Marian's clit. She tried to brush it away, but I held on firmly as I gently stroked her wet lust center.

Moving from breast to breast, I took turns licking and sucking on Marian's hard nipples. She began fucking me harder as I felt her clitoris swell. Her already tight pussy contracted in a spasm of pleasure as Marian began to shake from a violent orgasm. My usual ability to fuck until my wife claimed I'd given her a headache deserted me as I began trembling in simultaneous orgasm with Marian. Her tight box clamped down on my dick as I fired a full load of come deep into her pussy.

After resting for a couple of minutes, I asked, "So what's this bull I've heard about only having one orgasm?"

"This never happened before. I've always gotten off exactly the way I did with you and that's it. Usually the guys come right away and I'm so disgusted with the whole scene that I won't let him do anything else."

"Well, I'm about to do something else," I said, "which is eat your pussy."

"You don't have to," she said. "It really doesn't do anything for me."

"Sit on my face," I said, "and we'll see what it does for you."

Marian followed my orders and I buried my face in the dripping swamp of her pussy. Her juices and my come dribbled into my mouth as I licked my way from her tight teenaged pussy to her hot little clit. Working her into a gentle frenzy with my patient tongue, I increased my pressure as her breathing deepened. As her pulse began to race, Marian collapsed onto her knees and forced her bushy wetness tight over my face. Realizing that Marian might suffocate me with her pussy, I was ready to die a happy man as I brought my tongue to maximum speed. Marian's entire body stiffened as a low-pitched wail emerged from her throat. A volcanic orgasm lifted her pelvis just far enough to allow me to breathe.

"I've never felt anything like that before," she said after regaining her composure. "That was just incredible. Now you've got to let me suck your cock."

Not in the mood to argue with a beautiful woman who had her own plans, I leaned back against the sand and watched as Marian slowly took my penis in her soft, sweet mouth. I held back her blond hair so I could enjoy the sight of my ever-hardening phallus disappearing between her full, red lips. With each bob of her head, Marian took more and more of my cock into her mouth. As she worked her way deeper down the shaft, I knew her gagging reflex would eventually stop her from taking all of me. Wanting to help, I pushed my hips down deeper into the sand, so that she would have a little less of my cock to worry about.

Apparently feeling the movement of my hips, Marian reached around behind my butt and pulled my hips back up. She now had every inch of my lust to lick.

Somehow inspired, Marian took more and more of my cock into her mouth with each dive of her head. I nearly passed out from pleasure as she was able to bring her lips to the very base of my cock. As I began moaning, I brought her lips up closer to the sensitive tip of my dick and instructed her to suck hard.

As my come began spurting into her mouth, Marian resumed giving me complete deep throat. Once I'd filled her mouth with semen, Marian let some dribble out of my cock onto her hand. Smearing it on her breasts, she said, "Lick it off."

I immediately complied with her request and then kept right on licking my way south, until I'd brought her to another orgasm. She returned the favor by giving me yet another blowjob. By the time she was done, I thought my cock was about to fall off. I was used to having sex about three times a week, not three times in ninety minutes.

In the past six months, I've been working on my master's thesis and fucking Marian about four or five times a week. She's

stopped fucking every Tom, Dick and Harry in town and seems to
be getting her head screwed on straight.

As for my wife, I think she's about to run off with another man.
At first I thought I'd warn him, but now I've decided it's his problem. When she goes, I'll quit working on my thesis and start fucking Marian every day.

GEISHA BACHELOR PARTY

I'd like to share with you the bachelor's party given to me by
my friend Amy. I first noticed this pretty Asian coed sitting in the
corner of a college research class. About five-feet-two and
ninety-five pounds, she had a slim figure with small breasts, a narrow waist and long, slender legs. Her almond-shaped eyes, jet-
black hair and delicate lips gave her that beauty unique to
Oriental women, a certain subtle aura of grace. I introduced myself pronto. Amy drew me like a moth to a flame, and her attraction to me was equally instantaneous. We agreed to work
together on a class project, and got to know and appreciate each
other even more.

This might have been the start of a fantastic romance, but, unfortunately, we were involved with other people at the time. We
did become close friends, however, sharing our innermost secrets.
It was just a matter of time until we acted on our common love,
exploring the secrets of each other's body. Like a master musician,
my fingers and lips coaxed from Amy's writhing body the sounds
of ecstasy no other lover had ever been able to draw forth. She
proved equally adept at playing my fleshy flute, her hands and
mouth working skillfully to elicit every precious note I could
pump down her talented throat. Yet, despite these passionate sessions, we never went all the way.

About a year ago, I started dating a rather special woman and proposed to her by the summer's end. When I told Amy, she was shell-shocked—as if what she hoped would never happen was happening. I tried to reassure her that my forthcoming marriage didn't mean an end to our love, but Amy shook her head and said she had lost me. However, she said, before I was married, she wanted a last night with me, then quickly added that after that night we were through. Nothing I could say would dissuade her, so we agreed to meet on the following Saturday in the poshest hotel in town.

It was a balmy summer afternoon when I checked into the hotel and called Amy. She said she'd be right over, but the sun had set before she strolled through the room's door. Amy was stunning in a thin cotton dress that showed her exquisite body to best advantage, high heels, carefully applied makeup and long, loose hair. Before I could say anything, she dropped her overnight bag and fell to her knees. "I've wanted you so badly for so many years," she said breathlessly, "but I was never sure you wanted me. Be gentle when you use all of me tonight." I was speechless. Was this the same woman who had resisted me so successfully all these years?

Realizing this was a dream come true, I asked her to stand and lift up her dress. Although I have seen Amy nude before, this was infinitely more exciting. As the dress tantalizingly ascended, first her shapely legs, then her skimpy panties were revealed, the fabric already stained with her sexual excitement. My rock-hard cock threatened to tear a hole through my pants, but I calmly asked her to remove her panties.

Amy hesitated. Then, holding her dress up with one hand, she slowly peeled off her flimsy panties. As they dropped to the floor, I was astonished—her pussy was completely bald. She never had had much pubic hair to begin with, but whatever she had, had been neatly shaved off. Her clearly visible, ivory cunt lips nestled beneath her gently rounded belly, the swollen slit already moist and slightly distended. With downcast eyes and dress well above her hips, she looked like a naughty little geisha about to be rewarded.

As I circled and thoroughly inspected her, my fingers traced a light path down her shapely legs, up between her smooth thighs and finally over the soft curve of her hip. Amy shivered as she enjoyed my feathery caresses, her eyes closed, sighing softly. My hand then slid down her pubescent-appearing vulva, slipping into and spreading her smooth slit. Amy groaned and, clamping her legs together, instinctively pressed her clit against my trapped hand, her flowing juices drenching my fingers.

Bending her over, I asked Amy to grab her ankles. When she did, I flipped her dress high over her back and shucked it off her to expose her quivering love pie. I slowly undressed and saw that she was watching me from between her parted legs. Then, standing behind her, I let my full nine inches gently probe her slippery oyster, seeking her celestial pearl. Amy whimpered softly and reached for my straining cock. Her touch on it was feathery-light, fluttering from the glans to my balls so delicately I almost came on the spot. I jerked away so abruptly she reacted as if she'd done something wrong, but I quickly reassured her, saying she was just too nice. "Forgive me," she sighed, "but I've wanted you for so long."

Gone was Amy's self-control as she convulsively jerked just the lips of her slick, tight pussy up and down my swollen cockhead. "Please," she pleaded, "let me put it in." "Yes!" I almost screamed, and she reached eagerly for my huge, throbbing cock with tiny, trembling fingers. Her ebony hair clung to her glistening skin as she struggled, twisted and turned to get my huge cockhead into her. She must have had at least two orgasms, her legs bucking each time, before she succeeded in lodging the tip of my cock in her indescribably small, wet cunt's entrance.

After all those frustrated years, I could no longer restrain myself. I grabbed her hips and slowly but inexorably eased into her. Amy squealed and momentarily tensed up, then squirmed madly like an impaled fish. I couldn't believe it: I was finally fucking Amy!

If you've ever fucked Oriental women, you know how incredibly tight they are. Amy's velvet squeeze box was absolutely the tightest and best I've ever had. Her virginlike twat gripped my sheathed cock, contracting and throbbing, so that at first I couldn't move even if I'd wanted to. Yet, as I slowly stroked into her molten furnace, it gushed liquid fire that pooled at her puckered anus and ran down her legs. "Umm," Amy cooed, "I always knew you'd feel good, but this is sooo good." Within minutes, she was ready to come again, but before she could, I pulled out and begged her to completely strip. She had kept her bra on.

As Amy shucked her padded bra, I hungrily eyed her intriguing, tiny tits. She was a 34AA which meant she was pancake flat but what Amy lacked in bulk she more than made up for in the heightened sensitivity of her small nipples and their puffy, penny-size areolae. She panted rapidly when I gently nipped at one delicate cherry blossom with my lips and, by the time I began to lick circles around her other sweet strawberry, she was shuddering as if freezing.

Her body soon shook uncontrollably as another climax tore through her.

Spent by her intense release, Amy slipped limply into my arms. I kissed her passionately, then positioned her on her knees on the soft carpet. Kneeling behind her, I told her to reach back and spread her luscious vagina for me. Amy did so and remained in this position as I fondled her exposed, sweet delights. With Amy finally mine for the taking, I decided to push into her tantalizing hole. I began to fondle her tiny, flowering cunt, easing my index finger in to the knuckle.

She squirmed so much that I thought she had had enough. When my hand strayed to her fiery clit, however, Amy groaned, "No! Don't move." Then she moaned, "I want you inside me!" With her upended ass bumping into my belly, I pressed steadily forward into her indescribably tight hole. When I entered her,

Amy gasped repeatedly, then shoved a hand between her legs. As she frantically fingered her love button, her hips began to rock back and forth, and I was amazed as her tightly stretched pussy slowly devoured every inch of my cock. Suddenly she emitted a high-pitched cry, and writhed in the throes of a long, powerful orgasm. With her hot buns slapping hard against me, I shot my wad, too, and her constricting cunt madly milked me dry. We collapsed on the floor. After a few speechless minutes, Amy crawled into my lap, took my limp dick in her hands and said, "You're everything I imagined you'd be . . . and more!" With that, Amy lowered her head to lick me clean, sucking me vigorously until my dick was as hard as a rock, filling her sensuous mouth. Then, playfully looking up at me, she removed my cock from her lips, and with her slender fingers wrapped around and sliding on my thickness, seductively asked if I was ready for more. Much to her disappointment, I told this wanton wench it was time to get ready for dinner.

Dinner was in a dark corner booth of the hotel's restaurant. The plunging neckline of her dress gave me a clear view of her pink rosebuds—she'd left both bra and panties back in our room. After giving the waiter our orders, I eased her dress up over her lap. She pouted disapprovingly, looking over at the other tables to see if anyone was staring at us, but when I cupped the naked juncture of her delicious thighs, a lascivious smile appeared on her lips. Throughout dinner Amy wriggled and moaned softly, struggling to keep her composure as I played with her. I knew my touch really turned her on. When our waiter brought the check, she looked at him with lust-dazed eyes and sensuously licked her lips, leaning back to brazenly display my fingers buried in her hairless Oriental pussy. Smiling appreciatively, the waiter took a good, long look and asked that we please come again. Amy replied she would make sure we would come again and again.

Before I could close our room's door back up on our floor, Amy was stark naked and had stripped me of my suit jacket. She nailed me with an openmouthed kiss, her tongue dancing in my mouth.

Then she jerked down my pants to enjoy a healthy dessert portion of my cream-filled sweet roll. She grasped my swaying erection and led me like a helpless, panting puppy into our room and out to the balcony. There, in clear view of the adjacent rooms, Amy threw all her inscrutable reserve to the wind as she leaned against the railing and furiously ground her pelvis against mine. Then, placing a foot on a nearby sun chair, she teasingly spread her soft lotus petals with my red-hot poker, whispering urgently in my ear, "I'm so horny! Take me now!"

I looped an arm under her bent knee and pierced her soft, clinging vagina in one swift stroke. Amy's eyes flew open, then slowly closed as I repeatedly withdrew my cock a very slow, tight inch and put it back in abruptly. She whimpered with each thrust, then grasped my shoulders and locked her legs about my waist. Like a woman possessed, she humped me until her celestial gates slid down to tightly seal my sword at its hilt. Throwing her head back, her hair whipping from side to side in her ecstasy, she came again and again. As she convulsed with intense orgasms, my hot lava burst into her aching pussy and mixed with her sizzling juices. My howls mingled with hers in the still night.

Although I have tried to see Amy several times since that night, she has steadfastly refused, holding firm to her original resolve. It's been six months and I haven't given up. This coming Saturday I'll be at the same hotel and have told Amy I'll be expecting her. I fervently hope she stops by! If she doesn't, I will still always remember her fondly and her fantastic parting gift to my bachelorhood.

COITUS INTERRUPTUS

*F*or twenty-five years I've been married to a lovely woman, whom I'll call Linda. We have always maintained a very vigorous sex life, despite raising three children. During the early years of marriage we were able to utilize our children's school hours and their grandparents' baby-sitting availability to engage in some rather uninhibited sexual activities. Once our children had grown and moved away from home, we looked forward to relative peace and quiet so that we could really enjoy our X-rated movies on the VCR and the various sexual paraphernalia we've collected over the years, usually kept hidden in the back of the closet.

Unfortunately this was not how it turned out. Two of our children returned home due to marriage and money problems, and my mother-in-law, recently widowed and in poor health, came to live with us.

At first we accepted these circumstances with understanding and compassion, but as time passed both of us became increasingly frustrated at the lack of privacy or opportunity to pursue our sexual inclinations.

One evening last fall we were both in a particularly horny mood, and I suggested that we take a drive into the country outside our small Ohio town. My wife, knowing what I had in mind, liked the idea, and we headed out feeling like a couple of teenagers. A short while later I found a gravel road which seemed quite deserted. Because I have bucket seats and a center console in my car, we got into the backseat as soon as I parked.

It must have been the thrill of "parking" again after so many years, because both Linda and I were as aroused as we have ever been. After a very short period of foreplay, I had Linda's blouse and bra removed, and she pulled her skirt up above her waist. My hand went between her legs to massage her pussy through her sheer panties. She was soaking wet and ready to be fucked. I unbuckled my belt and undid my zipper. My cock was like a rock and larger than I could remember it having been for a long time. I slid Linda's panties down and positioned myself between her legs. But, just as I began to insert myself, I was blinded by a bright light shining in the window.

With a jolt, I jumped back from Linda and looked straight into the beam of a spotlight. "Excuse me," said the officer, "may I see some identification?"

I was in a state of panic and mumbled something I don't even remember. Reaching into my wallet, I offered him my driver's license. As I did so, I was able to make out his face in the light of the full moon. The township had hired him just last month, and I had been on the review board. He recognized me and said, "I hate to interrupt, but you'd better move on, Mr. G. It's not safe to park on these deserted roads."

I thanked the officer for his concern and we waited for his car to pull out before we got dressed and drove away. I suggested a drink and we headed for our favorite pub to calm down and relax. After one drink and the start of a second it was obvious that we were both even hornier now and eager to finish what we had started. Then an idea struck me.

"Why don't we go to my office? There won't be anyone there at this hour, and Scott has a great leather sofa in his office."

A few minutes later we arrived at the office complex where I work. We entered through the back and didn't turn on any of the lights, in order to avoid arousing suspicions. There were security lights on in the halls that allowed us to see our way into Scott's office. By the time we got there we were practically panting with desire as we made our way to the sofa. Once again I had Linda's bra and blouse off in rapid order. She was so eager that she was pulling off her skirt and panties while I massaged her breasts and sucked her large, swollen nipples. I quickly removed my shirt, pants and shorts. Linda lay back on the sofa and stretched out full length as I moved between her legs. We were like animals in heat. There was no thought of further foreplay. In a voice from deep in her throat, Linda growled, "I want you to fuck me right now and I want it deep and I want it fast."

I placed my engorged cock at the entrance to her cunt and began my first thrust. But before I had even completely entered her, I froze at the sound of keys in the outer office door and the clanging of metal buckets. My God, I realized, it's the cleaning crew. Moving faster than I ever had on the tennis court, I threw on my shirt, shorts and pants in record time. Linda ignored her bra and panties and literally jumped into her skirt and blouse. I switched on the light and sat down at Scott's desk just in time to catch Linda's panties and bra, which she'd thrown to me to hide. I stuffed them into my pocket and started arranging papers on the desk, while she sat on the sofa and grabbed a magazine.

Seconds later the crew entered the office. "Working kinda late, aren't you, Mr. G?" asked one of the two men.

I was still in a state of shock, but managed to mutter something about another long day. Unfortunately, as I spoke, I rose from the chair, and Linda's panties fell from my pocket, landing on the floor in plain view of everyone in the room.

As Linda and I beat a hasty retreat from the office and headed for our car, we left the two of them staring at each other open-mouthed.

As soon as we were in the car, we broke into hysterical laughter from the absurdity of the whole evening. I suggested another drink, and we headed back to the same pub.

As we sat sipping, now hornier than ever, I told Linda in my best Bogart voice, "Here's looking at you, kid, and somehow, some way, I'm going to get in a good fuck with you tonight!"

"I'll drink to that," responded Linda, and then her eyes lit up. "I've got the perfect place!" she exclaimed. "Jackie and Charley are on vacation, and Jackie gave me the key to their house to check on it while they're gone."

Faster than a speeding bullet, we were back in the car heading for Jackie and Charley's house. A short while later we let ourselves in and headed for their family room, where we knew a big, comfortable couch was waiting for us.

Our passions fueled by the excitement of being caught earlier, further stoked by the challenge of finding a "safe" place, we both felt like lust-crazed teenagers. By the time we got to the couch most of our clothes were off and my cock (which hadn't really been soft for the past three hours) was bigger than ever.

We had just made it to the couch when the police arrived at the front door. Jackie had neglected to tell Linda that they had installed a silent burglar alarm the previous week.

As before, we went into what was far too quickly becoming a routine with us—a frenzied hurry-up-and-get-dressed drill.

The two investigating officers were polite and patient as we showed them the key and explained that we were checking on our friends' house. Unfortunately my pants were still unzipped, Linda had her blouse on backwards and her hair was all over her face. To make matters worse, one of the officers was the same one who had found us earlier in the evening parked on the gravel road.

"I understand, Mr. G, I understand," was all he could say. We could see him struggling not to laugh.

Since that fateful evening we have found two safe refuges, whose locations I certainly am not going to divulge. After our experience that evening, though, both Linda and I agree that the thrill of illicit sex and being caught in the act certainly adds zip to your sex life.

CHAIN BANG

It all began when Beth caught me with my pants down. I'd seen no problem with a little nude sunbathing on the deck as part of my two-week vacation, but now the woman in charge of renting the condos at the lakeside resort I was visiting had just walked in on me. Great, I thought, I'm here only one night and she's going to kick me out. Before I could think of anything to say, Beth sat on one of the chaises and explained that she usually calls on guests to see if they are pleased with their accommodations. I stammered that everything was fine, and told her that I'd spent most of the previous day relaxing at the beach. Then, suddenly remembering my manners, and looking for a way to cover my nakedness, I asked Beth if she'd like something to drink. She said she'd appreciate something cold, so I went inside to put on a pair of shorts and get some orange juice. From the kitchen I jokingly asked Beth if I'd broken any of the resort's rules. She laughed and told me that most people enjoy having breakfast on their balconies. Relieved, and figuring that this episode could possibly turn into something memorable, I removed the shorts again and walked out on the balcony as naked as before.

When Beth saw me, she smiled and excused herself for a moment, saying she had to make a phone call. A few minutes later, when she returned to the balcony, she wordlessly unbuttoned her jumpsuit and let it fall to the floor. She then just stood there for a moment, as if to let me admire her body, which I certainly did. Although she was over forty, her large breasts were round and firm. Still saying nothing, she began caressing and squeezing her hard, brown nipples. One hand soon slid down along the curves of her torso and began to rub her blond bush. Her eyes now flashed a wanton look. "No, you haven't broken any regulations yet," she said, "but I'm wondering just how much you're willing to do to avoid violating our rules."

I was puzzled, but Beth didn't explain. She simply dropped to her knees and took my cock in one hand. With her other hand she stroked my balls as she worked my shaft to its full seven inches and then stuffed the head into her mouth. After some playful licking, she took in my entire cock and slid her head up and down on it, swirling her tongue around the base every time she reached bottom. Just as I was about to get down on the floor for a hot 69 with her, the screen door opened behind me. I panicked, but Beth never missed a beat. When I saw who had crashed our party, I recognized her as a woman I'd noticed on the beach, a brunette in her early thirties. Since she was totally nude, I couldn't help but notice that her tits were smaller than Beth's and her pussy had been shaved completely. She immediately bent over and drove her tongue into my mouth, and then pulled back and whispered, "Let's see how you do with two hot women."

Dropping to her knees, she positioned herself alongside Beth, who stopped blowing me to turn to the stranger and engage her in a prolonged French kiss only inches from my dick while both of them jerked my standing, wet cock. When their kiss ended, Beth began pleasuring my balls, allowing the brunette to suck on my shaft. Each of them was also fingering the other's cunt.

As my balls began to throb and a flood of come swelled within them, I was startled to hear still another voice behind me saying, "Let's make it a foursome. My name's Brendan." Beth and the other woman stopped what they were doing and turned to greet the newcomer. Much to my surprise, it was one of the young male lifeguards from the beach. He and I had similar physiques, both of us being tall and lean, but his cock was longer and thicker than mine. The women grabbed for it and began hungrily to lick and stroke it. Hard, it must have been ten inches long. Beth began working over his balls as the brunette ran her lips up and down the length of his shaft.

They stopped after a few minutes. Beth turned back to my dick while the brunette slid beneath her and started licking her pussy. The lifeguard stepped toward me so his meat was swaying just in front of my face. I'd done some cocksucking in threesomes before, so I wasn't uninitiated, but I barely managed to get five inches of Brendan's thick dick in my mouth. To help things along, I started stroking the base of his huge tool and rolling his balls in my palms. After about two minutes, we began moaning and bucking against each other. As he placed his hands on my shoulders and coaxed me into swallowing another inch, I saw the brunette out of the corner of my eye, furiously rubbing her clit, bringing herself to orgasm. Beth was pressing her cunt into the brunette's mouth, which was coated with Beth's cunt juices. The sight was too much for me, so I held on to Brendan's ass and Beth's head as my come poured over her tongue. When my orgasm subsided, Brendan's began. He came in waves with powerful thrusts and so much hot cream that I couldn't swallow it all. Beth hastily slurped up the overflow that dribbled down my chin.

When we took time out for a rest, I asked the others if we should move to the bedroom. There was a loud chorus of noes. Rising to my feet, I was greeted by the appreciative smiles of six nude spectators—two women in their thirties, two girls in their early twenties and two other lifeguards, both of them golden tan like Brendan and about the same age as he. After introductions, Beth congratulated me for having passed the first stage of the group's initiation, adding that one more phase remained before I could join the group as a regular. To put it mildly, I was a bit surprised. No more than thirty minutes earlier I had been quietly enjoying the morning rays—and now the balcony furniture was full of sexy bodies. Beth, continuing her explanation, said that I had been screened when I'd inspected the condo a month before this. Three other members of the group had been hiding in a closet while Beth and I had discussed rental terms, and the three-on-one seduction was planned for the morning after my arrival. My nude sunbathing made it unexpectedly easy for Beth to get the activities started. Everyone else just let themselves in through the front door, which Beth had left unlocked.

So what, I wondered, was the second step going to entail? Beth explained that it was a game they called Last Link. The game was the invention of four members—Beth, Priscilla (the brunette, now on the couch stroking a young stud's dick), Joan (an eighteen-year-old brunette with watermelon tits and a shapely ass) and George, another of the young studs. While making a routine inspection of vacant units three summers ago, Beth happened into a condo where Priscilla was teaching Joan the techniques of lesbian lovemaking. So deep into their pleasure were they that they continued lapping each other in a hot 69 for about ten minutes before noticing Beth's presence. After only an instant's hesitation, Beth joined them and the three women made love together for the rest of the morning. Quickly becoming close friends, Joan later sought Beth's advice on how to deal with George, her "summer boyfriend," who was continually try-ing to convince Joan to let him fuck her on the beach. Beth of-fered to arrange a morning tryst for Joan's first time with George, but Beth and Priscilla devised a scenario similar to the one I'd ex-perienced—during which they surprised Joan and George in mid-fuck and joined in the fun. After that, desiring more hard meat for what became daily meetings for group sex, Beth invited the other two lifeguards, and Priscilla invited a few oversexed house-wives who were looking for action on weekdays when their hus-bands were at work in the city. As many as fifteen people might join the orgy on any given day.

The "meetings" were held in vacant condos (Beth had access keys). The guys were chosen as much for their discretion as their cock size, and the women for their love of fucking and sucking ei-ther sex.

Which brings me back to the game they called Last Link. Looking at the faces on my balcony, I noticed that everyone was getting a little anxious. The guys' cocks were beginning to harden and the women were licking their lips in anticipation. I sensed that the game would soon begin. Beth explained to me that it was a contest entailing a series of blowjobs and cunnilingus acts. When a person orgasmed, he or she was out of contention and had to stop giving or getting oral sex. The last one to come was the winner.

When it came to admitting an initiate into the group, a rule stipulated that the candidate had to finish among the last three in order to qualify for membership. I said I understood, and drew for position, using numbered chips. Then, arranging ourselves in clockwise order, we lay in a circle on the floor. My eagerness was almost unbearable as everybody checked out their positions in the chain. I felt I had an advantage in that I generally take a while to orgasm during oral sex. I further assumed that the three young guys would be quick-triggered. I knew I would find out soon enough as I prepared to slurp on George's eight-incher. At the same time, a sweet-faced woman named Ann, whose soft, full breasts belied her forty-one years, curled her tongue and held it, poised for action, just above the head of my throbbing dick.

A mechanical timer signaled the start, and everyone dove in. Slurping sounds and heavy moans filled the room. I moaned loudly as Ann engulfed my entire member and superheated it in her throat. The action around me was torrid, but I didn't dare look around for fear of getting too excited and climaxing too soon.

About four minutes passed before Cindy—a young blonde that George was finger-fucking while tongue-lashing her clit—began screaming and bucking wildly as she reached orgasm. I immediately quickened the pace and sucked all but the last inch of George's cock in and out of my mouth. As Cindy's moans and groans died, George's member seemed to grow half again as large and he spilled his hot load into my throat. When he'd shot the last few drops, George and Cindy rolled to the side and the circle became smaller. Beth's sopping slit was over my face now. Silently vowing to finish the task that Cindy had begun, I drove my tongue into Beth's hole. She looked down for a moment to see who had replaced Cindy, and gave me a smoldering smile.

It was Ann who came next, and she took her mouth away from my penis to throw back her head and scream in delight. The sounds of all this hot sex affected us all, but I managed to quell the ache in my balls as Beth began humping my face. Wanting to return her earlier favors on the balcony, I used my tongue to caress her clit. At the same time I reached up and gently pinched her nipples while pressing her tits together. She quickly gushed her juices as she rode my mouth, and then rolled aside, exhausted.

As I sat up to find my next partner, Joan signaled an impending orgasm as she broke away from Priscilla's cunt and grabbed the head of Linda, the torrid twenty-four-year-old redhead who was at work on her clit. As Priscilla and I prepared to move in to join the three other remaining players, Charles, a slim guy with a ten-inch monster, dumped his load into Linda's mouth while pulling Brendan's dick out of his mouth. Wrapping his hand around his meat, Charles sprayed Linda's throat with another torrent of white jism and pumped a few last drops into her open mouth. An incredibly erotic scene, it proved too much for Priscilla, who had been fingering her clit while sitting there beside me. As she came, she worked her right hand through her bush and kneaded her tits with her left, clenching her legs tightly together as she shrieked with pleasure.

In only seven or eight minutes, the number of players had decreased from ten to two.

Although I had already qualified for membership in the group, I was determined to be the ultimate winner, too—the last link. The others moved in closer as Linda—my final competitor—and I moved toward each other. Another of the horny housewives, Linda had well-rounded boobs and rock-like nipples which stood out proudly as she spread the dark bush between her legs to show me one of the largest clits I'd ever seen. Mesmerized, I slid between her thighs and she deftly took my entire cock into her mouth. As I felt the head touch the back of her throat, I knew immediately that I'd met my match. Ann had been incredibly smooth, but Linda's ministrations were unbelievably sensitive, and the swelling ache began again to tighten my balls. I quickened the tempo and fought off the imperative urge to release my load in her mouth. I sensed that she was also close to an orgasm. She surprised me then by quickly rolling away and coming up on all fours with her ass pointed at my face. She spread her cunt for me as she looked back over her shoulder and said, "Fuck me."

Needing no further encouragement, I shoved my cock in to the hilt with a single stroke. My belly was pressed against her asscheeks as I grabbed for her tits and began wildly fucking. Although we had slammed together for no more than twenty seconds, our bodies were drenched with sweat when she screamed, "Oh, God! I think I'm going to come!" I leaned back and pushed into her one more time, pushing her into orgasm. Then I let go too, shooting my hot sperm deep into her pulsing vagina. Linda cried with joy, and we collapsed on the carpet together, unable to move for several silent minutes. Exhausted and satisfied, the ten of us soon curled up together for some gentle afterplay.

It wasn't until later that afternoon, as we relaxed on the beach in the warm sun, that I fully appreciated what had happened that morning. The highlight of my vacation, however, was a slumber party involving a dozen people. There were also two more games of Last Link. Needless to say, I enjoyed this vacation more than any other. I've already made my deposit for this summer. I can hardly wait.

FREE PARKING

*T*his year my wife's birthday—and events resulting from it—was special. We started out the evening by going out for dinner to a good restaurant and then on to a local nightclub for some dancing and entertainment, where we ran into Bob, a good friend of mine from work. As the night wore on, Bob and I took turns dancing with Cathie, my pretty wife.

Cathie looked fantastic as I watched her and Bob dance. She was wearing a little miniskirt that nicely showed off her long legs. Under her thin, slinky blouse, her braless forty-inch tits bounced seductively. Bob had a big bulge in his pants after every dance with her, and so did I.

Somewhere around two o'clock in the morning we decided to call it a night. Bob had drunk quite a bit, so Cathie suggested that we drive him home. When we pulled into the well-lighted parking lot of the apartment complex where he lived, Bob turned us on to some really good grass, and we spent some time talking. After a while Bob got out of the backseat of our small car and talked to us through Cathie's open window, on the passenger's side. I decided to get out myself, to stretch my legs and get some fresh air, and I leaned against the top of the car and talked to Bob over the roof.

All of a sudden his eyes widened and a strange look developed on his face. Then, even though Bob's arms were leaning on the car's roof, I heard his zipper go down! I looked through the windshield and got the surprise of my life! Through the open window, Bob's huge, semi-hard cock and balls were banging right in Cathie's face, and she was jerking him off! She looked up through the windshield at me and smiled as she licked the head of his swelling cock! My own rod instantly turned rock-hard.

I went around the car and sat on the hood in an attempt to block the view of what was going on, in case someone came out of the apartment building or drove up. This also gave me a good angle from which to observe my wife, sucking and licking my friend's big cock. The sight was fantastic.

Bob seemed nervous, but he nevertheless looked like you couldn't have pried him off the side of the car with a crowbar. I lit up another joint, and he and I smoked it as I watched my wife trying to totally engulf his huge cock, which would have involved her half-swallowing it. She was sucking and jerking him off with one hand while her free hand unbuttoned her blouse, which she pulled open so that Bob could see her big tits. Her hand caressed her erect nipples.

Next, she pulled up her skirt, and the light of a nearby streetlight revealed that she wore no panties and her cunt was soaking wet. She started finger-fucking herself, moaning loudly as she rubbed her clit. In a few minutes she came, moaning and groaning and trying to swallow more of Bob's big cock!

Bob looked like he was having trouble standing up as his hips pumped faster and faster into the open window of the car. "I'm gonna come, I'm gonna come," he groaned, and then his entire body stiffened as his enormous rod started jerking in Cathie's pretty mouth.

Now, my wife likes to eat come, but she wasn't prepared for the load that Bob was pumping into her greedy little mouth. She was trying to swallow it all, but he just kept on coming until it ran out of the corners of her mouth and dripped in big globs onto her bare tits.

I still couldn't believe that I was watching my wife pleasure a strange cock, but what was even more captivating was how pretty and sexy she looked while doing it. She held Bob's cock out of her mouth for a few seconds, and it shot long streams of thick white fluid all over the seat and on her blouse. Then she quickly took it in her mouth again.

Meanwhile two cars had pulled in and parked nearby as Bob was still coming. I was sure that it was obvious what was going on, as Bob must also have felt, because he pulled his cock out of Cathie's mouth and quickly stuffed it back into his pants. We said a quick good-bye, and Bob thanked Cathie for "the best blowjob that I've ever had." He rushed inside without a backward glance and I jumped in the car and quickly drove off.

About two blocks away, I found a dark spot and pulled the car over. Cathie was frantically fingering her cunt and said, "I hope you liked watching me suck your friend's cock. When he rubbed it against me while we danced, I got so excited that I wanted to suck him right there in the bar!" I moved closer to her and grabbed a come-covered tit. "It was an incredible turn-on sucking his big cock right there in the parking lot where anyone could see us," she moaned.

She gave me a deep kiss, and for the first time I tasted another man's come on my wife's lips. I became so excited that I quickly moved down to her tits and licked Bob's partial load off her swollen nipples. The smell and taste of his sticky come all over her face and tits drove me absolutely wild!

Throwing caution to the winds, we got out of the car. I bent Cathie over the front fender as I pulled her dress up over her hips. As I pulled my stiff staff out, she looked over her shoulder and said, "Oh, fuck me baby, fuck me." I grabbed her hips and in one stroke rammed into her wet cunt until her ass was tight against my belly. "Too bad those cars pulled in and interrupted us," she moaned. "I was hoping that you and Bob would be taking turns fucking me by now."

"You'd love to fuck that big cock of his, wouldn't you?" I said as I fucked her harder.

"Oh, yes," she groaned. "The next time we go out, I'll suck you both off in the parking lot at the bar, and then the two of you could even fuck me on the hood of the car like this if we were careful." I fucked her faster and harder until we both came, wishing Bob was still with us and waiting his turn.

On the way home all Cathie talked about was how exciting it had been for her to suck Bob's big cock right in the open in front of his house. "Let's go out dancing again next weekend," she said as she again toyed with her cunt. "I'll give you and Bob a real good time."

And the very next weekend, she did. With Cathie dressed very enticingly, the three of us went to a nightclub in a neighboring town. On the way there, she jerked us off, and Bob pulled up her dress and played with her cunt and tits.

When we arrived, I parked near the entrance, and we smoked a couple of joints before going in. The band was good, and soon we were all having a good time, in spite of the crowded dance floor.

After a couple of hours of dancing and drinking, Cathie said, "Okay, boys, it's time to go out to the car so I can suck you off." All three of us were more than ready. She had been stroking our clothed cocks on the dance floor and rubbing her big tits all over us. The blouse that she had on was so low cut that it barely covered her erect nipples.

Cathie quickly got in the car while Bob and I stayed outside, side by side on the passenger side. She rolled down the window. Bob already had his swollen cock out. I hastened to match his move, and he and I squeezed up to the window. Together, we smoked a joint as we felt Cathie's mouth and hands attack our cocks. We didn't discuss it, but I could tell that Bob was somewhat anxious, as was I, about the fact that, once again, anyone coming out of the bar or pulling into the parking lot could see exactly what the three of us were up to. Still, we were too excited to care as my ravenous wife licked our cocks.

I was ready to come and Bob was giving every sign of doing the same, when the doors of the bar flew open and out came three guys that Cathie had been dancing with inside. They headed toward their car, parked in the next row, but they figured out what was going on before they reached it. I expected Cathie to stop, but instead, the closer they got, the harder she sucked and more tightly she held on to our throbbing rods.

As these guys walked up to the front of the car, I looked down and saw that Cathie had opened her blouse, exposing her big tits and hard nipples! The audience obviously made her even more wild, and she increased her attentions on our cocks. The three strangers didn't say a word—they were transfixed watching Cathie through the windshield as she continued sucking merrily away.

In a wave of unselfconscious pleasure, I came all over her tits as her hand continued to stroke me. Bob was close behind, his big shaft once again filling my wife's mouth with jets of come. As she savored both of our juices, she watched the strangers out of the corner of her eye. She licked Bob's cock clean and then spread her legs wide, pulling up her short skirt to show us her bare, wet cunt and started fingering herself.

Bob's limp cock, now forgotten, slipped out of her mouth, and he quickly tucked it back into his pants. Cathie was immersed in giving herself pleasure, and she gave us quite a show, fingering her cunt and sucking on her own big tits until she had a moaning orgasm.

My wife continued to surprise me when she said to the three strangers, "If you boys would like to do more than look, I'll suck your cocks." Not needing to be asked twice, they crowded around the open car window and unzipped their pants. Cathie sucked off each of them for a few minutes, and all three reached in the window to feel her fabulous tits.

Then some heavy sucking quickly polished off two of them. I got the feeling that she saved the third guy for last because his cock was almost as big as Bob's. The four of us watched her tongue swirling around his big cockhead, and I felt my own getting hard again. She sucked fast and furiously, almost choking on him, until he let out a deep groan. He pulled out of her mouth and squirted as she continued to jerk him off. She was still licking his cock when Bob and I saw more men coming out of the bar! We jumped in the car and sped away.

"Find a motel real quick, baby," Cathie said. "Sucking all that cock has made me superhorny and my cunt's just dripping." As soon as we got a room, the three of us were naked in a big bed in record time. Cathie and I were giving each other head. Bob got behind her, and she stopped sucking my cock long enough to say, "Oh, Bob, give me that big cock. I've wanted it up my cunt ever since I first saw it last week."

I couldn't wait to see Bob inside of her, so I reached up and grabbed his rod and rubbed the head all around her wet cunt lips, inches in front of my face. "Give it to me, give it to me," she kept moaning as he gradually pushed the head in. I watched his huge cock slowly sink into her precious pussy up to his big hairy balls.

As he pumped her, she came a couple of times, but this didn't stop her from moaning for more. Watching his enormous member ramming in and out of my wife's cunt from only inches away was too much for me, and I came in her mouth. She swallowed it all, but just kept sucking me as if she were starving, and I thought she was going to bite my cock off as Bob fucked her harder!

He reached up under her to grab her tits, and used them to pull her farther down on his huge cock with each stroke. She was having one long, continuous orgasm, impaled on his massive shaft. Then I saw the base of Bob's cock swell even larger and his balls start to jerk. I reached up and took his balls in my hands, feeling his load pump into her. Afterward, we all just collapsed in a sweaty, tangled heap and fell asleep. After a good night's rest, we started it all again—but this time I fucked my pretty wife's cunt while she sucked Bob off. We didn't leave that motel room until late afternoon and we're already planning next weekend's entertainment.

RESCUE AT SEA

*A*s a flight medic on a helicopter ambulance crew in the U.S. Army, I am often faced with long periods of boredom between missions. This time it was a two-week stint at a training area eighty miles south of an army base in California. From this location the army supports the military and civilian populations with sometimes dangerous aerial rescues and helicopter ambulance services twenty-four hours a day.

The first twelve days passed with no missions, no flying and no sex. As the training area is forty miles from the nearest town and we are on two-minute call at all times, the best we could do for relaxation was to pump some iron and deepen our already deep tans.

The thirteenth day started off as usual. Wake up at 0600 hours, do a preflight check and warm up the helicopter by 0700, then eat breakfast, shower and out in the sun by 0830. Just as we had the barbecue pit set up for a nice rack of ribs for lunch, the phone rang with our first mission. A pleasure boat was taking on water six miles offshore.

By the time I got my flight suit on, the pilots had the aircraft running. En route, I had time to put on my harness and help the crew chief, Monty, prepare the rescue hoist to pluck the passengers from the sinking boat. Flying at over one hundred forty miles per hour, we arrived on the scene just in the nick of time. The boat in distress was a racing sloop, and its stern was almost completely underwater. Two women were standing on the bow, waving at us. Monty placed the Jungle Penetrator, the device that would lower me to the sloop, on the hoist. Then, while the pilots deftly kept the aircraft hovering at sixty feet of altitude, Monty skillfully reeled me down to the heaving deck of the sinking vessel.

What greeted me on deck when the Jungle Penetrator touched down got me thinking of a penetrator of a different kind—the eight-inch one I wield between my legs.

The two hapless sailors turned out to be what I can only describe as quintessential California girls. Their names, we later found out, were Cindy and Crystal, and each did justice to her T-shirt and bikini bottoms. Both were in their early twenties, with blond hair, ample breasts, tight asses and long legs.

I regained my professional composure long enough to strap Cindy into the Jungle Penetrator. I signaled Monty to bring us up. Cindy clung tightly to me during the short ride up to the chopper—and I couldn't believe my good luck. Monty was wide-eyed and openmouthed as he helped us into the hovering helicopter. As soon as we'd unstrapped Cindy, I went back down to pick up Crystal. By the time I had her strapped in, only ten feet of the bow was above water. It was standing almost straight up, which reminded me of something else that was sticking up, something made of flesh and blood. As Monty winched the cable in, Crystal and I had a great view of the boat as it slid entirely under the water.

Monty and I strapped the girls into seats, one on either side of the aircraft. I signaled the pilots to go to the nearest hospital, a standard procedure, and then I got my first good look at Cindy, who was seated on my side of the cabin. Due to the intense wash of the rotor during her ascent on the cable hoist, she had a case of the chills. Not only was she shivering, but her nipples were visibly erect under her T-shirt.

To keep her warm, I wrapped her in a woolen blanket. She motioned for me to lean close to her. Placing her mouth at my ear, she yelled above the roar of the engine and whirling rotor blades. "I'd be warmer with you in here with me!" To make sure I got the message, she spread her arms wide and gestured for me to join her in her cocoon of warmth. Even through my harness, survival vest and flight suit, the electricity of her embrace sent a direct order to my own soldier: Stand up and get ready for action.

As soon as the blanket was around us, Cindy reached down to massage my already erect cock. That was all the encouragement I needed to reach under her shirt and start vigorously rubbing her large tits. As I rolled her nipples between my thumb and forefinger, she reached up with her free hand and lifted the visor of my helmet. Now that my face was uncovered, she pulled the blanket up over my head and planted a soulful kiss on me, the rousing effects of which reached my toes. Since we were pretty well hidden by a privacy curtain from the others' view, Cindy stopped massaging long enough to unstrap my harness and unzip my flight suit to release my soldier from his prison—and she really knew how to make sure he fully enjoyed his newfound freedom. Bending her head down, she started to flick her tongue across his head with the delicacy of a butterfly's wings. This pleasurable torture put my hips in full motion, which Cindy put to good use as she engulfed my entire prick in her talented mouth. As I pumped in and out, she fondled my balls.

After thirteen days without sex, this was just too much to withstand. I gushed what seemed like gallons of come into her mouth, which she swallowed greedily. As the spasms in my prick slowed, I opened my eyes to see that the curtain had slipped and the copilot was watching me and applauding. Looking past the copilot, I saw that Crystal was riding Monty's pole. The sight of that, and of him sucking on her breasts, got my soldier ready for a renewed campaign.

Cindy and I lay on the floor of the aircraft. She spread the blanket and I kissed my way down to her pussy, stopping along the way to get a delicious mouthful of each breast. Upon reaching my goal, I pushed aside her bikini to get my first taste of her honey-pot. I licked her clitoris while my fingers worked their magic in her love canal. I could feel the strength of her thighs as she nearly crushed my flight helmet during her first orgasm. Now that she was sufficiently prepped, I was ready for my final maneuver.

Placing my hands on her shoulders, I kissed my way back to her face, stopping again at her large tits, this time to roll her nipples between my teeth and tongue. But neither of us could hold out any longer, and I plunged my cock deep into her with one swift stroke. The velvety smoothness of her snatch was matched only by the moistness. It felt fantastic!

Being in the military, I have had pleasures with exceptionally talented women from the world over, and I can truthfully say that Cindy's was the tightest cunt that has ever clenched my dick. Definitely no beginner, Cindy used her love muscles to alternately grip and release my meat. After five or six minutes, her pussy started to quiver in the throes of another orgasm, which sent me over the edge, too. With her legs wrapped around my waist, she held me firmly in place as I shot my second load deep inside her.

When the pilots saw that Cindy and I were done fucking, they gave us time to get cleaned up. Then we landed at the hospital and dropped the girls off. They promised to come by our Quonset hut that night to personally thank us again for saving their lives—and when they did, they rewarded us royally.

COLORADO CAVALIER

When I first moved to Colorado, I had for the first time in my life a considerable amount of money and no particular reason to rush into a job. So I decided to stay at a resort in the mountains near Denver to relax and generally enjoy life.

My name is Bill, and after recently becoming single again, I moved out west intending to begin life anew at thirty-one. During the week I had made a living as an engineer and on weekends as a photographer, photography being one of my true loves in life. I've always felt very fortunate that I have good genes and am lean and muscular.

This particular resort had a riding stable, and the owner after realizing that I was a decent customer by paying by the month, instead of the usual overnight fee, would let me ride free in exchange for guiding an occasional party up into the mountains on horseback. The arrangement was fine by me since I was getting the opportunity to photograph a lot of the countryside, not to mention the enjoyment of escorting many young ladies with deliciously firm asses and bouncing breasts along the trails. That is how I met Jennifer.

About a month before I met Jennifer for the first time, a beautiful pair of Oriental girls, Kisha and Tai, showed up and asked if I could take them riding away from the rest of the crowd. After we had gone a considerable distance, Tai asked to stop awhile so that she could ask a favor of me. Explaining that she and Kisha had been lovers for many years, and having noticed my camera, she told me they had always wanted pictures of themselves fondling and caressing each other. She wanted to know if I would be willing to be the photographer while they made love on horseback. I really couldn't believe what I was hearing, but since the mountain air does funny things to some people, and since they were both lush and lovely, even if they weren't into men, I gave them my blessing to do as they wished.

Turning around after I had unsaddled Dusty, a large dappled Arabian, I was greeted by the sight of these two truly good-looking girls, totally naked, breast to breast, their hands busy at play in each other's silky pussy. As I helped them up onto Dusty's back facing each other, the musky aroma of their wet pussies drifted through the air as, licking and probing, the girls reveled in their lovemaking.

Taking pictures as they kissed and their bodies rubbed against each other, I listened to their love sounds as tongues and fingers searched, squeezed and toyed with hardened nipples, open pussies and hungry mouths. As Tai pressed her fingertips against Kisha's swollen clit, tantalizing the little pleasure button that she loved to stroke and tease, Kisha shuddered and cried out for Tai to fuck her pussy hard and deep.

Breathing heavily, Tai asked me to hand her purse up to her, from which she removed an enormous double-ended dildo that Kisha began to beg to have buried inside her. Lubricating its length with her own love juices, Tai pressed the head of it against her lover's burning slit while Kisha reached down between her legs, spreading the entrance to her dripping pussy. Sliding the dildo teasingly up and down Kisha's gushing cunt lips, Tai suddenly plunged a full eight inches of the rubber cock into the steamy depths of Kisha's pussy. I watched it open even more and then cling to the shaft as it impaled her.

By this time Kisha was in total bliss. Tai now thrust the other end into her own overflowing pussy and they fingered each other's clit and took turns pumping the shaft that connected them in and out of each other's wet cunt. With pussies filled, hands furiously massaging clits and mouths sucking erect nipples, the girls came so many times that rivers of their juices trickled down to the ground until, finally satisfied, they held each other still.

The girls ended up with two rolls of excellent photos that day, and I ended up with a more-than-obvious erection. But besides being good-looking, they ended up being good-hearted and good-natured—they sandwiched me in between the heat of their bodies. With Kisha squeezing my swollen balls, Tai slid her hands up and down the length of my wildly pulsing cock and I erupted in pleasure. Load after load of hot, slippery come exploded from my cock. Their hands and my shaft were now soaked and sticky with come, but they realized that once would not be enough to satisfy my throbbing member. I now felt Kisha's hand close around my throbbing dick, pumping it until once again I shot thick strands of come onto her waiting fingers. With a mischievous giggle, Kisha stared at the glistening substance covering her hands and then began to fingerpaint on Tais' tits, using my come as imaginary colors.

But this story is about Jennifer. One lazy spring afternoon, Jennifer, a very attractive twenty-seven-year-old who came up just about every weekend, but who usually rode with several of her friends, appeared alone and asked if I would ride with her to an old mining town in the area. Now when I say old, I mean abandoned long ago, but many of the buildings were still standing and mine shafts and tunnels were everywhere. Actually, the town itself was in surprisingly good shape mostly because there were no longer any roads into it and therefore most people did not know it existed.

Without hesitation I said I would be more than happy to ride with her and began saddling up a pair of horses that would do justice to her body and features. Jennifer was a tall brunette, with almond-shaped eyes, a deeply tanned complexion, soft wet lips, beautifully full, rounded breasts with prominent nipples, a cute little ass and legs that seemed endless.

Before we left, she smiled coyly at me and excused herself to make one last trip to the bathroom. Upon her return, I noticed that she appeared to be walking rather cautiously. I attributed this to her tight jeans, which were firmly pressed into her pubic mound, and to a pair of almost new boots, which I knew must have hurt like hell. When she bounced up onto the saddle, she sighed softly and gasped, then wriggled around until she was comfortable—far more comfortable than I knew.

As we approached the ghost town, she asked if I would tie up the horses while she went inside one of the buildings to go to the bathroom again. When Jennifer did not return in a reasonable amount of time, I went to see what was keeping her.

Looking through a broken window of the building she had chosen, I saw her beautiful body leaning back against one of the walls, her jeans and panties pulled down to her knees, one hand fondling her tits and nipples and the other eagerly playing with her swollen clit and pussy. As I took in the scene before me, I noticed her jacket lying on the floor beside her and on it, a small strap-on vibrator shiny-wet with her juices. Now I fully understood what caused her difficulty in walking and her breathless moments on the way up into the mountains!

Not wanting her to realize that I had seen her masturbating, and being painfully aware of my own aching cock and balls, I slowly backed away and, when out of sight and sound, stroked my swollen cock to my own intense orgasm.

When she returned shortly, flushed and apparently satisfied, I began to plan an encounter that would be enjoyable for us both. After we had explored the area, Jennifer having been totally fascinated by the site, we began the trip back down, and I made the conversation much more personal and sex-oriented. By the time I walked her to her car, we had made a date for the following week to ride back up into the hills and camp out for the weekend.

When the weekend came, I was determined to start the adventure out right. I met Jennifer at the lodge with a big hug and a gentle kiss and was instantly turned on when she slid her wet tongue between my lips in a long, lingering French kiss.

As we talked and packed the saddlebags full of munchies and supplies, we decided to leave any extra clothes behind, our excuse being a lack of room to carry them but secretly knowing we wouldn't be wearing them anyway. The crispness of the air, the smell of the pine trees and leather beneath us, and the knowledge that we would soon be locked in an embrace as hot and wet as the lather on the horses made for a ride in which time and space seemingly had little meaning.

Upon reaching the ghost town, we put our food and sleeping bags in one of the old buildings, engaged in a little touching and kissing, and then with the taste and scent of each other fresh on our lips went about gathering some firewood. I might add at this point that there is little in life that I enjoy more than eating a woman, and if Jennifer's pussy tasted as sweet as her neck and lips, then much of my weekend was going to be spent nestled between her fabulous legs with my tongue buried in her moist slit. As we walked farther from camp searching for wood, we came across a small meadow with a stream running through it with wildflowers everywhere springing up from the soft meadow grass. Jennifer gave me a smile that melted my heart and announced that she wanted to swim nude, and then lie in the sun on the flowers to dry off and relax.

She faced me and started to undress. I watched this beautiful lady unbutton her blouse and slip it off her tanned shoulders. Next came her boots, which she pulled off with amazing agility, and then her button-up jeans. I watched as she popped open each button and tugged the jeans down over her hips, revealing a pair of scanty, string-bikini panties and the outline of her pussy.

Jennifer was definitely enjoying herself. She stood facing me in her bra and panties, legs spread wide and hands behind her back. She kiddingly asked me if I thought she had a nice body. When I assured her she did, she proceeded to show me the rest of it while watching the growing bulge in my jeans. I could almost feel the unbridled, aggressive enthusiasm for sex that was smoldering beneath her panties.

With excruciating deliberation she reached between the mounds of her breasts to the clasp of her bra. She unsnapped it and its lacy cups clung to her full breasts for a moment, then spread apart allowing each breast to be fully visible. Jennifer's tits were a perfect 36C, and even without her bra they stood firm and proud. Her nipples were large, erect and a beautiful dusty rose in color, in contrast to the creamy complexion of her breasts and otherwise darkly tanned body. I lay back and enjoyed as Jennifer proceeded with her seductive game. Neither one of us felt any sense of urgency, since this was a game better played tantalizingly slow.

With a swift, deft movement, Jennifer brought me back to the here and now by slipping her fingers beneath the strings of her panties and pulling up on them until the lips of her cunt were clearly visible and pressed against the thin fabric covering it. I could see the moisture from her pussy spreading across the front of her panties as she began to move her hips as though fucking. Finally she snapped the strings hard, tearing them and letting her panties fall freely from her rounded, firm ass.

As she stood totally nude before me, I saw that she had left her pubic mound with its fluff of brunette hair intact, but had shaved her pussy lips so that now they were fully exposed and glistening wet with her love juices. I smiled to myself since I have always kept my cock and balls likewise trimmed—an experience that I at first resisted but now find great enjoyment in. I knew she would love my clean-shaven body as much as I loved hers.

Jennifer's body was alive with desire. The breeze blowing across her hardened nipples and sensitive clit was making her shudder with involuntary spasms as she yearned for the satisfaction to be found from yielding flesh against flesh. Her striptease had taken all of a half hour, and now, almost panting, she asked me to get undressed and tease her as she had done to me.

My shorts and jeans were now soaked with the pre-come that had been steadily seeping from my throbbing shaft. I walked over to Jennifer, let my searching tongue brush against her neck and ears, flicker into her open mouth and briefly nuzzle her left nipple as my fingertips grazed across her open thighs. Feeling the heat from her body, I backed away from her as she sat down, legs open, eager to have her void filled. As she sat there running the tip of her tongue across her lips, her mouth was now as moist as her slippery slit. My balls ached to fill them both with hot, thick come.

Unbuttoning my shirt and pulling the tail of it loose from my jeans, I heard Jennifer begin to moan softly and saw her gaze was riveted to my golden hairy chest, shimmering with perspiration from the noonday sun and the heat of my body. Taking my shirt off, I began to squeeze my nipples, now as hard as hers, only much, much smaller. With this, she began to chant to me that she was going to run her hands over my chest, suck and bite my nipples and fuck my mouth with her tongue long and hard. She was squeezing her own tits and rolling her nipples between her fingers. After I had my boots off and undid my belt, I slid my zipper down, and her hands slowly slid down her body until they found the smoldering heat of her cunt. Now it was my turn to play and tease for a while, and, pulling my jeans down past my hips, I began to gently stroke my swollen dick.

I don't know if she had ever watched a man fondle his cock before, but as my hand pressed and rubbed against my thick shaft, I watched her fingers slip in between her swollen pussy lips. I watched as her fingers moved up and down inside her creamy cunt while the head of her pink clit pressed out from between her pouting lips. Listening to the sound of her fingers in her pussy and watching the juices flow out of it, I could only think about burying my face between her legs, taking her clit in my mouth and lapping up all of her wonderful come. By this time, my balls were ready to explode. The pressure of my jeans against my throbbing dick was reaching a dangerous level, and listening to Jennifer tell me how she was going to suck and fuck me for hours wasn't helping my self-control either.

As I pulled my jeans down to the ground, Jenn gasped as my seven-inch cock sprang forward and bobbed up and down in front of her. As we stared at each other, my cock pulsing in the open air and her mouth and pussy wet, open and inviting, I began to walk toward her. I leaned over her sitting body and, as she crushed her lips to mine, I felt her tongue slide into my mouth. As her tongue probed my mouth, she began to squeeze my nipples with one hand, pumping my cock with the other. With Jenny's hands busy at play, I began to fondle and caress her glorious tits and nipples, rubbing and squeezing them between my fingers. Kneeling down, with Jennifer's tongue still furiously fucking the recesses of my mouth, I began to trace a path from her tits to her sopping-wet pussy. I couldn't believe how hot her pussy felt as my hand covered its smooth lips. Jenny pressed it hard against my fingers and screamed for me to finger-fuck her little, wet pussy until she came. As my fingers touched her electric clit for the first time, she arched her back and flooded my fingers with moisture as she came in a rush of passion.

I couldn't handle the way she was pumping on my throbbing dick anymore, and when I told her I wanted to fuck her tits, she put my cock between those beautiful globes and squeezed them tightly around my thick shaft. Flicking my fingers up and down over her swollen clit while thrusting my cock between her creamy tits was too much for both of us, and, as she cried out that she was coming a second time, I shot thick streams of milky come onto her neck, her tits and her stomach, which she rubbed all over her body and licked from her fingers.

Reaching back and grabbing the cheeks of my ass, Jennifer pulled me forward until my still-stiff organ was inches from her face. While it takes me a long time to come the first time, I can stay hard for hours, and as Jenn started sucking on the length of my shaft, I became rock-hard. Just touching the underside of my cock with the tip of her tongue made shock waves of pleasure surge through me, causing my shaft to jerk involuntarily away from the heavenly teasing of her mouth. Jennifer seemed to love this sweet torment, rubbing the throbbing head of my cock all over her face and then letting it pulse freely in front of her to once again be toyed with. She then began noisily sucking and licking my cock, twirling her tongue around the head of it only to take it deeper into her mouth. I flipped around until my face was inches from her beautifully shaved cunt while she hungrily began sucking again.

Up close, Jenny's pussy was gorgeous beyond words, perfectly shaped and musk-scented, an eclair to be nibbled on the outside and licked deeply on the inside. Her outer lips, pouting and swollen, begged to be kissed. Her clitoris, pink and erect with passion, pressed its head from between her slippery labia awaiting the flutter of my tongue. Knowing that pools of sweet syrup awaited me within these appetizing surroundings, I eased my mouth toward the feast before me. As I blew my hot breath on her overflowing honey-pot, Jennifer raised her pelvis toward my mouth, telling me she wanted to feel my searching tongue inside her burning pussy. Plunging my tongue between her legs, I began to lick Jenn's vagina and her clit. She tasted wonderful. Her juices filled my mouth and trickled down my chin as I lapped her pussy.

I could feel my balls filling with another load of come. The pressure at the base of my cock began rising as Jenny alternated between sucking me and rubbing the head of my dick rapidly across her hard nipples. Spreading her pussy open with my fingers, I started to devote all of my attention to her swollen clit. I took it into my mouth. As I licked, sucked and gently bit her clit while playing with her smooth thighs and round ass, Jenn began to moan loudly. Squeezing and fondling her ass with come-drenched hands, I slid my fingers in between her lips and began to tickle her wet, hot hole. At this, Jennifer went absolutely crazy. With my tongue on her clit and my finger probing her cunt, she came in a flood of sweet syrup. Moments later so did I, filling her mouth with a torrent of hot sticky come.

Turning around and pulling Jenny down full length on top of me, I reveled in the feel of her tits pressed against my chest, my hard cock crushed against her pussy and the taste of our come mixed together as we kissed deeply. Whispering in my ear that her cunt was on fire for my thick cock, she closed her hand around its base and began to guide me inside her. The sensation of her cunt enveloping my cock was heavenly as the head of my shaft spread her lips apart. I could feel her pussy walls pulsing and contracting as I continued to slide deeply inside Jennifer, finally burying my throbbing dick to the base. Jenn settled down on top of me as she had on her saddle that fateful day, and I watched her tits bounce in the sunlight as she rode the length of my dick. I let her control the rhythm of our lovemaking, and after twenty minutes of her being filled with my cock, I knew she was on the edge of coming yet again. So I reached down and pressed my thumb hard against her clit with one hand, firmly tugging on her nipples with the other. Jenny bit her lower lip and screamed that she was coming, falling on top of me as she quivered in the throes of her orgasm.

Rolling out from under and getting on top of her, I explained to Jenn that I had yet to fill her sweet cunt with come. At this she wrapped her long legs around my waist and pulled me once again into the recesses of her body. Holding me tightly against her, Jennifer cried out as I plunged my cock harder and faster into her tight pussy. Knowing that I was reaching the point of no return, I told Jenn to reach down between us and play with her clit. My dick pounded at her pussy as her tits shook beneath me. When my aching balls finally exploded, it seemed as though come spurted from my cock forever, filling Jennifer totally and deeply. Crying out that she couldn't believe that she was coming again, she bit into my shoulder and came in a long series of orgasms, melting our bodies and mind into one. After what seemed like forever, we lay still in each other's arms, our sexual appetites for now fully satisfied.

I gently kissed her lips and breasts and we fell asleep in the meadow holding each other closely and peacefully. Our lovemaking session had taken all of four hours and, upon waking up, we finally had a chance to cool off in the stream and roll in the wildflowers.

Today our bedroom walls are graced with photos of Jenn and me making love in every position possible. Her favorite is a close-up, forever captured on film, of my cock pumping its load of creamy honey into her overflowing mouth, with some of it dripping down her chin to her nipples and running down her smooth stomach to form a pool in her cute little belly button. It always reminds us of our pool in the meadow.

TREASURES OF THE FAR EAST

*A*s a civil service adviser to the military, I've had several interesting tours overseas, mostly to the Far East. In each of these tours I met very select, attractive, sensual women. Since I was married, even though my wife and I were going through a trial separation, I did not attempt to form any kind of permanent relationship with any of the ladies I met. In fact, as attractive as the women were, I did not try to play any sexual games with them. Probably my slight aloofness made it seem like I was hard to get, and this may have been a challenge to their feminine wiles. In any case, without any effort on my part, I somehow became the target of some subtle seduction. I realize now that if I had been more honest and direct, I undoubtedly would have lost out miserably.

After my first six months in the Far East, I was sent to a remote but beautiful island that one could easily think of as a heaven on earth. It was the kind of place that you would fantasize about as a backdrop for a wet dream—swaying coconut trees, emerald-green water, salt white sand on the beaches, every kind of fruit known to man and an overflow of nubile women wrapped in batik. The island people were polite, friendly and as innocent as babes in paradise.

As I dealt with the foreign military, both female and male, it wasn't long before I learned the taboos of their culture. The one that would have bothered any virile and horny American was the strict rule that island females had to remain chaste until marriage. Virginity was their most prized possession. For an unmarried woman to be found deflowered would mean dishonor for her in both military and civilian life. The island men, on the other hand, were the epitome of the machismo of a male-oriented society, and as such, they were ignorant of modern sexual attitudes and gave their women very little sexual satisfaction. No foreplay—just the old "in-out" and off to sleep. To them, women, no matter how beautiful, were like chattel. As it turned out, these facts of island life which I personally abhorred proved to work very much in my favor.

The island women had heard stories about American men being the most knowledgeable in sex. That propaganda somehow had spread over much of the island. Their own men, they complained in their little gatherings, were grossly inadequate. Not only were the men selfish and undeserving, but their penises were very small, puny things. Female curiosity perpetuated the rumors about the size and ability of the American male.

My daily duty included acting as an instructor to certain female army and navy units. Most of the ladies had some training in English, but I knew their language well enough to answer questions from those who only spoke the native tongue. It seemed they were always eager to meet me and listen to my jokes—in any language—even though I was usually very businesslike in order to guard against any impressions that I might be an opportunist. In no time at all I became a trustworthy confidant and grew amazed at the questions the girls put to me.

Some of my favorite tête-à-têtes were with a girl of about twenty whom I shall call Vailima. She looked at me with such admiration, her luminous eyes aglow, that each time I spoke to her I felt a rush of glory and bursting pride that she had picked me as her bosom friend. I didn't want her to misinterpret my feelings, so I downplayed any attention she paid to me. (She could have thought of me as a father figure, as I was twenty years older.) I invited her to nice little suppers and we talked at length about her career, island music, her studies and trivia of every kind.

Eventually she got around to asking questions about American cultural views compared to her culture, and this led to the inevitable clinical discussion about sex. Her lead-in was so polite and unobtrusive that I almost didn't realize that she had managed to get me to discuss every prurient detail of sexual activity known to Western man. Moreover, surprisingly, she showed no sign of embarrassment. She even asked if I had any pornographic pictures, as she had heard that all American men look at them. Since she had already emphasized the taboo concerning premarital intercourse, I asked myself about her motives. But I couldn't imagine that she was anything more than innocently curious. And I hoped that she hadn't noticed that my member, having taken on a certain turgidity due to all our discussions about sex, caused me some discomfort by pushing against my zipper.

My admitting that I did indeed have pictures of the kind American men sometimes look at, led to my invitation to see them in my cottage. We walked there talking about the gardens that we passed, the smell of the flowers and the sound of rushing water in the nearby river. Upon reaching the cottage, I ushered her into the living room and onto a large soft sofa. But as I excused myself to go into the bedroom to get the pictures, she came to the door to look at all the decorations I had on the walls. She sat down next to me on the bed and tested its softness. The smell of her freshness so close to me stirred another yearning in my groin. My heart was beating faster as I withdrew the package of pictures I had stored away.

"Can you explain them to me?" she asked, looking like a student seeking an answer to a math problem.

She extended her hand and took several of the pictures. As she looked at each picture, her eyes widened. Her mouth suddenly pursed and a small sound of surprise escaped from her lips, as if she hadn't known what to expect. One picture depicted a threesome of two women and a man. She studied the picture for a long moment as if puzzled.

"What are they doing there?" she asked.

There was no use in pretending that I couldn't explain the scene with such an eager student to prompt me.

"The women are sucking each other's genitals while the man is penetrating one from behind."

"Is this the way you Americans do love? I thought surely it would be enough with one man and one woman."

I could not think of an easy answer.

She pondered her statement for a moment, and looked at a picture of a girl masturbating in front of another girl with no man in sight.

"It is better when you have someone to share the pleasure," she said. "This is the only kind of sex I know. My friends and I all do it. It is less complicated and it releases your feelings. But we don't stick things into ourselves like these girls do."

My curiosity was piqued.

"Is it because you are virgins and are afraid of losing your virginity?"

"Some girls sometimes forget what virginity means, and they are the ones who suffer later and can't get married. No man here will marry a nonvirgin."

The talk now had become so provocative and frustrating that I knew I couldn't keep my cool for much longer.

"How do you go about relieving yourself of the feelings you have if you are prohibited from doing so many things?"

"Nearly all of the girls in my barracks have discussed this problem at one time or another. I guess we all have agreed that we can play sex with each other. I have seen them in bed at night hugging and kissing. They like to get undressed and rub against each other. And I guess this is all right. It seems to make them happier."

"Do you enjoy watching them doing this?" I asked, my voice suddenly strained.

She thought for a long moment, her head tilted back, and looked at me through long lashes. Her large doe-like eyes seemed to glow.

"If I were to say yes, would this change the way you think of me?"

I surely didn't want to pontificate over morals and the so-called evils of the flesh or give the impression that I didn't approve. It didn't take but a second to respond. "Not at all. We've already established our friendship, and we're just being honest with one another." (What hypocrisy I had lumbered into! I was aching to strip off her clothes, lick my way over every inch of her delicious body and ask her to suck my dick.)

She smiled. Had I imagined that she had changed her position slightly to give me a small glimpse of the divine valley I so longed to smother with kisses?

"Would seeing such a sight be enjoyable to you?" she asked.

I smiled, and she had the answer.

"The next time I come to visit, I will bring a friend," she said, and rose to leave.

My member strained in frustration against my pants. She had managed to tease me into a state of frenzy.

"And will this friend be male or female?" I asked anxiously.

"I have no male friends in that category," she said, and walked away from me, looking over her shoulder to say good-bye as she reached the door.

"And when may I expect such a nice visit to come?" I asked, a little too eagerly.

"It will be a pleasant surprise soon."

She smiled broadly and left. A moment more and I felt a sense of regret building in my guts for being so slow and stupid in my approach. But then I realized she would do as she pleased. In all the time I had known her, in spite of her innocent appearance, she had demonstrated a decided independence in getting what she wanted.

The next two days at work were agonizing. I spent every free moment thinking about Vailima and her girlfriend. On the second day, when I reached the cottage after work, I hoped to find a message for me. But there was none, so I just showered and ate a lonely meal. By seven in the evening, with a dull weekend to look forward to, I was reading on the sofa when I heard a slight tap on the door. Through the window in the door I could see the outline of three figures. I almost ran to the door.

"I thought you might need company this evening," Vailima said. "If you are busy, we will understand." She smiled with such sweetness that I had almost forgotten my mission. "It is not so, is it?"

"You are most welcome to visit me. I'm glad that you are here." (This was the obligatory greeting of their culture.)

The two other girls that entered were about the same age as Vailima. She had chosen two of her most beautiful friends. Their figures all were perfect, with small firm breasts, slender bodies and long legs. They had dressed in their finest native clothes and wore gold bracelets and necklaces. The slight aroma of their perfumed bodies stayed in the air, setting off fantasy after fantasy in my mind.

I had to force myself into the mold of the perfect host. I offered them a place to sit and gave them crystal goblets filled with mild red wine. They sat drinking and peacefully looking at the many photo albums I had of my travels. I wondered when the important topic would come up. I turned to Vailima, and her smoldering glance told me that our secret discussion had been shared with her friends.

"Tusitala suggested that perhaps you would enjoy seeing some of our traditional dances. All three of us were taught these dances when we were very small. I think you will like them."

Without waiting for an answer, Vailima crossed the room to the cassette deck and inserted a tape she had brought. The music started slowly with an exotic, sensual beat. Tusitala rose from her seat and began the dance, her arms and hands moving in graceful arcs above her head, sweeping with suggestive gestures to her bosom. Her face remained sweet and childlike, yet her body was moving seductively, her pelvis undulating and slowly humping in my direction. Vailima joined her and imitated the same movements. Vailima finally encircled Tusitala's waist and drew her close for a light kiss on the lips. Then Vaea joined the dance, pressing against Vailima and cupping her upturned breasts.

By now the atmosphere both inside and out had become hot and moist. Rain had started coming down in a rhythmic chatter on the roof. We were suddenly cut off from the rest of the world.

The girls were taking off their clothes one article at a time, prolonging my frustration a little more. I found myself sweating in the humid, music-filled room.

The three bodies approached the end of the dance, and each movement became increasingly more intimate until all were completely nude. Without seeming to notice me, they were touching each other's breasts and reaching out to tongue each other's mouths. I heard little whimpers of joy as they melded together and lowered themselves onto the soft rug. When the music came to a stop, nobody noticed. My eyes were glued to the delicious spectacle on the floor. Vaea and Tusitala had locked their legs together and, while they were humping their pubes, Vailima positioned herself so that Tusitala could lick madly at her clitoris. All three were moving against each other in a steady rhythm, building to a climax.

From the moment I saw the three naked girls lowering themselves to the floor, I had remained transfixed, almost unbelieving. The throbbing in my groin alerted me to the pleasure I could have if I acted soon. My clothes came off in a hurry, but I didn't know where or how to start. With my bone standing straight up demanding attention, one movement in their direction could end the whole show if they became apprehensive about any designs on their virginity.

At this moment, the three writhing bodies were in the throes of simultaneous orgasms. As they humped frantically against each other, my cock squirted jism halfway across the room. There, I thought, went my chances.

As it turned out, the girls were still ready for some more fun, and I was anxious to get on with it. We retired to my large oversize bed in the bedroom and drank a little more wine. It wasn't long before Vailima started to beg me to show her friends the American porno pictures, which I did with great zeal. Not only that, Vailima suggested that we try some of the things depicted in the photos. As Vaea was the only one not a virgin, she allowed me to fuck her in any position I wanted while Vailima and Tusitala sucked her tits and licked her pussy from below.

It would be very hard to choose which of the three was the sexiest, as each was the answer to any man's dream. Vaea, with her beautiful cunt and soft, curly pubic hair, had nether lips as pink and juicy as ripe peaches. Tusitala, the smallest of the three, had hard, pointed tits and a luscious mouth. But nothing could beat the magnificence of Vailima, who had the legs, tits, ass and beautiful face of a starlet, plus sexy, flowing hair. She was so incredibly beautiful!

Needless to say, I spent as much of my free time as possible with the girls, as they considered me a safe solution to their problem. Each of them learned to be expert cocksuckers, and they constantly vied with each other to get my acclaim for best blowjob of the week.

Although I eventually had to return to the States at the completion of my tour, I knew I couldn't just leave the ideal situation I'd found. When I got back I completed my divorce, and not long afterward my ex-wife remarried. I'm glad she's happy in her new life, and I know I am. I continued to write to Vailima with the prospect of marriage and she accepted. I couldn't get another tour to her country, but she said she'd wait for me, and at last I saved enough to make the trip and marry her. We've been together for several years now, and I've never regretted my choice. Our sex life has never been dull. Though we don't look for others to join us, we nevertheless have had a few encounters with married women and single girls who found that we answered their needs. Vailima says that even if we don't have any more "experiments," she's satisfied with the man she loves. She had kept her promise and married me as a sweet, tender, ever-faithful virgin.

THE LURE

I was really pissed off as my pickup finally rolled through the Golden Gate Bridge tollbooth and Sally and I headed north on Highway 101 to redwood country. Even the sun coming up over San Francisco and silhouetting the buildings in shades of red and gold didn't do much to calm us down. Sally hadn't said one coherent word since we had left her flat in the Inner Mission district. All the way down Van Ness Avenue and Lombard Street she had groaned and sworn and kicked the floorboard of my truck. Just about the time we hit center span on the bridge, she turned to me and screamed at the top of her lungs, "That son of a bitch has been coming home drunk out of his skull four or five nights a week for six months and I told him, one more all-nighter and the party is over!" She glared over her shoulder at San Francisco, now bathed in the evanescent Californian morning light, spun her head around toward me again, and shaking her finger about two inches from my face, screamed, "That bastard is history!"

What had happened was I had spent a month planning this fishing trip up to the coast range with Harry. I didn't know him very well, but the guys at the shop all said he really knew where to find the best streams and they had all caught their limit when they had gone with him. Harry and I had gone out drinking after work several times. As we talked about fishing, he had promised to show me the ropes as long as we drove my pickup truck and I brought the booze. Most important, we had to drop off his girlfriend Sally with her sister in Eureka because he didn't trust her alone in San Francisco for three nights. I should have known there would be trouble, because twice I'd dropped him off at Sally's flat so bombed out of his mind he could hardly walk and I'd heard them going at it as I had hurried away, down the sidewalk to my car.

When I arrived at Sally's place at five in the morning as planned, I could hear them shouting before I even got to the door. As I reached for the bell, the door flew open and Harry stood silhouetted in the hall light like some weird space monster from a grade-B movie. He bounced from one side of the door to the other as Sally kicked and hit him from behind and shouted obscenities. Oblivious to her attack, he raised his hands and eyes to the ceiling, and summoning the little dignity he had left, he proclaimed through alcohol-numbed lips, "Fuck the world," and slid down the wall unconscious. It was clear that he was not going to go fishing for quite a long time. We both stared down at him as the silence and morning fog gradually enveloped us.

When we looked up our eyes met, and with anger still dripping from her tongue, Sally asked, "Well, are you still heading up north?" "Yeah, I guess so," I muttered. "I'll try to find the good fishing spots by myself." This time her voice was softer as she asked, "My sister is expecting me and I really want to see her. Could you still drop me off in Eureka like you had planned?" "Come on and get it in gear," I said as I turned and headed for the pickup. "I'm hitting the road right now." Before I had reached the sidewalk, I heard the door slam as she darted past me with her backpack and made herself comfortable in the passenger's seat before I could start the engine.

For the next two hours as we drove north through the Marin headlands and Napa wine country, I said about ten words while Sally raved about how Harry would come home drunk and give her a fast fuck and pass out, leaving her pussy aching for more. Then she went on and on about how horny she was and how she had had only about three orgasms in the six months he had lived with her and how she could easily have three or more a night with a good man. Then she went into even more detail about how she had tried to get his prick up when he had passed out so she could sit on it and get her cunt off, but it had never worked. However, the coup de grace occurred just two nights ago. With anger still resonating in her voice, she said, "The last couple of weeks he started bringing home X-rated movies to play on the VCR. Well, the night before last he came staggering in with a tape of *Deep Throat*, and he wants me to go down on him while he watches it. So I suck this bastard's cock for a solid hour, and just as the tape ends, I'm ready to jump on his rod for a real juicy fuck when he lets the whole load go in my mouth, rolls over and goes to sleep. Well I . . ."

Before she could finish the sentence I broke out laughing, the thought of it was just so funny. Her eyes blazed in anger as she stared at me laughing at her plight; but then her tight lips melted into a smile and we both laughed and laughed out loud. The mood of hostility and tension had been broken, and we began to talk more freely. After a while she said with relief in her voice, "What the hell! As the commercial says, you only go around once in life. Let's put the bullshit behind us and go for the gusto! Why don't you stop at the next rest station. We split so quickly, I didn't have time to do anything. . . . I want to change my clothes, comb my hair and brush my teeth. Okay?"

We pulled into the large rest stop north of Ukiah where Route 20 turns east toward Clear Lake, and she grabbed her backpack and headed for the ladies' john. She was wearing an oversize quilted ski jacket and baggy cord pants when she went in, but when she came out . . . incredible! Sally is tall, over five-feet-eight, and full-bodied, and as she walked across the parking lot toward me, I could do no more than gape openmouthed. She had been transformed into a goddess! She was now wearing a miniskirt that hung no more than two or three inches below her ass and accentuated her long, perfectly sculptured legs. However, my attention quickly shifted upward to the silk or nylon blouse that clung to her body as though it were painted on. It was un-adorned except for some lace across the bottom where one button held it closed below the fully exposed cleavage between her pair of 38Ds. Her breasts were so huge and so unrestrained by the blouse or a bra that they hung down nearly to her waist and swung freely as she walked toward me, smiling broadly and enjoying my stare. Her bright-red hair was combed out and hung below her shoulders as a fiery frame for her beautifully made-up face. It was clearly visible through the skintight blouse that nearly a third of each wondrous lobe was nipple, capped by a large head that stretched the material at least another three-quarters of an inch.

I gazed openly at her two beauties as she stopped no more than a couple of inches from me and looked into my eyes, saying, "Hi. I don't think we have been formally introduced. My name is Sally. You're Bill, aren't you?" I shook my head in the affirmative as I peered straight down the canyon between those nipple-capped love-mountains that she swayed back and forth and rubbed against the front of my shirt. Without waiting for me to speak she continued, "All this talk about orgasms and giving head has me so hot that my fuck juice is running down the inside of my thighs. Let's pull the truck over to that clump of trees where it's more isolated and you might just catch something with your rod beside some dumb fish."

I stomped on the accelerator and sped for the trees that shielded the view of the highway and the rest stop. Sally was all over me, grabbing for my now-throbbing cock and running her tongue around and into my ear as she whispered in a deep throaty voice I hadn't heard before, "Make me come, Bill. Please, make me come. Give me your hard cock and make my pussy explode. Oh, please, do that for me and you may have anything you want. I'll do everything you want if you'll just make me come."

She was buck-naked by the time the truck screeched to a stop. I slid over to her side of the seat and we both began to frantically pull down my pants. When they slipped over my boots, my prick flew to attention and hit her stomach. As she threw her right leg over mine and slid down my lap, her scarlet muff spread open to reveal swollen pussy lips glistening with cunt juices. My fully erect cock was clamped between our bellies. As she leaned back to inspect her prize, I couldn't help smiling at the look of surprise on her face. Her eyes bugged out and she inhaled suddenly as she repeated over and over, "Oh, my God! It's huge!" With all due modesty, I have become accustomed to that reaction from women who see my dick for the first time. Standing tall, it's about eight and a half inches long, but women mostly comment on how big around it is and they love the giant head that sits on top.

At this moment, however, I didn't want to bask in Sally's admiration of my prick. I wanted to put it to use, preferably in that dripping box just inches away. Sally must have read my mind, because she grabbed my cock with both hands as she rose up higher on her knees. I thought she was going to jam it into her pussy, but to my surprise and delight, she began vigorously rubbing the head back and forth over her clit. She drove me wild as over and over her clit massaged my come-hole and her stretched cunt lips tightly gripped the crown of my rod. The musky smell of her freely flowing fuck-canal filled the cab as she threw back her head and shoulders, thrusting her giant boobs into my face. In my frenzy I grabbed one in each hand and buried my face in her cleavage, kissing and licking my way back to the protruding nipple-tips and sucking them alternately like some newborn suckling calf.

Sally bounced wildly on my lap and frantically pounded my cockhead on her clit until she tensed and a violent shudder shook her whole body. I dropped the tit feast from my mouth as she grinned broadly. "Oh, Bill, I made it. I made it," she said with a hearty laugh. "I've come, and it's marvelous!" She nestled her fuck-hole on top of my still-pulsating prickhead and I gently reminded her that I had yet to share her climactic joy or even know the pleasure of penetrating her love-passage. With the same childish grin and a shy schoolgirl voice, she whispered, "But you're so big! I don't know if my fuck-tunnel can stretch that wide . . ." and after a few seconds' contemplation she added, "or that deep."

Her orgasm had gushed her come over my cock so it was well-lubricated. I grabbed her ass-cheeks and slowly eased my cock-head past her pussy lips into her vagina. She moaned with delight, "Yes, yes, yes. It's so good. But so big! Please go slow." I pulled harder on her ass-cheeks and slid my cock one inch deeper, then stopped. I repeated this nine times, and each time her pussy convulsed and her cunt muscles rippled up and down my rock-hard shaft. She whimpered as each successive inch stretched her vaginal walls to the limit. In that low throaty voice I have come to love, she moaned, "I never knew it could be this good and it never stops. I'm on a continuous come, so give it to me! Give me all you have!" That was all I needed to hear. I had held back to give her pussy time to expand, but now I could wait no more and drove my cock to the hilt. As our pelvic bones collided I felt the come bursting from my cock and my load shot into and out of her cunt. She jerked up straight on my cock, her backbone stiffened, and her eyes grew as big as saucers. In the most breathless way, she simply said, "My God! Oh my God!" and collapsed in my arms.

When we had recovered and were ready to go again, Sally slipped into my red plaid wool shirt that matched perfectly her bright-red hair and scarlet muff. She rested her head against my arm as we drove for about an hour through the beautiful countryside and into the redwoods. Each time I shifted gears, she rubbed her tit against my arm and marveled over the long orgasm she had had.

Suddenly she knelt next to me, threw off my shirt, cupped one ponderous boob in each hand while she pushed them up into my face and begged me to suck them like I had when we had fucked. I quickly took hold of her shoulder and pulled her down, yelling, "Hey, do you want to get us thrown in jail? The highway patrol can see you through the windshield." "Well, they can't see me down here," she said, as she lay back on the seat and began to play out the most bizarre, eroticized scene I have ever witnessed.

With her head resting on the armrest of the passenger door, she threw her left leg over my shoulder and her right leg onto the dashboard, spreading her cunt wide just inches away from me. She drove three long fingers full-length into the silky deep-red hair that coated her love-box and began humping her ass up and down on the seat. "I'm getting my cunt ready for you to spear it with that giant javelin you call a cock," she said, smiling mischievously. My eyes danced between the road in front of me and her beckoning pussy, beautifully encircled in that soft, sweet, scarlet down.

I have to confess that I was speechless for one of the few times in my life. When I responded with nothing but an openmouthed stare, she slipped her fingers out of her crotch and pressed one hand on the outside of each tit, pushing them up and together. In a sweet voice that combined teasing with mocking tones, she said, "I know my Billy wants to tit-fuck. He's tired of Sally's stretched-out cunt and wants to drop his gallons of hot come in the folds of these two bulging breasts." The suggestion of driving my hot rod down the grand canyon of her tits was an idea of considerable merit, and my mind raced ahead to the next turnoff. She continued her teasing, "Don't tell me my Billy doesn't want titties or pussy. He knows that mammoth pole won't fit down Sally's sweet little throat, so he must want to jerk it off all by himself." I finally controlled my voice enough to blurt out, "Just keep it hot, honey. I'm going to pull over at the next redwood grove and give you a forest fuck you'll never forget." Her eyes glazed over and her head rolled back on the seat as her fingers again slipped into her pussy and her other hand squeezed and pinched her bulging bright-pink nipples. Her teasing tone turned into desperation as she moaned, "Hurry, Bill, hurry! I want to make you come. I want you to fuck me as I've never been fucked before. Fuck me, fuck me."

The pickup's tires screeched and rocks flew as I tore down the exit ramp at Phillipsville on the Avenue of the Giants and ground to a stop at the first empty parking area. I dragged Sally naked from the cab and ran down the winding path between the towering redwoods. Shafts of sunlight breaking through the canopy of thick high branches lit the way and the pungent smell of wildflowers and ferns filled our nostrils. The silence and warm moist air of the forest overwhelmed us when we finally stopped to catch our breath. A lust handed down from our primeval past boiled in our blood. Naked now, I stood over Sally, who cowered between my legs and hissed like some wild animal as she licked up my thighs and over my ass-cheeks. Quickly moving forward, she kneeled before me and took my hard shaft into her mouth, pounding it down her throat for what seemed like an eternity. As if that was not enough, she slowly rose, wrapped her arms around me and clamped my prick between our bellies. Throwing her head back she almost growled, and said melodramatically: "Fuck me like the beasts that walked these paths a thousand years ago. Fuck me like the wild wolf that ruled these hills and screwed his savage mate to quiet his throbbing groin."

She slithered down my body and landed on her hands and knees in front of me, her large ass-cheeks spread and her cunt lips swollen and waiting. I obeyed this savage call and dropped down behind her, both of us resting on a blanket of soft cool moss with tall green fern branches gently caressing our bodies. As I leaned over my panting she-wolf, positioning my prick to enter her fleshy womb, I knew that this time there would be no inch-by-inch entry. Grasping her hips, I pulled them back as I thrust my cock forward, sliding all ten inches deep inside her. Her unrestrained howl of ecstasy as I coupled my savage mate sent a surge of primitive passion through my veins as I drove my member deeper and deeper into this baying bitch. She bucked up and down, pressing her ass back against me to take my shaft even deeper as the last traces of modern inhibition vanished and her howls of joy echoed through the trees and canyons of our wooded love-nest. Neither of us made any pretense of restraint as I now firmly held her hips, and with each stroke, withdrew my ramrod until only the head remained clamped in her vaginal vice, and then plunged the full ten inches up her convulsing cunt. Her love-juice now flowed so freely down her thighs that my pubic hair was soaked and the scent of it, mingled with the fragrances of the surrounding forest, raised me to a new, even higher level of excitement.

I paused for just a moment to survey the scene. As I relaxed my grip, Sally slid off my impaling prick and in one quick continuous movement rolled over onto her back, brought her knees up to her breasts, spread her legs far apart and rhythmically raised and lowered her parted pussy lips in time to my racing pulse. In one final gesture of submission she ran her hands slowly down the insides of her widespread thighs to her cunt, which she spread open with her fingers. Reacting to the instincts of our departed pagan ancestors, I flung my six-foot-two-inch frame on top of her and drove my cock, for the first time effortlessly, to the base of her cunt. Hot jets of jism surged from my prick as waves of orgasmic ecstasy racked my body. With her legs wrapped around my waist and her arms around my neck, we fused into one as I emptied load after load into her hot, welcoming pussy. My throbbing cock would not be tamed and with each stroke her legs clasped my waist even tighter and another load of come exploded into her pussy. She began to come, too, moaning my name. My modern-day temptress turned bitch-in-heat finally lay exhausted in my arms, but in my daze I pumped on, more from reflex than desire.

With my balls drained dry and my flaccid cock no longer able to probe its horny home, I rolled onto my back and luxuriated on the soft, cool moss blanket beneath me. She whimpered as she crawled around on all fours and drew her beautiful breasts across my face and down my chest. She was my wolf mate now and her whine was a song of love for the lord of her pack. Her tongue darted from place to place as she licked up my thighs and, burying her face in my groin, lapped up the potion of my jism and her own juices from my balls. She found my limp prick lying on my belly and after rubbing it round and round with her cheeks and lips licked it clean. Leaning back to shake her head, a cascade of long sun-bleached red hair floated down. Taking it in her hands, she tenderly wiped my lower region until it was completely dry.

We awoke as the sun was setting, and walked naked along the

path from our lair to my pickup truck, traversing thousands of years of history in a mere ten minutes. We dressed in knowing silence, exchanging warm smiles, and then followed the sun as we drove over pine-covered hills and onto the flatlands outside of Eureka. I pulled the pickup onto the beach at Arcata while we watched some kids from Humboldt State build a bonfire as the sun surrendered its last rays and sank into the Pacific.

Sally and I have been seeing one another for about a year. Every meeting is a new adventure in erotic excess. Each time I see her she has thought of a new position to try out, dreamt up a new fantasy to fulfill or bought some new sex toy to test out. She is so proud of my big dick that she sets up threesomes with her girlfriends to show it off.

No matter what we do or what erotic heights we reach, I'll always think of Sally the way she was that first beautiful day we watched the sun come up over San Francisco and sink into the Pacific in Arcata. I'll remember her walking toward me at the rest stop, her ponderous boobs swinging freely in her skintight blouse. I'll remember her lying on my truck seat with her leg over my shoulder and her cunt spread wide as she begged to be fucked. And I'll particularly remember the she-wolf in the primitive quiet of the forest resting on all fours, her ass high in the air waiting to receive her mate.

How could I ever forget? Could you?

GROUP GROPE MOTEL

*L*ast summer, on my forty-second birthday, my wife and I went on vacation to Yosemite National Park. On our way home we stopped in a small town in eastern California to spend the night. We got our motel room at about four in the afternoon and, with some snacks and a large jug of wine, we went out to enjoy the pool.

After we swam a little and drank a lot, we both were feeling a little horny. Another couple unexpectedly joined us. Since the motel was almost empty, we were the only ones in the pool. The woman was a vision of loveliness, with blond hair, blue eyes and a thirty-eight-inch bust at least. Both her hair and her legs were long and golden. She had on a very skimpy bikini that barely concealed her breasts and beautiful ass. She swam laps while her tall, lanky husband lay by the pool and drank beer, not saying a word. As she and my wife chatted, I studied her glorious body and got hornier and hornier.

Finally, the other couple left the pool and my wife and I gathered our things and went back to our room. The air conditioner wasn't working properly, so I went to the office to report it. The girl in the office, who wore an outlandish outfit and too much makeup, said she'd send someone to fix it.

When I returned to our room, I found my wife Samantha sitting seductively in the middle of the bed, naked and ready, sipping a glass of wine. Sam, who is thirty-eight years old, has a beautiful face and hair, and her five-foot-seven figure is perfect. Her rather puritanical midwestern upbringing had colored her ideas about sex. For instance, she didn't like me to eat her pussy because she thought such a practice was "dirty and sinful." (Although later she admitted she'd really disliked it because she couldn't get off when I did it.) She had sucked my cock only once in sixteen years. In the motel room, however, she startled me by saying she wanted my cock in her mouth.

I tore off my bathing suit and jumped in bed with her. We tangled tongues in a long, hot kiss while I fondled her firm breasts and pinched her nipples. She soon eagerly took my cock into her mouth—until it grew too big and fat for her to keep in there. My cock is barely six inches long but extremely thick and curved backward. I really hadn't missed her blowjobs in the five years since her last attempt because I have a problem known as Peyronie's disease, which causes my penis' unusual curvature, making an erection somewhat painful. Gradually this condition has caused a loss of sensitivity in the epidermal layer of my cock, which may seem ideal for an all-night fuck session (something I've not tried yet). Usually, after my wife has two or three orgasms and I have one, we're through for the night. But this night was different.

While Sam squeezed my cock, I gently rolled and pinched her clit. I slipped one and then two fingers into her juicy cunt. She was hot and ready. Realizing there was no chance of her letting me eat her when she was at this stage, I asked her to get my cock-head good and wet with saliva. When she'd done this, I pushed her down gently on her back.

It is sometimes difficult to get my fat, curved cock into her tight twat, but now it slid in easily and I immediately became aware of just how hot she was. Her dripping cunt was as hot as an oven. This was surely going to be an evening to remember. Little did I know how memorable it would truly be!

Sam locked her legs around me and began thrusting furiously with her hips. Before I had even really started, she experienced her first orgasm and screamed with pleasure, which she seldom does. I settled into a steady action of deep thrusting into her fiery depths, and she had three or four orgasms in the next five minutes. As usual, though, despite her enthusiasm, I was not getting close to a climax. I do enjoy giving her so much pleasure, however, and we fucked in three or four more positions and wound up lying across the bed, with her on top of me, dangling her legs off the edge of the mattress.

That's when we noticed a woman standing in our doorway, the one from the motel office, still wearing her garish outfit. She must have been watching for quite a while, because she had a feverish look on her face. Then my wife dropped the second bombshell of the evening by saying, "Either come in and join us or leave. You're letting the hot air in."

The intruder came in, closed the door and stood watching us.

I was amazed when Sam resumed the movements of her pelvis on my cock. She seemed really to enjoy having someone watch us. Enjoying it, too, I made long upward thrusts into her burning snatch.

Still standing by the door, the girl was rubbing her pussy through her clothes and squeezing her breasts. Her eyes were glued to us. I gave her a warm smile and a look that said "Come on and join us," and she responded immediately. As she dropped her pants to the floor, her shapely legs and slender hips came into view. She had no panties on and her dark pubic hair stood out boldly against her white skin. When she removed her sloppy top, she revealed even more breathtaking treasures—large, firm breasts with dark-brown areolas and hard nipples. As she removed the pins from her upswept hair, it cascaded over her shoulders. She was a perfect 35-23-35 beauty, about five feet five inches tall and twenty years old. The only fault was her excessive makeup, but I detected fine bone structure beneath it. She stepped over to the bed, turned her back to my wife, straddled my head and lowered her dripping pussy right down upon my face. With a dreamy look on her face she said, "Hi! I'm Debbie." Before I began lapping her cunt, I bade her welcome.

There was no hair around Debbie's cunt lips as there was on her well trimmed pubic mound. I dug into her cleft with my tongue, found her clit and sucked and nibbled on it. She wriggled her bottom all over my face. I was in seventh heaven. For the first time I was fucking and eating pussy at the same time.

Sam had meanwhile placed her hands on Debbie's shoulders and, as Debbie rode off to never-never land, Sam pressed her breasts into Debbie's back as Debbie leaned back against her. Sam began to moan and gasp for breath, as she's wont to do in the throes of a really good orgasm. When her spasms stopped, she fell over on her side and curled up with her pussy shining wetly between her legs. Debbie kept grinding her crotch into my face until she had at least two orgasms in quick succession, which caused her to moan and groan deep in her throat.

As she approached her third climax, she glanced around at Sam and said to me, "Your wife has a gorgeous pussy. Do you think she would let me suck it?"

Before I could answer, Sam sat up and said, "No way! Why don't you just fuck my husband and be content with that?"

Moving my soaked face away from Debbie's steaming snatch, I said, "Fine with me," and deftly rolled her onto her back beside Sam, in the middle of the bed, and stabbed my raging hard-on into her pussy. Debbie groaned again, threw her legs up over my shoulders and launched into a fast ride with me to paradise.

At first it was very strange, lying there beside my wife, fucking another woman—but when Sam reached down and began caressing my balls, it was heaven. Debbie grunted ecstatically with every thrust I made and screamed out loud during two more orgasms. Although she had the tightest cunt I'd ever been in, I was still nowhere near a climax. When I asked her to let me fuck her doggie-style, she said it was her favorite way. She excitedly got on her knees and helped me insert my cock into her burning tunnel. She was so good that I was only vaguely aware of all the noise we were making and of the fact that her head was banging against the headboard, and the headboard was striking the wall, until a thumping arose from the other side of the wall and a loud voice said, "Can't you hold it down over there? We can't concentrate on what we're doing!"

Sam, who was up on her knees now, caressing Debbie's shoulders and my balls, dropped her third bombshell by yelling back, "Well, why don't you join us and we'll all concentrate together?" I nearly swallowed my teeth but didn't miss a single stroke into Debbie's gorgeous cunt. When there was no response, I returned my full attention to Debbie's pulsating pussy and—finally!—my impending climax.

Suddenly the door burst open and in came two people—the vision I'd seen in the pool and her husband. I nearly fainted. They stepped over Debbie's strewn-about clothes and the vision said, "Oh, goody! It's the couple from the pool this afternoon. We will join you. And look what I've brought for you girls." She reached over and pulled open her husband's short robe. There hung about ten inches of raw prick, still glistening with her juices. Debbie groaned with desire, my wife swallowed audibly and my cock slipped out of Debbie's pussy just as I came, shooting my cream all over.

The vision, whose name was Tanya, squealed with delight and slipped out of her robe. Her beautiful body was now completely naked. She crawled onto the bed with me and Sam and Debbie and offered to clean my cock of any and all sperm with her beautiful mouth. Never one to refuse a lady, I watched her lick and suck my cock, which was slick with Debbie's juices as well as my sperm.

Debbie scrambled off the bed, meanwhile, and fell to her knees in front of Bill to worship his huge muscle. It had slowly gained enough hardness to stand out straight. It was a good ten inches long, as I've said, and about three inches around. The head was purplish and massive. Debbie crammed as much of it as she could into her mouth.

Tanya, still doing an excellent job on me with her tongue, was amazed at how hard my cock still was. Sam, who was kind of left out for the moment, crawled off to a corner of the bed without once looking away from Bill's giant prick. I knew she yearned to feel it between her legs but was frightened by its size.

Although I wasn't feeling much of Tanya's talented tongue and mouth, I enjoyed squeezing her luscious tits and feeling her firm young body all up and down. She was twenty-five years old and had a flawless body. And she had a hairless pussy—yes, not a hair on it—which explains how she could wear that skimpy bikini without any pubes showing.

I just had to get my lips on that slick cunt of hers, so I eased her mouth off my cock and rolled her over. She lay back and spread her legs wide. As I put my head between her thighs and looked up the length of her glorious body, I saw a hungry look in her eyes that wasn't there before. She had the most beautiful pussy in the world. It was so cleanly shaven that it had no stubble at all. Her labia stood out full and wet, gaping open before my eyes, with her juices running down.

I deeply inhaled her sweet aroma and filled my mouth with her cream as I licked and sucked every inch of her smooth crotch. Every time I touched her hard clit, her hips would buck and she would work her crack tighter against my mouth. She soon came with a long scream that stopped everyone else's action, including Sam, who was actually fingering herself on the corner of the bed.

Debbie and Bill now joined us on the bed and he inserted his horse-cock into her greedy pussy. He grunted, she groaned, and after five minutes or so, she'd managed to get only about eight inches in—but she was in ecstasy. Watching this spectacle was most exciting, and I felt an overpowering need to fuck Tanya. I plunged my hot rod into her bald pussy and we proceeded to screw wildly.

Debbie lasted only ten minutes with Bill. With me, though, Tanya soared through climax after climax and almost passed out once from sheer pleasure. Nevertheless, due to my handicap, I was still not close to coming. Finally, Tanya whispered to me that her favorite way of fucking was doggie-style. She promised she would make me come if I fucked her pussy from the rear. Happy to oblige, I eagerly got on my knees behind her. Tanya was so good in this position that, as she'd promised, I did come. In fact, it took only about five minutes. She had three more orgasms herself as I rubbed her clit with my finger and drove in and out of her cunt with my unflagging cock.

Incredibly, Sam began helping, too, by caressing Tanya's back and shoulders and, once in a while, rather tentatively pinching her nipples. As my big O came surging into my cock, I pulled out of Tanya. She twisted around to face me as I shot spurt after spurt of hot cream on her face, breasts and stomach. She rubbed it frantically all over her body and into her hot, hairless cunt.

Then came the pièce de résistance. Bill wanted to fuck Samantha. He stood there waving his telephone pole in front of her face and said that she owed it to herself to try it. Sam admitted that she wanted it in her pussy but was afraid of its size. I told her not to worry, that I thought she could handle it and that we all would help her.

My reassurance, together with her burning desire, overcame Sam's hesitancy. She spread out on the bed and we all gathered around to watch as Bill placed the immense head of his cock against her gaping pussy. I thought for a second that Bill's giant lance would never fit, but as he worked slowly and carefully, it gradually disappeared into Sam's sheath. I kept encouraging Sam to relax her pussy while Debbie and Tanya squeezed her tits and massaged her body.

I was entranced by what I saw going on between my wife's legs. Her pussy was stretched at least twice as much as ever before. What happened next was paradoxical, moreover, because Sam came a half dozen times while Bill toiled over her. It was one of the most exciting and passionate experiences of my life just to see this. My heart raced and my senses reeled as I watched my wife shed all her sexual inhibitions in order to be fucked for the first time by another man. As Sam and Bill approached a mutual orgasm, I reached in to finger her swollen clit. Her poor, stretched pussy seemed to be on fire as Bill's long ramrod pistoned in and out of her. When they came together, Bill shot great gobs of hot cream all over her body.

When we'd regained our composure somewhat, Debbie, standing next to me, said she was amazed that my prick was still half hard, and she set about restoring it to full strength. I remarked to her what a great situation this was: three beautiful women, two clean-shaven pussies, my wife free of her inhibitions and Bill with his horse-cock. No sooner had I said this than Debbie jumped up and exclaimed, "Holy shit! Why didn't I think of Jan and Sherron? They both love big cocks." And she ran to call them.

During the brief lull in action, we drank wine, snacked and took showers. When things started rolling again, Debbie and Tanya drifted into a hot 69 on the floor and Bill started looking around for his next partner. Soon a cute little redhead came in. Seeing everybody else naked, she stripped for action as she was still saying hello. She had small breasts and a great-looking ass and said how excited she was to be at her first orgy since college. She kept her pale-blue hose and garter belt on and they provided a lovely contrast to the dark-red hair of her patch. She was Debbie's friend, Jan. She was twenty-five and about five-foot-three.

I decided to make the newcomer feel welcome by leading her over to the bed and eating her cute little pussy. She tasted like ginger and she was the most active person I have ever feasted on. She twisted and bucked all over the bed before she came in a crashing, smashing climax that nearly broke my nose and neck. All the time she was coming, she kept shouting that she wanted a giant cock in her pussy, but the only one in the room was busy at that moment. Sam was masturbating Bill's giant schlong while he had three fingers furiously diving in and out of her cunt.

Wanting to be helpful, I told Jan that I would get her ready for the main attraction and I propped her ass up high in the air with two pillows and plowed into her flaming tunnel with my own hard dick. Jan and I fucked furiously while Bill was getting hornier and hornier because Sam didn't succeed in bringing him off by hand and could not get more than an inch or so of his massive cockhead into her mouth.

Finally, when Bill came over to us, I gave up my place in Jan's cunt and he poked his gigantic cudgel into her. She planted her feet against the headboard and pushed back against him, her eyes wide and her stomach actually bulging from the strain she was under, but she obviously loved every minute of it. The rest of us watched in fascination as Jan experienced a string of big O's, even though Bill couldn't get more than half of his cock inside her. When he finally came, we all saw her literally thrown back by each blast of his cannon. A flood of his cream poured out of her twat and soaked the pillows as he uncoupled from her.

As Tanya began eagerly cleaning Bill's prick with her voracious mouth, a loud knock came at the door. Debbie—still naked, of course—threw open the door and loudly invited the person who was standing there into the room. It was Sherron, whom Debbie helped undress in a flash. Sherron was young and slim, with large breasts and a great ass. She was a rich chocolate color with medium-length, black, curly hair. Having never had a black woman before, I was very excited at the prospect of eating and fucking this ebony beauty. The mere anticipation brought my half-hard cock back to life instantly.

As I gorged myself on Sherron's delicious cunt, Debbie presented her cunt to Sherron as if they had made it together many times before. As Tanya sucked on Bill's cock, Debbie moved Tanya around so she could eat her sumptuous pussy. Before you could say "sock it to me," Bill was eating Sam; Sam was eating me; I was eating Sherron; Sherron was eating Debbie; Debbie was eating Jan; Jan was eating Tanya; and Tanya was sucking on Bill's tool. Finally, Sherron broke away from the daisy chain and said she wanted both Bill's and my cock at the same time.

Bill lay on his back on the bed and Sherron mounted his monster from above, with much noise and movement, but she could only take about eight inches. Now I positioned myself in front of her and began to work my much shorter tool into her mouth. It went in easily, and then the fun began. Everyone joined in, squeezing, kissing and caressing our every sensitive spot.

Sherron was going wild, fucking him and blowing me with ever-increasing gusto. She'd done this before, undoubtedly, because she was so good at it. And was she noisy—grunting, squealing, groaning, even with her mouth full. She came five or six times, but even so, when she heard Bill announce that he was nearing orgasm, she increased her tempo even more.

I began coming just as Bill went off in Sherron's cunt, sending her off on another trip to ecstasy. I jerked and jumped and pumped semen into Sherron's throat for what seemed at least two minutes. When I pulled out and flopped over on the bed, Sherron was lying motionless with her eyes closed. Bill was still in her, but not moving, staring dumbly at the ceiling. And my wife had a devilish grin on her face.

What an experience! Not for years had I come three times in less than four hours! And never before had Sam or I ever participated in a group orgy. It was magnificent.

Best of all, it wasn't quite over yet, for Tanya's magnificent mouth and slick pussy, a little later, restored me as the whole bunch of us labored on for another two hours. Sam fucked Bill again and it was great for her. Bill fucked Sherron and Jan again. And I managed to satisfy not only Debbie, but also Jan and Sherron once more each before coming.

Sam was as happy as a lark when it was all over, and the other women said they had never before been serviced by two studs like Bill and me. We all agreed to get together next summer for a repeat performance. Debbie said she knows a Japanese gal and a Navajo princess who would love to join us. I'm already taking vitamins and eating lots of oysters.

CABIN FEVER

*I*f it hadn't been for the three inches of powdery snow that fell the night before, the horse would be moving at a quicker pace—though still not as quick as the beat of my heart. I had memorized the destination after studying the maps for several weeks—ever since Danielle had mailed them to me.

The horse seemed to sense my anxiety. Undoubtedly Danielle, waiting now at the cabin, was just as anxious.

The sun was beginning to set. I knew I'd have to hurry. The path ran gradually uphill and, in spite of my eagerness to reach my destination, I found it necessary to stop and rest the horse for a few minutes before reaching the top of the rise.

According to my maps, the cabin was near. My intuition told

me so, too. I could almost feel Danielle's intoxicating scent, feel her silky skin, look deep into her soft brown eyes. I took stock of my surroundings—and pushed on.

I mounted the horse again and rode steadily to the top of the rise, where I was relieved to see—about half a mile distant and barely discernible—smoke wafting from a chimney. The faint smell of a wood fire greeted my nostrils and I knew the cabin would be warm inside. The horse quickened its pace without being told.

I was sure that Danielle had been waiting all day for my arrival. I could even imagine what she'd been doing. The last few hours she'd spent in careful preparation. I could picture the exquisite result—the fireplace provided the only light in the main room of the cabin, casting an orange glow over the walls, floor, ceiling, furniture. Two candles illuminated the bedroom, giving off a faint lemony scent. Bearskin rugs adorned the rugged wooden floor. The dim candlelight played over the satin comforter on the round bed, which was sunken in the floor to create what we called our "love pit." Everywhere there were huge pillows of satin or velvet in shades of bone and white. The flickering light imparted to the room an atmosphere of serenity. The soft sounds of water in the black-tile hot tub in the corner of the room seemed to emphasize the sheer silence of the deep snow outdoors. What a vision!

In my mind's eye I could see Danielle waiting silently on the rug by the fireplace, trying to contain her impatience as she flipped through a magazine, feeling the painfully slow passage of each minute. Again and again she imagined that she heard me approaching the cabin, only to realize it was the beating of her own heart she heard.

Then, finally, I arrived. The sudden neigh from the horse was carried to her on the night air. I know, because I saw her appear at the open cabin door. She stepped outside to greet me, unaware of the bitter coldness around her. As I came into view, she saw the smile on my face—and her eyes smiled seductively. I dismounted and ran to her. We stood face-to-face, not touching. The space between us was like an island of warmth. Snow began to fall upon us in large, fluffy flakes. It wasn't until she saw the snow clinging to my eyebrows that Danielle realized how cold was the night. It made her shudder.

After I bedded down my horse in the tiny stable, she took me by the hand and led me into the warmth of the cabin. She unzipped my fur-lined parka and hung it by the door to dry. She poured a brandy and, with a smile, handed it to me. Never moving my eyes from her beautiful face, I drank it quickly. The amber liquid heated my insides. Only when I set the glass down did I reach out to cup her face. We gazed deeply into each other's eyes, savoring our togetherness.

I tilted my head slightly and pressed my burning lips to hers. We held the kiss and I wrapped my arms around her slender body and drew her against my own. I could feel her firm breasts pressed between us and the hardness of her nipples. A familiar heat rose through my thighs and warmed my entire being.

She slowly pulled herself from my embrace and, still without speaking, led me by the hand into the bedroom. There she sat me down on the window seat and knelt to remove my heavy boots. When my wool socks were lain aside to dry, she warmed my feet in her hands. Then she motioned for me to stand. She pulled my lamb's-wool sweater over my head and tossed it on a chair. She then began to unbutton my shirt. As each button was liberated from its hole, she kissed the chest hairs that sprang free. Soon my shirt was completely off. Restraining herself from rubbing her hands over my torso, Danielle seemed to be enjoying the sweet anticipation of love. She unbuckled the leather belt of my jeans and unzipped the fly slowly. She slid my jeans down my legs and breathed in the comforting scent of my sex, which made her smile contentedly. She removed my underwear, liberating my swollen cock. How she wanted to wrap her mouth around its head! I could tell how badly she longed to caress my balls and feel their hair tickle her face.

With a discipline I didn't know she had, Danielle rose and looked me squarely in the eye. Smiling, she led me to the steaming Jacuzzi. When she was sure that I was comfortably seated in the swirling bath, she took a bar of jasmine soap and started to wash my back. After rinsing my back, she soaped my chest, delighting in the way the hair retained the lather. She softly caressed my nipples and gradually moved down along my stomach. At her request, I stood and she lathered my buttocks, kneading each one and then working down my thighs.

I felt the tension of the journey leaving my body. Warming with arousal, I turned to face her. My bulging cock was even with her head. She continued bathing me, soaping my legs now from ankles to knees, washing away the weariness of many hours on horseback. Finally, she set the soap aside and cupped her hands under my balls, increasing the pressure of her grasp and then easing off. She allowed one hand to travel to my cock, which she stroked, feeling it grow harder and bigger. A low moan escaped my throat as she played her fingertips lightly over the head of my cock.

Suddenly I felt a stream of cool water on my cock. The contrast between the heat of the Jacuzzi and the cool water was almost too much to bear. Just as suddenly I felt intense heat on the head of my cock. It was Danielle's tongue, which slid down the entire length of my shaft. It was so big and so thick that she always loved the challenge of taking it all in her mouth. She poised her open mouth above the head and engulfed it. She slid her mouth down to the base, then back up again—and again and again—increasing her speed slightly each time. The sight of my meaty monster filling her month was so exciting that I knew I would soon lose control. Up and down, up and down, and suddenly I was groaning loudly as all the pent-up pressure was released from my balls.

Danielle let me come in her mouth. She sucked softly for a while longer, making sure she had every last drop.

When I'd calmed down, I placed my hands on either side of

her beautiful face and pulled her to me. She stepped into the tub with me and, wrapping my arms around her, I held her for a few minutes, just savoring the feel of her silky flesh against mine. The musky scent of her neck tickled my nose. The contrast of her dark hair against the skimpy white shirt she wore excited my senses. I was surprised to find that I was hard again, and I began to slowly rotate my hips against hers.

Danielle's breathing quickened. I lifted her in my arms and carried her back to the bed, placing her down among a clutter of white pillows. As I drank in her beauty with my eyes, I began to unbutton her shirt. She wore nothing underneath. Her dark skin against the whiteness of the shirt and the bed sheets was striking. I wanted her instantly, but I also wanted the moment to last forever. I also wanted to push her to the edge so that she would beg me to fuck her. Her eyes were beckoning already, and I brought my mouth down on hers. I licked her lips and the kiss became even more impassioned. Then I kissed her eyes and ears. When I reached her neck, she sighed deeply.

Danielle's breasts are small but firm. I've always loved the way her nipples stand out. They seemed to call to me. My breath warmed one and then the other. With my tongue I described tiny circles on her left breast while the index finger of my left hand did the same on her other breast. Danielle gasped when I gently pinched one nipple and, with even greater gentleness, bit the other. My heat was rising. I knew she was wet and I couldn't wait to taste her sweet juices, but I forced myself to slow down. Gradually I kissed my way down her tummy. The heady aroma of her sex greeted me and grew stronger as I approached her hairy mound. Downward I continued, lightly brushing over her dark pubic hair, until I was kissing the insides of her thighs. Her skin is so silky there that I lingered and stroked it with my fingertips.

Danielle gasped and whined when my tongue finally touched the center of her deepest passion. I drank her juices greedily as I stuck my tongue deep inside her. Her back arched and her hips rose so her pussy would meet my mouth. At this point I restrained myself to increase her already urgent desire. Removing my mouth, I lightly blew on her cunt.

In the candlelight I could see the glimmer of her wetness, and it was I who could wait no longer. As I raised myself into position, Danielle spread her legs wide to take me in. Just before I entered her, I lifted her hips and slid a pillow under her ass to improve the angle of entry. The head of my cock found its mark and I slid it just a little way in. I pulled it back slightly, then pushed it in a little farther, but not yet all the way. When once more I pulled it back, Danielle began struggling to hold my cock in with her muscles. "Please," she cried. "I need you now."

I delayed one eternity longer and then slid every inch of my huge cock into her. Her breath left her momentarily as she shivered with intense feelings of pleasure. Now I moved slowly in and out while she squeezed and loosened, squeezed and loosened her vaginal muscles. As we fucked, I kissed her lips and then her nipples, each in turn, traveling a triangle with my mouth—breast to mouth to breast to breast to mouth.

Between labored breaths, her eyes glassy with blissful pleasure, Danielle told me that she didn't know how much longer she could last. She seemed to have lost all sense of where she was as she grunted, "I'm coming! I'm coming now!" She said she felt as if she were about to burst wide open. The sounds of my own moaning and groaning, and my obvious loss of control, were enough to push her over the edge as with one final deep stroke we came together, neither knowing whose orgasm came first and caused the other to erupt.

Danielle writhed and groaned as the pulsating waves of pleasure started coming at gradually decreasing intervals. We both felt what seemed like a river running from where we were joined. We stared deeply into each other's eyes and smiled. I leaned my head down to kiss her once more when the excitement had subsided. Looking out the window, I noticed it was snowing fiercely now. Danielle and I discussed the possibility of being stranded in the cabin until spring. Then, still inside her, I began thrusting again, slowly, gently, and Danielle's beat rose again. Turning over, she sat on top of me.

How, she asked, could I be so big and hard again so quickly? It had always amazed her. And she had always amazed herself at how quickly she got turned on again. She teased me now with her cunt, moving over me and feeling me strain to keep my cock in her cunt. Her rhythm increased. She gave in totally to her passion and began bucking wildly and crying aloud.

I watched Danielle's face as she came, losing all sense of her surroundings. She called my name, encouraging me to come with her again. When the last pulse ended, she collapsed forward and rested her cheek on my chest. As I slowly pulled out of her, a small moan of disappointment escaped from her throat. With me cradling her affectionately in my arms and with our legs intertwined, we slept and dreamed of more snow-girt lovemaking together.

THE DUDE & THE DIVORCÉE

*M*y story began about two and a half years ago, when I returned the handbag that my friend Debra had left under her classroom seat. My name is Jim and I'm a twenty-four-year-old black student working my way through college in my hometown here in Virginia. I am six feet two inches tall, weigh one hundred sixty-five pounds, and have been told I am mature for my age and moderately handsome.

When I was leaving my political science class one day I saw that Debra had left her bag under her seat. I picked it up and ran after her, but she had already split. Finding her address in her wallet, I set out to return her handbag to her.

Debra is a blue-eyed brunette, about five-feet-five and a hundred and twenty-five pounds. She's in her early thirties. Her hair was shoulder length and always carefully brushed. She used cosmetics to highlight a very pretty face that her glasses partially masked. Her fingernails were colored to match her lipstick and she always dressed for class as if she were in an advertisement in *Vogue* magazine, which contrasted with the jeans, sweatshirts and sneakers worn by the other women students. She rarely lingered after class and, although she appeared to want to be friendly, she struck most of us as a fashion fanatic who bordered on being a snob and a coquette.

When I arrived at Debra's house to return her bag, I discovered that she lived in an upper-middle-income, largely white neighborhood. Approaching her door, I attracted the stares of some of her nosy neighbors. She was extremely relieved to recover her handbag and warmly invited me into her home. It was when she introduced me to her twin ten-year-old daughters that I learned she'd been divorced about three years earlier. I also learned that she worked as a secretary and that her boss allowed her time off to attend classes and finish college.

Since I had a hot date that evening with my steady girlfriend, I left Debra's house as soon as I could. Nevertheless, even though my girlfriend had been taking good care of all my sexual needs, I was mildly curious about Debra. I'd always regarded her as out of my league and so had never given her much thought. As I drove away, however, I realized for the first time what a great body Debra had. I got a hard-on just thinking about her pretty tits and her beautiful, well-rounded ass. But I could only wonder how this woman, ten years older than I, would react to any come-on I might make. I was very apprehensive about the racial prejudice that still exists in Virginia. I decided to cool it and play it slowly to see what, if anything, might later develop.

Although our meetings after that were friendly, Debra still played the role of the proper and serious student. Because of her attitude, I doubted that I could get her to develop any interest in me. But she looked better and better every time I saw her. Then, toward the middle of the semester, our instructor assigned research papers to be prepared by study groups of four. Debra and I, together with two friends of mine, were assigned to the same group. Each of us had to complete his or her own research and then integrate our findings in one term paper. Debra stayed after class on the day of the assignment and told me she was glad to be in my group and was looking forward to working with me.

A few weeks later, after we had separately completed our research, Debra invited the group to come together at her house one evening to finalize the paper. Aware that this would be a good opportunity to see what the score was with this woman, I secretly asked the other two members of our group to beg off, but not to tell Debra until it was too late for her to cancel the session. Since both had been invited to a party that evening, they agreed to call her at the last minute and say they could not be at the meeting.

On the way to Debra's, I picked up a bag of pot and smoked a joint. While I wasn't high when I got there, I was definitely less apprehensive than on my first visit. When I got to her door, she told me of the last-minute cancellations by our other members. I feigned surprise but reassured her that she and I could finish the work without them. She was wearing designer jeans, showing off her gorgeous ass, and she had on a red T-shirt. Although I had never before made out with an older woman like her, I knew then that I was going to make my play if the opportunity came along.

She suggested that we work on her dining-room table. The spacious dining room was separated from the sunken living room by two steps. I observed that the living-room sofa faced the fireplace. The room was lighted by one table lamp, giving it a very romantic atmosphere. However, her daughters were still up, watching some show on TV as they did their homework.

I sat at the dining-room table next to Debra and we discussed our research notes and figured out how best to organize the paper. We worked for about an hour. She was busy making corrections and outlining the contents of the paper while I pretended to be reading a research article she had recently copied. In truth, my cock was getting ideas and the only thing that really interested me was watching her gorgeous tits jiggle under her tight red T-shirt and dreaming about how it would feel to caress and squeeze that beautiful round ass of hers.

Debra must have noticed the massive hard-on in my pants, because she looked there several times, but she gave no indication that she noticed anything unusual. I became frustrated and feared that my inexperience with older women was beginning to show. Another problem was that her daughters were still up and could hear everything we said. Then, unexpectedly, she slipped me a note. "Do you have a girlfriend?" it asked. Next to the question she had drawn two squares, one to be checked if my answer was "yes" and the other if it was "no."

This sudden and perhaps juvenile tactic surprised me, but I determined to play along and see where it led. I checked the "no" square and wrote, "Are you interested?" Then I folded the note and laid it in front of her.

She read my question, wrote the word "maybe" under it and returned the note to me. I tried to hide my surprise. She removed her glasses, rose from the table and told the twins that it was their bedtime. She led them down the hall to their room and helped them into bed. In a short time she returned. But instead of joining me again at the table, she went to the living room and motioned for me to sit with her on the sofa.

Maybe the effect of the joint I'd smoked earlier was wearing off, but I was getting nervous. I still did not know what she expected or how I should act, but my cock was straining so hard against my pants that I had difficulty just walking the few short steps to the living room. Debra didn't make it any easier, either. The slight smile on her face told me that she was enjoying my acute discomfort and that she completely understood my condition.

Clumsily I sat next to her, but I did nothing. Finally recognizing I was not going to take the lead, Debra blurted out, "Well, are you going to attack me or what?" With that invitation, I put my arms around her and kissed her hard and passionately on the lips. My awkward eagerness and heavy-handedness must have caught her by surprise. She tried halfheartedly to pull away. But by now I was much too hot and horny to be teased any longer. I was going to take command of the situation.

Firmly but gently, I held her head back against the sofa. Stroking her long hair, I kissed and nibbled on her neck. With my tongue, I explored her ear. Debra's face was flushed. It was evident that she was enjoying the petting as much as I. A long, deep soul kiss caused her passion to rise further. Her breathing became heavy and she began groaning.

My hands found her tits and, while I fondled them through her T-shirt, her ass began to squirm. Charged by her excitement, I lifted her to an upright position and pulled her T-shirt over her head. She didn't protest.

A delicate lacy black bra covered Debra's tits. The sharp contrast of the black bra and my dark hands next to her white body stirred a degree of eroticism in me that I had never before experienced. It seemed to have a like effect on her. She was biting her lower lip and her blue eyes took on that glazed look of lustful passion. I pulled her to me tightly while again kissing her fiercely. When I released my hold, she reached behind her back and unhooked her bra, allowing it to fall from her shoulders.

In the soft lamplight I saw that her breasts were small, firm and upright. She had freckles on her shoulders and on her chest above her breasts. A small beauty mark punctuated the apex of her cleavage. Her rosebud nipples, seen against her milky white breasts, suggested arrogance. Eagerly I cupped her breasts in my hands and gently massaged them. I kissed each and circled the nipple with my tongue. Both nipples were soon erect. She cradled my head against her bosom and I was intoxicated by her subtle perfume. As I returned to nibbling and sucking on her nipples, she moaned and began frantically rubbing herself between her legs.

The mouthwork I was lavishing on her increased our already

hot desire. I held back as best I could because I wanted desperately to prolong this unbelievable ecstasy. She took the initiative by suddenly massaging my cock through my pants. A moment later she acknowledged that I was boiling when she pulled her nipple from my lips, knelt before me and unfastened my pants. Our urgency was so great that she pulled only one of my legs from my pants and spread my thighs. My massive black cock, freed at last from restraint, reared straight up toward her face. With one hand she squeezed it tightly. The head swelled larger than I had ever seen it. With her other hand she lovingly held my balls.

Debra began kissing and running her tongue up and down my cock-shaft. Now and then she delicately flicked her tongue against the head. After a while she moved down to my balls and began gently sucking them. Never before had I experienced such pleasure. If she had not maintained such a tight grip on my rod I would have spurted my load almost immediately. After teasing me like that and watching me writhe, she moved her mouth up to my throbbing cock again. Wet with her saliva, the head was soon a glistening dark purple. I watched her try to take the whole of my dark cock in her mouth. It was so big she had difficulty, but by gradually working her lips down along the dark shaft, she finally got it all in and began deep-throating me.

Debra is the only woman who's been able to do that for me. Sucking furiously and making loud slurping noises, her hair kept falling across her face as her head movements became more rapid and her lips alternately tightened and loosened on my rod. I met each of her movements with a thrust, fucking her in the mouth and throat. From the lustful sounds she made, I knew she was enjoying it just as much as I was.

All too soon, though, I knew I wouldn't be able to hold back much longer. From deep within me, I felt my come rising—and then I was overwhelmed by the longest orgasm I've ever had. For what seemed like five minutes I shot hot semen into her crammed mouth. The outpouring was more than she could handle. It oozed from the sides of her mouth and dribbled from her chin down to my dark thighs. Some of it got in her hair. She swallowed as much as she could hold in her mouth. Then, as if to make sure that none of my come soiled her sofa, she licked my cock and thighs clean.

Still quivering with excitement, Debra lay back on the sofa, placing her head on my naked lap and rubbing my semiflaccid cock against her face. I had never experienced such euphoria from a blowjob—but I had never had a blowjob before from such an experienced lover. It then occurred to me that this prim and proper lady had actually been a wild, aggressive tigress lying in wait to have her way with me!

Neither of us spoke for several minutes before she asked if I had enjoyed it. I told her honestly that it had been the best I'd ever experienced. Debra then got to her feet and picked up her bra and T-shirt from the floor. Clad only in her jeans, she disappeared down the hallway. I was uncertain of what was to happen next, but I knew I wanted more of this sexual feast—and I knew I owed this passionate woman some of the same kind of ecstasy she had given me. I removed the remainder of my tangled clothing and waited anxiously, hoping for an encore.

A few minutes later I heard music coming from the rear of the house. Debra reappeared in the hallway. Her hair was once again neatly brushed and she was wearing a full-length, blue-flowered satin robe. The robe was untied, exposing black bikini panties on her otherwise naked body. She motioned to me and I followed her to her bedroom. After closing the door I saw that the room was dominated by a queen-size bed. Along the wall was a large chest and a long mirror directly facing the bed. She cautioned me to be quiet and not awaken her children. Then she stepped back and looked me over as I stood before her in the buff. I felt like a slave on the auction block. She told me I was strong and handsome, and she called me her "ebony lover." When she lightly ran her fingernails along my limp cock, I felt my desire rapidly returning.

I pulled her against my naked body and slipped my hands

under her robe. We kissed hungrily again and I could taste a residue of my come in her mouth. As I ran my fingers up and down the bare skin of her back, she slipped her arms out of her robe and let it fall to the floor. Although the room was only dimly lit, in the mirror I could see Debra's pale whiteness pressed against my dark skin. The sight brought on a formidable erection, which I rubbed against her panties as I reached into them and grabbed the soft silky cheeks of her ass. Her nipples hardened almost instantly against my body as she began to grind her pussy against my fully awakened cock.

Finally I pulled her damp panties down over her hips. Debra stepped out of them and stood naked before me. There was a small patch of light pubic hair above her pussy. Her ass was fuller than those of the younger women I had known. I asked her to sit on the edge of the bed. When she did, I knelt in front of her. Reaching up between her outspread thighs, I felt the warm dampness of her pubic hair with the palm of my hand and inserted my fingers into her vagina. As my fingers probed deeper and deeper inside her womanhood, she began to shudder and shake. I fingerfucked her until she was thoroughly wet, then removed my hand and lowered my face to her lovely cunt, which now had a glistening opening the size of a half-dollar.

As I kissed and ran my tongue between her pussy lips, I felt her thighs tighten around my head. She pushed her cunt into my face as I licked her gash harder and deeper. My tongue probed the same inner depths my fingers had explored. Then I withdrew my tongue and searched for her clitoris, which I found swollen to the size of a pencil eraser and fiery red. I tongued it roughly, much to her delight, and sucked it as hard as I dared. She began convulsing so violently that I thought I was hurting her, but when I pulled my mouth away, she took my head between her hands and guided me back again to her pleasure zone. Soon, when she began to orgasm, the entire bed was shaking. She groaned so loud that I feared she would awaken her children.

In the mirror I watched her squeeze her tits and pull on her nipples. It was like watching an X-rated movie, except that I was now one of the actors. Excitedly, I straddled her and allowed my cock to replace my tongue in caressing her clitoris. She began pleading with me to put it in and fill her up. "Fuck me good and hard," Debra pleaded. Over and over again, she kept telling me that she wanted all of my big cock in her. Her pleading turned me on even more and I promised to fuck her better than she had ever been fucked by anyone before. "Please do it now," she begged. "Please fuck me."

I pushed her gently onto her back and placed her legs over my shoulders. I knew I wouldn't be able to get all my huge hammer into her at once, so I inched it in slowly. She kept begging for more of it, telling me how wonderful it felt. With each stroke I seemed to go deeper, and she arched her hips to meet each of my thrusts. Our rhythm increased in tempo until I had penetrated her so completely that the head of my rock-hard cock was touching her cervix. She cried out, not in discomfort but utter joy.

We fucked like this for twenty minutes or more before she begged me to hurry and fill her with my come. I increased the tempo and she began to climax violently. I shot my load deep within her. Her vaginal muscles contracted around my pulsating cock, milking my semen out. When we were both calm again and she slowly lowered her legs from my shoulders, my cock began retreating from within her and I felt my warm come dripping down her legs. Suddenly, unexpectedly, she slid from under me and ran to the bathroom.

While she was cleaning herself, I remembered the pot I had brought and went to get it. I rolled a couple of joints and brought them back to the bedroom. We lay together on the bed and smoked them as we talked and listened to another tape of soft music. Debra told me of her failed marriage and growing loneliness. She confessed that she had been horny and wanted me on my first visit, hoping I would seduce her. She said she had a greater sexual appetite now than when she was twenty and that it was not being satisfied by her regular boyfriend. She explained the need to be discreet about meeting new sex partners because of her job. Although she did not say so, I got the impression that she was being kept and would allow nothing to jeopardize her friend's generosity in paying for her expensive needs.

After we finished smoking the joints, she said she wanted more sex with me and promptly began giving me head. It wasn't long before she was on my cock, fucking herself wildly. She had another orgasm as I sucked on her titties. Before I let her rest, however, I mounted her doggie-fashion and rammed my hard cock into her pussy from the rear, pounding my belly against the cheeks of her magnificent ass as I fucked her. That night I came five times as she introduced me to every sexual position I had ever thought of—and more besides.

The sun was just peeking above the horizon when she asked me to leave. She wanted me to be gone before her children awakened. After taking a shower with her, I went to the living room and dressed. She put on her robe and followed me, telling me how great an evening it had been for her. She kissed me hard and then I slipped out her side door.

I drove to a friend's pad near the college instead of going home and, after I'd awakened him, we shared a beer while I gave him an abbreviated account of my evening with Debra. I then slept on his sofa most of the day. (Later I learned that Debra had typed and turned in the research paper that day. When the grades were posted, I discovered that each member of our group had received an A.)

I was able to get back together with Debra only twice before the end of the semester, neither of which occasions matched the loving lustfulness of that first night. I also learned the friend—to whom I had confided—had a big mouth. My steady girlfriend, Lenora, found out about me and Debra. Because Lenora kept close tabs on me during the following semester, Debra and I gradually lost contact. Several months later I learned that Debra had taken up with a weight lifter and that she was getting all the sexual attention she could handle.

Although I have enjoyed exciting nights with other women since the memorable one with Debra, I have never come close to duplicating the sexual satisfaction I experienced with her. Now I'm looking hard for another older lover who fucks and sucks like a hungry tigress.

THREE-FOR-ALL

*T*o begin with, I am thirty-one years of age, six feet tall and quite good looking. I have always had more than my share of lovely women along the way. Until several weeks ago, in fact, I thought my days of sexual discovery were for the most part past. But I was wrong.

It all began two weeks ago. By chance I encountered a young woman, Marti, with whom I had been now and then involved during college. Marti looked as beautiful as always. If anything, she had improved with time. We hugged and kissed and spent the next twenty minutes catching up. She was late for an appointment, so we made a dinner date for the following Saturday evening and she rushed off.

When the hour of our engagement arrived, I took Marti to a small, softly lit, intimate restaurant where everything went extremely well. We found it as easy as ever to communicate with each other. Several hours and two bottles of champagne later, we went to a disco for after-dinner drinks. The place was in full swing when we arrived. Marti and I spotted a place to stand and I fought my way to the bar for the drinks. Waiting for the bartender's attention, I was surprised by a pair of hands suddenly covering my eyes. Wondering who was their owner—and whose breasts were pressed against my back—I looked over my shoulder into the eyes of one of my favorite past lovers, Bonnie.

"Michael!" she squealed, and gave me a crushing hug. She

looked incredible. Her honey-blond hair was a sea of soft curls, falling to the middle of her back. Her body and sparkling green eyes were still as perfect as they'd been during those passion-filled evenings in my college apartment. I took Bonnie's hand in mine and led her toward Marti.

Marti appeared perplexed when I returned, cocktails in one hand and Bonnie in the other. I quickly introduced them to each other. Marti asked, "Are you the Bonnie I've heard so much about?"

"I imagine I am," Bonnie replied. "And you're Marti—college-days Marti!"

"That's me!" Marti laughed.

"Well, this is quite a coincidence!"

The conversation, influenced by entirely too much alcohol, became amazingly open and personal. Marti asked Bonnie how her luck had been with men in the city where she now lived. "My luck with men hasn't been so great," Bonnie said. "I've done better with women."

I knew Bonnie had experimented with bisexuality years before, and what she said now really didn't shock me. What did surprise me was that she would be so open with Marti. Although slightly taken aback by Bonnie's remark, Marti didn't seem repulsed or uncomfortable. Rather, she wanted to know about Bonnie's lesbian experiences.

Bonnie said her experiences had begun with an extremely feminine and beautiful roommate during her sophomore year of college. I was absolutely fascinated, listening to these two women. When we were joined by a few friends of mine, Bonnie and Marti ended their conversation. Marti asked me to take her home. We left and went to my apartment, where we immediately melted into each other's arms and made passionate love until the early morning.

As we lay holding one another close, Marti said that for as long as she could remember, she'd had a burning curiosity to experience another woman's body. Years before, as an eighteen-year-old, she had often invited her closest friend at school to sleep over. One night as she slept, Marti had awakened to the gentle caress of her friend's hands on her firm young breasts. Instead of turning away or startling her friend, she'd pretended to be asleep as her friend's fingers found their way to the damp cotton panties between her legs.

Marti had never reciprocated in those evenings of sexual adventure, but she invited her friend over many times again, always anticipating her touch and attention. She'd gone as far as letting her best friend's lips taste her nipples and her friend's fingers enter her virginal pussy. Their encounters had ended when her girlfriend moved out of state with her family. But those special evenings had left their mark upon Marti's sexual awareness. No wonder she was so turned on to Bonnie. Bonnie's perfect body, the softness of her blond hair and, most important, her total femininity made Marti's imagination swell with the anticipation of an encounter with her.

I was captivated by a vision of these two exceptionally beautiful women actually exploring each other's body. My cock began to harden rapidly. How outrageously erotic if this dream could actually become a reality!

"How serious are you about spending time with Bonnie?" I whispered. Marti didn't know quite what to say. "Bonnie is very free, you know. She's always been uninhibited. If you're really interested, I'm sure I could work it out for you. I'll speak to her, if you like."

Marti fixed her eyes on mine and asked softly, "If I agree to live out this fantasy, will you be there? Can the three of us make it together instead of just she and I?" She laid her head on my shoulder and added, "You've experienced her before. If you were there, it would make me feel much more confident and secure. I really want to," Marti confided. "I'm just so inexperienced."

"I'll talk to her," I said. "If the mood seems right, I'll see what she thinks."

With that, Marti held me close and we began to make love

again. When I left her in front of her house the following morning, I promised to talk to Bonnie.

I saw Bonnie that afternoon and, as I expected, she was excited and flattered by the whole idea. I explained Marti's special request that I participate in the sensual adventure. I cited the insecurity that Marti felt about being alone with her. Several minutes passed. I awaited Bonnie's response. My pulse quickened when a wonderful, rather naughty smile appeared on her lovely face. Leaning across the sofa, she slid her arms around me, gently kissed me and said, "How about this weekend! Will that be all right with you and Marti?" I almost fainted.

That Saturday evening, I waited impatiently in the hotel suite I had taken for this special occasion—champagne on ice, romantic music playing softly, lights dimmed, candles lit near the huge quilt-covered bed. The ladies were to arrive at eight. Dinner was at nine.

As I sat sipping champagne and enjoying the evening skyline view through the window, there came a knock at the door. I had seen Marti look lovely many times before, but never like this. She was exquisite. A shimmering black silk dress clung to her body as if it had been painted on. Her large nipples, already swollen, pressed visibly against the sleek fabric. The curve of her large breasts was accented by a single strand of white pearls. As I led her to a large armchair, I focused on her perfect legs and firm ass. Her shoulder-length hair framed her sparkling eyes and full red lips in the warm candle glow.

Just then Bonnie arrived. She walked slowly into the suite and her eyes immediately found Marti's from across the room. The curves of Bonnie's voluptuous body beneath the crimson red velvet she wore were obvious. Her pointed breasts were like Marti's, the nipples visibly rigid. The electricity in the air was explosive.

As we all talked and drank champagne, I saw them stealing glances at each other's straining nipples. I sensed their rising hunger to taste what they were looking at.

The evening slipped by. After dinner, Marti sat on the edge of the bed. I felt my heart race as Bonnie rose from her chair and went over to her. No words were exchanged as Bonnie's graceful hands began carefully to massage the other's neck and shoulders. I watched fascinated as Marti arched her neck so that her tresses fell onto Bonnie's full breasts. I heard the girls' breathing become deep and labored. My own breathing quickened and my temperature rose as I watched Bonnie's polished fingernails work beneath Marti's sheer dress. Marti began to moan, her large breasts cupped in Bonnie's hands. I watched, spellbound, as Bonnie helped Marti to her feet. Bonnie now sat on the corner of the large bed. Silently Bonnie lowered the black silk from Marti's shoulders. Neither woman took her eyes from the other.

I caught my breath as Marti's rose-tipped breasts finally swung free. The nipples were swollen and rigid. I stared as Bonnie's long tongue ran across their undersides, leaving wet trails shining in the candlelight. Bonnie began to run her hands up along Marti's long legs, disappearing under the black silk. Marti meanwhile unfastened the front of her dress until it opened, revealing tiny, black lace panties. Bonnie's mouth closed greedily around one of Marti's swollen pink nipples. Throwing her head back, Marti gasped. Bonnie's lips were now wandering across Marti's torso, kissing and licking.

By now I was panting with excitement, my cock straining the zipper of my pants. Bonnie took Marti by the hand and led her to one of the large chairs near the window. Marti seemed almost in a trance. Bonnie knelt between Marti's gorgeous legs, spreading them open and running her hands over them. Marti eventually lifted her ass from the chair to let Bonnie roll off the panties— soaked with her musky wetness—down over her perfectly formed thighs, calves, ankles and feet, still encased in black high heels. After what seemed an eternity, Bonnie attained her goal, the tuft of damp curls between her new lover's legs.

I got up and sat on the carpet next to the girls and watched breathlessly as Bonnie's fingers disappeared into Marti's waiting pussy. She firmly but carefully probed deeper with each stroke, until three fingers were entirely buried inside of Marti's throbbing cunt. Marti's body tremored and her eyes fixed on the other's angelic face. Slowly Bonnie withdrew her nectar-soaked fingers. Marti watched entranced as they moved to her breasts, smearing the juices of her heated cunt in circular traces across her hardened nipples. Leaning forward between Marti's thighs, Bonnie kissed the heaving breasts, pulling and squeezing the swollen nipples.

Marti was in ecstasy, shunting her head involuntarily from side to side. I was amazed—and so was Bonnie, I think—when Marti suddenly took Bonnie's fragrant fingers and hungrily stuffed them into her mouth. I looked on as her passion-inspired tongue cleaned her cunt juice from Bonnie's fingers. Bonnie moaned and removed her mouth from Marti's full breasts to the dripping cunt below. She placed her red lips greedily over the swollen clit between Marti's trembling thighs. Marti screamed as her lover engulfed the swollen pearl of her lust.

Never had I been more turned on. Bonnie's blond curls brushed the softness of the other's thighs. I could hear the moisture being sucked from Marti's cunt. I quickly stood and removed my clothes. Marti gaped at my straining cock as it was released from my pants. Her fingers encircled it and guided it into her open mouth. Bonnie's tongue was now probing the interior of Marti's inflamed cunt. I was transported by this dream coming true.

Bonnie's angelic face was pressed deep into the other's fragrant cunt. The wetness was visible on the smooth skin of her face. Marti spread her legs wider apart, welcoming the tongue that probed her pussy. Her hand was on Bonnie's slender neck, and she pulled her even closer, urging her to invade her pussy as deeply as possible.

My cock, never harder, was being forced into Marti's soft mouth. I soon felt the come inside me boiling. But Marti suddenly took my cock from her mouth. She stood up and helped Bonnie to her feet. She then told Bonnie to lie back in the chair where she had just been. Bonnie settled back on the soft cushions as Marti moved in between her thighs and began exploring Bonnie's breasts, pulling her nipples and rotating them between her fingers. Marti leaned forward and their mouths met. They were locked in a passion-filled kiss, Marti tasting her own sweet juices on Bonnie's face.

I watched expectantly as Marti slowly kissed her way down to the other's nipples. Without hesitating, her eager lips closed over Bonnie's rose-tipped breasts and straining, taut nipples.

Bonnie sighed. Turning her attentions to me, she pulled me close and sucked my prick greedily into her warm mouth. Marti quit mouthing Bonnie's tits and descended to the wet, fragrant cunt that was pressing against her. I watched intently as Marti— for the first time—lowered her beautiful face to the dripping pussy before her and pressed her nose and mouth into the pink slit. She moaned and whined as the taste of a woman's hot cunt invaded her senses. She lapped her new lover's cunt with increasing speed until Bonnie convulsed in a volcanic orgasm.

Bonnie and Marti, after leaving their impassioned embrace, helped me to the chair. My pulse quickened as they kneeled on either side of me, their lovely hands fondling my cock and balls. I watched closely as they took turns engulfing my prick in their mouths. Their hands were everywhere, stroking my buttocks, caressing my balls, gently running over the length of my shaft. I felt my orgasm building as Marti's fingers worked wildly on my cock. When the eruption of come began, Marti closed her lips over the head of my cock and filled her hungry mouth with my hot, pearly fluid. Bonnie quickly replaced her and did the same as my prick continued spurting.

Come was everywhere. Thick, wet drops clung to the women's faces and strands of it hung from Bonnie's blond curls. I caught my breath as she leaned across my thighs and pulled Marti's face to her own. She licked and sucked the warm come from Marti's lovely face. In a sexually charged kiss, they locked their lips together and exchanged my come between them. My mind reeled!

We continued our lovemaking for the entire night, utilizing every possible combination of positions. After we'd enjoyed more orgasms than we could count, we fell asleep, content and satisfied.

In the morning I awoke to find the girls nestled comfortably on either side of me. When they woke up, the three of us showered together, popped one more bottle of champagne and drank a toast to our special friendship. Then the three of us climbed back into bed and pulled up the covers, knowing we would enjoy many more special times together.

Part Two

Part Two

FILL 'ER UP

I was driving along Highway 61 toward New Orleans and noticed the fuel gauge was near empty, so I took the next exit and drove into the first service station I saw. It was in a place called Gramercy. After I filled the tank, I ran into the office to pay the bill and started running back when—wham!—I bumped into a woman who was bending over, tapping the wheel-bolt covers of a van with her fist. I put both my hands on her shoulders so she wouldn't fall.

"Terribly sorry," I apologized. "I'm late for New Orleans and didn't notice . . ." But then I did notice—and I stopped breathing and stared openmouthed. She was the most gorgeous, stunningly perfect redhead I'd ever seen or ever will see. Titian tresses cascaded over bare shoulders, framing lustrous eyes that spoke to me, although the sounds she made emerged from delicately formed crimson lips. Her modulated drawl told me she wasn't from the Deep South.

"I'm unhurt, really," she said, "so if you'd stop squeezing my shoulders . . ."

That shock of beholding such beauty had left me frozen in position, nearly speechless.

"Excuse me," I blurted. "I was afraid you might have fallen. Pavement could have scratched you. My clumsiness is inexcusable. May I help? Trouble with wheel covers?"

My bursts of tongue-tied speech seemed to amuse her as she smiled forgivingly.

"Well, I lost one a while ago, so now I check them a couple of times a day. If you're in a rush to get to New Orleans, don't waste your time."

She said it so pleasantly that I knew I couldn't let this glory-of-creation go.

"I was in a hurry only because I'm hungry. Know any good restaurants in the city?"

"New Orleans? Too many to mention. What kind of food do you like?"

"Whatever you prefer," I replied, trying not to sound flippant. "That is, if you'll dine with me."

It seemed an eternity before she smiled brightly and said, "I thought you'd never ask. I'm really tired of cooking in my van. My name's Teri."

"And I'm Pat."

We arranged that I'd follow Teri to the outskirts of New Orleans, where she'd park the van and ride with me in my car to the Latin Quarter. She knew of a really good restaurant there in a quaint old hotel. When we reached the suburbs she parked at a huge shopping mall. I waited while she locked the van. As she approached my car, her slit skirt revealing her shapely legs, I jumped out to open the door for her. The sight of her seated in my Honda almost overpowered me.

"You like my legs?" she asked directly as I climbed back into the driver's seat.

"Didn't think I was that obvious," I said. "Yes, they're peerless. Hope you don't mind. Afraid I've been staring. Just can't control myself."

"I'm glad. You're not so bad, either. Why isn't your wife with you?"

Although I knew it might end things too soon, I had to be truthful. "The final decree is due in eighteen days."

Looking at me with a radiant smile, she slid over close and placed her hand on my crotch, stroking me there lightly.

"You're a few months behind me as a divorcé. I know how hard the waiting can be. You must be starved for more than food by now. Have many girlfriends?"

Her deft fingers unzipped my fly and moved over my stiffening tool.

"Wow! That's bigger than I hoped! Let's see if it gets any bigger!" She continued stroking gently and it began growing. "Oh Pat! It does get bigger! What a man! Wow, I'm glad we met. I want it! Let's do it before dinner. The hotel's on the next block. Park in the hotel's garage so we can register and go right up to our room."

I did as she suggested. In the garage I had to fight back an urge to slip her dress up her lovely thighs as soon as we parked. I did slide my hand under her dress, however. She opened her legs and I felt her soft crotch, massaging it until it turned moist. The garage was dimly lit, and I considered screwing her in the car. No, I decided, Teri was too classy for that action. Just then she zipped up my fly and looked at me with a lovely expectant smile. We quickly registered and went to our room, where I immediately lost all control. I pulled her into a tight embrace. Pressing my open mouth to hers, I dropped my pants and raised her skirt.

"Unzip the back," she breathed. When her skirt fell, skimpy blue underpants were revealed to my hungry eyes. I led her over to the bed and at the same time removed her blouse. After throwing off all my clothes, I slowly undid her bra clasp, revealing firm, full breasts and erect, crimson nipples. Bending forward to kiss each one, then to suck and stroke them, I was lost in passion. Teri rubbed her crotch against my leg and then let her tight bikinis drop to the floor. She stood on tiptoe and raised her splendid ass slightly above my stiff cock. Then she slowly lowered her pussy toward my standing rod. It was wonderfully tight as it met my cockhead. After resisting penetration for a second or two, it suddenly opened and slid completely over the top of my engorged cock.

"Oh God," Teri gasped. "That feels good! Oh Pat, I knew we'd fit! Oh, push hard!"

I moved my prick in and out, withdrawing it momentarily now and then to roll the head against her clit. Teri was breathing in husky, ecstatic gasps. After I-don't-know-how-long, she pulled me with her to the bed's edge and sat there with her snatch pressed forward against my thrusts. We fit so tightly and held on so ardently that my rod stayed in her while we moved from one position to another.

As we screwed face-to-face in a sitting position, Teri leaned back slightly, her rosy breasts and erect nipples exciting me beyond belief. I pumped in and out like a ramrod, resisting orgasm until Teri was ready. When she suddenly shouted "Fuck me, honey!" I removed my cock, pressed her back on the bed and, as her legs spread wide, I jammed my throbbing cock as deep as it could go into her. Her cunt muscles were coaxing me to a frenzy, but I held on, driving in and out till I nearly burst. Suddenly her moans were louder. "Oh Pat! . . . You're really fucking me now! . . . Don't stop!"

My dick squirted violently just as her juices began squishing forth. I pumped her completely full. Then I squirted out more, so that my thick fluid was forced back between my cock and her snatch before it dribbled down her legs. It was a glorious climax! I couldn't seem to stop coming—and I didn't want to. Neither did Teri, who continued fucking herself on my throbbing dick. Gradually we slowed down, and my rod gave one last little squirt. I dropped my open mouth on hers for a loving, grateful kiss. "I hope you feel as good as I do," I whispered, hoping the moment would linger.

"I've never been fucked this well before. Where did you learn how to please a woman so completely?"

"Didn't have to learn. With you, making love comes naturally."

We kissed noisily, openmouthed, with my cock still pulsing gently within her. Then, somehow, I knew she wanted to wash up. I carried her to the shower. As she stepped in, I couldn't quit staring at her glorious nakedness. I scrubbed her back first, then her graceful ass, and then I washed between her pussy lips very gently, rinsing away my semen. This turned her on again. She took my hands, placed them over her snatch and backed into me. My cock plunged right into her snatch. She grabbed it and worked it all the way into her tight pussy. We began fucking immediately, right there in the shower, with Teri bent forward so that my short strokes rubbed her clit. She soon reached back around my rump and pulled me against her so that my dick reached farther into her. On each of my backstrokes, she would shove it in deep again. She began to moan in cadence with my excited, hard breathing—I knew we were nearing another crescendo.

"Oh Pat! You're giving it to me good! Fuck me! *Fuck* me!"

This time, again, we were right on. Her juices flowed copiously as my come squirted up her cunt. My cock pulsated wildly, gushing an immense load while she fucked back in full joy. Once again rolls of thick creamy fluid rolled down her legs, only this time the shower washed it right away. I kept squeezing my prick into her until the squirting slowed to a last happy spurt. I didn't want to let go, but she removed her hands from my rump and turned to give me a wet, noisy kiss.

Suddenly she dropped down and kissed my still-throbbing rod. "Pat, I've never sucked anyone, not even my ex. That's one reason he and I broke up. If you'd like, though, I'll suck you off." Her heavenly face was looking up at me, and I could do only one thing. I lifted her up and kissed her everywhere—her lovely breasts, tits, navel, her dimpled ass, her mound—but I didn't stick my tongue in her cunt. I'd never liked the idea of oral sex. Apparently, she didn't like it, either.

"There's only one place for your lovely lips." I said, and I kissed her endlessly.

"Pat, I've got to tell you that I saw you drive into the station and I stalled around. When you bumped into me, I know it was accidental, but I was glad for the chance to talk. I knew we'd hit it off."

So it began. Teri and I drove to Miami after she returned the rented van. We stayed together while I worked across the USA, fucking together several times every night. Then, in Seattle, an argument arose from a minor difference of opinion and Teri stormed out of the hotel. I saw my stupidity in seconds and ran after her, but she had vanished. I searched all night and even hired a private detective, but to no avail.

Just a couple of weeks ago I saw a van crossing the border, headed for Vancouver, while I was crossing south to Seattle. For sure it was Teri at the wheel. By the time I'd turned around and got back through Canadian customs, she'd vanished again.

HUMPIN' JACK FLASH

*M*y marriage and sex life with Laurie was satisfactory, but becoming more and more routine. Swinging was out because she couldn't accept my dorking anyone else. So was a ménage. "No bitch is going to eat my cunt," she said. "Another man, maybe."

That was food for fantasy! Seeing Laurie's beautiful pussy impaled, or seeing a big, blue-veined cock in her mouth—yeah, I could go for that! Unfortunately, she claimed she could never do it in my presence or with my knowledge. Since secrecy is too much like cheating, we found ourselves at an impasse. But a fire was lit!

Laurie and I center our social life around a private club. Besides the live music and camaraderie, there is plenty of pot smoking in the parking lot. Many of our friends would love to get in Laurie's panties. Some would come in their pants if they knew we often fantasize about them.

Fantasy was all it was for a long while. Then one day my friend Jack and I stepped outside to share a joint. Jack played drums with the band, but he was also a photographer. When I saw that his van was loaded with photography equipment, my mind went clickety-click! Laurie and I had fooled around with cameras, trying to take pictures of ourselves fucking and sucking, and I knew she got off on it.

After the next dance set, Laurie and I invited Jack out for a little herb. Naturally the conversation turned to photography and our lack of success at it. He took the bait and asked, "Wanna use my equipment?"

"Naw," I replied. "I can't take decent pictures. Why don't you take them?"

"Jim, are you crazy?" Laurie protested, but with a sparkle in her eye that wasn't from the cannabis.

Back inside, she asked if I'd been serious. "Hell yes!" I said. "What's it going to hurt if he looks?" Best ease into it slowly, I knew, but I also knew if she ever let Jack get that far, she'd probably get fucked by him.

After the club closed that night, the three of us hopped into the van and headed for the beach. Laurie was nervous. She said she wanted to change from her dress and high heels. Under her dress she was wearing nothing but a garter belt and long hose.

Our moonlight session began tamely. But we were already on a roller coaster with but one way to go, and Laurie soon consented to pose for some titty shots—and she's really got a pair of melons, size 36C with silver-dollar nipples. A bit more coaxing convinced Laurie to hike up her dress, exposing her black bush. More cajoling from me and her knees parted. Jack set up a battery-powered spotlight that found her pussy lips engorged and dripping. Very little effort was required to get her naked—and no effort at all to get her to masturbate for the camera.

I nixed Jack's suggestion that I fuck Laurie while he got it on film. "No," I said. "Let me take the pictures. You fuck her." Laurie's eyes popped open when she heard this, but she never missed a stroke on her clit.

Jack's cock is bigger than mine, but I was too wound up for jealousy. Using a zoom lens, I got to within inches of her gaping pussy being filled by his thick shaft. I snapped several shots of her humping her crotch to meet and take it all! Incredible! I soon laid the camera down, however. I was too horny for any more picture-taking. I needed release and considered beating off.

Then I thought about Laurie's mouth. She and Jack were going at it missionary-style, and she took my meat in her mouth like a wild animal. Humping, grinding, twisting, turning, her gyrations caused my dick to slip out and I was shocked when Jack immediately engulfed it in his mouth. No way could I back out as he sucked it all the way in and greedily swallowed the quart of come I couldn't hold back when he and Laurie reached tremendous climaxes.

Jack and I switched places after a brief rest. Fucking Laurie while she slurped and deep-throated his rod was fantastic. Before it was over, though, she held his one-eyed monster up to my face. I sure hope that sucking one dick doesn't make you a real cocksucker!

ITALIAN STALLION

*M*y name is Scott and I'm a horny twenty-year-old Italian who loves to eat pussy! I'm about five feet ten inches tall and weigh about one hundred sixty pounds. I have piercing blue eyes and light brown hair. I've always done more than all right with the ladies and, up till recently, I honestly considered myself God's gift to the fairer sex.

Fran is about five feet seven inches tall with beautiful blonde hair and sensuously amusing big brown eyes! She weighs about one hundred fifteen pounds and she's got a body that won't quit! She's a perfect "10"! I usually go for gorgeous blondes with blue eyes, but in Fran's case I made an exception, as who wouldn't after seeing her tantalizing walk and tasting her kiss of death (so to speak)?

It all started one rainy afternoon at her log cabin in Pennsylvania. I asked her if she'd ever had a back rub and, to my surprise, she said no—adding that she'd like to see what it was like. The reason for my surprise was that she had been married for seven years (now, at the age of twenty-five, she's a widow). I jumped at the opportunity to show her what she'd been missing for all these years. Having wanted to make it with her since first laying eyes on her, the mere thought of just touching this chick had my balls in an uproar! I knew that within the hour I'd be engaged in the hottest sexual encounter I could ever imagine!

I recalled a bit of advice from my favorite Italian uncle, Joe, who told me, "Always remember, Scotty, you gotta kiss it first." When Uncle Joe's words crossed my mind I envisioned Fran's hot cunt pouring pussy cream into the depths of my throat and I began foaming at the mouth.

During her first back rub, I could sense that Fran was really getting turned on when I "accidentally on purpose" fondled her hard, erect nipples. As my hands slid up along her shirt, she let out squeals of sheer excitement. Then I whispered into her ear that I wanted nothing more than to lick her sweet pussy. I remember telling her that she reminded me of a beautiful genie and asking her if I could make a wish. "Anything, master," she replied breathlessly. "Anything at all!"

The first wish popped into my mind. "I wish your skirt would disappear along with your shirt, leaving you with nothing on except your panties," I said. Her reply was, "Your every wish is my command."

God, was I hard at the sight of her translucent white bloomers! All I could think of was burying my face in that soft blonde bush of my newfound genie's. Next she pleaded, "Make another wish, master," and all I could think of was for her to spread her legs and beg me to kiss her pussy. She readily obliged, saying, "Kiss it, master. Drink my come, master. Oh, master, please drink my come."

By now I couldn't resist anymore. I had to have her! I tore her undies from her hot pleading thighs and went down on her. Kissing her inner thighs, I found pussy juice already streaming down them. I became aware of her delicate and irresistible feminine odor as I then dove into her golden-hued muff and quickly found her throbbing love-button!

Fran begged me to show her what us Italian guys are all about, and you can bet I did. Driven by pure passion and lust, I grabbed her by her hips with both hands and thrust my pointed tongue deep into her burning cunt! She bucked and screamed at the top of her lungs as I worked my tongue in and out of her. My Dago nose was bumping against her clit in rhythm to the song coming from the radio, "Too Fast for Love" by Motley Crüe!

We never did make it to the bedroom, but when I told her that she should make a wish, she said, "Fuck me, master! Come in me!" I felt I owed it to her, so right there on the floor, I climbed aboard and shot the mother load deep inside her. All I can say now is that our two-and-one-half-month-old son must have gotten his looks from his mom. He's already a little stud and, with his blond hair and blue eyes, I know he's gonna be capable of driving women wild!

BACKSEAT DRIVER

I was eighteen and so was she. I had loved her since eighth grade. We lived in a small town in the hills of northern Minnesota.

I loved her from a distance, without sexual overtones, until one hot summer day. Then, one day in July, she was walking down Main Street with a friend as I came out of the drugstore. I think my heart stopped as I stood spellbound, watching her. She had the most beautiful tan I'd ever seen. She was wearing black shorts and a white halter. As she walked by and out of sight, I felt the first true stirring of desire in my loins. This was the first time I'd felt any great need to have sex with a woman.

From that day forward, my love for her was accented by a burning sexual desire, which I did not fully understand. Virtually every night I masturbated while fantasizing about her and her beautiful black shorts.

It was later in our senior year before we ever dated. I was always too shy to ask her out. She had been going with the "rich kid" in town since she was a freshman. I'd remained a virgin. Athletics and schoolwork had dominated my time, for I hoped to earn a scholarship to a major university. Through it all, though, my total and burning love for her never waned.

Then, in December, at a school dance, she came up to me and said, "Aren't you ever going to ask me out?" I was very embarrassed and mumbled something stupid. She took my hand and said, "Come on, let's dance." The band was playing a medley of slow pieces and, as we danced, I felt my cock rising against my zipper. I almost died of embarrassment when my swollen member brushed against her leg every now and then. Slowly she began to press her beautiful, slender body against me until my erection was impressed against her abdomen. The ballroom (actually our school gym) seemed almost nonexistent to me. All I could think about was her sexy body and the sensations awakening in my cock. I heard my voice saying, "I love you," and I heard her repeat the words after me.

I'm not certain how we got there, but we were soon in the backseat of my '57 Ford, frantically feeling each other's body and kissing without letup.

She wasn't very experienced but knew far more than I did. She became a playful leader while I did little more than writhe and moan in anticipation. She undid her blouse and bra and her small, white, beautiful jutting breasts were suddenly mine to see. They were delicately traced with what remained of her summer tan. My breath came in uneven gasps as she pulled my face to them. I beard myself uttering the word "fuck" as I nibbled, licked and sucked her hardened nipples. She laughed gleefully and said, "Let's take off our clothes."

The sight of her naked body was almost more than I could bear. She was beautiful beyond my hottest dream of her. The whiteness of her lower belly contrasted sharply with the large V of soft, dark, curly hair below. My cock was so hard as I gawked at her naked body that I thought it would break. She softly touched the end of it and said, "You're losing your oil." Looking away from her pussy for a moment, I saw the droplets of pre-come falling one by one from the tip of my throbbing cock.

She slowly lay down on the seat and spread her legs so that I could see the pink between her pussy lips as they parted for me. She gently pulled me onto her and, as I swung one of my legs over her, my cock rubbed against her thigh. Immediately I started squirting come all over her legs and stomach. I gasped and moaned in ecstasy as my cock released all my pent-up desire. Before I finished coming, she placed my cock into her sweet pussy and I felt like the world could end at that moment without any regrets on my part.

I came twice more before pulling my cock from her love-nest. We kissed and talked for hours afterward and I managed two more orgasms, perhaps more aptly described as two painful spasms from an aching but lustful and quite empty cock.

WHEELS OF FORTUNE

I'm in my early twenties, stand five feet eleven inches tall, and have a muscular build, which is lucky for without it I would never have survived that strenuous and exciting night. It started at a party. Since most of my friends were working or out of town, I figured I'd have to go by myself and just play wallflower. Boy, was I wrong! Some people that I knew showed up, and before long, we were knee-deep in a drinking game. The game was going into extra innings when I decided I'd better cool it since I had to drive home. So I got up and literally ran into a girl I'd known in high school. We started talking, but it became increasingly harder to hear what she was saying as the party grew livelier. She suggested we go for a walk. We did, and it was really pleasant, but it ended far too soon—before I'd had a chance to do anything. In hopes it would lead somewhere, I offered her a ride to her dorm. I parked my cycle in the lot behind the building, where she got off and started to go, then abruptly turned around and came back to push me gently onto my motorcycle seat. While I sat there stunned, she knelt quickly between my legs, unzipped my fly, and pulled out my quickly hardening cock.

"I can never resist a gentleman," she said, more to my throbbing dick than to me, before she kissed it lightly. Her lips were so soft and caressing as she slowly slid her mouth up and down my manhood, her warm tongue lapping from the base all the way to the head of my dick. It wasn't long before I sent my come shooting down her hungry throat, while I stifled my moans and grunts in my hands. As carefully as she could, she slipped my dick back into my pants and zipped me up. When she stood up, she ran her tongue over her lips and captured an escaping drop of come from the corner of her mouth so seductively that I was instantly hard again. She gave me a peck on the cheek and hurried off. As I stood there stunned but satisfied, I heard someone clapping behind me. I laughed to myself and got the hell out of there to return to the party. The night was still young and I badly needed a drink.

I was just getting off my cycle when I saw that my roommate had joined the party. He was talking with a blonde who displayed a very full set of breasts and a beautiful round ass. I said, "Hello," and she smiled. When she saw my helmet in my hand, her smile evolved from friendly into excited rather quickly. She immediately asked if she could go for a ride, and who am I to refuse such a request?

I drove her around the neighborhood for a while, going fast enough to make her clutch my waist and press her warm, firm breasts against my back. Looking for a place where we could be alone, I parked in a dark schoolyard and asked her if she would like to check the place out. She quickly agreed as we walked into the shadows. Within a second I had covered her fabulous tits with my hands and pressed my lips against hers in a passionate kiss. Moving my hands across her flat stomach to her crotch, I caressed her wet pussy through her jeans, making her breathe faster and more heavily. I was kissing her neck and ear when she whispered rather forcefully into my ear that she wanted me to take my pants down right then because she wanted to do it. Again, who am I to argue? Moving deeper into the shadows, I yanked my pants to my ankles and eagerly sat down on the steps, while she hurriedly removed her pants and dripping panties. She nearly jumped on top of my rock-hard cock, and before I could catch my breath, she was rocking back and forth so hard that I thought she was going to rip my dick off. Just as I was falling in time with her rhythm, she started to buck and moan and scream in the throes of passion. Suddenly a car's headlights flashed over us. She gathered her senses and as fast as she had taken her clothes off, she just stepped back into them, leaving me sitting there with my pole waving in the breeze. I reluctantly put my clothes on and drove her back to the party, where she thanked me and disappeared into the house.

Feeling frustrated, I walked into the house and ran into the hostess of the party, a girl I had been seeing on again and off again for the past several months. Lynn asked if we could go somewhere private to talk. After twenty minutes of riding through the deserted streets, we came to a desolate part of town. I parked the cycle, wondering what she would do this time. She didn't disappoint me. As always happens when she drinks and rides a motorcycle, she was hornier than hell. No sooner had I stepped off my bike than she had wrapped one arm around my waist and was desperately massaging my cock through my pants with her other hand. Not willing to be left out, I quickly began massaging her soft, ample tits and pulling her shirt and bra up around her shoulders. I flicked my tongue teasingly around her swollen nipples, which usually drives her crazy. She was getting so worked up that she could barely talk without gasping for breath, and I wasn't all that steady either, especially with her hand inside my pants fervently pulling and stroking my cock. So we both zipped up and straightened up before racing back to her house.

When we got there, the party had died down considerably, and she led me rather sternly through what was left of the crowd to her bedroom. Once the door was shut, she quickly helped me remove my clothes, then slowly and seductively stripped off her own. Totally naked, she playfully leapt onto her water bed with her legs spread wide and her head thrown back. Taking my cue, I eased between her legs and slowly kissed and nipped my way from her toes up her long, luscious legs. Licking teasingly around her steaming cunt, I continued to her navel, which I tickled with my tongue, making her laugh. Then I trailed my tongue across her stomach, leaving traces of hot, hungry saliva, and ascended to her breasts, which were heaving with excitement. I kissed her more forcefully around her nipples, up to her earlobes and back down to her right nipple, which I suddenly sucked into my mouth, making her gasp with pleasure.

Just when I sensed she was on the verge of coming, I stopped and slowly trailed kisses to her pouting cunt lips. I sucked on one lip, pulling gently before moving to the other, then plunged my tongue deep within her pussy. Her body tightened as I fucked her with my tongue, brought her to the edge of another orgasm, and then stopped again, lightly kissing her clit as she cooled down. When she was calm enough, I started sucking her clit and playing with her nipples with both hands. This time I didn't stop. I sucked and nipped and licked her clit until she wrapped her legs so tightly around my head that I could hardly breathe. Finally, with a trailing scream, she came. Her sweet wetness had only partly quenched my thirst.

Prying my head from the vise grip of her legs, I quickly shoved my cock as deeply as possible into her still-quivering cunt. Lynn instantly dug her fingertips into my back and shoulders as I pumped away, bringing her just to the brink, then easing away until she screamed for me to fuck her and not stop. That I did. I fucked her until I felt my balls tighten and shoot my hot load deep within her pulsating, gripping pussy. We collapsed for a short rest before feasting on the second course and the third and the fourth. . . .

I don't quite understand the magic appeal of motorcycles for some girls, but the two go together well enough to convince me that I'm never selling my bike.

THE NIGHT IS YOUNG

I'm in my mid-forties, with a Dolly Parton figure (though I am a flaming redhead) which I'm very proud of. I still get admiring glances from men of all ages.

One weekend last summer, my son asked if he could bring his college roommate home to spend the weekend. I said sure and when they showed up, I was sitting by the pool in my bikini.

As Mike, the roommate, was introduced, his eyes roamed unashamedly over my body and I blushed in mingled embarrassment and pleasure that this young man was so obviously attracted to me. I suggested that they join me by the pool, and when they returned I could see that Mike was a fine specimen of young manhood. He had a body like Michelangelo's David, as perfectly proportioned as a Greek god, and there was a bulge in his swimsuit that left no doubt that he was very well-endowed.

I couldn't take my eyes off Mike's body as he dived into the pool and swam around. I must admit that my son's roommate had begun to inspire some very naughty thoughts in my mind.

After the swim, my son announced that he had a date and would be out late. He invited Mike along and said he could get an extra girl, but Mike said he was tired and had some studying to do for a summer course he was taking. He'd just stay here this evening and cram if I didn't mind, he added. I noticed the emphasis he put on the word "cram," and it made me tingle in anticipation.

Since my husband was out of town on business, Mike and I were left alone that evening. It was a warm night, and I didn't bother to change out of my bikini. Also, to be honest, I was really getting turned on by Mike's obvious interest in my body and wanted him to keep getting a good look at everything I had.

I made some dinner and we discussed Mike's schoolwork. He was a varsity track-and-field man and had won a number of events. I couldn't resist asking him if he had a girlfriend. Mike just smiled and asked me if I really wanted to hear the whole story. I felt I might be taking this a bit too far but was too curious to resist, so I said yes.

Then Mike began to describe in graphic detail his quite numerous and really torrid sexual experiences with coeds and older women, too. He said he really liked older women, that they were infinitely superior to their younger sisters. This young stud had really been around!

He talked for over an hour, and I began to get horny as hell. He was really good at describing sex, and I felt my pussy getting wet.

Suddenly, without warning, he came over, put his arms around me and gave me a long soul kiss as he fumbled with my bikini top and then began to fondle my nipples.

I was hot as hell but realized this had gone far enough and began gently to push him away. His hand then dived into my bikini panties and his fingers found my clit. I have a clit the size of the tip of my little finger and it is incredibly sensitive. In the state I was in, his touch was like an electric shock. I moaned in pleasure and felt all my inhibitions vanish. Mike then kissed me, lifted me in his arms and carried me into the bedroom.

As he laid me on the bed, he was already pulling off my bikini panties. I was too far gone with frenzied lust to do anything more than mumble a feeble assent as he dived between my legs and began to eat me. He tongued my clit in an expert manner and brought me to a shattering orgasm almost immediately.

As I lay back panting, Mike dropped his trunks and revealed his monster meat—it was at least nine inches long, as thick as my wrist, with a beautiful upward curve. I'd never seen anything so magnificent—or as appealing.

Before I had a chance to say a word, he had raised my legs above my shoulders and inserted just the tip in my dripping pussy.

He slowly began to pump just the head of his cock in and out of my pussy. It was driving me crazy—I ached to have the whole thing inside me.

Finally, I could bear it no longer and asked him to shove it in all the way. Mike just smiled and told me to tell him how much I wanted him to fuck me. The bastard knew how much I wanted him and was going to tease me, but I needed him so badly I went along with his game.

Soon I began to get crazy with lust and begged him to fuck me. In one great thrust, Mike rammed his monster in me up to the hilt and then just held it there as I began frantically to squirm, begging him to screw me. As I came to a fantastic orgasm, he began pounding away for all he was worth and soon I could feel his cock spasm as he shot load after load in my love-box.

We just lay there for a while. Then Mike began slowly to ream out my aching cunt. He was still hard as a rock and he asked me if I would like him to frig my clit. I moaned my consent as he turned me over and slowly inserted himself, inch by inch, back into my willing pussy while he expertly fingered my clit. Soon I was heaving back against him as I approached another climax and his monster began to penetrate all the way into my cunt. We came almost at the same time in an incredible burst of ecstasy.

We had been fucking for nearly two hours and both needed a break, so I mixed some martinis as Mike took a shower. While Mike was in the bathroom, my son called and said he was spending the night with his girlfriend and wouldn't be home until the next afternoon. I told him that was just fine and joined Mike in the shower to tell him the good news. We couldn't keep our hands off each other in the shower, and after washing each other off and drying, we adjourned to the living room. Mike put his arm around me on the couch as, totally nude, we sipped our martinis. Mike asked if I had any good videos and I blushed since my husband had quite a collection and I really got turned on watching them. I asked him what kind he liked and he said orgy scenes.

I felt honestly embarrassed even though this young stud had just had me every which way, because I get terribly turned on by orgy videos. And I've always had a constant fantasy about trying it out some day. I brought a stack and asked Mike to take his pick. He selected one where Vanessa del Rio takes on half a dozen guys, one of my favorites though I didn't tell him so.

As the action got hotter, Mike's hands roamed over my body, getting me hot again as we watched Vanessa getting it from three guys at once.

Mike began to tell me about his experiences, describing the studs he said he could get me anytime I wanted. I went absolutely wild again, losing all control, and was soon on my knees sucking his meat for all I was worth. He shot another tremendous load down my throat and I eagerly squeezed him dry and licked his beautiful cock clean.

We were soon in bed again doing a fabulous 69 until I could stand it no longer and got on top of Mike. I rode him like a bronco while rubbing myself off to another great orgasm. Then I collapsed, exhausted. I had never had more than two orgasms with my husband and he never got it off more than twice with me. As I fell asleep with Mike's arms around me, I knew this would not be the last time I saw Mike. I knew I'd want him again and again.

During the night I woke up to find Mike on top of me, slowly rubbing the tip of his cock on my pussy lips. I asked him how long I had been asleep while he was caressing me and he said he'd just started. I reached down and squeezed the tip of his cock and felt wet, sticky fluid. I raised my fingers to my lips and licked them off. It was my own pussy juice! Somehow, this turned me on incredibly and Mike lowered himself to my pussy and began eating me out again, licking up my juices. When his tongue began to work over my clit I knew I was headed for another incredible climax and began to beg him to get me more young studs. I went crazy again and a torrent of obscenities poured from my lips as Mike mounted me again and shot his fourth load in my cunt, all the while telling me how I was going to love having half a dozen of his friends screw my brains out. When we woke up late that morning, Mike, incredibly, was ready for more. I was too exhausted to do anything but lie there as he spent nearly an hour getting off a fifth time. As we lay there in each other's arms, the front door opened—my son was home! Mike made a beeline for his room, and I rushed into the bathroom and ran the shower. My son didn't notice anything, but that was the last time Mike and I had alone. As they left the next day, Mike slipped a piece of paper into my hand and gave me a wink. It was a number of a friend of his who would contact him when I wanted to see him again. My husband came home that night and we had the best sex ever—my night with Mike had done great things for our sex life. Of course, I didn't tell my husband.

I tried to resist calling Mike, but the next time my husband went out of town on business, I lasted about two hours before I was on the phone dialing Mike's friend. But that's another story.

Mike has moved out of the dorm and now has an apartment of his own. Though he has lots of girlfriends, he usually finds time for a date with me when my husband's out of town.

Mike has introduced me to a couple of his friends who join in from time to time, and I've found that having two or three guys at a time is a lot more fun than just fantasizing about it! Best of all, my husband's and my sex life is better than ever. If only he knew!

MR. FIX-IT

I am a truck driver and I often spend many lonely hours crossing some empty desert or another. But every once in a while I get an eyeful of some babe sunning herself as she passes me in her car—or, even better, a girl giving head to a guy as he drives down the road. Things like that really wake me up!

But the experience I would like to relate went beyond mere looking.

A few weeks ago I was hauling a load of cut lumber from Vancouver to Los Angeles. I was cruising through the barren San Joaquin Valley of California when I noticed a bright-red Triumph coming up behind me. I could see the driver in my mirror, a cute young thing with long blonde hair. As the car pulled even with me, the girl flashed a smile as she looked up at me through her open sunroof. She was driving in my favorite position—left foot on the seat with the knee against the door, dress pulled up almost to her crotch, with her long, tan legs and bare feet soaking up the rays and with her right hand at the bottom of the steering wheel. Her left arm was resting on the windowsill of her door. She wasn't going much faster than I was, so I gave my rig a kick and was soon pacing her, getting a good look and hoping she'd show me more.

Some girls, once they know what you are up to, will take off and leave you in the dust. Not this one. She just kept even with me, flashing that sexy smile. Naturally, I smiled back at her, glancing ahead every few seconds to make sure I wasn't about to run into anyone. Fortunately, the traffic on I-5 was pretty light, but every once in a while she would have to speed up and pull in ahead of me to let faster traffic pass. But she always came back, each time showing a little more leg and pulling her left foot closer to her crotch.

Soon her foot was resting on the dashboard between the steering wheel and the windshield post. Then she really got daring and stuck her left foot out the window, resting her ankle on the side-view mirror. This allowed the wind to blow into her car and her dress flipped up around her navel, exposing her skimpy panties to my view! I gave her a shocked, horny look and she gave me that hot smile and threw her head back with a laugh, her blonde hair cascading over the headrest behind her. Then she ran her tongue along her teeth. She made no move to smooth her dress down! I gave her a big blast on my air horn to show my approval.

Another fast-moving truck was closing in behind her, so she pulled her foot back into the car and sped up to pull in front of my truck. As the truck passed, I gave the driver a bored-looking wave, hoping he was in too much of a hurry to notice my "lover" in the red Triumph. He was—and he didn't. As he passed the car, the woman tossed something out through her sunroof and it snagged on my right-hand windshield wiper. I flinched (I once had an owl slam through the windshield, so I am a bit jumpy about things coming at the glass) before I realized it was her panties! I couldn't believe it!!

A long line of cars passed us, following in the slipstream of the faster truck, so it was some time before my friend could move her car back over and get next to me. She had put her foot back on the mirror and her legs were spread as far as they could possibly be in the car. I got my first look at her beautiful pussy, its lips pouting out invitingly. At this point the girl began to play it cool, ignoring my presence and not looking up at me. Steering her Triumph with her right hand, she began to stroke her pussy lips with the other. Soon her hand was going a mile a minute, pulling on her clit and shoving two fingers into her pink cunt. Her left thigh began to quiver and she was chewing on her lower lip. Her sheer white dress became soaked with perspiration and I could see that she was braless. She began to hump her hand and I began to have doubts as to whether either of us was in control of his or her vehicle at that point!

She came (pun intended) back down to earth and slowed her fingers to a gentle stroking motion. She then pulled her foot back into the car and pressed her heel against her wet cunt and licked her fingers clean. Then she looked up at me with that wide smile, waved and sped off.

I was just catching my breath when I saw the Triumph swerve to the shoulder about a mile ahead of me. The right front tire had blown out, but she was able to keep the car under control and stop it safely. Being the gentleman that I am, I pulled onto the shoulder and parked behind her car to help her change the tire. She sat there, beet red in her embarrassment (I'd caught her with her pants down, as it were), but I complimented her on her performance and, as I changed the tire, she relaxed. She got out of the car and stood next to me as I worked, making small talk with me.

After I had put her spare on and jacked the car down to tighten the lug nuts, she sat on the fender, giving me another beaver-shot as we talked. Her pussy was dripping wet again and only inches from my face. She smelled delicious. I cracked some dumb joke and she laughed, putting one foot on my shoulder as I tightened the last nut. Unable to resist the temptation, I pulled my gloves off and slid my hands up her legs and into the wettest pussy I have ever felt!

She immediately stopped laughing and began to moan, leaning back against the windshield post to give me complete access to her cunt. I leaned forward, pulling her to the edge of the fender, and buried my hot tongue in her slit. She tasted better than she smelled! I suddenly realized we were in full view of passing traffic and I pulled back. Fortunately, it had gotten pretty dark and no one seemed to have noticed us! She began to laugh again and got a full-blown case of the giggles. She laughed so hard that she said she had to pee. Since there were no rest rooms around for miles, I told her to go squat beside my cab where nobody could see her and to let it go, which she did.

I put the flat tire and tools in her trunk, closed the lid and walked up to her. It had apparently taken a while for her to get over her giggle-fit, because she was still squatting on the ground. "Gee," I said, "as long as you are down there, it's time to pay your bill for having your tire changed." I expected her to laugh it off, but she looked up at me with very serious eyes. I didn't blink but looked expectantly into her eyes, holding her gaze. She didn't look away but reached for my belt and said yes.

This was an immediate turn-on for me, as I have always fantasized about finding a beautiful woman who would do almost anything. I was hard already, but the way she'd said yes and the look of animal lust in her eyes almost made me come right then. I decided to play her, to see how far I could take her.

While she undid my belt, I reached down and pulled her dress off over her head and dropped it to the ground. It landed in a puddle of oil below her pussy, but she made no move to pull it out. My pants dropped to my ankles and I pushed down my shorts. She began to kiss the tip of my cock. She stroked my shaft with one hand and held on to my hip with the other, licking a drop of pre-come and trying to force her tongue into my peehole. She then began to lick my balls.

It had been a hot day and I could smell the sweat wafting from my crotch and I was suddenly self-conscious. But then she said, "I love the smell and taste of a man's sweat!" and began to lick under my balls and my self-consciousness went out the door. Between slurps, she told me how she had always wanted to "get down and dirty" but her husband was a wimpy "neatnik" who wouldn't let her touch him unless he was freshly showered. She wanted to revel in the taste of a "real man"—taste everything he had to offer, clean every inch of his body with her tongue. Still looking into my eyes, she said, "I'd do absolutely anything for a man who knows what he wants and is not afraid to take it!" Then she slid her mouth over my cock.

I couldn't believe what was happening! A man would have to be dead to not hear the invitation in her words and see the pleading in her eyes! I looked around to make sure we could not be seen, and, since we were completely shielded from passing cars by my truck, I went for broke. I slipped my meat into her mouth and she did not pull away. She shifted her body from the squatting position to her knees, both to steady herself against my thrusts and so she could lift her chin a little and give me access to her throat.

I moved my cock as hard and as fast as I could, sliding it easily down her throat and burying her pert nose in my pubic hair. My balls were heavy with come and made slapping noises each time they hit her chin, which was wet with saliva. I pulled out every five or six strokes so she could breathe. She loved it! So did I— and I soon let loose the largest load I think I ever have, filling her hot mouth. I held her head with my dick in her mouth until I had stopped shaking and the last few squirts had rinsed out her tonsils. She looked up at me with wild eyes, and I saw a stream of come leaking out from around my dick.

"Why don't you swallow that?" I whispered to my beautiful cocksucker. "You've never drunk a man's come, have you?" She shook her head. Again she looked at me with those blazing eyes and then gulped down my cream. It was difficult with my soft cock in the way, but after three gulps she managed to swallow it all (that's a really neat feeling, by the way).

"Did you enjoy that?" I asked. She nodded, her arms wrapped around my waist to steady herself. "Better than your husband?" Again she nodded, this time with a muffled groan. "Would you like to do it again?" Another nod and groan, and she made no attempt to pull away.

"Mmmm," she said. "I've always wanted to taste everything a man had to give, and I love it!" She put her fingers to her chin to wipe the last of the spilled jism into her mouth, but I asked her not to, to leave it there. By then I was hard again and began to slowly stroke my meat. She threw herself on my penis and began to fondle and lick it, and soon had it buried deep in her throat again. She was voracious! I surrendered myself to her hungry mouth and just stood there as she worked it in and out, up and down, making mewling noises deep in her throat until I exploded again. Again a few drops remained on her chin.

"Now please leave it there until you get to wherever you're going," I told her. She said I could count on it, and I helped her to her feet. I picked up her wet dress and walked her to her car. A truck went by and, as soon as we had a clear shot, I walked around to the driver's door of her car and opened it for her so she could slide her naked ass behind the wheel. I tossed her dress into the backseat and bent to give her a good-bye kiss, realizing it was the first time we had kissed. I tweaked her left nipple and took one last finger-dive into her wet cunt. Then I brought my fingers to her lips and she licked them, thanking me for the experience.

The last I saw of her were her taillights fading down the road at a hundred miles an hour. I never knew her name, but I still have her panties hanging from my sun visor. Every time I drive down I-5 I look for her, but I know I'll never see her again. Too bad. I've been giving a lot of thought to teaching her to drive my truck. She can do better than settle for a wimp.

SCREEN TESTES

*M*y girlfriend and I are both very into sex and particularly enjoy masturbatory fantasies, which is one reason we really like to watch sex videos such as *Oral Majority 1, 2* and *3, Nymphette,* etc. We have often thought about doing some videos ourselves and recently got the chance. Since we both live in the San Francisco area and since most sex videos are shot either here or in Los Angeles, it was relatively easy to get linked up with a suitable video studio. Although not a full-length video, it was still quite fun.

We showed up at the photo studio and were met by a beautiful young lady who helped us fill out paperwork. Then she said she needed to interview us both before the shoot to make sure we were right for the parts. First she took Lisa into a room and asked her, among other things, if she knew these would be "wet sex" videos. The interviewer, whose name was Mary, explained that this referred to ejaculation by the male actor. She went on to explain that this involved the shooting of sperm on either the actress's torso, breasts or tummy and that these are also referred to as "full relief" shots. In these shots the actor, who becomes very excited during foreplay, is encouraged—when he is ready—to let his pent-up semen rush to freedom and squirt out, splattering wherever it pleases.

Lisa explained to Mary that she was aware of all this, since she and I frequently rent sex videos. In fact, I was kind of amazed when Lisa candidly explained to Mary that scenes in videos—like that in The Brat, starring Jamie Summers—where there is lots of erotic talk between the actors and actresses, really turns us on. And (I was surprised she volunteered this) Lisa said she really enjoyed watching the semen squirt as the actors climaxed outside the actresses. To her, somehow the amount of semen ejaculated was a measure of the actor's manliness and the sexual power of the actress.

By this time, Lisa's nipples were beginning to harden and poke against the thin material of her top (I think Mary was aware of this). Anyway, after complimenting her on her beautiful body, Mary asked if she would mind taking off her top so Mary could examine her breasts. But first, Mary told Lisa, she wanted her to just stand there with her sheer top on so Mary could observe her partially covered breasts. The top was so thin that Lisa's full, medium-size breasts were visible to Mary, who commented that it looked like Lisa had nice, pointy, high-centered nipples with medium areolae. Lisa knew that it was important to impress

Mary, so she offered to remove her top to provide a better look. Mary was very impressed and asked Lisa to touch her nipples so she could see them hard and erect. They were beautiful—pink, about a half inch long and a quarter inch in diameter—just like little penises crying out for stimulation.

Mary candidly asked Lisa if she realized what a delectable target her breasts would make for a swollen penis. Lisa smiled and admitted that my penis had splattered its three teaspoons of semen across her breasts many times. Mary smiled back and emphasized that the videos they were shooting called for copious male explosions on the actresses and that audiences very much enjoy watching wet climax shots. (I knew Lisa concurred one hundred percent!) Mary then told us that sex films had come a long way. Dialogue had become more important because it, too, stimulates the viewer. As a result, she explained, "There is much more erotic talk leading up to the wet climax shots. We want to tease the viewer to the max but also make him or her aware of the fact that the teasing always leads up to a wild, wet climax." Mary pointed out that, since the advent of "safe sex," masturbation has become well accepted, and that their aim was to help the viewer enjoy the masturbatory experience "just as he or she enjoys a fine meal."

Well, Lisa and I agreed. Obviously very impressed with Lisa, Mary said she needed a quick peek at Lisa's rear end and genitals. Lisa pulled her jeans down and stood there in her thin, almost transparent, panties. Mary admired the contour of Lisa's tight little butt, but when Lisa turned around, Mary's eyes lit up. Lisa's skimpy panties were very wet! She was obviously quite excited—and she was a little embarrassed, too, that Mary was seeing her in this state. Mary just stood there wordlessly, her eyes virtually devouring my sexy Lisa.

Lisa stood there and let Mary stare. Her breasts and pink nipples were gorgeous and her swollen genitals were flowering open against her almost transparent panties. It looked like Lisa's pussy was hairless, just like a little girl's—except Lisa is twenty-two years old. Most of the actresses these days like to keep their vaginal lips bare for the camera and obviously Mary wouldn't have to tell Lisa that. Mary smiled coyly as she examined Lisa's spreading pussy-petals through her panties. Mary must have sensed that I was getting awfully hot from watching all this and she told me to take off my slacks so she could examine my lower body. I was rock-hard now and my pre-come had been oozing steadily into my underwear as I watched Mary examine Lisa. By the time I pulled my slacks off and stood at attention for Mary, my penis was jutting out like a flagpole.

This was becoming an increasingly sexy situation and, not having ejaculated in four days, I was really looking forward to making Lisa a lot wetter and me several ounces lighter. I knew Mary would probably want to watch me squirt, because sex-video audiences like to see male actors make the actresses really wet, and Mary said she wanted to use men who discharge lots of semen. Well, I hadn't ejaculated yet, but the pre-come was really oozing from the little slit in my penis and dribbling down onto the rug. I think Mary thought I was about to pop, because she half smiled and quickly handed me a couple of tissues. I told her that I was leaking pre-come only because I was coveting Lisa's now totally naked, beautiful body, which was really turning me on. Mary asked Lisa to ever so gently insert her fingers in her vagina to make her sex lips flower open even wider. Mary (and I) could see plainly that Lisa was getting excited, and Lisa couldn't resist the temptation to gently rub the little pink helmet now protruding from the top of her inviting slit.

Mary said that this "interview" would be similar to the movies she would ask us to appear in, so she asked if we would mind if she watched as I penetrated Lisa. Her only request was that I shouldn't come inside Lisa, because she wanted to observe the ejaculation. I knew how important this was. As I've said, Lisa and I especially like the wet climax shots in sex videos and there is nothing worse than waiting in anticipation for the explosion, only to see a couple of weak dribbles. Lisa and I particularly like

to watch Peter North–type explosions on actresses, and we knew
we could show Mary just that.

Well, Lisa was really excited now. Her open labia were very
swollen and hanging outside her equally inflamed inner lips. Of
course, as I looked at this beautiful nymph, my penis just got
harder (if that was possible) and continued to drip a thin, clear
drool of pre-come onto the rug. (Gosh! What if pre-come stains
rugs?) Mary was exciting us more with the suggestive comments
she was making. She smiled and asked me to stand real still. Then
she got down on her hands and knees and cupped my testicles in
her palm. She squeezed ever so gently and commented that they
seemed full enough of semen to be crying out for ejaculation.

Mary asked Lisa to bend over and then gestured for me to slide
into Lisa's cunt from behind. Boy, I was looking forward to that
feeling of being inside her. My penis brushed against her thighs,
leaving thin trails of crystal clear pre-come fluid. Lisa giggled. In
the coolness of the room, the pre-come trails were cooling
quickly and kind of tickled her. As I stood close, I reached around
to her beautiful breasts and massaged her pretty pink nipples between my thumbs and forefingers. It was so exciting that I felt a
tremendous urge to ejaculate right there on the outside of Lisa's
cunt lips. I quickly grabbed my penis and squeezed hard at the
base to stop it from spurting until I was really ready. Thank goodness it worked! Oh, sure, I was still leaking pre-come, but at least
my semen hadn't spilled prematurely.

As I penetrated Lisa I felt the walls of her love-tube tighten
around my penis as if daring me to shoot off inside her. Lisa was
on the pill, so a series of semen bursts inside her would give her
only pleasure. Even so, I knew Mary wanted to watch the ejaculation just as Lisa and I do when we rent videos. Besides, Mary
wanted to be sure that I performed the Peter North–type explosion that Lisa and I had talked about. When Lisa rolled over on
her back and I stood up, Mary gestured for me to kneel over Lisa.
As I did, Mary grabbed the head of my penis and played with the
little slit, spreading pre-come all over the purple red knob. Mary

smiled down at Lisa's beautiful body. Lisa's pink nipples pointed straight up from the strawberry areolae of her firm, perky breasts. Her hairless slit was by now very inflamed, of course. Mary smiled and remarked that so far we'd shown that we had the sexual capacity to fit right in with her other actors and actresses. She mentioned that occasionally Carina Collins, Candi Evens and Peter North appeared in her videos and she asked if we'd like to work with them. Lisa and I said we'd love to.

Mary grabbed my penis again and began slowly masturbating me as she reached over with her other hand to Lisa's genitals and began manipulating her clit. Lisa and I were so hot we couldn't stand it, so Mary suggested I kneel over Lisa—like I was getting ready to penetrate her in the missionary position—and just let Mary stroke my penis to climax. I remarked that I would probably spray all over Lisa's breasts and tummy. Mary grinned and said she hoped it would be as good as we told her it would be. Anyway, Mary kept stroking until I announced I wasn't able to hold back anymore. She then quickly grabbed Lisa's panties and placed them on Lisa's tummy to give me a "target." She commanded, "Fire when ready!"

I could feel the semen straining to erupt. I heard Lisa yell, "Oh, here it comes, Mary!" as the first squirt shot onto the panties. The next squirt had more pressure and hit Lisa's breasts. Then ribbon after ribbon of thick, pearly white semen sprayed all over Lisa. Mary just sat there in disbelief, watching. "Oh, my!" she finally said. The milky white sperm drops made Lisa's pretty pink nipples shine wetly. Mary touched the creamy drops with her fingers and was pleasantly surprised at how hot they were. There were numerous little puddles on Lisa's tummy and, of course, the panties were drenched. Lisa's cunt lips were still quivering from Mary's masturbatory ministrations on her clit.

Mary then said, "Let's see how you get off, Lisa!" and started stroking Lisa faster and faster. Lisa's hips began bucking as she pumped against Mary's finger, her face contorted with pleasure. Beads of sweat began breaking out all over Lisa's torso, mixing with my milky sperm. Soon she lifted her body off the floor entirely and came.

Mary seemed very impressed and asked if we'd like to work with her video performers. We were overjoyed. "The sooner the better!" we said.

THE COCKTEASER AND THE SCREAMING PRICK

I was eighteen and a senior in high school. It was back when all the girls wore super-short miniskirts up to their asses that drove all the guys wild, including me. There was this one girl in my class my age, Sandy, who had a fantastic body and sure knew how to strut her stuff. She was tall with long blonde hair, big firm tits and a tight little ass that was always visible when she bent over even slightly in her micro-miniskirt. The problem was that she was one of those gold-digger types who only went out with guys who had new cars and plenty of cash to spend on her. She was a tease, strutting her stuff all around, because you knew you couldn't have a taste of that luscious body unless you had some big bucks.

The guys loved to watch her go by, but she pissed me off. One day she sat across from me in study hall. When she got up to go to the library, she swung those sleek long legs around from under her desk and gave more than a flash of the hot pink panties she was wearing. That got me really hot and bothered, but it also got me angry because she acted like she was too good to even talk to me.

One day I had just about had enough of her teasing. It was between classes and she was standing in the hall, flirting with a guy whose father owned a local construction business. She was leaning against the stairwell railing with that great ass of hers peeking out from underneath her miniskirt. The guy she was talking to left and she just stayed there looking down into the stairwell, knowing very well that her ass was drawing attention. Three of my friends were with me and they groaned aloud at the sight of her lacy white panties underneath her sheer panty hose. But I couldn't stand it anymore. As we walked by I reached out and got a firm grip on one of her ass-cheeks, gave a little squeeze and said to her, "Um, just the way I like 'em, nice and firm." She spun around instantly in a fury and said, "You son of a bitch!" I quickly replied, "You fucking tease! Quit asking for it if you don't want any!" My friends were standing by in shock, with their mouths just hanging open. I'll never forget her comeback in a million years. Without batting an eye she looked straight at me and said, "I want it bad, you just don't have enough flesh to satisfy my appetite." Howls of laughter went up from my friends as she turned victoriously and walked away. I was momentarily stunned. She won the battle, but I knew I would get her back.

From that day on it was never the same. Every time I saw her, we would jab each other with the crudest sexual insults we could think of, drawing raised eyebrows and jeers from both her friends and mine. One day we passed in the hall and I said, "Hi, cunt." She replied, "Hello, prick," and that was it. On another occasion she spouted some insult and I said, "Eat me." She turned and looked right at me and said in front of about ten witnesses, "Listen, I could suck you so hard it would make your mouth go dry." Everyone shrieked with laughter, and I was again left speechless.

This little contest went on for several weeks. Sometimes I would be the one embarrassed and sometimes she would be. But I could tell from her reactions that she was enjoying it as much as I was—and our friends loved it.

Then came the day I will never forget. There was a Halloween carnival and dance being held in one of the school's cafeterias. Some of the students had dates, but most of us were just looking for a little excitement. I was there with two of my best friends. We clowned around at the carnival and had a pretty good time. When the dance began, we each danced with several different girls. They had a live rock band, the music was really loud and soon everyone was working themselves into a frenzy. That's about the time I spotted Sandy and her equally snooty friend Rhonda sitting near the back of the room, acting as if no guy there was good enough for them. Sandy was dressed true to form. She wore a tight pink blouse that buttoned up the front and really showed off those magnificent tits of hers. As I looked closer I could see a little lacy bra beneath the almost transparent material. She had on a super-short black miniskirt that revealed every inch of her long satiny legs, which she had crossed over her tight little pussy. She was definitely a turn-on, but I ignored her as best I could and danced with a couple other girls who were close friends of mine. Still, just knowing she was sitting there aggravated the hell out of me.

Then the band announced that they were going to play a couple of slow songs and the lights went dim. The band started playing softly. I was looking around for a partner and spotted Sandy still sitting in the same chair. I thought to myself, "Oh, what the hell, give it a try." I walked over to her and was just about to ask her to dance when she turned her head, glared at me and snapped, "What the hell do you want?" Quick with a reply, I bent over and whispered in her ear, "I want to come inside of you." She was stunned. Without asking, I took her by the arm and led her out to the dance floor. I looked into her eyes. She wasn't embarrassed—she was melting with desire. I placed my hands on her waist and pulled her to me. She wrapped her arms around my neck as if we were old lovers and started swaying to the music. I could feel her firm breasts heaving against my chest. I had an instant hard-on. She pressed against me so forcefully that I knew she could feel every throbbing inch of me.

As the music went on she really started getting into it. She eventually worked my right leg in between her legs and started a slight up-and-down humping motion on my upper thigh. Her tiny skirt rode up slightly and I could feel her wet warmth on my leg as she ground her panty-hose-covered pussy into me. I reached underneath her skirt and grabbed her ass with both hands. She moaned softly and rested her face on my shoulder. There were other couples all around us, but no one noticed our activity because the room was so dark and crowded. When I began to caress her tight ass with my fingers I realized that I could feel nothing but a thin layer of nylon. She was not wearing any panties—only panty hose that were sheer to the waist! Then, just when I was about to slide my fingers down her ass into her wetness, the lights came on and the song ended. Suddenly she jerked her head up, pushed me roughly away and said, "You bastard!" I was taken entirely by surprise and just stood there and watched her walk back to her seat where her friend Rhonda was still sitting. A friend of mine came to me and said, "What's wrong, Romeo? Trying to get in her pants again?" But I was too bothered to give him a reply. I was hot and could feel my juices dribbling from my massive tool. And I was pissed off too! How could she be such a teasing little bitch?

I walked off the dance floor and looked over at her again. She was sitting there with her legs tightly crossed and her arms folded smugly across her chest, acting as if she were the princess of the ball. But I knew that her hot pussy had been gushing just a minute ago. What a bitch! If she had thought that I had had a new car sitting out in the parking lot, she would have eagerly hopped into my backseat and fucked my balls off.

I was just about ready to ignore her again when I saw her lean over to her friend and whisper something. Then she got up and went through a door which led into the adjoining kitchen area. Since this area was restricted, I wanted to know what she was up to. So I waited a few seconds and then followed her. The kitchen was completely dark but, after my eyes adjusted, I saw that she had gone outside through an exit that led to the truck loading dock. I quietly stepped out into the darkness. The area was fenced off from the school yard, surrounded by tall evergreen trees. I couldn't figure out where Sandy had gone. Then I heard a familiar low moan from the dark corner of the loading dock near a small stack of packing crates. I squinted my eyes and made out Sandy's form, facing away from me. She was moaning because she had her skirt pulled up and seemed to be furiously frigging her hot pussy with her right hand. What a magnificent performance she was putting on, and all for me!

My cock was throbbing and so hard that I couldn't just stand there anymore. As I came up slowly behind her, she became aware of my presence, quickly smoothed down her skirt and stood up. I walked right up behind her, pressed my body close to hers and whispered in her ear, "Need some help?" She silently responded by easing her body back into mine. She wanted me badly! She started to turn to face me, but I wrapped my arms around her waist and pulled her ass to my crotch. She began to rotate her hips and I slowly massaged my way up her belly until I had both of her beautiful tits cupped in my palms. She leaned her head back on my shoulder and moaned. I could feel her stiff nipples through her thin pink blouse and her lacy bra. I leaned over and bit her gently on her neck. She let out a little squeal and pressed back into me more forcefully. Then she took my hand from her breast and placed it on her upper thigh. I began to massage her leg just below the hem of her skirt. I could feel the wetness that was seeping down from her passion pit and I could faintly smell its gentle scent in the fresh autumn air. I worked slowly upward until I had her hot pussy quivering under my fingers. The front of her panty hose was so soaked with her juices that my fingers were wet. She was almost screaming now. There was no stopping us.

As I continued to finger her nylon-covered cunt, I used my other hand to undo my pants and drop my shorts. I pulled up the back of her skirt and my cock sprang up between her legs and snuggled up into her hot wet junction. She reached down in front of her and grasped my cock, sticking out from between her legs. I began to piston back and forth as she held it tightly against her sopping mop. She was really getting hot. She would lean forward, roll her head around, then throw her long blonde hair back over her shoulder and lean back into me again, moaning louder with each of my strokes.

Finally she could stand it no longer. She stuck her thumbs inside the waistband of her panty hose and jerked her nylons down around her knees. She leaned over the stack of crates with her ass sticking up provocatively, looked back at me and said in a low lusty voice, "Do it!" I placed my cock between her now naked thighs and felt the warmth of her hot flesh. I figured that she wanted my steel shaft jammed up into her hot little hole, so I decided to do a little teasing of my own. Besides, I knew I wouldn't last long if I plunged right into her and I wanted this ecstasy to last just a little longer. I reached around in front of her and pulled my cock up between her cunt lips and slowly began to rub the length of my shaft against her protruding clit. She started bucking wildly and said, "No, I need you to put it in me!" But I just kept right on sliding gently back and forth in between the folds of her hot muff. She arched her back and leaned her chest against the crate she was using for support. She groaned in frustration a couple of times and tried to work the knob of my prick into her dripping tunnel, but I wouldn't let her have it. She was going to have to beg for it!

Finally she looked back over her shoulder with a fire in her eyes and said, "Fuck me, you bastard!" That was good enough. I eased back and placed the tip of my huge dong at the entrance to her quivering hole. Then I thrust forward and my whole length sank into her depths in one mighty stroke. She screamed out loud. It was tight, but she was so lubricated that I went in all the way. My size was more than she expected, but as I began my thrusts, she matched me stroke for stroke. I reached forward and got my hands on both her tits inside her blouse as I continued to pound away at her box. Her breathing got very rapid and shallow in between moans. Soon my balls were boiling with liquid and I knew that I would last only a few more strokes. I pounded hard. Then she really got wild. She started screaming, "Oh, shit, oh shit, oh fuck, oohh fuck, ooohhh . . ." That did it! In the middle of her intense orgasm I blasted the biggest load of jism of my entire life! Wad after wad pumped out into her steamy depths as she continued to moan softly.

My prick began to go soft, but I continued to stroke slowly in and out of her cunt until at last my limp noodle slipped out of her. While we were both trying to catch our breaths, our juices were running down the inside of her thighs. We stayed there in that position for several minutes, hearing nothing but the pounding of our hearts. Finally I put myself back in my pants and she pulled her soaking wet panty hose back into place. She turned around to face me for the first time in the encounter. She planted a passionate wet kiss on me, snaking her tongue in between my lips. Then she just looked at me for a moment with those big blue eyes. We went back to the dance but she went her way and I went mine. We became good friends that year but never again repeated our sexual encounter. Today she is married to a well-to-do broker. Wouldn't you know it! All in all, Sandy has to rank as one of the best lays of my life. Although I now rarely see her, I'm told she's reverted to her cockteasing ways—who knows, I might get lucky again.

HOT RODS AND RUBBER DOLLS

*S*aturday was a typical northern California spring day. I decided to enjoy the sun and generate some sweat at the same time by riding my mountain bike. After I got to my favorite riding area, I took off at a fast clip down a winding trail. As I climbed a small knoll, something off to the right caught my eye. I stopped short, only to glimpse what appeared to be a naked woman near the top of the hill. My curiosity, as well as my lecherous mind, urged me to head in that direction. I was trying to be quiet, hoping that my eyes had not deceived me. I didn't want to blow a chance at spying on some babe in the buff.

In fact, I decided to walk the rest of the way. I laid down my bike and crept slowly, silently, toward the summit. When I reached the top of the hill, what I saw caught me off guard. About fifteen yards below me was a very attractive redhead. My first impression had been correct—she was indeed naked. But what really made my eyeballs pop out of their sockets was that she was fucking one of those blowup sex dolls! Here was this voluptuous woman balling a hunk of rubber! I couldn't help but laugh out loud at the sight. I thought she heard me for a moment when she stopped fucking briefly and looked up the hill. I just lay low for a couple minutes before taking another look. I didn't get up and go over to her because I was deeply curious about what kind of crazy sex she was going to have with her rubber Romeo.

When I glanced her way again, I saw that she had gone back to French-kissing her "lover." Carefully she ran her tongue around the doll's puckered lips while lustfully moaning out loud. From my vantage point I could see that this woman was endowed with a hefty set of knockers. Even from fifteen yards away, each of her nipples appeared to be the size of my thumb! Her pussy had been cleanly shaved and I could clearly see the large outer lips of her cunt. She positioned the doll on top of her and placed its erect penis between her legs. I remember thinking that she may have filled it with water instead of air, because the doll appeared to be quite heavy. What a bizarre scene! After a few minutes of masturbating her pussy with the doll's cock, she ran its dick slowly up along her body, stopping at her breasts. She rubbed its erection between them, pushing them together and lifting her head to watch the action. Eventually she moved the imitation cock up so she could take it into her mouth, and she gave the thing one of the wildest blowjobs I've ever witnessed.

By this time, my own dick was throbbing with excitement. I pulled down my shorts, grabbed it with both hands and, in a frenzy, started to jerk off. My balls were swollen with come that was just pulsing to shoot out, and I wasn't about to stop stroking. I turned my attention back to the woman just as she rolled over on top of her blowup doll. I could even hear what she was saying. Was it ever dirty! With the plastic man's cock in one hand and his face in the other, she was calling him a "weak bastard" and rasping, "I'm going to fuck you so hard your balls will turn black and blue." Picture this very feminine-looking woman fucking a sex doll, mouthing these filthy words. Then she did exactly as she said she'd do to her inflated sex toy. Her humping was so fast and furious I thought for sure her buddy was about to burst. All I could feel was envy for a piece of rubber—that and the buildup in my groin. I couldn't hold back any longer and my come surged through my dick, spurting all over my bare belly and chest. I went rigid as my orgasm jolted my entire nervous system. After that, my eyes glazed over and I passed out.

I thought I was fantasizing again when I felt a warm, moist sensation on my lower abdomen. I opened my eyes enough to see the very same woman running her talented tongue across my belly toward my dick. Was I dreaming? I leaned forward and saw that it was, indeed, the redhead. She asked if she had been the one who'd caused all the mess, referring to the come that was splattered all over my belly. Not quite believing what was happening, I just shook my head yes. With her hungry mouth sucking on my limp cock, she aroused an animal lust in me like I've never felt before. I lay back, closed my eyes and smiled. I'm not made of rubber . . .

WORKING LATE

*K*aren and I had been working in the same office for over a year before we met at lunch one day and discovered that we had much in common. It didn't take long before we were meeting for most of our lunchtimes. Karen stands about five feet two inches tall, has long blonde hair that reaches down to the small of her back, soft blue eyes and full, pouting lips—a real doll.

During the summer, she often wore tight-fitting miniskirts and T-shirts that looked like they were spray-painted on her body. Several times I'd met her dashing across the parking lot to get out of a sudden, soaking summer rain. The damp chill would cause her nipples to stand erect in her skimpy bra and her shirt to cling to her ample breasts, which rose enticingly with her every breath. Hiding my erections during these encounters was often a problem.

Our relationship began in earnest one night when I was at my desk, long after regular working hours. Growing drowsy, I got up and took a walk around the hallways to see who else was burning the late-night oil. As I was passing the elevator, the doors opened and Karen emerged.

Karen was wearing a one-piece cotton sundress that clung to her luscious body suggestively and was short enough to provide spicy glimpses of milady's thighs. Actually, she might almost as well have been wearing Saran Wrap, for her dress was soaked and virtually transparent. Her nipples appeared as hard points on her beautiful breasts, and the lace fringes of her underwear were visible, perfectly framing her luscious cunt lips.

"Just when I found that my car wouldn't start, the rain came crashing down," she said. My raging hard-on and I both thanked the powers-that-be. "Do you think you could give me a jump start?" she asked.

"Of course," I stammered. "I'll be done in just a bit." I tore my gaze from her fetching breasts, which seemed to be crying out to me to be kissed and squeezed. My heartbeat was racing as I returned to my desk and resumed working. Karen followed. She sat on the edge of my desk, almost as if it was her intention to drive me wild. Maybe she was horny, maybe she had tied on a few, lowering her inhibitions, or maybe she was a lot more courageous than I dared to hope. After a few minutes, she lay back languidly and pulled her dress farther up her thighs.

As I sat in awe and watched her breathe, she spoke. "Have you ever thought of all the different places in this building that would be great for having sex?" she asked. I couldn't believe what I'd just heard! I thought I would lose my load right then and there. "How about it?" she proposed. "It's late and the place is deserted. And you did offer to help me."

That was all the urging I needed. Without a word, I shut off my desk lamp and stood up. I laid my hands on her thighs as I positioned myself in between them. I raised her dress and moved my hands up her smooth thighs to her lace-covered snatch. Her rain-dampened panties slid over my fingers and, with my thumbs, I began lightly stroking her crack. I could feel the heat of her body as I reached around her firm ass and pulled her closer. She reached up, pulled my head close and kissed me as I'd never been kissed before. She then unzipped my pants. Her small hands trembled as she wrapped them around my straining member and pulled it forth. I pulled her toward me across the smooth desktop and got into position to start fucking.

"Whoa! Hold on!" she said. She got off the desk and deftly pulled her dress over her head, letting it fall to the floor. That done, she knelt and helped me remove my pants and undershorts. Seeing my eight-incher standing tall, she sucked it between her full lips and flicked her tongue back and forth across its swollen tip. I felt her hot breath at the base of my shaft as she sucked and kissed every inch. My first load had almost arrived when she suddenly stood up and walked out into the hallway.

"That was just to make sure you're really ready!" she said as she left the office. I promptly followed. She went to the drinking fountain and splashed water on her breasts before turning to face me. I could see a passionate desire in her eyes. Her breath was shallow and labored. The cool water of the fountain had brought her nipples to full attention, and I began to kiss them. She sighed deeply with my every kiss and caress. I reached behind her to grasp her firm ass and to remove the last of her garments. She moaned and purred as I pushed her panties slowly down her thighs, and she stepped out of them. Placing my hands on her ass again, I pulled her against my rigid cock. She began massaging it. Only an enormous exercise of willpower kept me from going over the edge.

But then, with no warning, she tore herself free. She ran away from me and vanished around a bend in the corridor. I hurried after her, eager to find her and quench the flames of my desire in her moist, pink love sluice.

Standing out before me like a divining rod, my cock seemed to direct me to her. She was waiting in the storeroom. The door closed quietly behind me as I entered the darkened room. Without warning, her lips were on mine, burning with lust and desire. I hugged her hot body to mine and she wrapped her legs around my waist. My throbbing prick effortlessly penetrated her warm, moist cunt. Immediately I felt that amazing, massaging grip that every horny woman possesses in her vagina.

Holding her ass, I directed her up and down on my straining tool. Whenever her legs tightened about me, the muscles in her snatch gripped the shaft of my cock tighter. I could feel the suction growing as our thrusts increased in strength and tempo. I'd never felt a pussy so fantastically tight before! Our rocking motion pulled at the foundations of my being as the fantastic Karen screwed me for all I was worth. The delicious pleasure mounted as her sex juices began to run down my legs.

Karen arrived at her first climax with a rush. She arched her back, let out a deep moan, and pushed her breasts up toward my face. I continued driving wildly into her. Her wild abandon soon sent me over the top. With a low grunt as the air whooshed from my lungs. I pressed my savage member as deeply as possible into her box and shot my sperm into her voracious depths.

I slowly withdrew from her and slumped to the floor. She sat beside me and we both gasped for air, grinning like idiots.

After a few minutes, I heard an impish giggle and saw Karen

get up and walk toward the door. "Why don't you just relax for a minute while I go and retrieve our clothes?" she said. When she'd left the room, I stood up and headed down the hallway to the conference room, where I collapsed into one of the chairs. I guess I must have dozed off, because the next thing I remembered was feeling the weight of Karen's body on my lap. I opened my eyes and saw her bare backside. "We can't possibly have any more fun until I get you ready again," she said in that fetching tone of hers. Then she began slowly moving her ass back and forth across my rising dick. Her sighs filled the room as I reached around her and began massaging her firm breasts and rock-hard nipples. With one hand I began caressing her cleavage. With my other hand I reached down to her pink cleft and began massaging her hard clitoris.

As Karen's bucking and moaning increased, my dick sprang up to its full height and begged for attention. The sweat on her thighs helped her slide across my lap almost effortlessly. The friction of my prick against her beautiful ass felt delightful. Reaching down, she deftly slid my mammoth member into her well-lubricated snatch and began to ride me with zeal. Her panting grew louder and louder as she neared another climax. With one hand she was rubbing the base of my pecker and delicately massaging my nuts while her other hand was guiding my touches upon her burning flesh.

Just as Karen orgasmed we were startled to hear a key in the door and someone turning the knob. Fearing discovery, Karen— still in the midst of her climax—quickly got off of me and hid under the large conference table. When the cleaning lady entered the room, I laid my wet trousers over Karen's white dress. The cleaning lady looked at me curiously. I tried to explain that I had accidentally soaked myself in the thundershower and had come upstairs to dry off. Under the table, Karen took my stiff cock into her mouth and began to lick and suck it. I did my best to cover up my trouserless condition from the intruding woman while Karen brought me ever closer to my second orgasm with her lips and tongue. As the familiar pressure rose in my nuts, I was forced to account for my involuntary thrusting motions, lest the intruder catch on to what was happening. I explained that I was cold and shivering, and I pointedly asked her to turn out the lights when she left. But still this woman remained to chat! I couldn't have borne it if Karen were to stop—her blowjob was making my face tingle as that delicious pressure reached a crescendo in my balls. Sensing the nearness of my climax, Karen dramatically increased the tempo, all the while maintaining a perfect silence below the table.

"You don't look so good," the cleaning woman said. "Maybe you've taken a chill!"

I was about to assure her of my well-being when I ejaculated with frightening force. As gobs of my hot load filled Karen's mouth, my hands shot out across the tabletop and my eyes began tearing. As my hips pushed forward, I involuntarily caused Karen's head to bang against the table. The cleaning woman jumped back as if I had leapt at her, brandishing her vacuum hose as if to ward me off, and fled.

After she had slammed the door, I looked under the table and saw Karen sitting there with a big satisfied grin on her face. "Thanks so much!" she said. "I have meetings in here all the time, and doing this is about all that I can ever think of." As I helped her out from under the table, she gave me a long kiss. I assured her that whenever she felt this daring again, I would be more than happy to oblige her!

THE COUPLE AND THE BACHELOR

*M*y wife Liz and I are both thirty years old. We are an attractive couple. Both of us are in great shape, with well-tanned bodies, and we like to remain that way. We live in a quiet subdi-

vision and have a secluded patio in our backyard where we sunbathe nude every chance we get.

The house next to ours was recently occupied by a new neighbor, a bachelor. After about a week, Liz and I decided to extend
a friendly invitation for him to come over for a get-acquainted
drink. Liz said she would go over during the afternoon and introduce herself while I was at work. She said that she had very little
on when she went next door to extend the invitation, which is
how she usually dresses in the summer. All she wore was a tiny
halter top that was just about transparent, and a pair of short
shorts. The halter afforded a great view of her tits and dark-
brown nipples, while the shorts left almost half her ass in plain
sight. When I got home, I asked Liz how things had gone. She
said that our new neighbor, Phil, would be over after dinner for
drinks. She also told me that he was attractive, about forty years
old and living alone. He had seemed very nice and easygoing, and
he was happy that someone had come over to visit.

Phil arrived at about eight o'clock with a bottle of wine. I introduced myself. Liz was upstairs showering, so I opened the wine
and poured a glass for Phil and myself. While we drank and
waited for Liz, Phil told me he worked as a consultant to a large
company in the area, and that he'd always wanted to move out
here. Liz came down about twenty minutes later and joined us.
Liz likes to dress sexy. Very much an exhibitionist, she wore a
long nightgown slit up the front almost to her crotch and so low-
cut on top that it revealed more than a little of her beautiful big
tits. Judging from the grin on his face, Phil was pleased to see her
again. When she sat on the sofa across from Phil and me, we had
a great view of her long legs, which were exposed by the slit in
her gown. Liz has the best body I have ever seen. She has a perfectly conditioned 35–23–37 figure and stands five feet ten
inches tall in her bare feet.

We were all very relaxed and enjoying each other's company.
It was turning out to be a great night. The wine was helping
things along. I mentioned to Liz that I thought she was wrong

about Phil being forty, and Phil said he was actually forty-two. In utter disbelief, she asked him how he kept himself so young-looking. He said he exercised a lot outdoors and loved being in the sun, which was apparent from the nice tan he had. Liz told him how much we enjoyed sunbathing in our backyard. She didn't mention that we usually do it naked, though. Phil said he preferred going to the beach to tan, adding that he wished there was one nearby. Liz told him that he was more than welcome to try out the backyard beach and join us on our patio the next afternoon. Phil thanked her and said he'd be over.

After some more talk, Liz got up to get us all another glass of wine. As she leaned over to hand Phil his glass, her tits almost fell out of her gown. He couldn't take his eyes off of her, and I couldn't blame him. As I've said, Liz enjoys being an exhibition-ist as much as I enjoy being a voyeur. When she sat down on the sofa again, her gown was so far above her knees that we could see she wasn't wearing panties. Making sure we had a good view of her tits as well, she moved the material of her bodice very dis-creetly aside, so that both breasts were all but revealed down to the upper edges of her areolae.

When we were ready for more wine, Liz said we'd finished the bottle. Since it was still early, I volunteered to go out for more. Phil said he would take a ride with me. On the way to the liquor store, he told me how attractive Liz was and how lucky I was to have her. I remarked on how much she would appreciate hearing him say that to her directly. Phil said that, if I didn't mind, he'd express his admiration to her when we got back. I told him just to relax and tell her whatever was on his mind, because Liz and I were always very open with each other. I think my assurance helped Phil to relax a lot.

Soon we were back, sitting around talking, the two of us men watching Liz. When Phil did mention how attractive he found her, Liz smiled happily and said thank you. He surprised me then by adding that she had a body he would love to see more of. Liz was seated facing us and, as she crossed her legs, we were able to get a glance at her crotch, but only for a split second. Her top was pushed further aside, however, giving us a full view of her areolae. Liz certainly knew exactly what to do to drive us nuts. This went on for the rest of the night, till Phil said that he should be going. As we walked him to the door, Liz told him to be sure to stop by the next day to work on his tan. He said he'd be there and thanked us both for a very nice evening.

After Phil's departure, Liz and I stayed up and talked awhile. She said again that she couldn't believe Phil was over forty and she wondered if he was as good at sex as his body led her to believe. She had always wanted to have an older man, just to see what it would be like. I said that this might be a golden opportunity for her to satisfy her curiosity. (As I've said, we are very open with each other, sexually as well as otherwise.) I also said I was sure—judging from what he'd said—that Phil would not mind putting his body at her service.

Next morning, we got up early and laid out several blankets on the patio. Then I went to the corner store for beer and put it in a cooler on the patio. A radio completed our sunbathing gear. Liz and I, not wishing to force matters, decided not to greet Phil in the nude, but rather to wait and see what happened. I wore a bikini that barely covered my cock and ass. (If I couldn't be naked, at least I'd cover as little as possible.) Liz chose to wear the skimpiest bikini that she had. Made of a satiny material, it always gets men's attention. The top consisted of a tiny string that barely covered her tits and showed most of her nipples. The bottom was a G-string that didn't cover her ass at all. The best part was that the G-string covered nothing more than the slit of her completely hairless (shaven) pussy.

Before I went outside to get things ready, while I was oiling myself up with suntan lotion, the doorbell rang. It was Phil, and he asked if he was late, seeing that I was already oiled up and in my bikini. I said no, and commented that it was already eighty degrees, but it was only ten o'clock in the morning. I noticed that Phil was checking me out. He told me that he liked the bikini I was wearing. I thanked him and thought nothing more of it. Phil then said that under his shorts and tank top, he was wearing a bikini similar to mine. I told him that I thought it would please Liz that both of us guys were wearing bikinis.

When Phil and I walked outside, Liz came over to say hello to Phil. His eyes almost bugged out when he saw her in her string bikini. She told him to take off his outer clothes and relax. As Liz walked back to the patio, Phil noticed that there was nothing covering her ass-cheeks, and he just followed her as she shook them all the way there. Liz decided that we should all have a beer, and when she bent over the cooler to get them, the view of her ass was fantastic. Phil thanked Liz for the beer and told her how well her bikini showed off her fantastic body. Liz said she was glad that he liked it—and her body as well. Phil took off his top, revealing a hairless and very muscular chest. Liz watched intently as he took off his shorts. His bikini was almost as small as mine, and he had a nice big bulge in his crotch. Liz said that he also looked good in his bikini, and that she liked what it showed off. Phil's trim, hard body was nicely tanned.

Liz said she was going to put on some oil, and she gave Phil the other bottle to use. Phil and I were mesmerized as we watched her slowly massage the oil into her skin. She started with her shoulders and then did her tits, sliding her oily hand under the string bra and getting her huge nipples hard. She worked down across her stomach toward her pussy, teasing us like mad. Liz then stood up, rested one foot on a chair and rubbed oil up the length of her leg to her crotch. She repeated this performance with her other leg. Phil and I watched as she seductively turned around and massaged oil into her buttocks and the crack of her ass. When she finished, she asked me to put oil on her back. I did so gladly, kissing her neck as well.

At this point, I wasn't the only one with a hard-on. It was obvious that Phil had one, too, as Liz noticed when he started to oil himself up. She wryly commented on how he and I seemed to be enjoying what we saw. Phil said he was enjoying it very much, at which Liz offered to oil his back for him. When we were all oiled up, Liz suggested that we play some Frisbee before it got too hot. It was a good idea on her part because it gave Phil and me a good chance to watch her tits bouncing. We also had some great shots of her ass whenever she bent over to pick up the Frisbee. It was a miracle that her tits remained in her skimpy top.

We tossed the Frisbee around for about half an hour, then sat down for a few beers and some conversation, which eventually turned to sex. Phil said that he had never married and did not have much chance to date because of his heavy work schedule. He also said he didn't have any other friends out here and was glad to know us. Liz said that maybe she could help him out. She explained that she and I have an open marriage. Much to my surprise, she also told him that I was bisexual. (Although I am, I didn't expect her to bring it up.) Her next statement was even more surprising for she said that I could help him out too.

Phil wasn't at all upset. He simply said that he had been curious about bisexuality for some time. He also mentioned to Liz that he would give anything to have sex with an attractive girl like her, with a body like hers. Liz just smiled. It was obvious that the sunshine and beer had mellowed the three of us out, and that things were opening up. We sat around and drank several more beers, getting pretty loaded. After a while, Liz suggested that we lie back and work on our tans.

Liz was between Phil and me as we lay on our stomachs, soaking up rays. She offered to oil us up again if, when she was done, one of us would do the same for her. That was fine with Phil and me. Deciding to do me up first, Liz gave Phil a nice view as she kneeled by me, facing him. When Liz got to my crotch, she gently gave my balls a squeeze. When she was done spreading oil on me, she leaned over and gave my ear a nice wet tongue-kiss.

When she asked if Phil was ready for his oiling he was lying on his side with a huge erection visible. Seeing the bulge at his crotch, Liz quipped that it looked like he was ready. She told him not to be embarrassed, that she was happy she made him feel sexy. Phil relaxed and asked if he would get the same kind of oil rub as I'd had. She said he surely would, but she gave him a much slower massage, especially when she got to the part of his thighs closest to his crotch. I saw her rub his ass and give his balls a squeeze. Phil even let out a soft moan. At the end of her massage, she even kissed his ear as she'd kissed mine. I got a giant hard-on just from watching all this.

Liz then asked which of us was going to return the favor and oil her body. Phil looked at me questioningly. I told him to be my guest. I knew that this was what Liz wanted. With his erection still intact, Phil rubbed oil upon Liz's smooth skin from her shoulders to her toes. When he got to her string top, Liz told him to untie it. The string fell off of her, enabling us to see the sides of her tits, which were pressed against the blanket as she lay on her stomach. When Phil reached her ass, he tactfully moved on by it to her feet, but Liz said to him, "Hey, don't forget my ass, if you please." Phil replied that he wanted to leave the best part for last. He gave her feet a nice massage and started to work his hands back up her legs. Liz began to moan and squirm around as Phil's hands approached her crotch. She was also spreading her legs wider and wider apart. She told him to take all the time he needed—and, believe me, he did. Liz's legs were spread as far apart as I had ever seen them, which gave Phil a great view of her ass and pussy, neither of which was much concealed by her bikini. When he began massaging her inner thighs, he let his fingers glide across her smooth skin. Then he knelt between her legs and let his fingers slide between the cheeks of her ass. Liz was really moaning and squirming as Phil finished up with a kiss like the one she had given to each of us. Liz thanked him for an excellent job and said that, if he was willing, she would like him to repeat that later on her front side. Phil said he would love to oblige, if it was all right with me. I said that whatever Liz wanted would be fine with me. Phil thanked us both, and we lay in the sun for another hour and a half, the whole time downing beers.

Finally, Liz said that we'd better turn over so we wouldn't get sunburned on our backs. As we stood and stretched, Phil excused himself to go to the bathroom. While he was gone, Liz asked if I minded the way things were going. I said no, not at all, that I'd enjoyed just watching. She assured me that I would not be left out of the fun later that day. I said I wasn't worried about that, and she gave me a kiss and said thanks for understanding.

When Phil returned, I left for the bathroom. When I reached the door of the house, I saw Liz and Phil engaged in a deep kiss. They didn't hesitate at all—it must have been the beer, or maybe they'd kissed before. I went inside without saying anything. When I returned, they were still kissing, so I waited until they were done before I rejoined them. We sprawled on our backs, and Liz said it was her turn again to apply the oil. She started with me. I hadn't lost my erection from before—it was even larger, in fact. Starting at my shoulders, she spread oil upon my upper torso. At one point, she grabbed my nipples between her fingers and gave them a pinch. Then she put her mouth on them and sucked and gently bit them. She knew I was dying for her to do that, and she kept it up for several minutes before moving on with her hands.

Watching all this, Phil got another huge hard-on. Liz told him to be patient because he was in for the same treatment. But he began rubbing his cock through his bikini as he watched. When Liz reached my crotch and saw the bulge there, she asked Phil if he would mind if she peeled my swimsuit off of me, explaining that we normally lay out naked anyway. He said it would be fine with him. With that, Liz pulled the bikini off of me, exposing my rigid prick, which stood straight up. I have a good eight-incher with a large pink head. Liz teased a little by caressing my cock and balls, then continued the massage down my legs. When she noticed the drops of pre-come on my cockhead, she leaned down and licked them up. But then she stopped and asked Phil if he was ready.

Judging from how swelled up his cock looked in his bikini, he was beyond mere readiness. After making sure that I had a good view, Liz gave him the best massage I had ever seen. Phil was moaning louder than before. I was a little surprised—and disappointed too—that she did not take off his bikini when she got to it. When Phil looked at her questioningly, she told him that she wanted to leave the best part for last, which made him smile happily. When she did take Phil's bikini off, it seemed to take forever. I was just as anxious as Liz was to see his prick—and we were both rewarded by the sight of the largest cock either of us had ever drooled over. It had to be at least three inches longer than mine. The head resembled a dark purple plum. Liz began to rub oil over it with both of her hands, working up and down the length of the shaft and then cupping his balls. It was several minutes before she finished with a hot kiss upon the head. It was amazing that neither Phil nor I had come yet. I think that beer must inhibit sperm production somehow.

Liz asked Phil if he was ready to give her the repeat massage he had promised. Phil told her to lie on her back. Before she did so, she said she wanted to give us a better look at her titties. With that, she reached behind her back and untied her top (which she had earlier retied). Her firm round tits were revealed for our joyous inspection. Her nipples were hard, almost an inch long, and begging for attention. Phil commented that he had never seen bigger nipples and that he loved their rich brown color. Liz suggested that he shouldn't waste time talking about them.

Phil poured oil on her and began to rub it in, trying not to rush directly to her tits. Finally, though, he began to play with them. Liz begged him to pinch and pull her nipples. The more he played with them, the more she loved it, moaning louder all the time. Phil kept pleasuring her tits for at least ten minutes before massaging the rest of her. He seemed apprehensive about taking off her bikini bottom, until Liz forthrightly requested him to do so. He then untied the waist string. Liz raised her midsection a little so as to make it easier for him to remove the little triangle of fabric. When he got a full view of Liz's bald pussy, he couldn't believe his eyes. It was the first shaved cunt he'd ever seen, he said, exclaiming how beautiful it looked with all the hair removed. Liz said she was glad he liked it. I moved over for a better look and saw that her pussy was dripping with juices. Phil noticed this too. Without asking, he knelt between her legs and began to lick her entire snatch. Liz began going wild. She thrashed around and made little squeals of ecstasy as Phil pushed his tongue between her cunt lips.

I began to masturbate as I watched the show unfold in front of me. Liz must have had several orgasms during the few minutes that Phil was eating her cunt. When he stopped, she looked drained. She said it was time for her to do more than just look at the two big cocks within her reach. She suggested that, unless Phil and I objected, she wanted to give us both head at the same time. It was fine with us, we told her. So she had us stand alongside each other while she knelt in front of us. Taking hold of our pricks, she pulled us together until our pricks were touching. I looked at Phil, who said it felt good to have another cock against his. Liz rubbed them gently against each other for a while. Then she began to lick them both at the same time. I hadn't thought it possible, but Liz managed to stuff both of our dicks into her mouth at once. It wasn't easy, but she did suck on a few inches of both simultaneously and licked the heads with her hot tongue.

Phil and I could have gone on like that for hours, but Liz finally had to stop. She got on all fours and asked Phil to fuck her doggie-style. She then asked me to eat her at the same time Phil was fucking her. I lay beneath her, my head under her pussy, and I spread her meat apart as I watched Phil's long, hard cock sliding in and out of my wife's cunt. It was a sight I had never seen from this angle before. After he had gotten his entire shaft in her. I began to lick her clit and kiss as much of her pussy as I could. The whole time I was doing this, Phil's prick was running across my tongue, and his balls, which were huge, were slapping my face. Phil and Liz soon were thrashing wildly. They began to fuck each other harder and harder. Nevertheless, Liz somehow leaned her head down and began to suck my cock. She and I had never been in a position like this before, but we were loving it—as, I am sure, Phil was too.

After about five minutes of getting head from Liz, I announced that I was ready to come. Phil said that he couldn't hold back any longer himself. At almost the same moment, we both exploded. I fired my hot come in Liz's mouth, and she greedily swallowed every drop. Phil, meanwhile, kept pumping his load deep into my wife's pussy. Still licking her there, I tasted Phil's sperm when it began to drip out. When Phil finally withdrew that huge cock of his, Liz asked me not to move because she had a treat for me. I remained under her, and she lowered her pussy until she was sitting on my face. I knew then what my treat was. Phil's come was dripping profusely from Liz's pussy and into my mouth. She normally has lots of juice for me to enjoy, but now there was so much more—and it tasted especially good—with Phil's come mixed in. I swallowed every last drop.

After I'd had my treat, Liz said we should get out of the sun. The sun and the beer were getting to me too, so I said we should move to the hammock, which is strung beneath some shade trees in the corner of our yard. Phil and Liz thought that was a great idea. We all lay down again in the hammock and fell asleep. We were out for an hour or so and woke up feeling great. We discussed what had happened and agreed it had been great. As we talked, we all got horny again. Phil and I soon had hard-ons again, and Liz began playing with her nipples and fingering her pussy.

Phil and I sat back against the ropes and stroked ourselves as we watched. When Liz was done coming, she said it was our turn to masturbate while she watched. Phil and I moved to the opposite side of the hammock so she had a good view of our hard dicks. We began to jerk off as she gently played with her tits and pussy. I had an urge to grab Phil's cock, but I wasn't sure how he would react, even though he'd said he was curious about what a bi encounter would be like. As though she were reading my mind, Liz said that maybe I could help Phil out. He looked apprehensive but said it would be all right with him, so I pulled him toward me until our chests were touching. The hammock was like a giant pocket, holding the two of us together like two peas in a pod as we gently rocked back and forth. At that point I forgot that my wife seemed to be infatuated with our new neighbor; in fact, I forgot she was even there. I was completely focused on Phil's beautiful, hairless chest. I kissed his nipples and bit them gently. I inhaled his strong, salty man-smell as I reached down and began to rub our cocks together, stroking them both at the same time. Then I reached around and cradled his buns, which were still slippery with suntan oil. Before I even had time to think about it, Phil was kissing me, hard on the lips. His tongue found my tongue and his chest rose and fell against mine as his breathing quickened. I was beginning to understand what my wife saw in him—he was a great kisser. I could have kissed him the rest of the afternoon, but there were more pressing matters to attend to, like that throbbing love-missile Phil was pressing against my stomach. I backed off and lowered my head to his huge cock. This wasn't easy, but I finally got myself in position.

Phil was trembling as I put my mouth over his great cockhead. I teased it for a while as I licked, kissed and nibbled on it. Then I ran my tongue along his shaft, pausing now and then to suck his balls.

Liz must have been feeling left out, because she jumped out of the hammock mumbling something about faggots. I took Phil's rod out of my mouth to ask him if he felt like a faggot. He laughed and told me to suck harder. I was really getting into it, with my nose buried in Phil's pubic hair and his cock halfway down my throat, so I don't know when exactly Liz left. The next thing I knew, I heard the backdoor slam and Phil said she'd gone inside. I didn't care.

Eventually Liz returned with a jar of honey. She said it was time for lunch. I took Phil's cock out of my mouth and asked her what she meant. Instead of answering me, she caught hold of the hammock ropes and pulled us closer to her. Then she tilted the jar and poured a thin stream of honey over Phil's stomach. I watched, fascinated, as the golden fluid pooled in his belly button and slowly rolled down his upright cock. Tossing the empty jar aside, Liz stood on tiptoes and leaned over this honey-coated feast. I joined in and, together, we gave him a fabulous tandem blowjob.

When Phil grunted that he was about to come, Liz said that she wanted to eat his come, so I started to lick his balls as he came in Liz's mouth. Just then Liz lost her footing and grabbed for the far side of the hammock. Her weight capsized us and before I knew it, we were all in a pile on the grass under the hammock. Phil's cock was still in her mouth and from the way she was swallowing I could tell he was still coming. At last Phil let out a low moan and collapsed on the grass. My wife grabbed his wilting stem around its base, slowly pulling its length from her mouth, and then licked him clean.

She gave me a kiss. I found out then that she had not swallowed all of Phil's come. She pushed some into my mouth and we shared it.

That was the end of a perfect day for all of us. It had also been an exhausting day. However, it was not the last that we spent together. We've never bothered with clothes since then, and Liz and Phil have free rein with each other whenever they want to, which is often. It isn't unusual for me to come home and find them fucking. Sometimes I just watch and at other times, I join in.

Phil and I also like to have sex together on occasion, and next weekend I'm going to help him hang a hammock in his backyard.

THE GIFT OF TONGUES

I was a mere eighteen years old then, and I have had many similar experiences since. But none were as memorable as this. I am a male, six feet six inches tall, and weighed only one hundred and eighty pounds back then. I have curly red hair, blue eyes and a lot of freckles all over my face, arms and shoulders. Not ugly, mind you; in fact I've been told so often that I am handsome that I am now convinced of it.

As I remember her, Molly was about five feet four inches tall, and maybe one hundred and five pounds, if that. She had chestnut-brown hair, cut in a short shag that was popular in the 1970s, with brown eyes to match. She had small but shapely breasts, and her womanly curves had not yet filled out completely.

One day not long after we started going together, Molly and I went up to the boardinghouse where I was living. At first we just sat on the sofa in the upstairs living room, cuddling and talking. Then I took her by the hand and led her to my room. My roommate Mark was at work in the shipyard, as were all of the other boarders, so we were all alone.

After closing the door, I turned to Molly and, not saying a word, bent over to give her a gentle kiss of reassurance. I felt her relax as my lips touched hers. I sat down on the edge of my bed and motioned for her to kneel on the floor in front of me, between my knees. Looking directly into her eyes, I very gently traced lines with my middle fingers of both hands, in small circles on her cheeks, spiraling outward until I reached her ears. I touched her small, slightly upturned nose, the flare of her nostrils, her lips. As my fingers caressed her lips. Molly began to rub her hands up and down my thighs.

I lifted her head to meet my lips and I kissed her. I kissed her gently, flicking my tongue lightly across her lips with short, brisk licks. I kissed her several times. As my tongue probed the inside of her mouth, finding her tongue and swirling around, I allowed my right hand to run down the front of her blouse till I reached the first button.

I deftly undid each button, gently drawing my finger along her flesh as it was exposed. When the last button was undone I removed her blouse, slipping it over her shoulders while keeping my lips pressed firmly to hers. Starting from her hands, which had reached up to grasp my shoulders, I ran my fingers along her arms to her neck. I caressed her shoulders, my hands meeting behind her neck.

Still kissing her, I unclasped her bra and let it dangle from her arms. I rubbed the flesh of her back where her bra had been, moving my hands up and over her shoulders and down to her firm little tits. I cupped those ripe peaches and gave them a gentle squeeze, running my thumbs over the nipples, feeling them grow erect with excitement.

When I finally ended our kiss, Molly was breathing heavy with excitement. "Wow!" she exclaimed. "Where on earth did you learn to kiss like that?"

I didn't say a word. I only smiled and lifted her to her feet. Looking up into her eyes once again, I undid the snap of her jeans and pulled down the zipper, all in one fluid motion.

With practiced ease, I peeled her jeans down over her slender hips, inhaling the sweet aroma that assailed my nostrils from her dampening crotch.

Before removing the last piece of her clothing, I cupped the slight bulge that her pubic mound created in her panties. Her panties were soaking wet, and I could feel the heat emanating from her fiery slit.

My fingers shook in anticipation as I slid them up the front of her panties to grasp hold of the elastic waistband. Very slowly, I peeled Molly's panties down over her hips. Gazing up into her eyes, I reached around her and cupped her ass-cheeks, one in each hand, and bent forward to run the flat of my tongue along her dewy slit. Molly shuddered as my tongue made contact with her sensitive nubbin. She tasted even better than I had thought.

When I stood up, Molly climbed on the bed and lay down, motioning for me to come to her.

I positioned myself so that I was straddling her torso. I lowered my hips to where I could press my cock into her cunt, and leaned down to give her yet another gentle kiss. But this was not to be so, as Molly wrapped her arms around my neck, pulling herself up to me and firmly planting her lips on mine in a deep and very passionate soul kiss. I could hear her moan with desire as her tongue snaked out of her mouth into mine, dueling with it in a mad dance of sheer lust.

When she broke the kiss, Molly flopped down on the bed, breathing very heavily. "Do me!" she gasped. "Do my pussy! I need it so bad!"

I simply looked at her and smiled, but then moved down so I could use my tongue on her entire body. I slipped a knee between her thighs so she could have something solid to hump on while I took care of her upper torso, slowly covering every square inch of her luscious flesh with my active tongue, being careful to avoid her temptingly hard nipples.

Finally, I flicked my tongue across the sensitive nubs, causing her to buck and squirm beneath me. Molly was begging me to stop and move down to her honey-pot, which was soaking wet as it rubbed against my knee. I gave her nipples one last suck before moving down her belly with my tongue and lips. When I reached her navel, I stopped and began to lick circles around the deep depression. Molly raised her knees and used her hands on top of my head to try to push it down to her steaming snatch, but I simply stopped all tongue action until she realized that I was in control of the situation.

Spiraling inward, I dipped my tongue into the depths of her belly button, probing all around the inside. Molly gasped as my tongue found the bottom. She later told me that nobody had ever done this to her before. I guess not many people know the joys of navel sex.

From her navel, I then made my way down her groin to the brown triangle of Molly's pubic thatch. She began to hump her hips against my knee with an urgency that I found quite stimulating. I loved seeing her like this. Yet my aching cock still longed to plunge into the recesses of her fiery cunt. I could sense that she was near the brink of oblivion as I used my fingers to part the pouting petals of her juicy twat.

I gently tongued my way up one side of her outer labia, rounded the top of her slit and moved down the other side. I then dipped my talented tool into her honey-pot, wagging it back and forth, from side to side.

I could sense that Molly was getting closer, so I finally moved my mouth up to zero in on her visibly erect clitoris. The little nub glistened with her juices as I began to flick my tongue in circles around her button. Molly's breathing became ragged and short the nearer I licked. She began to churn her hips up to my face, trying to make the sensitive contact that would surely send her flying over the edge.

Finally I gave her that contact, but only briefly, teasing her to a fever pitch. She was begging me to tongue her clit, muttering obscenities in between gasps of air. I continued to tease her until she was frantic. And then I lay my tongue flat against her swollen clit, humming low in my throat. That was enough to do it. Molly went sailing off into outer space.

"Oh! . . . Oh, yes! . . . Yes! . . . That's it, lover!" she cried as she began the first series of powerful orgasms. "Eat it! Lick my cunt! Lick my pussy, motherfucker! Come! Coming! I'm . . . I'm . . . I'm coming!" Her body began to convulse uncontrollably with each racking wave of ecstasy.

"Oh baby! Baby . . . baby! . . . I love it!" she continued, as her head thrashed from side to side, her eyes tightly closed.

Molly continued to writhe in release as I alternately tongued her spasming clit and dipped into her clutching cunt. Her pussy was overflowing with fluid, and I did my best to lap it all up. When I returned to her joy button, Molly soared to even greater heights, grabbing me by the hair and mashing my face into her vulva. It was hard for me to breathe, but I didn't care because of the joy I was bringing to this delightful little creature.

After what seemed like an hour, she started to come back down to earth, releasing her grip on my head so I could come up for air. Once I got a lungful, I continued to tongue her cunt and returned to her clit to give it a gentle flick. Her whole body shook as a post-orgasmic tremor surged through her. I repeated this several times, shortening the interval between flicks of my tongue. Then I flattened my tongue against her vulva and began to wash it back and forth over her clitty. Molly responded with one long, shuddering, continuous convulsion.

Looking up at her, I saw that she had begun to cry. She explained that this was the first time she had ever come like that. Also, this was the first time she had really wanted to fuck but couldn't, because she was really shallow and small "down there." She said that whenever she tried, it caused her great pain, because she could not handle a normal-sized dick, let alone the monster that she imagined me to have.

I moved up to lie next to her, pulling her close to me and soothing her sadness. "Babes," I began, "my body may be long and lean, but Mother Nature has played a cruel joke on me."

"What do you mean?" she asked.

"This," I replied, getting off the bed to stand up and pull down my pants, revealing the slender six inches of cock that have been the cause of my learning to be so skilled with my fingers, tongue and lips.

"Oh, wow!" she exclaimed with delight, as she moved to the edge of the bed to face my throbbing member. "It's beautiful!" she added as she opened her mouth to engulf my entire shaft. Her cunt might have been shallow, but she sure had a deep throat.

Molly began to suck my steely rod with the earnestness of the well-loved. Her tongue swirled around it as she concentrated her attentions on the purple head, sending waves of pleasure coursing through my entire being. It didn't take much of this type of mouth action to bring me to a climax. She grabbed my ass and totally buried my cock in her sucking mouth.

With one hand, Molly grasped my dick around the base and began to jack it in time to her bobbing head while, with the other hand, she cradled my balls and began to squeeze gently.

With a stifled cry, I erupted in her adorable mouth, sending jet after powerful jet of white-hot semen splashing against the back of her throat. Molly just kept sucking and swallowing. She continued sucking until I had gone limp in her mouth, and then released it with a pop. Looking up at me for approval, I noticed a few droplets of sperm at the corners of her mouth, which she promptly licked off.

"Fan-fucking-tastic!" I sighed.

I never got to fuck Molly, although we stayed together for a couple of months after that. I know that I will always remember her with fondness and, even though the odds are against it, I keep hoping that someday we might meet again.

PRIVATE SHOWING

I am a twenty-two-year-old attractive blonde (five feet five at one hundred twenty pounds with blue eyes and a 34-22-34 figure) and happily married. I have never desired to sleep with another man since I have been married, and I have never been untrue to my husband. Until recently, that is.

One evening while my husband and I were lying naked in bed and cuddling, we began discussing our fantasies. My husband asked me what my most erotic and frequent fantasy was. I replied that I had always dreamed of making love to another woman. When I asked my husband to confess his most desirable fantasy, he replied that he often dreamed of watching me have sex with another man. I was a little shocked, but curious about what exactly he had fantasized.

He told me that his fantasies of me with another man did not include someone that we knew, but a stranger, someone who I would never see again and who would not threaten our marriage. While I played with his cock, I asked him to describe what he would like to see me do with another man. He did, and the evening ended as we straddled and made love.

I thought about his fantasy for the next week or so. At first the idea made me feel a little uncomfortable. However, I found myself thinking about it more and more and getting quite excited whenever I did. I soon found that whenever I would masturbate with my vibrator, I would fantasize about screwing another man. I love to masturbate with my vibrator, especially when my husband watches me. I usually start by gently rubbing and massaging my breasts until I get my nipples as erect as I can. Then I let my right hand slide down to my pussy, and I start to play with my inner lips. As my pussy begins to moisten, I slide my middle finger inside and get it wet so that I can easily rub my clit. As I start to approach orgasm, I take my vibrator, insert it and slowly slide it in and out. Then I quickly place the vibrator on my clit and explode into an orgasm. I can make myself come up to six or seven times when I use my vibrator, whereas I can only come once when my husband goes down on me.

It wasn't long before I told my husband that I would like for him to watch me make it with another man. He repeated that he did not want to see me make it with anyone we knew, but at the same time, we were both hesitant about getting a total stranger. Several weeks passed without anything else being said, until just prior to my birthday when my husband came home one evening and said that he had a plan. The plan would allow me to have sex with another very attractive man and, at the same time, allow us to remain complete strangers.

First, my husband called one of those singing telegram services and proceeded to tell them that, because he had to work late on my birthday, he would not be able to take me out as we had planned. He told them that in order to make it up to me, he wanted to hire a male stripper to come out to our house and sing "Happy Birthday" to me. He said I would be home alone, and that if the dancer explained who he was, I would let him in the house. On the night of my birthday and prior to the stripper's arrival, my husband instructed me to wear my short blue robe with nothing underneath. I placed some books on the couch so that it would appear that I was studying while waiting for my husband to come home.

As the time for my stripper's arrival neared my husband positioned himself in a closet that provided him with a clear view of our living room. When the doorbell rang, I answered it in a timid and cautious manner. The man explained who he was and who hired him, so I let him in, acting as if I had no idea what was going on. I excused myself for being dressed in only a robe and explained that I was getting ready to take a shower. I said, "If this isn't going to take long, I won't bother to get dressed."

He said, "It won't take long at all."

I led him into the living room and I sat on the edge of the chair. He had the entire room to dance and strip in front of me. He was by no means an average-looking man; he was the most gorgeous stud I had ever seen. He was six feet tall, had blue eyes, blond hair, broad, muscular shoulders, a washboard stomach and the tightest ass a girl could ask for. He had the facial features of a model and a smile that made me weak in the knees.

As he turned on his music and started to dance, I made sure that I was completely unexposed. He was wearing a karate outfit, and he seductively and sexily began to remove the karate belt. The top of his karate outfit fell open, and I was rewarded with my first glimpse of his handsome chest. He slowly danced over to me and lightly draped his karate belt around my neck as he leaned over to give me a small kiss on the lips. As he did so, I ran my hands up his chest. I was sure that by now my breasts were partly visible, as I was no longer making an effort to keep my robe closed. Next he danced back a step or two and removed his top, then his pants. He was now wearing only a pair of briefs. I could feel that not only were my nipples hard, but my pussy was so wet that the juice began to run down my crack. (This has only happened once or twice before in my life.)

He continued to dance for a while, turning around, enticing

me with his sexy ass. He started to dance forward, bringing his crotch closer and closer. I finally reached out, cupped his beautiful ass with my hands and ran my tongue from the top of his underwear to his belly button. His bulge got noticeably larger. I asked him if he got that hard every time he stripped and he admitted he had never gotten a hard-on before while on the job. By now my robe was hanging open freely, and he took my hand, inviting me to dance with him. As I stood up and began dancing, he removed his briefs, exposing the skimpiest and sexiest G-string I have ever seen on a man. Seeing this, I removed my robe and began to dance closely next to him. His G-string barely covered what appeared to be a large and very attractive dick, which I could not wait to get my hands on.

There I was, dancing in the nude next to this gorgeous stranger dressed in only a G-string. The music ended and I stepped forward, put my arms around his neck and gave him a kiss. I could feel his hard-on pressing against my stomach, and a small drop of pussy juice began to run down my inner thigh. He stated that usually when he finishes stripping, the audience has on more clothes than he does, but that he enjoyed the change. I replied that I wasn't modest and that I was actually quite turned on. I asked if he would like something to drink as I turned and walked into the kitchen.

I poured him a glass of water, and as I was walking back into the living room, he was starting to put on his briefs. I said, "Wait, doesn't the birthday girl get to tip her stripper?"

He said, "Of course," and dropped his briefs on the floor. I went over to my robe, removed a ten-dollar bill from the pocket and walked over to him. I reached out with my left hand and pulled his G-string forward far enough so that I could get a good view. With my right hand, I slid the ten-dollar bill down and wrapped it around his balls. Then I slid my hand up to his dick and pulled it out of his G-string. I began to slowly stroke his large cock as I leaned forward to give him a long, passionate kiss. Our tongues eagerly began exploring each other's mouths. I continued to stroke his lovely cock as he put his arms around my naked body. I took my left hand and guided his hands down to my ass. He finally touched my soaking pussy. As he deftly played with it, I began stroking his cock faster and faster. We stopped kissing, and I whispered in his ear. "Please let me suck your cock. I want you to come in my mouth and then fuck my hot pussy."

He walked over to the couch and asked. "Do you always get this wet?"

I breathlessly replied, "I've never been this wet before in my life." I got down on my knees and slid his G-string all the way down. I asked him to sit on the couch, and I began to hungrily suck his cock like my life depended on it. With my right hand I began to feverishly rub my clit, but not for long because within minutes he began to unleash gobs of come down my throat. I was only able to swallow a little: the rest was smeared on my left hand and his cock. I took the come on my left hand and rubbed it all over my right tit and asked him to lick it off. He did promptly, going as far as savoring and swallowing his own juice.

We then lay on the couch together, kissing and exploring for the longest time. He kissed my neck while his hands massaged my breasts. I started to play with his limp dick and swollen balls. He moved his kisses lower until he was sucking my nipples. By now he had two fingers moving in and out of my pussy in a steady, continuous rhythm. His tongue ran down my stomach until his head was positioned between my legs. I was begging him to eat me out. He teased me by licking my inner thighs and running his tongue up the crack of my pussy. Next he began sucking my inner lips. I moaned in sheer ecstasy. It wasn't long before he was uncontrollably sucking my clit and darting his tongue in and out of my moist opening. It normally takes my husband ten to twenty minutes to make me come when he goes down on me, but this time I didn't last longer than five. I clenched his hair and tightly held his head between my legs as I ground my clit against his tongue. I came so much that I soaked the couch underneath my pussy. His mouth and chin were covered with my juice as he came up to kiss me on the lips. I was breathing heavy and had small red patches on my chest. I stuck my tongue into his mouth and tasted myself, rubbing my jutting clit all the while.

As we were kissing, I reached down and guided his cock into my hot pussy. He moved in and out slowly, increasing his rhythm. I was meeting each of his thrusts with my rising hips. He continued his hard, driving jabs for what seemed an eternity until he finally exploded with a shuddering orgasm. I felt his come running out of my pussy and trailing down the crack of my ass. Finally, he collapsed on top of me and we lightly kissed. We lay there quietly until his limp dick gradually slipped out of my hole.

After a little while I said it would be a good idea if he left, since I was expecting my husband home soon. I lay back and relaxed as he got dressed. I walked him to the door. We French-kissed deeply and then said good-bye. As he left, he gave me his card and asked me to call him if I ever needed his services again. With a smile, I told him I sure would.

After the stripper left, I went back into the living room and found my husband waiting for me on the couch, completely naked. I approached him and stood in front of him. He sat up and began to massage my pussy, which still had some come inside it. He sucked on my right nipple as I held his head firmly at my breast. My husband sat back on the couch, and I positioned my pussy over his mouth. He gently parted my pussy lips with his fingers, and his tongue began to caress the inside of my pussy. He was supporting my ass with the palms of his hands as I moved back and forth on his tongue. Finally, he began sucking on my clit and fingering my hole. It took me longer than usual, but eventually I shuddered with my second orgasm of the evening. He continued swabbing my clit with his tongue.

I then sat back and slid my husband's hard dick into my moist pussy. He was extremely excited, yet able to last for what seemed a lifetime as I moved up and down on his stiff dick. My husband seemed to fuck me with more vigor that night than ever before. He continued to fuck me until finally he shot the largest load of come ever into my wet pussy. We both collapsed in exhaustion. Then, sheened in sweat, we fell asleep. It was the finest birthday present ever, and I have been devising ways to make my husband's next birthday as exciting as mine was.

TRIVIAL PURSUIT

*M*y wife stands five feet three and weighs about one hundred and twenty pounds. Her measurements are 34-28-35, and she knows how to move every succulent inch when we make love. She has big, brown eyes and a tantalizing smile that never fails to draw men's attention.

I am six feet tall, weigh about two hundred and thirty-five pounds, have dark brown curly hair and the same color eyes. My vital statistics, for those who may be interested, are: chest, 50; shoulders, 54; waist, 38. I have an average-size cock. My wife and I keep in shape by being active in various sports, such as volleyball, tennis and, for my wife, a Nautilus health center.

The incident I want to describe occurred last year when Lisa, then twenty-six, and I, then twenty-eight, were trying to conceive our first child. After figuring out when conception would be most likely for her, Lisa devised some kinky escapades to get things rolling. Well, after a few months of trying, she still wasn't pregnant. I told her that the next month would be mine to plan. She was to leave everything in my hands. Lisa somewhat reluctantly agreed (I am known for my kinky imagination). I assured her I'd try not to get too out of hand. As the weekend approached, I came up with a suitable plan for some good fun and games.

I wanted to make this as unforgettable as I could. On Saturday I told Lisa to be ready by eight that evening. I asked her to keep an open mind, which I knew wouldn't be difficult because Lisa's pretty open-minded as it is. That's what helps to keep our marriage going. As eight drew near, she said she was going to take a shower and get ready. As soon as she was in the shower, I jumped into our van and sped to the nearby market. I purchased a can of whipped cream and then went to the local video store to rent some X-rated movies. I picked up three we had never seen before. I hurried back to our apartment with plenty of time to spare. I placed one of the tapes into the VCR and fast-forwarded to the first sex scene. I shut the machine off and hid the other two tapes and the whipped cream so Lisa wouldn't see them. Next I took out our favorite toy, a seven-inch vibrator, and hid it in the living room. I placed a couple of blankets on the floor in front of the television.

Lisa finished her shower and went into the bedroom to change. She was strutting around with the most devilish smile I'd ever seen. She was curious, but also a little leery of my imagination. When she said she was ready, I told her we were going to play one of her favorite board games, Trivial Pursuit. Only this time the rules were going to be slightly different. If you missed an answer, you had to remove a piece of clothing, and when you no longer had any clothing left, you had to do whatever the other person said for five minutes. She was a little hesitant about the last stipulation, but decided to go along with it, anyway. I thought for sure that I was going to literally lose my shirt since Lisa is so good at this game, but, instead, it was Lisa who couldn't think of the answers. First, off came the socks. Then the sweats to reveal my favorite black-and-red-trimmed teddy underneath. I got hard seeing how her nipples pressed against the fabric of the teddy. When she lost the next round, she slowly stood up, reached between her legs, and unsnapped the snaps. She wiggled out of her teddy, bending toward me and smiling, and revealed another bikini. She looked so sexy I almost shot a load right there in my pants. When she stood straight up, her breasts wiggled so succulently that my mouth watered. I almost felt like saying the hell with the rest of the game and screwing her right then and there.

I lost the next five rounds straight and was down to my bikini underwear. Lisa lost the next round and removed her bikini to expose another bikini. This was the skimpiest thing I had ever laid eyes on. By then, I was lusting for her like a schoolboy in heat.

I lost the next two rounds and stood before Lisa with one mother of a big hard-on. It wasn't difficult to notice that she was also excited. Her nipples were jutting and her areolae were all puckered up, waiting to be sucked. Lisa was delighted when she noticed I had trimmed my pubic hair and had shaved my balls. She smiled and said, "Ummm," slowly running her tongue over her lips.

Lisa lost her next turn. She stood up and moved seductively over to my side of the table, turned her back to me, and bent over invitingly as she pulled down her panties. She wiggled her cute little ass and looked over her shoulder to watch as I ogled her. She straightened up and turned around to display her pussy, which had been shaved to form a cute triangle. The next round Lisa lost again, and for the next five minutes I had her French-kissing me with her beautiful, full lips. With her tongue, she slowly moved down my chest, stomach and, finally, my cock. She ran her tongue up and down the underside of my shaft, then she stuffed the entire length into her mouth. One thing about my lover, she *loves* to give head, and, believe me, nothing beats a woman who enjoys what she is doing.

I lost the next round, and my beautiful little wife instructed me to lick and suck her breasts. She loves when I do this. She moaned and shivered with pleasure as I feasted on her soft globes.

After I finished with her tits, we played another round. She won again. She lay back on the couch with her ass propped on the edge of the ottoman and her legs open slightly, just enough for me to see her tight little nook.

She had me suck and kiss her whole body, but I had strict orders not to touch her pussy. This drove me crazy. It drove her crazy, too. I could smell that special aroma that comes from a woman when she's aroused. It drove me wild. I won the next round and had her sit on the floor with her back against the couch. I told her to watch the video on the television as I caressed her breasts and nibbled her ear. She was moaning as we watched the couple humping and slurping on the screen.

The next round was mine again. We repeated the previous scene, only this time she was to caress her own breasts and finger her own stiff little clit. To my enjoyment, the next scene on the video was a threesome, with two men fucking and sucking the same woman. I especially enjoyed this scene since I've often fantasized about having a threesome with me, my wife and another man. By the end of the five minutes, Lisa's juices were all over her hands and inner thighs.

The next few rounds involved the can of whipped cream. We covered each other with it and then took turns greedily lapping it off. I had avoided Lisa's clitoris. I knew if I concentrated on that delicious, protruding button too much, she would go off like a firecracker. But now it was time for my real surprise. When Lisa lost the next round, I had her lie on the blankets and I started the VCR. I then brought out the vibrator, and she looked at me sultrily with her brown eyes. I turned on the seven-inch vibrator, which we had nicknamed Pierre. It hummed softly. I ran it all over her body. First, I had her lie on her stomach, facing the television so she could watch the action while enjoying the massage. I moved Pierre along her neck and shoulders, then I slowly moved our friend down to the small of her back. Slowly, I moved the vibrator down over her succulent buttocks, down her legs to her feet. After spending some time on her feet and calves, I ever so slowly brought Pierre up her thighs to her firm cheeks. Tenderly, I began to knead and massage them. Then, to her surprise, I ran Pierre along the crack of her ass. When I spread her legs, I could hear the moist smacking of her gorgeous, inner lips parting. Kissing her neck, shoulder and back, I moved Pierre down the crack of her ass and along her pussy lips. With each passing stroke, Lisa would let out short gasps and moans. I had her turn over. We repositioned ourselves in a 69 so that my blood-engorged cock was hoisted directly over her moist, inviting lips, and I had a close-up view of her nicely trimmed, soaking pussy.

I went back up to her chest and ran the vibrator over her edible little nipples and then back down to her pubic mound. This time as I moved near my wife's delicious pussy, she took hold of my cock and began to lick and suck my shaft and balls. When Pierre reached Lisa's thighs, she parted them ever so slightly, releasing once again that intoxicating aroma of her womanhood. Her pussy was wetter than I had ever seen. She was drenched with her own juices. I took Pierre and began to slowly massage around her pubic area. Then I moved down to her swollen outer lips, still avoiding her clitoris. Lisa gasped and squeezed my cock with her mouth as I slid Pierre back and forth from her pussy lips to her creamy thighs. This drove her crazy. During all of this, I began to talk to her about having another man here to help please her. Even though she gets upset at me when I bring this up any other time, while I was gently rubbing her pussy with the vibrator, she became really turned on.

By now her moaning had drowned out the action coming from the television. While Lisa was sucking and fondling my cock and balls, I began to slowly apply more and more pressure until the vibrating head of Pierre disappeared inside her slick confines. Slowly, tenderly, inch by inch, I moved Pierre in and out of her. With each stroke, she moaned and gasped for air, yet she never released my cock from the warm, soft confines of her mouth. Soon I began to feel the familiar tingling in my balls. As I continued moving Pierre in and out of her, I began to finally lick and nibble on her gorgeous clit. It was sticking out so much that it looked like a small penis. She frantically gobbled my cock while my intense tonguing brought her to the verge of climaxing. Then I slowly moved the soaking vibrator out of Lisa and turned to face her. She was flushed and her eyes radiated with pure lust.

I pulled her on top of me into one of our favorite positions, and I slid right into her soft, velvety interior.

We began to French-kiss and caress each other as we moved toward our impending climaxes. Her pussy juice was dripping down my balls. She sat straight up and started rocking back and forth while caressing her own breasts. My cock felt like it was going to explode. I began to rub her body with my hands. The look of pure pleasure on Lisa's face was one that I'll never forget. She lowered herself so I could suck on her luscious tits. I moved my hands down and began to squeeze the firm globes of her tantalizing ass. She was so drenched with juice that the entire crack was as slippery as her love-canal.

She slipped up and down on my cock and rubbed her tits against my chest. She went over the edge and climaxed with the strongest orgasm that she had ever experienced. I was right behind her. I slid my throbbing shaft all the way into her inner recesses as I climaxed and pumped my juice deep inside her. She and I lay side by side, facing each other, hugging and kissing, saying how much we loved one another.

It was nine months later that Lisa gave birth to our first beautiful baby girl.

THE BEST MEDICINE

*T*oward the end of World War II, I came home from Europe with several wounds and decorations. After a lengthy stay in the hospital I was granted a recuperation leave. I decided to spend a few weeks with two old-maid aunts who lived some fifty miles away on the edge of a very small town. It was very healthy with the fresh air and all.

In the same town there lived two girls with their family, one twenty and the other eighteen. The younger was very pretty and away at school. The older, Pam, was not that pretty, being a bit on the masculine side. She spent a lot of time at my aunts'. They had a horse she liked to ride.

One day I was in the barn getting ready to jack off. I was sitting on a bench, leaning against a stall, my hard dick in my hand. Pam walked in just then. She stopped halfway, stared at my dick and slowly walked over to me. I asked her to have a seat. She said she had never seen a hard-on before.

Embarrassed. I slipped my cock back into my pants. I started up a conversation to relieve the tension in the air. She talked about her complete lack of social life, how she never had any dates. She was depressed all the time, and didn't know what to do about it.

I told her that what she needed was an education in human relations. She agreed. I suggested she come to the house the next day. I knew my aunts would be out of town. Right away she seemed very interested and agreed to come over.

Sure enough, my aunts weren't gone five minutes and she came over. She seemed a bit nervous, and I made jokes to try and relax her a bit. I chose the front bedroom so we would be able to hear if anyone came around.

We went in, closed the door and pulled down the shades. She sat on the bed, a very apprehensive look on her face. I pulled off my shirt, shoes and pants, leaving on only my undershorts. I sat next to her and started to unbutton her shirt. When I got to the last button she stopped my hands and took a deep breath. I knew I'd better slow down or I'd scare her away. I spent some time kissing her and gently massaging her back, loosening her up. After a few minutes of that she didn't try to stop me as I slipped her shirt off her body, seeing her very small breasts.

I leaned over, moistened my lips with my tongue and kissed her on the mouth. She moaned. I kissed her again, longer, harder, opening my mouth slightly. As she responded to my kisses, I undid her bra. I flicked my tongue over her lower lip. She responded by opening her mouth and letting the tip of her tongue touch mine. She was getting into it now as I slipped her bra off, revealing breasts the size of small oranges, with very large nipples.

By this time my dick was hard and poking out of my shorts. Very gently I pushed her down on the bed so her feet were dangling over the side. I moved up and started kissing her again. Very soon she had opened her mouth and was receiving my tongue and giving me some of hers. I pulled away from her and started on her breasts. She couldn't take much of this before she started rolling and bucking on the bed. I moved my head down to her thigh and started working my way up to her pussy. By the time my hand reached her crotch, she was shaking.

I got up. I unbuttoned her shorts and, in one motion, pulled them and her panties off. She lay before me, a virgin waiting for whatever came next. I started rubbing her body, never once touching her pussy. She had long, strong, slender legs, a flat stomach and a small bush of black hair. My kisses started again. I worked my way up to her pussy, once again not touching it. By the time I got there she was a bundle of rolling, rocking, feminine spasms. Finally she asked me to touch her, which I proceeded to do with first my fingers, then with my tongue. She orgasmed and let out a high-pitched scream that should have brought the police. Not only had she never been sucked before, this was her first orgasm. She freely admitted to having rubbed her pussy a few times, but she had always stopped well short of climax.

After she had rested we started talking about what we had done. She was still a virgin and my dick was still very hard. I asked her to jerk me off, all the while explaining to her what was going to happen. She was fascinated with the prospect. I took over just before shooting and directed my come onto her naked thighs. She was delighted with having my semen all over her. I told her it was all protein. I got some on my finger and sucked it down. I asked her to do the same. She did, evidently liking it.

I put my dick, still very erect, into her mouth. She took it willingly and proceeded to suck on it. It wasn't long before I was once again shooting, and she took all of it, giving a little of it back to me in a kiss.

This ended the first day of her "schooling" but not her education. A short while later I popped her cherry, and we were soon fucking regularly. I also showed her how to 69. The only problem was whenever she came she'd really scream her head off. We always had to fool around in out-of-the-way places to avoid being found out.

Then she moved away to the city. I saw her again, five years after our affair had come to an end. She told me she was living with a beautiful young woman who was her lover.

So much for modern education.

CLEAN AND SUPPLE

*W*hile touring the western Pacific as a U.S. marine, I encountered numerous exotic playthings that greatly inspired my lust for the erotic. Even though each was outstanding in her own way, one *sensei* (master) allowed me, her young pupil, a brief glimpse into the window of pure eroticism. Travel through southeast Asia was no new experience, considering I'd spent the better part of my twenty-two years growing up in third-world countries.

Our ship had been anchored off of Pattaya, Thailand, for four days when my friend Carl and I decided to take a much-needed break from all the drinking and carousing. We were searching for a nice, secluded massage parlor when we stumbled upon the fabled "Sabailand."

Our resident expert guided us through a maze of candlelit tables and nude statues. We turned a corner in the parlor and I felt my lungs constrict sharply as my eyes viewed the most incredible sight I had ever seen. Of course, my lungs weren't the only part of my anatomy to respond to the vision before me. There, separating me from Valhalla, were three plate-glass windows. Behind the windows, in various colorful stages of undress, were seventy-five of the prettiest women I'd ever seen. Discs numbered from seven to two hundred fifty-nine were pinned on the girls' fishnet bikini bottoms and elaborate silk teddies, which barely left anything to the imagination. I hastily asked our guide if he could bring me a glass of native beer while I regained my composure and scanned the faces and bodies for the one girl that would satisfy my intense hunger.

After I finished my beer, I'd made my decision. Upon my request the guide walked up to the windows and, through an intercom, requested that number two hundred twenty-six relinquish her spot on the carpeted dais and meet her new customer. After allowing us only to exchange a mere few words and names with the ladies of our choice, the guide whisked Carl and me up an elevator to the third floor.

With a twist of a key and a flick of a switch I entered what could have only been a dream. In front of me was a large tile floor which led to a deep bathtub on my right. On my left was a massage table. As I imagined what was going to happen to me on the table, I felt a tap on my shoulder. In sexy, broken English, my little demigoddess explained that I was to undress and climb into the tub of soothing hot water. She laid down the air mattress she had brought in with her and slipped slowly out of her clothes to reveal her perfectly shaped breasts, supple waist and long slender legs.

I, too stunned to be at all embarrassed, saw the engorged head of my member protruding above the water while she commenced cleaning every inch of my body, paying close attention to my erogenous zones. Not a part of me was left unnoticed or untouched.

Next, she bade me to lie down on the air mattress while she concocted her mystical Asian potion. She had filled a basin with warm water and dumped a dozen or so bars of soap into it. Then she added a final, mysterious ingredient and then whipped up mounds of billowy, strawberry-smelling suds that she heaped upon my yearning body and hers.

Thus slicked down, she slid her body up and down my back while using her hands to further her massaging expertise. What followed were a myriad of yoga-type movements that left no doubt in my mind that she truly was a professional. Placing one muscular leg under my body and clamping down with the other, she massaged my legs and loins with hers, leaving me breathless, relaxed and eager for more.

I then rolled over so that she was straddling me. Placing her hands on my shoulders she ground the insides of her thighs and her perfectly mounded mons up my involuntarily tightening stomach, over the crest of my chest and up higher.

As she resumed this motion back down my torso and onto my thighs I knew she was reaching that incredible crescendo. With her head thrown back and a low, earthy moan emitting from her lips she grasped my straining cock as if she were pulling herself out of the grip of a raging whirlpool. She seemingly tried to pull herself hand over hand up my rigid pole only to slide down again due to the soapsuds. Again and again she attempted this maneuver until she felt the cauldrons start to boil. Then, through half-closed eyelids and semiconsciousness, I realized she had stopped and was beckoning me to climb into the tub once again, where she rinsed off our soapy bodies.

And then, while I waited what seemed an agonizingly cruel eternity, she toweled us dry and led me by the hand to the massage table. When she beckoned me to lie down, I realized that I would soon turn to jelly if I let her massage me any more. I refused and gently but firmly laid her down on the table.

Slowly spreading her supple thighs. I knelt poised—like a warrior preparing his coup de grâce on some fallen enemy—over her gaping vagina, slickened now with more than just soapsuds. And with more energy than a tiger leaping on its prey, I plunged into her waiting depths. My pulsating pillar of manhood showed no mercy, having been denied its just reward for so long, as I thrust in and out of those gripping walls . . .

. . . And as the fireworks of the two hundred and tenth July Fourth blinded me, she screamed the voice of thousands caught in the path of an erupting volcano, as my lavalike semen coursed through her womb.

I'm on my way back to Thailand in four months and can't wait to see my *sensei* again. There's nothing like a really good bath.

OVEREXPOSED

One sunny Saturday, my morning was filled with errands. My last stop was a pet store specializing in exotic animals, to buy food for my Amazon parrot. I purchased the seed and asked the young man at the front counter about a problem I was having with my bird, who seemed to be losing his pep. The man directed me to the back of the store, where another, more knowledgeable clerk was working.

I saw a slender young redhead sitting on a stool in the back room, with a large white rabbit in her lap. Her bright green eyes were astounding, her smile radiant. Her natural red curls, with just the faintest golden highlights, softly framed her angelic face. She was a tiny creature, and looked so sweet sitting there, petting her furry white bunny.

I explained my parrot's problem to her, and she asked me a few questions. She said I needed to pay more attention to him—to give him special treats and sing to him. She was friendly, so we began to talk at length about our mutual love for birds. I noticed two excellent, extremely well-lit photographs of exotic birds on the wall. When I admired them, she gave credit to her boyfriend, Toby, who she said was a professional photographer.

"Does he ever photograph people?" I asked.

"Quite often," she replied. "I've modeled for him many times."

"I'm considering having some nude photographs of myself taken," I said. "I'd like a memento for my old age, and I won't look like this forever." I'm twenty-nine and have a terrifically sinuous body that I've always been quite proud of. I stand five feet five inches, have natural blonde shoulder-length hair, an ample bustline, a twenty-five-inch waistline, and I weigh one hundred and sixteen pounds.

I continued to converse with the comely redhead, and she gave me her boyfriend's business card and insisted that I call him. We smiled and waved good-bye, and I took a lingering look at her standing in the doorway. Beneath her thin cotton blouse she was braless. The rays of sunlight streaming in surrounded her creamy, flawless skin as if it were an aura, making her appear even more angelic.

That evening, at a drive-in, in my boyfriend Marc's car, I explained to him my desire to have some nude photos taken of myself. I unzipped his pants and rubbed his cock gently, teasing his balls with my fingertips. Marc has a masterful cock. He's also an expert at cunnilingus. He moaned as I ran my tongue along the ridges of his cock and over its head. When I described the little redhead from the pet shop to him, he got really hard. Right through my tight blouse, he placed his lips over my left nipple and sucked at it. He told me that having the photos done was a great idea, but he wanted to come along to watch.

"I want to make sure that Toby doesn't get the wrong idea," he said.

"I wouldn't have it any other way," I replied, teasing.

He reached under my blouse and unsnapped my bra, freeing my breasts. He then lifted my skirt and, with his usual precision, slipped his roaring engine into me. I trembled and came instantly—we hadn't been together for almost a week. Marc took his time and continued to stroke me slowly, like a pro. But then the second feature started and we wanted to watch it, so he licked and nipped at my erect nipples until I came a second time. He plunged his engine even deeper into my wet pussy before he exploded wildly.

I waited a day before calling Toby. He sounded professional and enthusiastic on the phone, so we set a date for a photo shoot the following Saturday, and he gave me his address.

When Saturday rolled around, Marc and I drove to the address Toby had given me. It was a large duplex apartment along a cul-de-sac in a wholesome suburban neighborhood. The redhead answered the door when we knocked, and introduced herself.

"Hi, I'm Audrey. We didn't get around to introductions when we met in the store last week."

"Nice seeing you again, Audrey. I'm Gina, and this is Marc."

"Welcome, both of you," she beamed, and opened the door to let us in.

She walked barefoot across the plush navy rug. The furniture was all white and soft beige. She wore cutoffs, and a hint of her round, white ass was visible. She told us to have a seat and said she'd be back in a minute with something cold to drink. When she turned to leave the room, I noticed Marc's eyes following her, sizing her up seductively.

"She's even better looking than you described," he said carefully.

"Almost supernatural," I said to myself, wondering if I should have left Marc home.

I may have been imagining this, but when she returned with our drinks, it looked as if another button on her blouse was undone. She was wearing a thin cotton blouse similar to the one she had been wearing when I first met her, but this time I could clearly see the texture and color of her small red nipples sticking up underneath. She was dressed very provocatively for one with such an angelic aura, which only made her more intriguing.

"Why don't we go into the studio? It's cozy there too," she said in a relaxed voice.

There was one black wall and one white wall in the photography studio. Equipment was set up in the far corner. Toby turned and smiled at us, but was busy adjusting the lights, so he didn't say anything. Huge, overstuffed black-and-white pillows were scattered all over the floor. Audrey plopped down on one of them and patted the pillows on either side of her.

"Have a seat. Relax. Toby likes to combine his photo sessions with a party atmosphere. You'll get much better pictures if you're not nervous," she explained. She lit up a joint and passed it to me. "I think you'll appreciate a few tokes of this," she said.

"I'll be okay," I said as I took a hit. "I've had more medical students gawking at me in my gynecologist's office."

I passed the joint back to Audrey. Toby moved in front of me with his camera and said to me softly, "Take your clothes off now, okay? Or would you like to do some poses half-clothed?"

"That would be nice, but this is all I have on," I answered, and lifted my form-fitting jersey dress over my head. I never wear underwear, and had on only a single garter and high heels.

Audrey and Marc sat down together in the corner. I began to pose, first lying down, then sitting in a ladylike manner. But Toby walked over to me, tapped my knees so that my legs fell open and quickly took a shot of my snatch.

"Those aren't the kind of shots I had in mind," I said, shocked.

"That was just for fun," he laughed.

Then he took pictures of my naked body from many angles—shots from behind as I knelt or stood, and side views of my breasts and erect nipples. Then I got down on all fours and he took close-ups of my tits from every imaginable angle. I wet my finger and rubbed it over the tips of my nipples to make them glisten. We were having so much fun that we barely noticed that Marc had taken Audrey's shirt off and was playing with her tits.

When Toby asked me to stand up for some full frontal shots, I instantly froze. So he said to Audrey, "Could you break it up there for a minute and help her with this?"

Audrey walked over to me slowly and pulled my body close to hers, kissing me on the lips. When she tongued my mouth I put my arms around her. She reached down and placed her delicious lips on my tit, while I reached for her pointed breasts and perky nipples, which were still warm from Marc's hot hands. I helped her take off her panties, then rubbed my hand over her furry little box. I sucked luxuriously on one hardening nipple while gently holding her other breast in my hand. We rubbed our pussies together to excite each other's clit.

Audrey put her hand between my legs and fingered my slit. She opened my red-hot pussy lips with her thumb and little finger, and tapped her middle finger erratically against my slippery flesh. She slid her finger into my pussy while she pulled my pleasure orbs to her mouth and sucked them like a hungry little kitten. We sank onto the pillows, and she held her sweet-smelling snatch open so that I could explore it with my lips and tongue.

I had eaten pussy only once before, but I rolled my tongue in circles around her hot box and licked her clitoris until it glistened. Suddenly I sensed how steamy the room was getting. Toby was frantically snapping photos, and when I looked over at Marc, I saw that he had taken off all his clothes. His penis was standing straight out, and though I've deep-throated him many times, I had never seen his virile instrument this huge before. As he watched Audrey run her smooth fingers over my body, he began to stroke himself impatiently. She leaned toward me and ran her tongue along my belly up to my chest, where she sucked fervently on each of my nipples. It felt great.

Marc approached us as I reclined on the pillows. Audrey's fiery mouth was still sucking away at my tit, where she contented herself until my nipple and her lips teemed to be one. I cupped my hands around her breasts and gently shook them; the shimmying made her nipples even harder. I noticed Marc's eyes on her tight little ass and I thought he was going to fuck her from behind. I would have loved to watch him fuck her doggie-style while she and I kissed and fondled one another. But instead, Marc joined Audrey, sucking my other breast into his mouth.

Suddenly, Marc and Audrey were locked in an embrace,

French-kissing passionately. I took this opportunity to slide between Audrey's legs again. With my tongue I parted the silky,
golden-red curls of her pretty pussy lips and let my teeth glide
over her throbbing clitoris. I sucked deeply until I was light-
headed. When I looked up, I saw that they were still kissing, and
Marc was massaging her supple white tits with his beautifully
tanned hands.

She lowered herself to kiss my eyelids, then said, "I want to get
a better look at Marc's cock. I think we've been neglecting him."

When her attractive green eyes beheld his huge cock, she
gasped. She grabbed his cock with her long, feminine fingers, put
her lips over the head of it and began to coax him with her experienced tongue. I ran my hands over her smooth, pear-shaped
bottom and patted her pussy with my hand. All this while, Toby
was having a field day with his zoom lens but, to tell you the
truth, we were barely aware of him.

Audrey energetically slid her lips up and down Marc's massive
cock. I was amazed—her mouth almost doubled in size, but she
never broke stride. She seemed happy and eager to be the perfect
sucking machine. I wondered if he had ever been inside a pussy
that felt that good. Unmercifully, I tickled his balls with my
tongue until he pleaded, "No, no. Please, no."

He didn't want it to end yet, so I let go of his gems and sam-
pled Audrey's luscious tit again. She was sweeter each time I
tasted her.

Toby couldn't handle it any longer. He dragged me away from
Audrey, laid me on the floor and began licking my pussy. He
thrust his tongue in and out, and jiggled my protruding clit back
and forth. He paid attention to every inch. His hands and tongue
were a tormenting mixture of smoothness and roughness, and I
closed my eyes, feeling as if I were drifting into outer space.

When I opened my eyes, I saw the full length of Marc's rigid
cock still sliding in and out of Audrey's mouth. Her hands
clutched his perfectly hard ass as he guided her back and forth
over his slippery erection. She was making lovely sucking sounds,

and I thought she would come simply from the pulse of his excited cock in her mouth. But Marc wanted his turn, so he spread her legs wide and buried his head between them. Opening her labia with his fingers, he searched for hidden treasure with his magnificent tongue. He licked and sucked her seam until, from the sounds she made, it was clear that she was having one orgasm after another, each one more intense than the last.

When Toby heard her impassioned cries, he slipped his tool inside me and moved it back and forth provocatively. The ridges of his powerful cock filled every crevice of my vagina. He plunged in deeper, then smiled as he took my breasts in his hands and squeezed them together. The come gushed from me, while Marc, ignoring Audrey's pleas, poked his tongue deeper into her pussy. She threw her head from side to side in ecstasy. Toby gave another thrust and then exploded. Come spurted from his pulsating penis in a seemingly endless flow.

Marc, who always has to have the last word, decided it was a good time to satisfy himself. Toby picked up his camera again, setting the shutter for fast action. Marc lifted Audrey and sat her on his perpendicular cock. He held her there, and she wrapped her long legs around his firm body. Her pussy was in spasms. He bounced her up and down on his hot tool for a few minutes and kissed her creamy white throat. Then they rolled to the floor still entwined. Marc held on to Audrey's waist and lifted her up and down on his smoking cock. I thought they were going to spontaneously combust. Suddenly, Marc shot his juice into her lovely pussy, and their bodies shook with pleasure—her tiny frame strained against his enormous member. She collapsed on top of him, and he fondled her gorgeous white ass. Toby finally ran out of film and we all sat there together, happy, naked and spent, and lit up another joint.

Audrey, Marc and I would like to plan another party like this—if Toby ever comes out of the darkroom.

IN CONCERT

I recently went to a large outdoor concert with my boyfriend, Mitch. There were supposed to be about fifty thousand people there, but judging by the way we were crunched together I'm sure there were a lot more. It was a hot summer night, so I wore a miniskirt with no underwear and a loose fitting T-shirt that did its best to hide my braless, 36C breasts. We were standing about a hundred feet from the stage, packed like sardines.

Once the music started, we all began swaying to the beat and singing along. Suddenly I felt something in my hair, and I quickly turned around to see what it was. When I did, I was startled to meet the most stunning green eyes I've ever seen in my life. They belonged to an absolute hunk. I froze for a moment, overtaken by his looks. He was wearing no shirt and only a tight pair of jeans. His short dark hair, combined with his tan, muscular body, sent a chill all the way down to my cunt. The unmistakable bulge in his jeans didn't help matters. I quickly turned around because I was beginning to blush and didn't want him to see.

I kept taking short glances behind me, and soon realized those incredible eyes were constantly on me instead of the stage. The crowd had started to shift, and my boyfriend was in front of me and to the side, with people standing between us. The sun slipped down soon after and left a giant full moon hanging above the large stage. My mystery man got more courageous as night fell.

While dancing to the music, I felt him moving against me in unison to the beat. Since I didn't move away, he must have thought I approved. Not that there was much room to move in anyway. I could feel his bulge grinding against my ass-cheeks as we rocked back and forth. I was a bit nervous with my boyfriend only four feet away. But whenever Mitch turned around he could only see my head, so I really didn't have to worry. Believe me, it's not like me to do something like that, but the wetness between my legs was driving me crazy. If only the guy hadn't been so hot, I would've been able to control myself.

When I peeked around again, I saw my mystery man mouth the words, "You're beautiful." Again, I turned away, blushing. He never stopped his grinding. Then he reached under my T-shirt from behind and played with my back and sides. I was so into it at that point, I began pushing my ass back against his solid cock. As he felt my approval, his hands started tickling my stomach, just below my bare tits.

I was too shy to touch him, but I knew he needed no encouragement. He removed his hands from my stomach for a few seconds. Then I felt his bare cock rubbing against me. He took my hand and placed it under the front of my miniskirt. I felt his cock poking through my legs from behind. I separated my thighs a bit so he could rub his long shaft against my soaked cunt. During all this, my boyfriend kept looking over at me. I'd smile and he'd go right back to watching the concert. Little did he know . . .

My secret stud had put his hands back inside my shirt and was lightly rubbing the tender underside of my tits. I was holding his cock, rubbing the shaft against my pussy lips. Soon I could feel my first orgasm arriving as his large head slid over my fiery clit. My body shook as he lightly held my breasts and, with his thumb and index finger, rolled my fully erect nipples like a radio dial. I did my best to control my gripping orgasm. As it subsided, Mitch looked over at me. He must have thought something was wrong, because he made his way through the crowd and over to me.

I panicked for a second, throwing the stranger's hands off my body. His cock was still hard and touching my cunt. I tried to move forward but he grabbed my hips and held me there. Mitch stood right in front of me and asked if everything was all right. I quickly said, "Yes. Why?" He said I looked like I was in pain or something. I told him not to worry and enjoy the show like I was.

While I was talking to my boyfriend, the hunk behind me had grabbed the swollen base of his cock and was searching for the opening to my pussy. I closed my legs, knowing if he found it I would be powerless to conceal my pleasure, and my boyfriend would discover us. I had to ask Mitch to turn around so I could rest my hands on him. He turned and I grabbed his hips. At the same time, I moved my ass farther back to accommodate the stranger's prick. Everyone was so close, there was no way anyone could have seen us. I felt him lift the back of my skirt up over my ass. He then took some time to massage me.

I was so wet I had no trouble accepting his large tool when he finally penetrated me from behind. I pushed back until he was all the way inside. His cock was much bigger than my boyfriend's. It brought me pleasures I'd never known before. The group started playing their most popular song and everyone went wild. Mitch thought my screams were for the band. He turned around to tell me what a great show it was. All I could reply was that it was the best. What I really meant was the giant cock pounding into me from behind!

My stranger had a tight hold on my hips and was working his cock in and out of me with absolute expertise. I could do nothing to hide my screams as orgasm after orgasm coursed through me. Mitch turned around in the middle of one of them and began kissing me, still not suspecting a thing. I stuck my tongue into his mouth. The sensation of having a complete stranger's dick up my cunt while French-kissing my boyfriend, who had no way of knowing what was going on, was one that I'm sure I will never forget. Mitch broke our kiss and said I was making him horny, and that he was going to give me the fucking of my life when we got home after the show. I said I had everything I needed right there with me, referring, of course, to the fuck-machine behind me, who hadn't let up during our entire conversation.

Mitch smiled and said, "You naughty girl, we can't do that here." That was enough. I turned him around and told him to enjoy the last part of the show. It took all I had to keep my cool.

My stud had incredible stamina. We must have been going at it for about thirty minutes. I desperately wanted him to have an incredible orgasm, so I stuck my hand through my legs, past his thrusting cock and down to his large sac. With every stroke, I would lightly squeeze his sensitive balls. That seemed to do it. I glanced back and saw the extreme pleasure in his face. He dug his cock as far as it would go, let out an animal moan and then I felt his come shooting deep inside me. We didn't move until his penis shriveled up and popped out. I could feel his warm come inside my pussy. He pulled my skirt back down over my ass and gave me a tap. I reached back and gave his bulge an approving squeeze. We still hadn't said a word to each other, but then he leaned toward my ear and said I had the best pussy he'd ever fucked. Then he licked my neck.

The concert ended soon after, and everyone slowly went their own way. Mitch grabbed my hand and began pulling me through the thick crowd. A second before I was whisked away, I turned to my stranger and told him he had the best cock I had ever had the pleasure of fucking. And with a quick smile, we parted company. I have never again seen my mystery lover, but you can be sure when I do, there will most certainly be a repeat performance in more intimate surroundings.

TEST FLIGHT

*A*s a pilot in the air force, it's one of my jobs to give instructional rides to all the new flyers in our squadron. One cool, March morning I drove to the base, and upon arriving saw that I was scheduled to a check ride with a Lt. Joey Collins. As I got my paperwork together, a stunning redhead, whose sleek five-foot-ten, one-hundred-forty-five-pound frame filled out her flight suit beautifully, came into my office.

"Is this where I'm supposed to sign in for my check flight?" she asked.

"It is," I answered, but not until I looked up and saw that the name tag on her suit read "Collins." I guess the puzzled look on my face was familiar to her. She told me that her last instructor saw the name "Joey" on the sheet and was also expecting a male pilot—until she checked in.

I took her out to the flight line after going over our weather charts and filing our flight plan. After we inspected the plane, we climbed aboard. The crew chief buckled her in her restraint harness and I got strapped into the backseat. We taxied out to the runway. As we rolled out to the centerline, she said over the intercom that this was always the best part of flying for her. I asked her why, but she said she wouldn't be able to tell me until we were already up in the air.

Well, I didn't have to wait to know what she was talking about. As soon as she slid the throttles to maximum and lit the afterburner, I instantly knew: The vibrations from the turbines and afterburner sent a raw buzz from my feet to my nose and I knew she was feeling the same buzz in her crotch!

She finally released the brakes after getting a green light from the tower, and as we took off she let out a long, sexy moan. I felt the stick jerking beneath my hand and realized she was having an orgasm. She confirmed it when she said, "Thanks for the help keeping it straight and level." I told her I wouldn't hold it against her, since I knew she was nervous.

But she calmly replied, "I'm not nervous, sir. I just had a big 'O,' if you know what I mean."

We talked some more as we climbed to altitude. I told her that I once knew another female pilot who had done the same thing on takeoff, and that if she wanted to come in my cockpit it was cool with me.

We completed the flight in about fifteen minutes. After we landed, I told her to report to my office to go over her performance as soon as she took her shower. When she walked in a little while later, I nearly spilled my coffee all over my fresh shirt. She had on a pair of jeans so tight, it looked like she'd been melted into them. Tucked into the narrow waistband was a khaki

T-shirt with no bra underneath. She had a great figure and carried herself with the grace of a model.

She smiled and took her seat, first shutting my office door and locking it! I quickly told her I was expecting the base commander, and suggested that it might be better to go over her flight later that evening over dinner. She agreed, and told me to meet her at the end of runway seven at eight o'clock. When she left, chills were coursing through my body.

The whole time the commander was with me, all I could think of was Lt. Collins and how I couldn't wait to take that hot little pilot for a ride of my own. When I got home, there was a message on my recorder from her: "If you're really a jet jock, then have your cock at runway seven by eight o'clock. I'll put it through more moves than an F-16!"

I took a long shower and splashed on some cologne. With a bottle of good champagne tucked under my arm, I slid into the driver's seat of my '67 Corvette. I suddenly realized that the car wouldn't be very comfortable for much necking, let alone fucking or a good 69. But I was confident that we'd find some way to get comfortable.

As I drove past the guard at the gate, she saluted me, and with the top down, I drove off to meet Lt. Collins.

The road I was headed for was off-limits to civilian vehicles, but I told the security police I would be watching some students practice their takeoffs and landings, and they waved me on. I clipped my lights as I pulled to the outer apron of the runway, and sat watching the sunset while listening to some classic Zombies on the tape deck.

I saw a car coming. My cock got hard just from the thought of what was in store for me. As Collins pulled up in her red Miata, I got out of my 'Vette and told her that we might have a problem, since neither of our cars was big enough for much activity.

"No sweat," she said, and quickly pulled a sleeping bag and a couple of blankets from her car!

She stepped up to me and I pulled her close, sucking her

tongue deep into my mouth. While we kissed, I opened my eyes
to see her already writhing with lust. We spread the blankets and
sleeping bag open, and soon we were both stark naked. I slipped
my mouth down to her tummy and had started licking my way
cuntward, when I realized she had shaved her pussy. It felt so
good to rub the smooth skin while feasting on her clit, which was
sticking way out. I hummed "The Star Spangled Banner" as she
put my head in a massive leg lock and commanded me to keep
sucking!

After she came several times, she finally released her hold on
me. "Get ready to have your cock sucked," she said. "I mean really sucked."

And suck she did! Her throat must have been bottomless. She
was rocking up and down on me like an oil rig, when all of a sudden I noticed a set of lights coming toward us. I was so close to
the edge, though, that I didn't say a word until I felt the last of
my hot come blast down her throat.

Then we both heard a car door slam. Lt. Collins jerked her
head up and gasped. Since we were both officers, I knew I could
take care of whoever was checking up on us. Still, it could prove
to be an embarrassing situation. But as it turned out, it was the
pretty, young security officer from the front gate who'd waved me
through earlier. She beamed her flashlight on us just as we were
diving under the blankets.

She started to ask if everything was okay, when she suddenly
giggled and said, "Joey?"

"Is that you, Anita?" Joey stammered. It seems they were
roommates in an off-base apartment. Anita walked back to her
car and got on the radio, then came back and told us that she was
"officially" on her dinner break. She and Joey talked for a minute
while I walked back to my car to get the champagne. When I got
back, Anita was taking her shirt off and Joey asked me if it was
all right if Anita joined us. I didn't even bother answering. All I
did was grab them both and pull them down to the blanket with
me.

They took turns sucking my prick, and then ate each other out. With a little persuasion, I got Anita to sit on my cock and ride it while Joey rode my face with her pretty, shaved cunt. I shot my load up Anita's tight box just as Joey flooded my mouth with her tangy juices. All the while we were doing this, there were planes taking off and landing not fifty feet away from us, roaring their engines and shooting flames out of their exhaust. It seemed that each time a plane took off, my cock was ready for another go with one of these two fine ladies.

Anita told Joey she wished she knew someone who could take her for a ride in one of those planes. Joey replied, "You do now!" She told her that I was a pilot and a flight instructor and that I'd be more than happy to take her up. Without hesitation, I agreed to do just that.

Now that I'm not stationed on that base anymore, I often think back to that night on runway seven. Shortly thereafter, I took Anita for that plane ride. (We ended up fucking before we even took off!) The three of us spent many happy weekends together that summer.

By the way, Joey and I got married last year, and yes, we still enjoy flying!

RIDE 'EM

I bought a horse on a whim, and then found out I couldn't ride him. He was an ex-racing thoroughbred named Miracle, and he would ride away with me. Either I found a good trainer, or I'd have to sell him. I decided to try the trainer route first.

Her name was Trish, and the people at the stable where I boarded my horse told me that she was the best trainer around. She was petite, with curly red hair and a tight little ass. When I first saw her she was wearing a pair of tight, white britches and tall, black riding boots. I introduced myself and explained my problem, and she agreed to look at my horse.

Trish was impressed by Miracle's size and asked if she could ride him. "Fine," I said, and helped her tack him up. She was very businesslike. I, on the other hand, couldn't help but notice her tasty ass and the way her pert breasts pressed against her shirt. She popped right on top of him with no assistance. Trish was muscular but still very feminine, and I was strongly attracted to her. I envied Miracle as she mounted him effortlessly. I wished it was me she was about to ride.

My horse put Trish to the test, taking the turns fast and bucking erratically. But she countered his every attempt to throw her, and pretty soon had mastered the beast. After about forty-five more minutes of riding his graceful form, she got off and said, "He needs to learn some manners, but he really can move." I asked if she would train us together. She agreed and we set up a lesson, adding that this session was a freebie. But I insisted on doing something, so she let me buy her dinner.

That evening, her transformation from stable hand to elegant woman was spectacular! Her shimmering red hair lay in ringlets around her shoulders. I looked closely, for the first time, at her green eyes and high cheekbones. She was wearing a silky, black dress that was gathered with a clasp at her breasts. High heels and black stockings completed the outfit.

Trish was quiet and shy as we drove to dinner—quite a difference from the woman who had so handily tamed Miracle a few hours earlier. I found the contrast appealing indeed. The meal was delicious, and although we made small talk as we ate, by the time we'd finished our second bottle of wine all I could think about was how hot I was to make love to her. Remembering how well she had handled herself in the saddle, I knew she'd be a spirited partner in the sack. Hopeful that we'd have a long and rewarding night together, I ordered dessert.

We shared a great big wedge of cheesecake dripping with strawberries. I offered her a piece on my fork. Taking my hand in hers, she slid the cake into her mouth and slowly withdrew the empty fork. A bit of strawberry juice lingered on her lips. It was making me very horny and she knew it too. As I moved to remove the juice with my napkin, she deftly caught it with the tip of her tongue. She smiled coyly and giggled at my growing discomfort. I shifted nervously in my seat.

"Now it's my turn to feed you," she said. Taking the fork, she offered me some cake. As I took it in my mouth, she let out a muffled sigh of pleasure. This really unnerved me, and I blushed. She giggled again, and this time I laughed back.

We really began to enjoy each other's company. As I offered her piece after piece of cake, I felt a nudge on the inside of my calf. She was working her toe up my pants leg. I almost dropped the fork as I watched her tease another piece of cake into her sensuous mouth. We laughed at our flirtations and moved closer together, feeding off of each other's desire.

As she leaned toward me, I got a good look at her nipples, erect and straining under her dress. I moved my hand to her leg and gave it a gentle squeeze. She looked approvingly in my eyes and opened her legs slightly. I moved my hand to her inner thigh and began to stroke her leg. She squeezed her legs together and moaned with pleasure at my touch. Her fragrance began to intoxicate me. Our heads moved closer together—but just as we were about to kiss, the waiter approached the table with the check. Trish began to laugh. I asked her if she was ready, and she replied, "For the last half an hour, at least."

Before we got in the car, I pulled her to me and kissed her passionately. It was as if a floodgate had opened and released our pent-up passions. Hungrily we explored each other's mouth as our fingers searched out the sensitive parts of our bodies. Realizing that this was not the place to consummate our passion, we got in the car.

As I drove, I told her I wanted to make love to her. "Yes," she answered, putting her hand on my thigh, "so do I. But first we must stop off at the stable. I need to check on a horse. He pulled

a tendon earlier today and I want to see if the swelling is down."
She moved her hand over my growing bulge. "I just hope it's not
as swelled as this is right now," she said of my throbbing member.

I was embarrassed by her brazenness. Trish apparently enjoyed
sex as much as I did and was not afraid to show it. I'd never had
the good luck to be with such a woman, and I was ready to enjoy
every moment.

The stable was dark and quiet. Taking Trish by the hand, I
kissed her again. Laughing, she pulled her head back and said, "I
bet you've never made love in the hay before." Well, she was
right. Before I could say anything, though, she pushed me away
and ran, giggling, into the barn, tossing her shoes off behind her.
I followed in hot pursuit. When I found her she was hiding behind a door. I picked her up and carried her to an empty stall that
had been cleaned out. On the way, she snatched up a blanket. I
put her down and she covered the ground with the blanket. Kissing hard, we eased ourselves down. The only sound, other than
our pounding hearts, was the stirring of the sleeping horses.

I slowly ran a hand under her skirt. As I ran my hand along the
inside of her creamy thigh, I realized she wasn't wearing any
panties. I began to squeeze and explore. She unbuttoned my shirt,
then sucked and bit my nipples. Our hips gyrated in unison. With
my free hand I unfastened her dress and peeled it away, as if
pulling petals off a rose.

Trish had a beautifully toned body. Her breasts were petite but
firm, the nipples erect and proud. Her pussy was framed by closely
trimmed wisps of red hair, and glistened in the moonlight streaming in through the stable door. I removed my shirt and our bodies met, their warmth insulating us from the cool night. We
kissed and fondled each other with unbridled passion. The horses
began to stir as our moans grew louder.

She rolled me onto my back and unbuckled my pants. Sliding
her hands inside my briefs, she pumped my throbbing prick. In an
instant she had stripped me naked and was rubbing the head of
my cock between her fingers. When I tried to suck her nipples

into my mouth, she pushed me away and said, "Just relax. We have all night." Starting at the center of my chest, she traced a wet path with her tongue down to my stiff cock and guided it into her waiting mouth. With her tongue she tickled the head and shaft. Slowly, she worked my engorged cock into her hot, hungry mouth. The pleasure was intense. I was completely at her mercy!

I ran my fingers through her hair and caressed her body. It felt so good I didn't want it to end. I felt a familiar rumble in my balls that told me I was close to climaxing. I told her this, but she wouldn't let up. All she said was, "Relax and enjoy it." I ran my fingers through her hair as I climaxed. With half a dozen spasms of pleasure I came in her mouth. She continued sucking and swallowing until the last drop was gone.

Getting up, our strength slowly came back. I took her in my arms and said, "Now it's my turn." I kissed her, tracing circles around her lips, ears and nipples with my tongue. Sliding my hand between her thighs, I stroked and squeezed them gently. Her moans told me I was on the right track. I ran my fingers through her pubic hair and searched out her pussy. It was moist and responsive. She squirmed under my caresses. I worked my finger in and out until she was dripping with pleasure.

After sucking each breast in turn, I drew a wet path with my tongue to her waiting pussy. Gently spreading her lips, I found her clitoris with the tip of my tongue. I maintained pressure on her breasts by pinching her nipples between my fingers. She gyrated, bucked uncontrollably and begged me to increase the tempo. I did so, and she responded with a shriek of pleasure that echoed through the quiet of the stable.

"Boy," she said when she'd caught her breath, "I sure needed that."

It wasn't long before we were ready for another round. This time I slid on top of her and rubbed my hard cock between her legs. She wrapped her fingers around it and whispered, "So what do you plan to do with this?" In answer, I slipped my rod past her velvety cunt lips with one quick stroke.

She kept her fingers wrapped around the base of my prick as I worked it in and out of her grotto. She was tight but wet. As our passion grew, so did our rhythm. She whispered in my ear, "I love to feel you fuck me. Do it hard." I pumped with all of my might and we soon exploded in mutual ecstasy. Our bodies covered with sweat, we lay in the dark, completely satisfied.

Eventually we got up and picked the straw from each other's hair and body. We got dressed and looked over her horse. He was doing fine. Then we returned to Trish's place, showered, and enjoyed a restful sleep. In the morning we were refreshed and started the day off by making love. I guess I lucked out. Not only did I find an excellent horse trainer, but I got a great lover in the bargain.

WIVES ON THE WAVES

*I*t began innocently enough. I was working through my vacation as first mate on a forty-foot cabin cruiser in the Caribbean. The captain, my friend, was kind enough to keep me employed all of my summers through college. As a charter, we usually had from four to six people aboard for short cruises. Generally our passengers were middle-aged businessmen and their wives or girlfriends. On one particular cruise I really lucked out, having two young couples on board for an extended weekend. I certainly didn't expect any sex, but it was nice to see two beautiful women sunning themselves on the deck, even if their husbands were also on the boat. While serving brunch to the two ladies our first morning out, one of them kept staring at me—and at my bathing trunks. This struck me as odd, considering she had an attractive husband below who was, presumably, sleeping. I might as well interject here that I am five feet nine inches tall, and have brown hair and brown eyes. I am in good shape, although I'll admit I'm certainly no Adonis.

When they finished eating, the women asked me to sit with them for a bit. Henry, the captain, was managing the ship, so I felt comfortable relaxing for a few minutes. They introduced themselves as Christine and Nancy. I told them my name and we exchanged pleasantries. I finally got up enough nerve to ask where their husbands were. Christine leaned forward to speak, and in doing so her towel fell off her shoulders, expressing a pair of incredibly full breasts. She blushed and put the towel back in place, although I must say she didn't seem in any big hurry to do so.

Christine and Nancy told me that their husbands were bisexual and, as Nancy put it, "hot for each other." Both wives were willing to let the men have their little getaways, like this one, as long as they didn't go off to find any other men. As part of the deal, the trysts always took place in an exotic setting, and the women always got to come along for the ride. And this, they explained, was one of those rides.

The two beauties went on to say that while they didn't mind getting it on in a group, straight girl-on-girl action didn't excite them much. I pointedly asked if they wanted to party with Henry and me, and was pleased (even a little shocked) to hear them both say yes.

I excused myself and went to tell Henry the good news. He smiled but, brandishing his wedding band with a sigh, told me I was on my own. "Knock yourself out," he said with envy dripping from his voice, adding that I could use the crew's quarters in the bow of the boat.

I ran back to the ladies, escorted them down to the cabin and carefully locked the door behind me. I got out some tequila and poured three generous shots. We continued to get acquainted, with lots of physical contact between the shots of tequila. Soon Nancy and Christine had my trunks off. Their hands and mouths were all over my body. It was a dream come true.

Those two sumptuous, raven-haired women did things to my cock I still think about to this day. Nancy positioned herself between my legs and gave my balls a tongue bath, while Christine offered the same treatment to my cock. Christine, in particular, had an incredible mouth. Her tongue never seemed to stop moving, it felt as though my prick was being given a nonstop massage. Looking down, I was so turned on I almost passed out.

I asked Nancy to remove her bathing suit and have a seat. She laughed and asked me where. I flicked my tongue in response, and soon she was astride my face, her thick, pink love lips parting for my tongue. The exotic smell of her cunt filled my nostrils. I had never been so happy in all my life. The sensations, tastes and smells were driving me insane with lust. My tongue and lips danced over Nancy's pussy so quickly and with so much intensity that for a minute I didn't notice what had happened: Christine had taken a seat as well—right on my throbbing cock!

It didn't seem as though any of us would ever tire out, so intense was the fucking and tonguing taking place in that little cabin. I'm proud to admit that I always last a good, long while in bed. I can exercise excellent control over my orgasms, which guarantees that my partners and I always get our fill. When I finally do come, though, I'm like a wild animal. And I knew that time was approaching.

Nancy was really getting into riding my face, and Christine was slowly easing her way up and down my cock. With one hand rubbing her clit and the other stroking my balls, she looked incredible. Her hair was tossed back. A dew of sweat covered her smooth body. Her eyes were glazed over and her tight stomach was heaving in what I knew was the beginning of an orgasm. She looked more sensational than any actress I'd ever seen in an erotic video. But what made this picture perfect was the frame: I was watching the whole fantastic scene through the gap between Nancy's luscious thighs!

Soon Christine was bucking frantically, grinding herself all the way down against the base of my shaft. She came, and I felt her juices massaging my cock as they dripped out of her satisfied pussy. I felt an incredible sensation beginning in my stomach and spreading through my entire body. I swear, I blacked out for a split second when I came. But come I did, blasting jets of hot sperm into Christine's cunt.

Nancy collapsed by my side on the bed, and I quickly lifted her leg and began feasting on her again from a different angle. I was happy to feel Christine's lips again at work on my prick. The best surprise, however, was glancing up to see Nancy eating Christine's sopping-wet pussy. What a turn-on! I couldn't help myself and emptied another load into Christine's mouth.

After a while we all collapsed in a heap on the bed. The smell of sex threatened to overpower the tiny cabin. I opened a porthole to let in the cool sea air, thinking of poor, married Henry upstairs in his captain's chair.

Soon Christine suggested a shower and a swim. The shower turned into another suck-and-fuck fest almost as intense as the first, but nothing will ever equal that first time with those two special women. I shake my head sadly when I think of what their husbands missed out on.

HEART & SOUL

A few years ago I tended bar in a soul club that catered to a mostly black clientele. I was the only white person that worked there, although, since I have a shaved head and a dark, rich tan, people often mistook me for black in the club's dim light.

The minute Anita walked into the room I knew she was special. She carried herself like royalty and her clothes and jewelry spelled class. She was super fine, and she knew it.

There was chemistry between us from the start. We spent the entire evening talking. I couldn't let her get away without asking for a date, and with a dazzling smile and a soft laugh she said, "Yes."

When the day of our date finally arrived I picked Anita up at her home. After I met her family we left for the restaurant. But something was wrong. She seemed stiff and uncomfortable. She sat against the door with her hand on the handle.

Suddenly it dawned on me. "You didn't realize I was white, did you?"

There was a quiet "No." Her eyes never left the road ahead.

I asked her if she wanted me to take her home. Again her answer was "No."

Anita never totally relaxed the entire evening, but from this awkward beginning came a long and eventually beautiful friendship.

Anita was proud of her ethnic heritage. As a Black Muslim she was extremely angry about the way the white power structure treated her people. Our discussions on the subject were often heated.

One night she said, "Greg, you know we don't often tell people, and we are not too proud of it, but I've got a grandmother who is part white."

After a few minutes of silence I responded, "What would you say, Anita, if I told you that we don't often tell people and we are not too proud of it, but I've got a grandmother who is part black?"

For a while she just looked at the floor. Then she murmured, "I didn't say that, did I?" For all she taught me, I was able to show her that the very thing she hated most—prejudice—was lurking in her own heart.

James Baldwin once wrote that white men lust after black women because they want to be the "master," to subjugate and violate them. I am not sure where Mr. Baldwin got his information, but he sure wasn't talking about Anita and me. She made it rough on me. She kept making rules, erecting barriers as if she wanted me to become discouraged and quit. Many times I almost got to

1

PENTHOUSE UNCENSORED IV

the point where I was ready to give up on her, but something about Anita kept me coming back.

After several dates Anita began to notice my frequent use of slightly risqué humor. "Sex is a big thing with you, isn't it?" she asked. I admitted that I thought it was an important part of a male/female relationship, something of great beauty when shared.

She nodded and said, "Okay, next Thursday." It was as if she had just made up her mind to have the car lubed. I protested that it was not necessary, preferring no sex at all to a cold, passionless "service job." But she had made up her mind, and nothing I said would make any difference.

Thursday came and we decided to take a brief out-of-town trip. Anita didn't want anyone in our community to even think we were lovers, much less catch us going into a motel. Unfortunately there was a convention in town, and after being turned away from several motels we headed home. I thought I heard a small sigh of relief. As we passed a Holiday Inn we decided to try one last time.

When I returned to the car, she looked up with a faint smile and said, "No luck, huh?" When I dangled the room keys, she shrank back into the seat, her smile gone. I felt an odd mixture of irritation and amusement. It was obvious the last thing Anita wanted was to hop into bed with a white man.

After we found our room Anita rushed to take a shower. I smiled again as I heard her lock the bathroom door. When she emerged, in a cloud of steam, she was wrapped head to toe in towels. She imperiously announced that I could now use the shower.

I half expected her to be gone when I came out, but she was watching television with the blankets tight around her chin. The mound of towels on the floor indicated she was naked beneath the covers. I sat down on the edge of the bed and we both pretended to watch the show.

Without saying a word, I turned and looked at her. She said, "Don't rush me." I smiled and pretended to watch TV again.

After a few minutes I leaned over and kissed her. Not our usual goodnight peck, but a moist, sweet kiss. All the walls came tumbling down. No black, no white, just a man and a woman. As I slid beneath the covers our naked bodies melted together.

I pulled back. I had dreamed of this moment for so long. Slowly I gazed at her nakedness. She was an ebony Venus, exquisite in every detail. Each beautiful breast was full and round, with a dark, swollen nipple that looked like a ripe blackberry. Between her satin-smooth thighs was a glistening wedge of dark curls. When I finally looked up there was a smile on her lips.

As I began kissing and licking her inner thighs, she leaned back and opened up to me. Her pussy was like a beautiful exotic flower. Each petal was trimmed in ebony while the center was a rich pink. As my tongue caressed her, sweet nectar flowed to my lips. Her hands urged me on. As I licked her clit, spasms shook her body. She began to moan and arch to meet my hungry mouth.

I moved up until I was looking into her half-closed, lust-filled eyes. The head of my swollen cock pressed against her hot, moist cunt. Slowly I slid into her. With each inch, her eyes grew wider. At first I took my time. Each stroke was long, slow and deep. She felt so good. Her pussy was tight, holding my dick like an old friend.

As our passion grew, our speed increased. Breathing became shallow and rapid. Sweat poured from our bodies.

Anita cried out, "Oh yes, oh yes! Fuck me baby, fuck me!" I was only too happy to obey. I felt the pleasure building. I tried to hold back, but there was no stopping. Grabbing her beautiful ass, I buried my rod deep inside her. My cock erupted, pulsing with each spurt. She wrapped her arms around me with a moan, and I felt her body shudder.

Now when someone mentions race relations I can't help but smile a little. I've learned a lot about the subject from Anita, and I like to think I've taught her a thing or two in return.

OFFICE ORIENTATION

Our receptionist is an eighteen-year-old girl who is the epitome of innocence. She looks almost like a librarian, but a very sexy librarian.

I saw in her eyes a thirst for life and its challenges. As the human resources manager for a large Midwest company, it was my job to give direction and nourishment to her desires. Since she was new to the corporate world, I decided I would really take her under my wing.

Her name is Debbie. She has a great body, but the clothes she chose to wear seemed like attempts to hide it. During the course of our many conversations I discovered the reason. She was very shy, having lived a relatively sheltered life in a small, rural community. I realized she needed more than simply company orientation. She needed orientation to life.

We made plans to spend a weekend together. I wanted to take her shopping—let her know what it is like to "go out with the girls." When the weekend arrived I picked her up at her apartment and we headed for the mall. I told Debbie that we would find clothes that were a bit more stylish than what she was accustomed to wearing. She excitedly agreed.

We stopped at a large department store and proceeded to the ladies' department. I picked out a few sensuous outfits for her, and we both went into the dressing room. Debbie tried them on. As she was changing I caught my first glimpse of what she really looks like—a beautiful young woman, fully developed in every sense of the phrase. Until then I had not paid much attention to her body because it had been so disguised. She had the figure of a goddess. Her breasts were firm and uplifted, with nipples that seemed to point at me. Her cunt had sparse blonde hair that revealed much of her pussy. I felt it was a sin for her to not show off her fine attributes.

I was feeling familiar stirrings within me as I watched Debbie try on the different outfits. I had never felt that way toward a member of my own sex. I felt confused: contradicting thoughts were fluttering through my mind.

I decided we were going to spice up her outfits a bit more than I had planned. I took her to the lingerie department.

I picked out some garter belts, bras, panties, teddies and a few other accessories which, I explained to her, would help her feel good about herself. I told her I usually wear them myself because they are so comfortable. Debbie was skeptical at first, but decided to go along because I was being so nice to spend time with her.

After I picked out some items, we headed back to the dressing room. She fumbled with the garter belt, so I helped her attach it to the stockings, accidentally touching her thighs in the process. I wanted to grab her, yet I was afraid of how she might react.

I am not sure who shuddered more when she pulled the G-string up her long thighs and, innocently enough, pulled too far, sliding the silky material into her cunt. I enjoyed watching her as she slid a finger in to retrieve the G-string from her warm, moist depths. I could tell she was as excited as I was.

Next I helped her put on a skimpy little bra I had picked out. I enjoyed the softness of her breasts, and I spent a little extra time making sure the fit was good. Her nipples were hard and erect, pointing out at me in an inviting way. We looked deep into each other's eyes as I finished her fitting. I was about to tell her we should be going, when she raised her finger to my lips to silence me. I gently began licking and sucking her finger. Surprise and lust were written on her face as I moved from her finger to her nipples, then down to taste another woman's pussy for the first time in my life.

Debbie lay back on the little stool. I was on fire as I pulled the G-string to one side and slid a finger into her honey-pot. I lowered my mouth and drove my tongue into her as far as I could, savoring her sweet taste. She came instantly, with a loud moan that brought a salesclerk running in to see what was the matter.

"Is everything all right in there?" she asked.

We both started giggling. "Everything is dandy," I answered.

We heard the salesclerk leave. I gave Debbie a soft kiss on the lips, gently sliding my tongue into her mouth. I held her breasts in my hands and felt the soft firmness. I caressed her nipples and she arched her back, moaning in delight, wrapping her arms around me and pulling me toward her so that our tummies and breasts touched. I was aware of a growing wetness between my legs, and wanted nothing more than to have her press her hot, young mouth against me and suck my sweet nectar like there was no tomorrow.

We quickly got dressed and walked out of the dressing room. Since the G-string was soaked from her arousal, I put it back on the shelf and grabbed another one. The salesclerk who had heard us in the dressing room gave me a sly look and smiled. I smiled back, starting to again feel hot stirrings between my legs. Having sex with another woman was having a bigger impact on me than I thought it would. I was becoming insatiable for my own sex!

We quickly paid for the merchandise and hurried to make the appointment with the hairdresser.

After we reached the salon I instructed Jackie, the hairdresser, to give Debbie a more contemporary look. I sat down to watch.

I watched Jackie and admired the firm flare of her hips and her shapely breasts. For the third time that day I started getting hot over a woman. Debbie noticed me staring at the stylist, and I think she felt somewhat jealous. As I sized Jackie up, Debbie began slowly spreading her legs under the bib so that I could see right up to her cunt. The G-string slid into her pussy. Her legs were encased in white lace stockings held up by the garter belt. Debbie lifted her knees slightly to give me a better view.

I was having a difficult time maintaining a conversation with Jackie. I think she knew that I was staring up Debbie's dress. Then Debbie began tracing the line of the G-string with her middle finger. Seeing this, I moaned. By this time Jackie was fully aware of what was going on. She said after she finished Debbie's hair she would be glad to "help me out," if I cared to wait around until lunchtime. I told her, with a chuckle, that I didn't think I could last that long.

Upon hearing that, Jackie locked the door and drew the shades. I was glad that we were lucky enough to be the only people in the salon. Jackie removed her clothes and insisted that Debbie and I undress as well. Debbie sat back and enjoyed orgasm after orgasm as Jackie and I licked her all over, nibbling on her most sensitive places. Then Jackie climbed up on the chair and sat on Debbie's lap, facing her, letting her breasts dangle in front of Debbie's mouth. She hungrily lapped and fondled Jackie's breasts.

I had a feast before me—two wet cunts staring me in the face. My tongue and fingers brought them both to orgasm, and they collapsed together.

I started to finger my own cunt while waiting for Jackie to quickly finish Debbie's perm. I was so wet I began smearing the juice all over Debbie's lips, giving her a taste of my pussy.

Finally it was done. Debbie looked incredible. The farm girl had been transformed into a woman of the 1990s. We quickly grabbed our clothes, put on just enough to cover ourselves and headed for Jackie's place, where we would be more comfortable.

As Jackie drove, I went down on Debbie again, bringing her to more orgasms. I loved the way she cried out when I ran my tongue along her hot clit. God, she could buck and bounce.

"I want to eat you," she told me. I had no problem with that. I lay down on the backseat and she got down between my legs. I was in heaven as she slowly ran her tongue along the soft folds of my pussy. When she wrapped her lips around my clit, my ass shot up off the seat and I was crying out, so loud I surprised myself. I came and my juice dribbled out of my pussy. Debbie licked it up. Smiling, she said, "Good to the last drop."

"You know, you two are driving me crazy," Jackie said. She was doing all she could to drive with one hand while manipulating her cunt with the other. Debbie and I reached over the seat and began fondling Jackie's tits as she drove.

Jackie's apartment is on the first floor, and she has underground parking. After parking the car we ran into her apartment and picked up where we left off. We didn't even make it to her bedroom for a couple of hours. The living room floor was fine with us.

We were three sex-starved ladies with a wealth of sexual energy at our disposal. We tried everything possible. Jackie had the most experience with woman-to-woman sex because many of her customers come on to her. It seems many of them get excited during the long hairstyling sessions, in which Jackie innocently rubs her body against them while doing her work. Jackie has made a lot of money taking special care of her "regulars."

Being intimately involved with some customers has enabled her to perfect the fine art of shaving and sculpting pubic hair. She had a photo album full of pictures of her work. Debbie and I got horny all over again after we looked through it.

Jackie taught Debbie and me plenty about the art of making love. She had a huge trunk of goodies—sex toys—that brought us to new heights of delight. We used every device at least once. We enjoyed what we did with the two-headed dildo the best.

After going at it for hours, we all fell asleep together. When we awoke a short time later we raided the refrigerator. We had built up hearty appetites, and knew we would need the strength for our next session.

At work Debbie and I keep our distance, which is often difficult. Debbie occasionally takes days off when I am out recruiting at colleges. She accompanies me as a representative. I have her dress very businesslike, but only on the outside. If her jacket were to be opened, anyone watching would be in for a surprise. I always get wet just thinking of how little she has on underneath.

Debbie's ability to charm has been instrumental in helping me hire a number of male and female coeds. Once, during a lengthy recruiting trip, we had not found time for loving. It was late in the afternoon and we still had one more interview—and on top of that, a long drive ahead of us. We were more than a little bit grouchy when the last girl showed up. You can imagine how delighted we were to discover how beautiful she was.

The room was arranged so that Colleen the candidate and I were facing each other. Debbie sat next to Colleen.

Debbie fidgeted in her chair as she began the opening remarks and basic questioning. I watched to see how well the candidate handled herself. When I caught Debbie's glance I licked my lips and looked at our candidate, Colleen. Debbie knew right away what to do. She spread her legs just enough to allow me a view of her panty-clad crotch.

Debbie then adjusted her suit jacket so her breasts were visible. Her nipples stretched against the silk blouse. Colleen continued to answer our questions. Debbie then arranged her chair so that she was facing Colleen, giving her the same tantalizing view of her pussy I had. Colleen became nervous and struggled to keep her attention from Debbie's crotch. The more Debbie fidgeted, the more her skirt slid up her thighs, exposing the tops of her stockings.

Colleen tried to avoid looking at Debbie by turning toward me. I picked up the conversation. This gave Debbie, a true exhibitionist, the chance to open her blouse, exposing a half-bra that uplifted her perky breasts. Debbie deftly removed her jacket and blouse, and then unhooked her skirt, letting it fall. She was standing behind Colleen wearing only her bra, G-string, garter belt and stockings. She began masturbating. I tried to pay attention to the candidate. Colleen, meanwhile, could not help but hear Debbie's activity. Nevertheless, she refused to turn around. Her face was flushed and she was breathing hard.

I said there was one more question I wanted to ask her. I watched a look of relief come over her pretty face.

I asked Colleen if she was interested in learning more intimate aspects of corporate culture. She stared at me silently for the longest time. I could imagine the thoughts going through her head. They were probably similar to those I had had while in the dressing room with Debbie.

She blurted out, "Yes."

I instructed her to turn around. I wondered what her reaction would be after she saw Debbie standing there with a finger in her clean-shaven cunt.

Colleen gasped. I began caressing her from behind as Debbie's fingers quickened their thrusts into her cunt. I took Colleen's suit jacket off. She didn't resist in the slightest, and merely continued watching Debbie and licking her lips. Next I unbuttoned her blouse and skirt and removed them. I kept caressing her as I undressed her.

Debbie then approached Colleen and hugged her. Colleen still had not said a word. Debbie pulled Colleen's hips against her own, and they ground their cunts together.

Colleen was beginning to loosen up. She let out little sighs and ran her hands all over Debbie. I was not going to be left out. I quickly took my clothes off, reached between their legs and started fingering and licking their cunts. Colleen's was tight and juicy, and she tasted marvelous. It took only moments to bring her to orgasm.

Debbie gently pushed Colleen onto her knees in front of her. With one hand, Debbie pulled her G-string aside and with the other she pulled Colleen's face into her cunt. Colleen's nervous inexperience was quickly replaced with energetic enthusiasm. Her tongue quickly brought Debbie off.

We had to get out of the interview room before the placement-office staff became suspicious. We put on only our suits, stuffing our underwear in our purses, and quickly left to go to Colleen's apartment. The ride there was enjoyable, as we continued petting in the car. Colleen had adapted so well to our advances, I couldn't help feeling impressed.

Colleen led us to her bedroom and we all undressed. We began an intense fucking session. It wasn't long before Maria, Colleen's roommate, walked in on us. We were not about to let her run away. Maria nervously resisted our advances, but gave in shortly after Colleen's tongue darted into her pussy. Then I placed my cunt over Maria's mouth, and Debbie caressed the girl's body. We managed to bring her to one sweet orgasm after another, within seconds.

Debbie and I were quite satisfied when we left Colleen's, and eagerly delighted that Colleen and Maria had joined our group.

STRIP TRIP

I'm just an average girl. When I walk down the street, men don't turn around to look at me. But an experience I had recently proved to me that anything can happen, especially if you take the initiative.

One of my good friends was getting married, so a few of us took her out to an all-male revue. We made sure that we were sitting at tables in the front row so we could stuff bills under the guys' G-strings and slide our hands inside their bikinis.

Once the show started, all I could think about was what it would be like to actually have sex with one of these men. Judging from the way they moved their bodies, I figured that any one of them would be great in bed. They all looked like they knew how to hit the right spot, how to push a girl over the edge of ecstasy. I had a plan that might work, but knowing my luck, I thought it would turn out to be just another fantasy I could think about while I used my trusty vibrator.

I went to the ladies' room and took out five one-dollar bills. Then I took a red pen and wrote a message on the edge of all the bills. It said: "Hi! Would you like to have a party with a very horny lady? If so, come to Susie's at nine-thirty tomorrow night." Then I wrote my address and added, "I'll be waiting." I returned to our table and set my plan in motion. The next five studs who danced within my reach got a bill with my message on it.

The following morning I got my hair done and had a facial. I bought three different kinds of wine, and I bought the sexiest and sleaziest outfit I could find. It was made out of black lace and nothing else.

When I got home I dressed, drank some wine and waited. I sat and watched the clock, second after second, minute after minute, hour after hour. When it was only five after eight, I heard a knock on the door. Great, I thought, here's somebody I'll have to get rid of fast.

I answered the door and my heart stopped. Standing in the hall was not one, but three of the male strippers from the night before. I couldn't believe it. Here I was, standing with three incredibly gorgeous guys. I just froze and didn't say anything.

One of them asked if I was Susie. I replied, "Yes. Come in, please."

The guy who had asked my name told me that he was Dave, and introduced the others, Jeff and Brad. Dave went on to say that they were sorry they'd showed up early but it would give us all more time to get to know each other. I offered them each a glass of wine.

Before we knew it, one glass led to another, and before long we were all very relaxed and talking as if we all had known each other for some time. I was feeling very fine and I confessed to them that I was very turned on by their performances at the club.

Jeff stood up and said, "Well, we'll perform for you right now." Brad tuned the stereo to a different station and began to dance around. I was getting very hot. Jeff pulled me up to him. I took over from there. I grabbed Jeff, pulled his body close to me and kissed him. As I was kissing him, I felt the other two strippers' hands on my body. One was working on my shirt buttons and the other on my skirt zipper. Things started going the way I'd hoped.

I had only wanted one of them but I sure wasn't going to turn the others away. I'd thought about having two men at once, but three? I felt like I was the luckiest woman on earth. I was naked and wondering what was going to happen next. Then Don lowered me onto the couch and plunged his thick cock into my pussy.

I was in heaven. Don was fucking me with long strokes, slow and easy. Jeff and Brad each had one tit in their mouths. I never thought I would enjoy having an audience. But to be truthful, the thought of all three of them watching me turned me on even more. When Don shot his load inside me, Brad and Jeff both kept sucking my tits.

I wanted more. I stood up, pushed Jeff to the floor and jumped upon his hard tool. I was riding him when I felt a pair of lips close over one of my breasts and suck my nipple. That got me thinking. I wondered what it would be like to have one cock in my pussy and one in my mouth at the same time. Brad was sucking my tit, so I reached for Don's cock and pulled him to my mouth. As I sucked Don's cock, I reached down and started stroking Brad's cock.

We carried on like this for at least another hour. I was fucked by each of them and sucked by each of them. And you know what? I was right. They *did* know just the moves that could push a woman over the brink. I never came so many times in my life, even counting marathon sessions with my vibrator. By the time we all fell asleep on the floor, I don't think there were any positions we hadn't been in.

When I woke up at dawn, my three studs were gone. But they'd left something behind. Next to a bottle of wine, I found three dollar bills. Each of my studs had left one with his name, phone number, and address written on it in red ink, and an invitation to call any time.

I haven't decided what to do yet. Maybe I'll call one of them. On the other hand, I've got plenty of one-dollar bills.

FRENCH GIRL

I'm married, forty, with two kids. My wife and I are happy. But we haven't had sex since our second was born three years ago. I love my wife, need her, and wouldn't leave her. Yet our lack of a sex life together made the episodes I'm about to relate all the more intense.

Last summer we were visited by Annette, a nineteen-year-old daughter of good friends. She's from Paris. She was touring the States, hiking and sightseeing, and stayed with us for a week. Annette was pleasant and friendly. Her English wasn't perfect, but it was fairly good. She baby-sat our kids a couple of nights so we could go out. After that week, she planned to hike from a trail near our home, meeting up with other French students at a hostel some miles to the north.

Let me tell you about Annette. She's five foot two, a bundle of energy with short, chestnut hair. She has deep green eyes, a thin, hourglass shape, and never wears makeup. Her breasts are small but very firm, with scarlet brown nipples. Her pubic hair is elongated and wispy. She's not at all like the women portrayed in explicit movies. In comparison to her, they're cold platinum. Annette has freckles over her back, arms and legs, and a slightly oversize nose. She's real.

I saw her, considered her youth, appetite, comeliness, and had the natural thoughts. I also felt the natural inhibitions. Besides the mixed emotions, there wasn't opportunity. But early one afternoon, my wife took the kids to a party at a friend's house. She was only supposed to be gone for ninety minutes. I watched over a cooking roast, its hearty odors making Annette and me hungry. We read. She sat in a chair across the room. I admit I was watching her as well, trembling and growing hard. I finally broke through my indecision, got up and pulled a chair up beside her. We talked about her day, her visit. We talked about small things, anything.

I went around the back of her chair and started rubbing her shoulders. She didn't ask me to. She didn't object or encourage. She sat there silently. I slid up the midlength sleeves of a Madras shirt, stroking her upper arms, her lower arms, caressing her hands, her fingers. I asked, "Do you mind?" She said at once, "No," and shook her head slightly, her hair bouncing as she did. "It feels good," she admitted. My heart leapt.

I moved around in front of her, sitting on the floor between her crossed legs, bare from the thighs, revealed by khaki shorts. I touched her legs, to and fro, above her knees, inside her thighs. I caressed them, and bent over and kissed them, lightly, gently. She spread her legs, and I gave them the same gentle, loving attentions.

Suddenly, we heard the garage door opening. I quickly moved to the other side of the room. I said to Annette, "Sorry." She looked at me with disappointed eyes, and nodded. The most difficult thing to mask was my very hard cock, and perhaps, our mutual nervousness. I don't think my wife noticed, and it subsided. No other opportunities presented themselves that week.

Annette left us early the following Sunday, giving us friendly hugs and perfunctory kisses, thanking us for our hospitality and company.

My wife was planning to visit family with the kids that entire week. I was to attend to job and home. They hadn't seen her parents, who live a three-hour drive away, in over a year. I had no objections at all. I helped pack and load up the car, saying, "Drive carefully" to my wife and admonishing my kids. "Be good at Grandma's and Granddad's."

I went inside and made some lunch. I consumed half the afternoon with chores.

At three o'clock the doorbell rang. I thought it was probably some collector for charity. Frankly I was annoyed at the interruption. I scowled as I opened the door, and then my jaw dropped.

It was Annette.

She asked, "May I come in?"

"Why, Annette!" I said in clutched surprise, swallowing hard. "Yeah, of course." My thoughts were racing. I restrained them, for fear of frustration. Might I have misread events? Quickly I said, "Sure," stepping back, beckoning her delectable form through the door. I added, "Is something wrong?"

She stepped inside, her hiking boots falling heavily against the tiles, and she kept her eyes from mine. I closed the door behind her. She took two steps toward the living room, then must have realized she still had on her hiking boots. She said, "Madame and the boys went to Grandmama's, no?"

I said, "Yes." My dick was thinking predictable things.

Annette turned and looked me full in the eyes. She said, " 'I had to come back, Bill." She stepped toward me. I was frozen in place, my arms stiff as boards. "Can you please, Bill, touch me some more, as you were?"

Her tone was pleading. I stepped forward, put my arms around her and kissed her. She trembled, emitting soft cries of delight. We struggled with her boots, and I carried her upstairs to the bedroom.

We took a lot of gentle time that afternoon, that evening and night. After undressing her, I caressed and licked her to a moaning, shouting crescendo, avidly licking her clit, darting my tongue into and around her. Afterward she urgently guided me inside her, where I exploded immediately. I remained. She rocked, she rolled, I stayed hard. One quality I value most about a woman is the rhythm she uses while fucking, her moans and sounds. I call it her "love song." All women are different. Discovering that rhythm is a lot of fun. For me, it's the secret to staying hard and squirting them full of come twice, thrice. Annette's French-accent love song was beautiful, with her "Ah, hah, ooh, mah, cons, cons!"

I woke the next morning about half past six, running a bit late for getting to work by quarter to eight. I left Annette slumbering, naked. I did it with some hesitation and desire. My cock was getting hard again just from looking over her in deshabille, her firm ass, recalling how I stroked it, how she rubbed it against my prick in a tease, her disheveled hair, and her salacious, satisfied smile. I took a shower, went to another room, got dressed and skipped downstairs, where I quietly fixed myself some breakfast. I left breakfast out for Annette, along with a note suggesting that she reheat it.

I was readying to leave when I saw pretty, white feet padding down our center stairway, followed by adorable, freckled legs. Annette was dressed in one of my white shirts, open in the front, and nothing else. I kissed her hello, explaining how I had to go, arms wrapped around her. She kissed back warmly. I frowned, saying, "I'm sorry, Annette, I *have* to be at work today. I'm looking forward to this evening, though, very much."

Annette said, "Yes, I understand. You must work." Then she stepped back a half step, thinking, smiling to herself. She said, "I think I give you something so you cannot forget me before this evening no?"

I couldn't imagine what she had in mind. Having learned that her ability to innovate sexually was exquisite, I was definitely not going to discourage her. She undid my black leather belt, slowly zipped down my fly, and dropped my dress pants to the floor. At this point, I started to grow. She knelt and pulled my briefs, sliding them down ever so slowly. I was rock hard, pointing outward. She rose from her knees and padded over to the kitchen table. She picked up a saucer, spooned some marmalade into it, and returned.

She knelt again, smiled sweetly at me, and dipped a long-nailed index finger into the marmalade, bringing the coated red-painted nail to her open lips, and sucking it off. "Hmm . . . it is good," she commented sensually. She repeated the dip, but this time she daubed the jelly over the top of my dick. She got some more, and put it farther down the shaft. She put down the dish and gently, expertly, began to smear the jelly all over my manhood. I just spread my legs apart and enjoyed the sensations, the moments when her nails touched my sensitive skin, making me jump, and her giggle.

Then, with a sigh, she knelt, opened her mouth, and started to lick up the marmalade. She did it very slowly and gently, not wanting to miss the slightest bit. At first I could hardly tell she was touching me at all, but the mere idea drove me crazy. She cooed, "How you say, 'Yum'?" We laughed together as she continued. I must tell you, as this went on and on for fifteen minutes, Annette saw me quivering, shaking, reduced to utter helplessness at her actions. *Anyone* could have come into the house at that moment and I wouldn't have cared. Annette was my universe. My cock exuded drops of come. Annette said, "Bill, you are delicious." She smiled at me devilishly. "Now for the breakfast," she said, opening her mouth, and took me into it, her tongue working underneath the head. She turned hers slightly, and simply sucked, no longer moving about, but sucking hard, wet, warm. I was buzzing with desire, and my dick felt like it would explode. I gave a great trio of groans when I came, spurting into her mouth like a fire hose.

I thanked Annette and went off to work. You can guess what I thought about during the drive. A buddy of mine pointed out that I must have dropped some marmalade on my slacks during a hurried breakfast. I almost laughed, but I caught myself, and said, "Yes, I'll have to take it to the cleaners."

It was genuinely hard to keep focused on work all day. I think the moment with Annette I recalled the most was a quiet time very early in the morning when she cuddled her head against my shoulder, stroking the hair on my chest. I daydreamed about that through lunch. I think every satisfying encounter has a moment when you look in each other's eyes and realize the lovable, sharing, giving being behind them. This was Annette's moment, or rather, mine of her. I got out of work at five that night, eager to go home.

As I unlocked the door, I called, "Annette," but there was no answer. I checked through the mail and dropped my coat and briefcase. I called again, "Annette?" She could have gone out for a walk, but I got an uneasy feeling that I'd find some kind of remorse-filled note in the bedroom.

I walked into the bedroom, and, seeing a feminine form in the bed, covers pulled up over her head, thought that my questions had been answered. "Oh," I said, "there you are," but realized she might be sleeping. Quietly, I got undressed and lifted the quilt, sliding under it. As I approached the warm body. I put my hand on her hip, stroking the top of her ass. She lifted her head and turned to me, long blonde hair covering the pillow and tops of her shoulders. This was not Annette.

"But . . ." I said. "Where's . . . ?"

My mystery woman smiled, leaned forward and kissed me, pressing her softness against me. I returned the kiss, still wondering, but enjoying the surprise. I kissed her neck, then shoulders, sliding down to lick and caress large, white breasts, looking like whipped cream–topped sundaes with cherries melted atop them in a cranberry sugar sauce. She sighed and oohed. As I touched and licked, she moved her left hand lazily about my chest, down my side, along my taut abdomen. She moved a warm palm down a leg to the front of my thighs, encountering my stiffness by happenstance. She stroked her discovery as I gently nibbled and circled my tongue about her nipples, almost tasting the cranberries. She lifted a leg and wrapped it about mine, hugging me closer to her, slipping her free hand to the small of my back.

I kissed between her breasts, her stomach, saying how beautiful, how delightful she was. She said, "Bill, I'm dripping," with a heavy French accent. She knew my name! Her name was Miou, I learned later. She lived only a few blocks away. Annette had given her the key. But at that point I was too unruly with passion to think about explanation. She opened her legs like a butterfly might its wings, yielding her pink warmth to me. I first admired and touched her cunt, her silvery mound of hair. I found her clit among ample folds, kissing either side of the opening with long tongue, then making for it, seeking shelter from the storm. I gradually converged at the top, gently eating, sucking, twirling her pink button, saying, "Hmm, yum," delighting in her taste. She was indeed wet, and had a familiar, natural-smelling fragrance about her. She was hot, for she crested in no time, muttering incomprehensible, wonderful-sounding French words.

She took my head in her hands, and led me over her, impaling herself with me. Miou flipped me over, still inside her, and sat on top of me, crisscrossing her legs. She began to move her pelvis about, rocking me and spinning my prick, pumping up and down so the bed began to shake. She stared blankly ahead, focused upon the sensations. I felt like my dick was an inflating balloon, and I did my share of rocking, trying to reach as many parts of her insides with it as I could. Our rhythm went up, around and down, pushing, relaxing, pushing, pushing. Miou breathed out with a slight cry, then repeated it, "Ahh-eh, ahh-eh!" getting more insistent each time. I groaned loudly. I blew off, arching my back, digging my heels into the bed with the tension. She kept pounding as I settled back, and then threw her head and her hair back with a jerk, groaning as the waves of pleasure rolled over her, compensating her for her efforts. She collapsed on top of me, and we slept almost immediately.

What was special about Miou? She made me feel very male, even by sleeping there, white sheet intertwined and twisted seductively about a leg, half covering her pubic hair, pelvis, and a single breast. I watched her charms move up and down with her gentle breathing. In the window-framed moonlight she looked like some Venetian goddess. I got up to use the bathroom and get water. I pulled on my briefs, out of habit and for comfort. As I walked about, I felt I was all balls and dick, as if these organs were volumes bigger than I realized. I was so conscious of them, so happy I could delve and thrust and shake and rub Miou with my dick, shoot her full of jellied jism, and that she was delighted with my doing so.

Work the next day was even harder than the one previous. On the way home, I stopped by an organic-food store to pick up some bread and things. There was an "Under New Management" sign on the outside. I found what I wanted, and then waited by the register, ringing the bell there. When no one appeared, I just walked about, killing time. They were probably out back in the warehouse, unloading, I thought. Ten minutes went by, and I started to get impatient. I found a door leading to the dock and opened it, softly calling, "Hello?" I heard vaguely familiar sounds from within. I took a cautious step forward. I peeked around a corner and saw a naked, dark-haired, handsome young man, eyes closed and mouth open in pleasure. Annette was kneeling at his feet, naked and tan, her firm ass resting on her heels. She caressed his hairy legs. She had his long prick in her mouth. Then she took it out, licking it slowly along its long shaft to the bottom, and then back again. She didn't put her mouth over it, just worked her dark pink tongue over its very tip, over and over, lapping up pre-come, saying teasing words in French to the one she was pleasuring. There were clothes scattered on the ground. I stayed quiet, observing, enjoying the voyeurism. My dick grew again, and I was tempted to jerk off, or even to join them. But instead I just watched.

The man—whose name I later learned was Gerard—opened his eyes and reached down for Annette's shoulders. Gerard is very strong. He's not at all heftily built, but he is tall, all bones and muscle. He lifted Annette to his shoulders, one leg over each, Annette's pubes before his face, and began eating her out. Annette stroked Gerard's hair. I was fascinated by the torrid scene before me.

Gerard let Annette down gently and lashed her nipples with his tongue. Gerard then kneeled and directed Annette to kneel as well. His very hard dick stood up like a flagpole as he leaned backwards. Annette stepped astride of Gerard. She took his straight prick within her, her legs far apart, and began to move up and down. He groaned once, exhaling some indescribable words.

This was quite a scene. Annette rocked up and down on Gerard's dick, loving it, beating herself to a climax. She and Gerard came within a half-minute of each other, Gerard finally collapsing onto his back on the floor.

Rising, Gerard took Annette in his arms, thanking her and kissing her. He pulled up his trousers, and Annette started getting dressed. I ducked back into the main store and waited by the cash register.

Gerard came out, and with a heavy French accent said, "I'm sorry I kept you waiting." I said there wasn't a need for apologies. I said it was well worth the wait. He looked at me, puzzled. Annette came around the corner, only half-dressed, her shirt still open, showing braless breasts. She had recognized my voice.

I said, "Annette, how have you been?"

Annette smiled and explained the whole story. She had taken a long walk through the neighborhood, and found the organic store. She stopped in to shop, and found Miou behind the register. Quickly Annette discovered that Miou spoke French, and was in fact from France, having moved here recently with her husband, Gerard. They were both happy to have found someone from home, and rapidly exchanged gossip. Miou confided that she was disappointed with American men, at least during her short time here. She knew some that would love to bed her, but they were too shy. In France, she explained, she found several satisfying, extramarital engagements. Gerard, she said, approved, even joined in once with a man and his wife. He thought it kept their bed life alive.

Annette told Miou she knew of an American man who would treasure her, if only she could make it with Miou's adorable husband. Miou smiled slyly, Annette said, much to Gerard's surprise and pleasure—he was hearing this for the first time too—and heartily agreed. Annette gave her the keys to my house. Miou ended up in my bed, and Annette spent the night with Gerard.

I get a postcard from Annette from time to time. She's married now, and has a kid on the way. Gerard and Miou still own the organic-food store, and I see them once or twice a year. Gerard and I still share Miou and she loves it. *Vive la femme! Vive la France!*

A SOLDIER'S STORY

T he air force had canceled my reservations at their posh hotel. Baggage in hand, I headed for the nearest motel.

I ended up making a slight detour to the NCO club, where I bumped into a married couple I'd met the night before. The man was personable, in his late forties, and blessed with an attractive wife who was many years younger than he. Despite her looks, I didn't like her. After watching her in action, I'd decided she was nothing more than a prick tease.

While exchanging pleasantries, I told them about how I had been bumped by the air force and had no place to stay that night. They immediately offered the use of their couch. "I don't want to impose," I told them, but they insisted. After a while I accepted their offer, even though I wasn't crazy about the lady.

Arriving at the apartment, my host said he was going to take a shower and go to bed. I found myself alone with his young wife. We had a long, animated, sometimes hostile conversation until the wee hours. I was still not impressed.

The next day we went to the club again. Returning to the apartment, my host again announced he was going to shower and retire. His wife also took a shower, while I watched television. She returned wearing only a skimpy robe. She sat next to me on the couch and brushed her hair. I offered to do the honors. She had beautiful hair. It smelled delicious. As I gently ran the brush though her locks, I became increasingly aware that she was smoothly naked under the thin robe.

Our conversation drifted to more sensual topics. I realized she was rather sensitive underneath her tough exterior. She wasn't the coldhearted person I had originally pegged her to be.

Difficult as it was, I kept the beast in my pants in check. After all, I was their guest.

After she went to bed, I lay in the moonlight thinking about the situation. Then, out of the corner of my eye, I saw an almost ghostlike image. It was her, in a gossamer chiffon negligee, almost transparent in the moonlight.

Before I could move or speak she placed her warm, moist lips against mine. Her passion flowed into me, spreading and warming. Then, just as suddenly as she appeared, she was gone.

I lay there on the couch for what must have been thirty minutes. My pulse was pounding, my body feeling as if it had been electrified. Confused, a thousand questions raced through my mind. Finally, I decided I had been right. She was a prick teaser. I was angry. Angry at her, but also angry at myself. I *wanted* her. I wanted her so bad.

The next day we again went to the club, and again returned to the apartment. True to form, my host announced he was going to take a shower and retire. She, on the other hand, said she needed some things at the store. Her husband tossed his car keys to me and asked if I'd drive her. A little reluctantly, I said, "Sure." I wasn't in a hurry to have her light my fire again, especially when I knew she wasn't going to cook anything.

Silently, we walked outside and got into the car. I started the engine and headed toward the street that would take us into town, where she could get bread, milk and a few other things she needed. Neither of us spoke while I drove. I kept replaying the events of the night before, trying to figure out what kind of game it was that she was trying to play with me.

Then I felt her gently place her hand on my knee. Not taking my eyes off the road, I savored the feeling of her palm firmly pressed against me, running up and down the length of my leg from knee to crotch.

"You're probably wondering about last night," she said.

"You got that right." I answered. "I really don't appreciate being teased like that. And," I impatiently brushed her hand off my knee, "do me a favor and cut the crap before you go and give me another hard-on like last night."

"Did I do that?" she asked.

"What the hell do you think?"

I heard her let out a sigh. "I'm sorry for getting you angry," she said. "It's just that I wanted you so bad. I had to just . . . just kiss you. I didn't want to risk my husband walking in on us."

"Your husband isn't here now, is he?" I asked. I let my remark hang in the air as I pulled into the parking lot of an all-night convenience store. I shut the car off and we both sat in silence, neither of us making a move to get out.

I felt her fingers fumbling with my belt. Then she was undoing my fly. I lifted my ass off the seat so she would be able to pull my pants and underwear down. My cock was already stiff when she took it in her cool hand. She lowered her head and gently took my cock into her moist mouth.

I closed my eyes and let my head fall back against the headrest as she gave me head there in the car. She took her time, licking my entire cock, sucking just the head, gently cupping my balls in her hand.

"Hey, you're pretty damn good at this," I said.

She didn't take her mouth away to reply, and I didn't mind one bit. I felt an orgasm approaching as the hot come sizzled in my balls. Faster and faster her mouth rose and fell on my cock. My pubic hair was soaked with her saliva. I grunted and shot my load into her mouth. I was thankful that she didn't pull away, and instead drank my come.

I am not sure how it happened. The next thing I knew we were standing alone in a dark motel room. We didn't speak. Slowly, I walked toward her and took her in my arms for the first time. If this was a tease, it was a good one.

I knelt and slowly began to remove her clothes. She started to speak, but I put my fingers to her lips. I didn't want words to shatter the moment.

I'd never really paid attention to her body, but as each layer of clothing was pulled away, I became more interested. Her skin was satiny smooth and pale in the failing light. Her breasts were full and round, with hard nipples that begged to be kissed. I slowly rolled down her panties, unveiling a rich, lush pelt, scant inches from my face. The subtle fragrance was headier than any exotic perfume. I looked up and she seemed embarrassed, unsure. My prick-teasing vixen was, in reality, a shy little girl.

Quickly shedding my clothes, I took her in my arms. This time it was my kiss that held her passion. Her skin was warm, smooth and soft as it pressed against me. My prick was begging to slide between her creamy thighs, but I held off. I wanted this to last a long time. She needed to understand that teasing is not nearly as good as pleasing.

I carried her to the bed and laid her gently on the crisp, cool sheets. Her dark hair framed her beautiful face. Her soft brown eyes were filled with uncertainty. She tried to cover herself modestly. Slowly, I explored her body with my lips and tongue. From her gentle forehead to her toes I licked, sucked and kissed every nook and cranny.

She threw her head back and her body started shaking when my tongue lightly grazed her hard clit. The lips of her cunt were slick with her love, and her natural perfume filled the room.

She was the first woman I'd ever met who had a truly beautiful pussy. It was almost a work of art. Up till that night, I had only feasted on a woman to be obligatory. But with her it was a labor of love. She was so sweet and silky. With each stroke of my tongue, her body arched and quivered. Her moans became louder and her hands urged me on.

Sliding up her sweating body, my rock-hard dick pressed against her stomach. She looked at me, her eyes pleading for me to make passionate love to her. I slowly raised my body and moved my cock between her thighs. I placed the blood-engorged head against her moist, velvety thatch.

I smiled and asked her if she wanted me to put it inside. She nodded.

"No, baby," I said. "I want to hear you say it."

Her words seemed to drip with passion. "I want to feel you, all of you, deep inside me."

Slowly, I lowered myself into her. I could feel her muscles holding me, rippling as, ever so slowly, I started long, deep thrusts. I wanted this to last, it was too good to rush. She, despite her apparent naiveté, was a natural lover. She moved with ease, matching my every stroke.

We began to move faster, her body and hands urging me on. Her lips left a trail of wet fire on my neck. Faster and faster, I could feel the pressure building. As I raced toward the finish, my dick burned with anticipation, my balls sizzling as they filled with hot come. I knew I wouldn't be able to hold off much longer.

Suddenly she gave a loud moan and held me tight. Her hips thrust up, burying me deep inside. I felt her cunt spasm.

It was then that my dick exploded inside her, pulsing with each spurt. It felt as if my whole body was draining into her through the head of my dick.

We collapsed. Our bodies were covered with sweat. We lay there for a while, just looking at each other. Then, gently, she gave me a little kiss.

For two days we explored. Hot-oil massages, steamy showers—the list of what we did is endless. We wrapped ourselves in sensuality, completely forgetting about everything else. Finally, it had to end.

I couldn't let her go back to face the music alone, so I decided I'd go with her to her husband.

When we arrived at the apartment, it was empty. I mean empty! Not a piece of furniture, not even a scrap of paper, was left.

BETH AND THE FRAT BOY

I saw one of my fraternity brothers talking to a carful of fellow students in the parking lot behind the house. There were two attractive women in the car. I thought the blonde in the backseat was especially sexy, so I gave her a smile. Her name was Beth, and as she tipped her sunglasses farther down her nose to give me a view of her luminous green eyes, I imagined how she might look in sunglasses alone: a smooth, silky body begging for my tongue. Thank goodness my fraternity brother and I were late to class. If I'd stayed any longer, I would have embarrassed myself by getting a pulsing hard-on.

I mentioned to my fraternity brother that I thought Beth was hot. I needed a date to our formal the following weekend, and he said Beth was definitely available, so I called her that evening. We talked for half an hour before I asked her to the formal. I told her what a great time we were going to have—the party atmosphere, the great tunes, the booze and the wild dancing. Her voice sounded soft, sexy and deep, and I began to rub my dick through my shorts while talking to her.

The day of the formal was pretty wild. As is the tradition at our fraternity, we have a celebration before the dance. We were doing shots of tequila—lots of shots—and playing touch football. I had wisely gotten dressed before I got too drunk: I knew what it was like to be in such bad shape you can't even tie the laces of your shoes! Now I had a great buzz going and could barely see the passes I was catching.

Before I knew it, it was nine o'clock. My tux was stained from the football game, but it was too late to get another one. I ran across campus to Figman Hall, which was Beth's dorm, and knocked on her door. I had a big smile on my face and smelled like a man: cologne and sweat, grass, dirt and tequila. Thank goodness I was chewing a piece of mint gum. The door opened and a little brunette said Beth would be right out and asked if I wanted a beer. I had no willpower. "Sure," I said.

Beth came out with a big smile on her face and said, "I'm excited about the party tonight." She had wavy blonde hair with some extra mousse in it to make it really stiff. She had a light, flawless complexion and the cutest little nose which turned up at the end. It reminded me of my penis, which was starting to get erect.

Beth was wearing a black party dress cut way above her knees. She had on a silver-gold belt revealing a small waist, and she wore no bra to cover her firm breasts. Her nipples were hard and pointing out. I gave her a kiss on the cheek and hugged her so that I could savor those luscious melons pressing against my chest. I felt a tremor in my crotch, but was still too drunk to get a real hard-on.

We walked in the front door of the fraternity house, and I took Beth's hand and led her down the stairs into the basement where we have our parties. We went immediately to the bar, and I got Beth a gin and tonic that was mostly gin. I poured myself a gin with no tonic at all. This was a party! We sipped our drinks and started to talk about school, our voices barely able to penetrate the loud music. A few minutes later the disc jockey began playing a really good tune. Beth and I put our drinks down and headed straight to the dance floor. I looked at her glass and noticed she'd practically sucked down the entire drink.

The next song was a slow one. Beth pulled me close and put her arms around my neck. I put one hand on her back and the other right above her perfect ass. As the song progressed, I concentrated on pressing my body tightly against hers. Her tits were making their presence known, and to my delight she gyrated her hips ever so slightly against my crotch. I took that as a hint, moved one of my hands to her ass and started to rub with vigor. We must have been putting on quite a show, because most of the other couples had stopped dancing and were watching our passion ignite.

Not wanting to be an exhibitionist, I suggested we take a break. I looked right at her crotch, then into her lustrous green eyes. She looked back at me and ran her tongue seductively across her upper lip. No words needed to be spoken. I grabbed her hand and half-led, half-pulled her through the throngs of people as we made it up the three flights of stairs to my room. As I was trying to unlock the door she reached under my ass, between my legs, and tickled my scrotum with her long fingers. She played with my balls with such delicacy that it made me shudder with delight. I leaned over and kissed her deeply, my tongue practically reaching her tonsils. I was so excited that I had a hard time getting the key in the door. She had to steady my hand with hers. I turned the lock and rushed into the room. I reached around and locked the door securely.

I grabbed her arm and pulled her to me, caressing her ass and pulling her crotch to mine. The effects of the alcohol were diminishing and I was sporting a lively boner. Beth glided her crotch over my ice-hard dick, moving in a circular motion so intense I thought she would split the seams of my trousers. She broke away from our long, deep kiss and went to work on my ear, slurping and sucking it like she was trying to make it come!

Beth was working both of us into a frenzy. I massaged her bra-less tits while rolling and pinching the nipples with my fingers. She leaned over, blew warm air into my ear and whispered, "I'm so horny I can't stand it." While still tongue-fucking my ear, Beth took her right leg and hooked it around my back, shifting most of her weight and practically jumping on me. I kissed her again and told her I was going to make her come until the sun came up. She moaned and replied, "Oh, I can't wait to feel your cock!"

I felt her cunt through her black dress while undoing her belt. Beth undid my shirt, slowly at first, then ripping it off me so that the buttons popped off and shot across the room. She reached into my briefs and massaged my cock, playing with the pre-come that had oozed from the tip. I kicked off my trousers and shoes, and quickly whisked away my socks while Beth tossed her clothes behind her. We stood skin-to-skin, except for our briefs, kissing each other and working our hands feverishly, unable to get enough of each other.

I kneaded her breasts and started sucking her nipples. Beth's areolae were the size of silver dollars and her nipples were as hard as my dick. I left her saliva-coated nipples and moved up to her neck. We began to grind our crotches together, dry-humping to the music our hormones were providing. Beth ran her long fingers down my back. I was getting goose bumps all over my body.

By now the strong, sweet aroma coming from the patch of wetness between her thighs permeated the air. In a voice hoarse and full of passion, she looked straight into my eyes and said, "I want you to fuck me. I want to feel your cock inside me. I want you to . . ."

Before she could say another word I slid two fingers into her sopping cunt. I pulled off her panties and used a third finger to jiggle her clit. I worked it in a circular motion, making her gasp and squeal as she rode my hand with gusto. Beth stiffened and then moved again, stiffened and moved again, keeping up this stop/start routine until she came. The amount of liquid that shot out of her was unbelievable. I'd never known a woman could ejaculate like that. My parents were right. College was full of learning experiences.

I pulled my fingers out so I could taste her honey, then put them near her mouth so she could also have a taste. She sucked my fingers the way I hoped she could suck cock, giving them long, wet licks and taking them deep into her throat. We fell to the floor, the fires of our lust raging. She lay on her back and spread her legs far apart, knees up. I stroked my dick, hovering over her mouth.

"Do you want it?" I asked.

"Yes, yes!"

"Where do you want it?" I teased, lowering myself until my cock was just out of reach of her lips. She snapped at it, trying to take it into her mouth, but I quickly pulled it away. She giggled and tried again, but again I kept her from tasting the knob of my cock.

"Please give me your cock. I want it now," she said. I looked down to see she was pumping a finger in and out of her pussy. What a turn-on!

"I know what you really want," I said. "You want it in your pussy, don't you?"

"Yes."

"Tell me about your pussy, Beth. Tell me what it's like."

"It's hot, sticky, and very wet," she began.

"And tight?" I asked.

"Tight as a fist," she said. "It's going to squeeze all the come out of you."

"That's good," I said, "because—"

But before I could finish, she grabbed my cock and stuffed it inside her. "Enough talking!" she said. "Just fuck me, baby!"

Her cunt felt so good around my bulging cock and I wanted to savor the feeling. I held her still for a second, letting the incredible heat of her pussy consume me. She locked her legs around my back and pulled me deeper into her. Her pussy felt like the mold where my dick had been cast—a perfect fit. I pressed my mouth to hers, feeling her erect nipples press into my chest. The continual slurping sounds of my dick plunging in and out of her moist cunt filled the room.

I was really putting it to her, so at first I didn't hear the knocks at the door. But as the pounding grew more insistent, it dawned on me that my roommate, Mel, wanted in. Beth and I were almost at the pinnacle of pleasure too. Damn! I covered her beautiful body with a sheet, grabbed a towel to cover my swollen, throbbing dick and, with a scowl, answered the door.

Mel stared back at me, his girlfriend at his side. They looked desperate, like they really needed a place to fuck—I guess her room was unavailable. I told them to come back in a while, then motioned to Beth to let them know I wasn't alone.

"We don't mind," said Denny, Mel's girl. "It could be a party." Denny was a hot number and at any other time I would have jumped at the chance to be in the same room while she was fucking Mel. But I'd just met Beth and didn't want anyone else around, at least not for a little while longer.

"Come back in an hour." I said. Drunk, horny and disappointed, Mel and Denny left.

I went back to Beth, apologized for the interruption and resumed kissing her. I couldn't wait to finish what we'd begun. But I must have been drunker than I'd thought, because all of a sudden the room started spinning. I mean really spinning. I had to lie down on the floor.

"Are you okay?" Beth asked.

"Just give me a minute," I said. It was right about then, I guess, that I blacked out.

I don't know how much later it was when I awoke, but I knew I'd been out for some time. My head was still spinning too, but for a different reason. Beth, naked and gorgeous as ever, was lying on her stomach, her face buried in my crotch. Her wet mouth was busily sucking my hard cock. I had blacked out many times, but I'd never been revived like this before! She gave a playful blowjob, flicking at the head with her pink tongue and taking long, lollipop licks at the shaft. My dick felt like a red-hot poker sitting in a fire.

"Oh good, you're back," she said when she saw me stir. "I was hoping that would do the trick." Satisfied with my recovery, Beth changed positions and straddled me, lowering herself seductively on my cock. "You said something about making me come until the sun came up. We still have a few hours left." With that, she impaled herself on my sausage.

Beth rolled her hips, filling herself with every inch of my prick and rubbing her clit against me. She moved from side to side and up and down, like some wild carnival ride. I could see the orgasm building up inside her. Her hips bucked faster and her head was tossing left and right. "Fuck me, fuck me!" she said through deep breaths. "Deeper! I want it deeper!"

I grabbed her ass and pulled her to me as tightly as I could. She told me to suck her titties, and that did the trick. No sooner had I taken her left nipple between my lips than she screamed, "Yes! Oh yes, come with me!"

Beth slithered up and down my cock, milking out my load as it exploded into her. The feeling was exquisite, and the sight of her riding up and down my pole kept me hard long enough to ram her to another pair of orgasms She didn't stop moving, but instead urged me on by planting her luscious tits in my mouth. Finally, her back arched and she came again, her entire body crashing down onto my chest.

We regained our strength enough to get dressed and vacate the room for Denny and Mel. We made our way to Beth's dorm, hoping her roommate wasn't in so the night wouldn't have to end.

BAHAMAS GETAWAY

A few months ago while on vacation in the Bahamas, I had an experience that left no doubt in my mind why French women have such a reputation as expert practitioners of the art of love. I was staying at a small, very private resort hotel on one of the outer islands that attract very little of the usual tourist trade. The hotel accommodated only about twenty-five people. Each evening, the management offered a dinner seating for its guests in an elegant dining room with a magnificent view of the pink, coral-sand beach below.

It was our first night there. My friends and I were well into our second round of before-dinner cocktails when the sexiest, most gorgeous woman I have ever seen in my life strolled into the room and seated herself at an adjacent table. This woman was in a class by herself. Tall and slim, with the lean, muscular look of an athlete, she had dark, lustrous, shoulder-length hair and penetrating blue eyes. She was wearing red nylon running shorts just tight enough to show off a perfect ass, and a transparent white blouse through which I could easily see the dark circles of her nipples.

Throughout dinner my cock was twitching like crazy, as though it could sense the world-class pussy of the woman sitting at the next table. I couldn't help but stare at her. She was talking with the three women and two men with whom she was dining. They all were speaking English with distinct French accents. I offered a silent prayer of thanks when, from the scattered bits of conversation I overheard, I figured out that she was not romantically involved with either of the men.

Several times during the meal she glanced over, caught me watching her and smiled before looking away. Unfortunately she didn't show up later on in the cocktail lounge as I'd hoped she would. Disappointed, I lulled myself to sleep that night stroking my meat, dreaming about the far more interesting things I could be doing with her if she were in bed beside me.

Early the next morning I went for a run on the beach, then decided to cool off with a leisurely ocean swim. As I emerged from the water, refreshed, my prayers of the previous evening were answered. Coming down the stairs and heading for the beach, wrapped in a white terry-cloth robe, was the woman. I watched as she pulled a canvas beach chair closer to the water, dropped her sunglasses and keys onto it, then casually stepped out of her robe. I blinked several times, hoping to God that this wasn't just a dream from which I would wake up alone with my dick in my hand. It was real, though—she was standing there wearing only the tiniest bikini bottom.

My prick started to stiffen while I gazed at her full breasts swaying slightly as she walked into the water, and I nearly came on the spot when she turned away from me and bent over to get her hair wet, showing me the most glorious set of buns I had ever seen. I suddenly realized that this was no accidental meeting and that she knew exactly who I was and what she was doing. I began to have great difficulty keeping my seven-inch tool inside my tight swimsuit as I watched her move through the shallow water to where I was standing.

"*Bonjour*," she said. "I am Jeanette. Do you remember me from last night?"

"Hi, Jeanette, I'm Barry. And you've got to be kidding. Only a blind man could forget someone who looks as good as you do," I replied, trying my hardest to look at her face and not at the pair of perfectly shaped tits that were bobbing in and out of the water in front of me. "I didn't think a woman could look any sexier than you do. You really have a fantastic body."

"I'm so happy you like it," she said. I noticed her looking down through the crystal-clear water and realized she was inspecting the huge lump growing in my swimsuit. She was smiling when she looked back up and said, "It looks like you have some impressive features yourself." I felt her cup my balls in her hand and then trace a fingernail along the entire throbbing shaft of my cock. Before I knew what was happening she had pulled down my suit and was slowly stroking my hardness to full erection. As she continued to fondle me she said in a husky voice, "It's always an added treat to find out the man I've chosen is well-hung."

I wasn't exactly sure what she meant by "chosen," but I figured it couldn't be too bad if she'd planned to start the day by massaging my cock before breakfast. I put my arms around her and kissed her, taking a breast in my hand and feeling the nipple harden beneath my fingers. Moving to the smooth contours of her ass, I pulled her close to me, pressing my hard dick against her mound.

She moaned softly and moved against me with an urgency that was driving me crazy with lust. There was no doubt that if this continued for about two more minutes I was going to be standing waist-deep in the water no more than fifty yards from the shore, fucking this woman like a madman. As good as that sounded, I could see that there were now half a dozen people on the beach, all of whom were showing an interest in what was going on. I knew that, even in the Bahamas, there were a few things that could get you in trouble if you did them in public. So I disengaged myself from Jeanette, pulled my swimsuit back up and told her that we needed to continue this back at the hotel.

We made it back to her room in record time. The next thing I knew, I was sitting naked in a deck chair on her private balcony while she knelt between my legs and gave me what was probably the best head in the world. There is no other way to describe it. Jeanette made unbelievably hot, insane love to my cock with her lips and tongue. She'd take my entire length down her throat while gently squeezing my balls, and then with excruciating slowness would let my prick slide out of her mouth until just the big, purple head was inside her lips and she could caress the slit with the tip of her tongue. She seemed to be able to sense exactly when I was about to shoot my load. She would slow down, just lightly kissing the shaft or running the slippery head over her face until it was wet with my pre-come, then plunge it back down her throat. I'd never known anyone who had such a talent for giving head.

After about twenty minutes of this, my balls felt like they were going to explode if I didn't get some quick relief. "Honey," I moaned, "if you continue doing that I'm going to come like a volcano."

She paused momentarily, letting my cock slip out of her mouth, and looked up at me with a big grin on her face. "Barry, darling, you shouldn't worry. You are going to come many times today, as am I. This is only the first. You American men are always so concerned about the timing of your orgasms. Just relax and enjoy it. Believe me, I certainly intend to."

With that, she took my throbbing tool in her hand and began to jerk me off while at the same time flicking her tongue over the sensitive underside of my cockhead. I completely lost control at that point and started coming like a fire hose, shooting stream after thick stream of semen. She never missed a beat and kept steadily sucking on my schlong.

"Oh yes, baby, yes!" she cried. "God, I love watching a man shoot off like that. It turns me on so much I just can't stand it." She squeezed out the last of my jism and slowly licked it from the head of my cock. "Now I need to come, lover. Make me come, baby. Please eat my little pussy and make me come right now!"

She quickly stood up, turned around and bent over so her dripping cunt was right in my face. I went right to work, grabbing her hips and giving her sweet-tasting slit the tongue-job of my life. In about two minutes she went off like a rocket and let out a high-pitched wail that I was sure would bring the hotel manager knocking on the door. She bucked and wiggled so much that I had a hell of a time keeping my tongue on her lust-swollen clit. But it didn't seem to matter as she climaxed three or four times in succession, each one more intense than the last.

After a warm, lingering kiss on the lips, she grabbed my penis and gently tugged me up and out of the chair. "Time for a nice, hot shower," she said, and headed back into her room with me in tow. Inside, she gave my cock a squeeze and told me to get started while she ordered breakfast. I might add it turned out to be a hot shower in more ways than one. By the time we were done she had sucked me until I was stiff again, and then begged me to fuck her from the rear while the warm water cascaded down our bodies. I had been with some horny women before, but I was getting the idea that, as the day progressed, Jeanette was going to provide me with her own personal definition of "insatiable."

Later, over a leisurely breakfast on the balcony, Jeanette told me that she lived in Paris, near the Louvre, was married to a Swiss businessman and was in the habit of taking an annual, separate vacation—the sole purpose of which was to have great sex with a strange man. This was done with the full knowledge of her husband, who took a similar trip at the same time. She had chosen the Bahamas this year and he had picked Copenhagen where, as she put it, "some hot, blonde, Danish nineteen-year-old is probably fucking his brains out right now. And I hope he is loving it!" She said they both found it to be very beneficial to their marriage, kind of like getting their erotic batteries recharged once a year. Apparently she'd decided when she saw me at dinner that I was the sexual companion she wanted on this trip. I briefly wondered what I could have possibly done to deserve such luck, but by then I felt Jeanette's hand starting to stroke my prick again and decided to leave the analysis of my good fortune for another time.

The next three days were an unbelievable blur of nonstop sex. We fucked, sucked, probed, licked and touched in every way I could imagine, and in some I couldn't. We did it in bed, on the floor, on the beach at night, in the hotel pool, even in the ladies' room at the airport on the day we left. Jeanette acted like she just could not get enough of my cock. If it wasn't in her cunt, she had it in her mouth. And if not that, she was jerking me off with her hands or feet or having me fuck her between the tits. During those times when my dick was recuperating, she would sit on my face while I tongued her to orgasm after writhing orgasm.

When she kissed me good-bye at the airport, she told me to look her up it I ever found myself in Paris. You can guess where I'm planning to go on vacation next!

BOX LUNCH

*W*hen I met Victoria, I was thrilled to discover that we shared the same occupation. We drive eighteen-wheelers, hauling produce all over the country, so we ended up running together for a few months.

Victoria isn't your average trucker. She takes great pride in her appearance. Polished fingernails, perfectly done makeup and styled hair are part of her daily routine. She is about five foot four, one hundred twenty-five pounds, with silky-smooth skin and shiny, dark brown hair. She is very striking. We were really attracted to each other and soon we were involved in the most intimate relationship either of us has ever had. This story is about an afternoon tryst that was so hot that the recollection of it makes me rock-hard.

Last spring I had to take some time off from work due to health reasons. We had been apart for about three weeks and had spoken on the phone only a few times.

Early one morning I received a phone call from her. She told me that she wanted to go for a picnic lunch and canoe ride. I organized the afternoon with eager anticipation.

We met at one o'clock. I wanted to jump into the sleeper of the truck right there and then partake of her fruits. She was wearing a pair of short cutoffs that showed the curve of her firm cheeks and a bright, red blouse. This only increased my desire for her. After she promised that she had something special in store for me, I was persuaded to wait.

The day was warm and sunny—not a cloud in the sky. We paddled along for about two miles. The lake was as smooth as glass. Suddenly Victoria stopped paddling and turned around in her seat, sliding to the floor of the canoe. She said that she was getting hot and undid all the buttons on her blouse. She opened her top just enough so I could see that she was wearing nothing underneath. She exposed a good portion of her breasts, letting the material just barely hide her nipples. By this point I was rock-hard and, as I was wearing only a bathing suit, little was left to her imagination. I really wanted to get the show on the road and diving into her muff would have been a great way to start, but she just sat there sunning herself. Occasionally she would massage her breasts and tweak her nipples, then she would slowly run her hands down her taut, flat stomach and under her cutoffs. She would leave her hands there for a moment or two, rotate her hips against her hands and then stop. I was going nuts with desire. Watching a woman play with herself is something that always turns me on.

I paddled to a spot by the cliffs. We parked the canoe and grabbed the gear that we needed for our lunch. There was a trail up the cliffs that led us to a very secluded spot overlooking the lake. Victoria said that this was our spot and started to lay out the blanket and organize everything. I gladly helped, knowing what was in store. I was ready to start my lunch. I figured a beaver sandwich would be a tasty appetizer. Victoria stood up and took her blouse off, then she seductively slid out of her cutoffs. She asked me to put some suntan lotion on her back, which I promptly did.

After taking care of her back, I worked my way down to her hips. Then I wrapped my arms around her, my oiled hands reaching for her breasts. After massaging her breasts until her nipples were as hard as bullets, I moved my hands down her tight stomach toward her love-nest. She pulled away, insisting that I run down to the canoe to get the cooler. Protesting that my cock was ready to explode, I reluctantly ran back to the canoe.

On the way back up the hill I heard moaning sounds coming from the area where I had left Victoria. When I got back to our site I saw a performance that I shall never forget.

Victoria was lying back on the blanket, her body glistening in the afternoon sun. She was well on her way to orgasm. I stripped out of my bathing suit, ready for action. Victoria was running her hands from her tits to her pussy, teasing herself. She rolled her oiled nipples between her fingers, then pulled them until they slipped out, hard and erect. Then she ran her hands down to her thighs, just above her knees. Her hands slid back up, right to her pussy lips. She pressed hard against her mons. Once more she slid her hands down her thighs, prying her knees apart and drawing them up. She drew her hands back up to her love triangle, moaning with pleasure. Slowly she began to gyrate against the pressure of her hands, building toward her climax. Sitting down at her feet I watched, trembling with excitement. She was too far gone to notice me.

With one hand she spread her lips. The other moved in unison with her hips as she fingered her clit. Suddenly she stopped. She took the finger that was doing all the work and stuck it in her mouth, sucking hard on it. When she drew it out, it was dripping wet with saliva. She reached down once more, this time sliding the finger up inside her cunt. At this point I could wait no longer. I leaned forward and dropped my tongue to her clit. She groaned and started coming. Although she had three quick orgasms back to back, I knew that she wasn't finished.

I knelt in front of her, grabbed my cock and rubbed the swollen head against her super-sensitive clit. She started coming again. I leaned forward and buried myself right to the hilt. She groaned with pleasure. After a few more strokes she came again. Just as she was at the peak, I exploded inside her.

After a few minutes of basking in our euphoria, she pushed me onto my back. Even though I was still fully erect, I was too spent to do anything. We lay side by side for a couple of minutes, then Victoria took over. She sat on my stomach, facing away from me, and started pumping my cock with her hands. Then she guided me back into her pussy, slowly moving her hips in a circular motion. This continued until I was ready to peak again. She stopped, sat upright, drew her knees up beside my hips and leaned forward. This gave me an excellent view of her pussy. With each stroke she took, her pussy lips pulled against my shaft, trying to suck every drop of come out of my cock.

With her pussy oozing, she began inching backwards toward my head. Although I had gone soft, the moment her pussy lips reached my tongue I was hard again. I stretched my tongue up to meet her clit and it was less than a minute before she was coming again. After she came she fell forward, totally exhausted. I ran my hands up her thighs and then slid them to her cunt, spreading her pussy lips apart. When I inserted two fingers into her hot twat, she started rubbing her face into my balls and stroking my cock.

She ran her tongue around the head of my swollen member. As I started rotating my thumb against her clit, she sank her lips down to the base of my cock. Then she spun around so I could watch the best blowjob in the history of mankind take place. After watching for a few moments, I was ready to pop again. Victoria sensed this and increased her speed. She massaged my balls and that was it. Groaning aloud, Victoria sucked every last drop out of me. After a while, we fell asleep in each other's arms. We slept for the rest of the afternoon.

When we woke up, we jumped into the crystal-clear lake. At dusk we headed back to the canoe and the mood for some more tender lovemaking overcame us. We made slow, gentle love in the canoe—the perfect way to end our perfect day.

WILD STRAWBERRIES

I'm a twenty-year-old male in the military. If there's such a thing as a food fetish. I've got it!

This happened about two years ago, and for as long as I live I will never forget it. I was living at home with my parents at the time.

It was Friday night. My parents had left earlier that evening and were going to be gone all weekend. I figured I'd have a party so I called a couple of friends and told them to come on over.

Pete and Dan showed up around nine. We started downing a bottle of tequila. About fifteen minutes later, Bernie showed up with Jane, a tall blonde with a nice body. After the introductions, I headed into the kitchen to mix two more drinks for the late-comers. Bernie followed me.

We talked while I prepared the drinks. "John, how would you like to give Jane the fucking of her life?" Bernie asked me.

Jokingly, I said, "You brought her, you fuck her."

He laughed and said, "No, I mean all four of us. Why not? We're all best friends, and she's one of the horniest women in town!"

I thought about this for a while, then said, "On one condition, I go first." He agreed.

After a few more drinks and some excellent smoke, I went into the kitchen and started making some preparations. Digging through the fridge, I grabbed three pounds of frozen strawberries and a few bananas. Next, I went to the garage and got some thick plastic bags to cover the bed with. When I was done, I went back into the living room to see how everything was going.

They were still sitting around. I whispered to Bernie that he should take Jane downstairs and help her to relax a bit.

As soon as they left, I threw the strawberries in the microwave to thaw them out. When I was done, Dan and Pete came in wearing shit-eating grins. Not long after that, Bernie came running up the stairs. He said, "She's ready." The three of them hurried back down. I was halfway down the stairs before I remembered the strawberries, so I had to run back up and get them. By the time I took them out, they were warm and squishy. I damn near got my rocks off just thinking about what was going to happen! Grabbing the fruit, I flew down the stairs, practically spilling the huge bowl of strawberries in the process.

I followed the trail of clothes to my bedroom. What I saw in there made my cock rock-hard. Jane was lying on her back with Pete's huge prick in her mouth. Her legs were spread invitingly and she was jerking Bernie and Dan off. I stripped as fast as I could, lit some candles and turned out the lights. I grabbed the bowl, walked over to the bed and started pouring. I began with her tits and worked my way down. She let out a muffled moan as the warm, sticky strawberries oozed down her stomach, slowly inching toward her mound. I emptied the last of the bowl onto her beautiful snatch. As I slowly spread her creamy thighs and started licking the strawberries off her pussy, she moaned and bucked, grinding her cunt into my face. She came at least twice. The four of us hungrily licked her clean.

I grabbed a banana, peeled it and slowly started to slide it into her wet pussy. She arched her back and thrust her hips forward to meet it. She went crazy as I fucked her with the banana. I was so into it, I didn't notice that the other three had left. When the banana was coated with her juice. I shoved it as far as it would go and started eating it out of her. I slid around into a 69, jammed my cock down her throat and fucked her mouth for all I was worth. It didn't take long for us to both come in one explosive orgasm.

We kissed and I rubbed the strawberries into her skin. She got a real laugh out of this, and she enjoyed it too. I scooped lots of the sticky fruit on top of her cunt and then I fucked her. My cock was nice and slippery from the strawberries, and I slid in and out of her like lightning. I popped one of her sticky, sweet-tasting nipples into my mouth, and I sucked it while I rode her hot box. When I was about to explode, I pulled out and shot my load.

Not long after that there was a knock at the door. Bernie came in saying, "My turn," and smiled. I could barely get up. I walked out and closed the door. I was covered with strawberries and squashed bananas and pussy juice, and I was thinking that this would be a weekend I'd never forget.

Since then I've tried various other foods—whipped cream, honey and butterscotch pudding. I want to try spaghetti, but I haven't yet found a willing partner.

DUTCH TREAT

*W*hen I joined the army last year I figured it would broaden my horizons. However, after I was promoted to lieutenant and learned I would be transferred to the Netherlands, I must admit I was apprehensive. I didn't know the language or the customs, and was afraid I'd feel alienated. But I soon learned that the Dutch were friendly people who liked Americans. Just how friendly they were I was soon to find out.

My story begins about two months after I arrived in Holland. It was a Friday night. I had been invited to join some Dutch officers for dinner and drinks. Since I knew I wouldn't be able to stay out too late, I opted to drive my own car. I followed them out to what I thought would be a local tavern. We drove through several small villages and down barren country roads. Finally we arrived at our destination. They bought me several mugs of my favorite beer, and soon we were laughing and joking. For dinner I ordered a hearty Dutch specialty, which I enjoyed immensely. After several hours of good food, good drink and good company, I said my good-byes. I would have liked to stay with them for a while longer, but it was already after midnight and I had a full day of work ahead of me.

When I left the tavern, a terrible storm was raging. The night was black as ink, and the rain was coming down in sheets. I wasn't sure if I was going to be able to find my way home, but I was going to give it my best shot. After about thirty minutes of driving in what I had thought was the right direction, I realized I was totally lost. I couldn't even find my way back to the tavern.

I drove on, hoping to find an inn where I could get a room for the night. I was cruising along on a dark, narrow country road when I spied flashing lights ahead. My sagging spirits lifted—I figured that it was the neon sign of an inn or motel.

Much to my disappointment, the flashing lights turned out to be the emergency lights of a stalled camper. I pulled over to see if I could help. I climbed out, pulled my jacket over my head and went over to knock on the driver's window. No one responded to my knock. The camper seemed to be empty. Now, soaking wet as well as lost, I got back into my car and drove on.

Not too far down the road I spied someone moving along the side of the road. Obviously this was either the camper's owner or a local ghost. I pulled up alongside the ghostly specter and tapped on the window, beckoning to the person to get into the car. The door opened and a drenched figure wearing a bulky trench coat and a gray fedora climbed in. It was then that I realized my passenger was a beautiful young woman.

She caught my eye. We stared at each other for an eternal second. She finally broke the silence. With a smile she said, "Thanks for giving me a lift." She had a wonderful British accent.

"My pleasure," I gallantly responded. It appeared that my luck was beginning to change.

"Well, it's not a good night to be out in the rain," she proclaimed, "but it is a good night to be rescued by a handsome prince." This made me blush, which made her chuckle. Still blushing, I sheepishly admitted that I was lost and asked if she knew of a place to stay for the night. She replied, "I am also a stranger to these parts. We'll look for a place together." So the two of us drove on.

About five kilometers down the road we came upon a crossroads with a small farmhouse nestled off to one side. The lights in the house were all off, but we decided to stop anyway. The storm had started to let up a little. I got out and rang the bell. After several rings, a light went on and an old man answered the door.

I tried to explain that we had lost our way and needed a place to stay for the night, but the man didn't understand my English, nor my broken Dutch. I called to my companion to come help me out. She got out of the car and spoke to the man at length in Dutch. Evidently she finally convinced him of our plight, because he ushered us in out of the rain and up the staircase to the second floor.

He spoke to her again as he unlocked one of the rooms, then he left us. We entered and found a large antique featherbed, a dresser, a table and chairs, some towels and a washbasin. I looked around for another room or bed, but this seemed to be it. She was confused by my distress. "Where do I sleep?" I asked.

Pointing to the bed, she said, "Right there, of course."

"Well, where are you sleeping?" I responded.

Without blinking an eye, she said, "I'm sleeping there too. Will that be a problem?"

"No," I quickly replied.

She explained that this was not an inn, but a private home.

The room we were in was a spare room that was used by relatives when they visited. She went on to explain that she had told the man that we were newlyweds, and he had taken pity on us, offering us a bed for the night, as well as a hot meal. "You see," she continued, "only if we were married would he have let us stay together in this room." Coyly she asked if she had done the right thing. My smile convinced her that I completely approved of her plan of action.

The tension in the air was broken by a knock on the door. The man's wife entered, carrying a tray with a steaming tureen, a pot of tea and some plates and mugs. She put the tray down on the nightstand, and my companion thanked her. The woman said good night and withdrew.

The tureen was filled with a thick, savory goulash. The tea was strong and sweet. "Let's eat before the food gets cold," I said, suddenly hungry.

"You eat. First, I'm going to get out of these wet clothes," she replied. As I ate, I watched as she took off her overcoat. She was wearing an emerald-green evening dress. It was still damp and clung tightly to her body. She was about five feet seven and one hundred twenty pounds, with medium-size breasts, a small waist and slender hips.

She hung the coat up and stopped to look at me. I was still staring at her. She smiled and pulled her gray fedora off. This unleashed a mass of lush auburn hair, which tumbled halfway down her back. Reaching behind her, she unzipped her dress and let it fall to the floor. I caught only a glimpse of lacy black lingerie before she wrapped a towel around her body. I immediately started to get a hard-on. Taking another towel, she patted her body dry and worked it over her damp hair.

I poured her some tea. She sat down across the table from me and brought the cup to her lips. A warm glow came to her cheeks as she sipped the steaming liquid. I got hard just watching her. She realized this and smiled, enjoying my discomfort. When I finished my stew she said, "You'll catch a cold if you don't get out of those wet clothes."

Not wanting to argue, I got up and moved over to the bed. She watched, amused by the reversal of roles. I stripped to my briefs. It was obvious that, even from across the room, she could see the bulge straining against my briefs. As I reached for the last dry towel, she stood up and moved toward me. "It looks as if you could use some assistance drying off. Let me help you," she said. She took the towel from my hands.

She began to work vigorously on my body. As she rubbed, her towel came undone and fell to the floor, revealing a black, lacy, front-closing bra and matching bikini panties. I stared at her lovely globes, heaving with every breath. Constrained, they clearly longed to be free. I tested the waters by cupping a hand around one of those beauties and giving it a gentle squeeze. She smiled and moved closer. I deftly unfastened her bra. She shrugged the straps off her shoulders.

We kissed for the first time, timidly at first, then long and hard. She rested a hand on my ass and gave it a squeeze. Her breasts were hot against my chest. She moaned softly as I cupped her ass-cheeks and pulled her tightly against me. We moved in unison, our bodies pressed together. All that separated us from ecstasy were two pieces of terry cloth. She was dripping with passion. Gently I massaged her mound of Venus. Moaning with pleasure, she began the rhythmic dance of love.

Sliding her tongue from my mouth, she circled my erect nipples before gently licking them. My cock throbbed every time she moved. I sighed with pleasure. Her tongue cut a wet path down my chest. She slid my briefs off, then stopped, poised in front of my pulsing member. Making an O with her moist lips, she kissed the tip of my cock. Looking up at me, she said, "Now I want to thank you properly for rescuing me from the cold night." She slowly slid her lips over my electric rod. It was all I could do to just hold on.

When she pulled back, my cock emerged from her mouth glistening wetly. But then her lips were tugging it again, taking in a little more each time until, finally, there was no more to take. I panicked with excitement. Beads of sweat were forming on my brow. I grasped her by the shoulders and guided her to her feet. Her lips glistened with pre-come and saliva. Her eyes were wild with passion.

"Not yet," I said. "It's too early to finish. Besides, now it's your turn." I kissed her long and hard. Our tongues searched each other out. I drew little circles around her erect nipples with my forefinger. They sparked with every touch, as if charged with static electricity. I pressed my lips around her nipples and tickled them with the tip of my tongue. She swooned, and I had to support her.

My strength waning, I slowly eased her down onto the mattress. Standing over her supine body, I slipped her panties off. Gently spreading her legs, I glided my engorged member into her waiting pussy. She was very tight, so progress was slow. I worked my cock in a little at a time. I was halfway in when she reached out and pulled me down on top of her, smothering me with kisses. Then, with one mighty thrust, I rammed my rod inside her to the hilt.

With a groan of passion, she whispered in my ear, "Fuck me. Fuck me hard." Bracing myself, I repeatedly slid my pulsing member in and out of her dripping pussy. She moaned softly as we both exploded in ecstasy. We lay intertwined, exhausted, until we fell asleep.

The next thing I remember was hearing a rooster crow loudly and seeing rays of sunshine darting through the windowpane. A knock on the door brought me completely to my senses. I suddenly realized I was in a bit of a predicament. You see, I usually wake up in the morning with a hard-on. Normally this is not a problem. However, we had fallen asleep in the same position that we had made love in, and now I found myself stuck inside my companion while someone banged on the door. I tried to pull out, but the juices of the previous night had dried up. My bedmate howled with laughter at my futile attempts. She reached for a mug on the night table and poured cold tea onto the problem area. The shock of feeling cold tea on my cock was enough to separate us.

I jumped to my feet, pulled on my pants and opened the door just a crack. I spied the same old woman from the night before with a breakfast tray. Pushing me aside, she entered the room, set the tray down and took the dinner plates away. My "wife" just sat there on the bed, naked, not saying a word. I looked at her in total disbelief, and we both burst out laughing. All she could say was, "Well, shall we eat?" After breakfast we made love again. Satisfied, we washed up and got into our clothes.

Finding the farmer, I thanked him for his kindness and paid him well. As we were leaving I looked up at our bedroom window and saw the old woman staring down at us. We waved and blew her a kiss. She smiled and waved back. I bet she was blushing a little. I know I was. We returned to my companion's camper and picked up some of her belongings, along with a few maps of the area. After we figured out where we were, I drove her home and headed back to my base. We see each other regularly now, and I am thinking of extending my stay overseas.

ALL HANDS ON DECK

No sexual experience I've ever had can compare to the one I enjoyed this past weekend. I had to write this as soon as possible because I don't trust my memory and if I wait to write I might leave something out. I certainly wouldn't want my husband to miss out on reading about my weekend fucking seven different men.

His favorite fantasy is to see me with other men, and I hadn't indulged him for a number of years.

My coworker Rachel had told me that part of my initiation to my new firm would be to let Herman, the owner, have a turn with me. After hearing her describe his equipment, I was definitely ready when Herman called and invited me on his boat for an overnight sail to the Cape.

On Saturday morning I packed a small bag, put on my new bathing suit under a pair of skimpy shorts and headed for the marina. My new suit is a white string bikini that shows off my ass. The top is a little too small, but I wanted to look as good as Rachel, who has one of those figures you wished you had—long legs, slim thighs, a tight butt and big tits. She has it all, but I've kept my five-foot-four body in great shape—and while I can't compete with her thighs, I definitely have her beaten in the boob department. My tits measure 37D and since I had kids, my nipples have become very big and prominent. I usually try to hide them, but not this day. I shouldn't have worried, because when I got to the boat I found only Herman, his partner Lou and a guy named Rob, whom I had never met. Herman told me that Rachel didn't feel well and had decided to stay home, but that I could handle her duties. "What duties?" I asked. Lou replied, "Drinks, drugs and decoration, what else?" He then laughed and introduced me to Rob. Rob was twenty-five and worked as a contractor. He had strong arms and hands to prove it.

Things got pretty busy then, and while the guys steered the boat I found a place to get some sun. I was dozing off when I heard Herman call for me. I went back and found the guys passing a joint. I asked, "Who's driving the boat?"

Herman said, "Don't worry about anything," as he passed me the joint. This stuff was powerful and hit me almost immediately. Pot affects me the same way as alcohol in that it really gets my juices going. I could feel my nipples expanding as I held the rich smoke in my lungs. After a few more hits I went below and brought up a pitcher of Herman's famous kamikazes. We were all having a great time, laughing and talking, when Lou said, "Well, I see drinks and drugs. Where's the decoration?"

Herman chimed in, "Yeah. Take off your shorts and let us see your ass."

I slowly stood up, unbuttoned my shorts and let them drop to the floor. "Okay?" I asked. There was silence for a long moment and I felt their eyes boring holes through me. Then Herman said, "You're beautiful, but we all have our shirts off and you're still wearing your top." He came over to me and, with one quick move, untied my top so it dangled from my breasts.

Lou grabbed one of the strings and slowly pulled it until my top slid away and my tits were exposed to the guys' lustful gaze. "We have to be careful lest these beauties get sunburned," Herman said. He handed Rob a bottle of tanning oil and said, "Why don't you do the honors?"

With a sexy smile Rob slowly dripped the lotion onto my tits. "Does it feel good?" he asked. I could only nod as he slowly massaged my tits.

Every time he touched my nipples I felt an electric shock run straight to my pussy. I could feel the juices oozing from between my legs. I spread my thighs apart in hopes that one of them would get the hint, but it became obvious that these guys were pacing themselves. I knew then that the next twenty-four hours were going to be wild.

Herman and Lou left us to adjust the sails, but Rob stayed with me and continued teasing my nipples. By this time I was on the verge of orgasm, and couldn't stop myself from sliding my hand up his leg and wedging it into his crotch. I yanked his suit down, grabbed his cock and slowly pumped his shaft. He was really well-hung! His cock felt like a lead pipe in my hands and, as I squeezed him, a drop of pre-come blossomed at the tip. I smeared it all over his cockhead and was pleased to hear him groan at my touch. I pulled him closer to me so I could get him in my mouth and give him a blowjob. I sucked and licked him until he pulled away, saying that I was going to make him come too fast. I said, "You can always come again. Do it now." I sucked him into my throat until he shot his load. I could barely keep his seed in my mouth. His come dribbled out of my lips and dripped onto my breasts. He pulled out and smiled at me as I lay down to rest. When Herman came back he said to Rob, "You might as well keep your suit off, because you'll never get that big hunk of meat back inside." Rob laughed and said, "Not when she's around, that's for sure."

I knew I was acting like a slut, but I was too hot to care. When Herman reached down and squeezed my pussy I thought I would come on the spot. Suddenly he took his hand away and dropped his shorts. His big cock dangled before me, begging to be eaten. Even soft, it was huge. The shaft was thick and heavily veined, and his balls were big, round and firm. My inspection of his magnificent cock was interrupted when I felt his fingers trace the outline of my pussy lips, pressing the nylon of my bikini into my damp slit. I opened my mouth, took his soft cock inside and licked him until he began to grow. It grew to such mammoth proportions there was no way I could hold it all. Soon only the head was in my mouth. His huge shaft stretched out a good eight or nine inches in front of me. I massaged his meat with both hands and it wasn't long before I tasted his come.

Lou approached me and asked if there was anything left for him. "Just her pussy," Rob said as he walked away. Rob stayed on deck as Herman and Lou took me below to Herman's cabin. Lou pulled off the rest of my suit and showed me his cock, which was the biggest I had ever seen. It was at least ten inches long and even thicker than Herman's. Lou knelt down to lap at my pussy while Herman nestled his dick between my tits. He was so big that every time he thrust forward I was able to take his cockhead into my mouth again. When I started to come, Herman pushed Lou out of the way and slowly pushed his cock into my pussy. I felt every heavenly inch as he stretched me wide open. My pussy had never felt so full. I wrapped my legs around him when he finally hit bottom. My clit tingled as orgasm after orgasm burst through me. He pulled out, then plunged back in and pumped harder and harder until I thought I would die from the pleasure. Suddenly I felt him stiffen. His cock throbbed as he pumped me full of come. When he pulled out I felt a rush of juice ooze down my leg. As he left the room he said, "Why don't you catch some more rays before we really start to party?"

Lou kissed me and offered another joint, which I sucked on eagerly, but what I really wanted was more cock.

After I cleaned myself up, I went back up to the deck in only my bikini bottom. I spent the rest of the afternoon working on my tan while the guys worked on steering the boat and getting us all stoned. The pot was great and I felt totally relaxed, but my mind was filled with thoughts of sex. I thought about my husband—if he knew what I had been doing he probably would have invited his entire softball team over for a party. I could just imagine all those men wanting to fuck me, their hard cocks drooling in anticipation, pumping me until I came. The images were so vivid that I couldn't help but touch myself.

"Need some help?" I opened my eyes to see Herman standing before me, his long cock swinging between his legs. I smiled and reached for him, but he pulled me up and took me below, where Rob and Lou were preparing some snacks for cocktail hour.

Rob was naked and Lou's suit was so small it could hardly contain his cock. Herman said, "You guys nearly missed a great show," as he pulled out a bag and handed it to me. I looked inside and found a variety of sex toys and lubricants. "Now you can finish what you were doing," Herman said as he led our little group to his cabin.

The men got comfortable in anticipation of my performance. Rob's cock started to expand as I reached into the bag and pulled out a dildo. It was about fourteen inches long and shaped like a cock, with a large head and thick shaft. I lay back on the bed and positioned myself so they could see my pussy as I began to play. I started to spread my lips apart, but my pussy was sticky from the fucking Herman had given me so I had to slide my finger along the crease in order to expose my clit. As I lightly flicked at my clit, I looked at the men and saw their cocks swelling in appreciation. I grabbed the dildo and rubbed it on my pussy until it was slippery with juice, then slowly inserted the big head. At first it seemed as if it wouldn't fit, but my pussy gradually opened wider until I could slide half of it in with each stroke. My clit was totally exposed now, and with each thrust of the dildo my body tensed with ecstasy. Herman reached over and flicked a switch, which turned on the vibrator inside the dildo. I thought I would pass out as I came over and over again. I continued to pump it until I reached a level of excitement I had never known before. I was totally out of control, and I found myself begging them to fuck me. Herman removed the dildo and rammed his huge cock into my cunt.

The pleasure was so intense I couldn't help but scream. Herman came with a shout and pulled out as I continued to twitch. Lou immediately took his place and filled me with his cock in one thrust. It felt so good to have another hot, throbbing cock inside me that I thrust up against him so he could plunge even deeper into me. He obliged by fucking me harder and harder. I was starting to come again when he pulled out. Herman pulled me on top of him and took another turn pounding my pussy. As I rode him I felt my juices running down my thighs. The squishy sounds of sex filled the cabin. He played with my tits as I bounced on top of him. Suddenly Herman rolled me over and positioned me on my hands and knees. After he had reinserted his huge shaft inside me, Rob knelt in front of me so I could lick and suck him.

Rob and Herman stopped moving for a moment. Then they began to move in rhythm—Herman steadily fucking my cunt and Rob fucking my mouth. It was the most intense feeling I have ever had. I felt another orgasm building, and panted and bucked as I went over the edge. They came as well and I felt rivers of come fill my body.

After they pulled out, Rob came over with a towel and helped me clean up. As he tenderly wiped me off, he leaned over and gave me a long, slow lick from head to toe. Even though I was exhausted, the feel of his tongue made my juices flow again. I gasped in pleasure at his touch, and was very disappointed when

he stopped and went on deck with the others. I must have fallen
asleep after that, because the next thing I knew I heard different
voices outside. I looked at the clock and found that it was nine-
thirty at night.

I looked out the window and saw that we had hooked up with
another boat. There seemed to be a wild party going on. Lou was
on the other boat smoking a joint, and Herman was calling for his
"grog" like a pirate. I quickly went up to join the party.

I was greeted with a loud cheer. Herman said he figured I was
asleep for the night. He introduced me to the crew of the other
boat, and I was pleased to see that they were as young and good-
looking as my friends. I got a bit apprehensive when I realized
that I was the only woman, but my nervousness disappeared after
a drink.

I sat up on the deck with Lou and a man from the other boat
named Jim. While we shared a joint, Lou rubbed my shoulders.
Jim said, "I could use a little of that," so he sat down between my
legs and I massaged his shoulders and upper back. Lou began to
get a bit playful, squeezing my nipples and stroking the sides of
my breasts. It felt good, but I kept silent because I didn't want Jim
to know what was happening. When Lou tried to pull my shirt off
I had to raise my arms, so Jim turned around to see why I stopped
his massage. He received a bird's-eye view of my big breasts
spilling out of my bikini top. He turned back around without saying a word, and I resumed working on his muscular shoulders
while Lou resumed working on my tits.

I felt Lou untie my top, then felt his nimble fingers all over my
naked breasts. As he touched me I got more and more turned on.
Unconsciously my hands slid around Jim's body to feel his muscular chest. I knew he was enjoying it because his breathing
quickened, and he had to change his position to create more
room for his growing cock. Lou had taken his cock out of his
shorts and was slowly dry-humping me from behind with long,
slow strokes. I reached between Jim's legs and gabbed his cock.

He gasped when I touched the large, swollen head that was

protruding from the waistband of his shorts. I could feel the sticky pre-come oozing from his slit as I squeezed his thick shaft. I panted, "Let me see it," so he quickly turned around and spread his legs for me. I pulled his shorts down and squealed with pleasure as his heavy cock sprang into view. I started to suck on him, and he groaned loudly as I slid my mouth up and down his shaft. Lou took advantage of this position and slid his cock into me doggie-style. Jim didn't last very long. After only a few minutes he stiffened and shot his load down my throat. He thanked me and walked away, leaving me with Lou's cock still thrusting into my swollen pussy and his hands cupping my tits.

Jim must have told his shipmates about what happened, because it wasn't long before I looked up to see two more guys from the other boat standing before me with their hard cocks in their hands. I ended up sucking both of them to orgasm before Lou finally came.

Lou and I went to the back of the boat to find Herman and Adam, the captain of the other boat, waiting for us. Adam asked if I'd like a tour of his boat, and as we carefully walked over and went down to his cabin, I knew exactly what he wanted. His boat was larger than Herman's, and his cabin was outfitted with a stereo system and a bar. He made me a drink, then we sat down on the edge of the bed and talked. His eyes continually dropped down to my tits and the hard nipples jutting through my shirt. When he'd look back at me I returned the favor by looking directly at his crotch and his growing bulge. Suddenly he reached up and lightly flicked one nipple, then the other, which sent shocks to my clit. He pushed me back on the bed, pulled my shirt up and sucked my nipples. After a few minutes he stood up and pulled off his shorts.

Adam's cock was hard, thick and hot. I pulled him between my legs and guided his missile into my pussy. I couldn't believe how easy it had become for me to fuck another man. Just the sight of a hard cock and I was ready. Adam pumped me with fast, hard strokes until he came. He pulled out immediately, only to be replaced by Jim, then George and Eric (the two men I had blown earlier). I lost count of how many times each one entered me and how many times I came. The evening was a blur. Finally Herman came aboard and carried me back to his boat.

I fell asleep in Herman's cabin and didn't wake up until we were nearly home. The morning was bright and beautiful, and while my body was tired, my pussy still oozed and tingled.

My husband met me at the dock and I could tell right away that he knew what had happened. I introduced him to Herman and the guys, then all of us headed for a pub to celebrate our successful voyage. But that's another story.

A GIRL CALLED SPIKE

*W*hen I was twenty, I used to ride with a gang of bikers. We had a ball, partying every night until the sun rose. Biker parties are the best—there's always plenty of wild chicks running around.

I'm not a bad-looking man, but I am honest enough to admit that I'm not every chick's fantasy come to life either. I'm five foot seven, weigh almost two hundred pounds, have brown hair and brown eyes. I rode a Harley back then and, believe me, no woman ever came between me and my bike.

Anyway, at one party I was introduced to a woman named Jeannie. Jeannie, at the time, was thirty-one and built like a goddess. She had shoulder-length blonde hair, green eyes and weighed about one hundred twenty pounds. She was only five feet tall. Everybody called her Spike for some reason.

After someone introduced us, she stuck to me like glue. I didn't mind. She was hot.

Later that night Jeannie and I, along with a couple of friends, decided to head out to a concert. As the night wore on, I became quite attached to Jeannie. We started talking as if we were old friends, even though we had known each other only a short while. The concert ended and we all got ready to split. I kissed her, and we promised to meet at an upcoming party.

That Friday night, when I arrived at Stinkin' Steve's house for the party, I was surprised to find that there were about forty guys and only six women there. Jeannie was one of them. It took all of ten seconds before the two of us were seriously making out.

The party got into swing real quick. Beer flowed like water. We also had Jack Daniel's and Wild Turkey. Nice, thick joints were passed around.

Jeannie and I were sitting on the small couch near the corner, and we were getting friendly. I noticed at that time that all the other women were nowhere to be found. I paid no attention since I had Jeannie.

At about six that night, Jeannie told me to follow her. We headed toward one of the back bedrooms. While we were on our way, we could hear loud moaning coming from another bedroom. We looked in and saw the three women and a group of guys going at it like there was no tomorrow. We watched for a while and received quite a sight, but soon grew more interested in each other.

I have to tell you, this woman was a fireball of passion. Now, I'm no John Holmes, as I've stated earlier, but I think I am more than able to please a woman. As soon as we were behind the closed door, Jeannie was on the floor fighting to remove my clothes. All I could do was sit back and enjoy. She quickly had my cock so far down her throat, I was amazed. While working on my cock, she slipped out of her top. I don't think it took her more than one minute to get fully undressed.

I was still dressed, with my cock hanging out of my fly. I told her to stop for a second so that I could get out of the rest of my clothes.

We got into a 69. I must say, she had one of the sweetest cunts I have ever tasted. She worked on me for a good twenty minutes before allowing me to come. And when I did, she shoved my cock all the way down her throat so she could get every drop.

She was smiling after that. I pulled her down onto her back, crawled on top and went to work sucking her cunt. She started moaning and telling me to fuck her already. Well, I believe in making a woman happy, so I quickly agreed. I got on top and slid my cock into her as slowly as possible. I didn't think she would ever stop coming. Her legs shot up over my shoulders. Once she had settled down I used long, slow strokes.

We must have been screwing for a solid hour before I could feel my orgasm approaching. I slowed down so that she could catch up to me. It was great when we exploded together.

It seemed only a few minutes had passed before she grabbed my cock and pulled me up onto her chest. She placed my cock between her tits. I began thrusting back and forth. Jeannie sucked the tip of my cock. She really enjoyed getting tit-fucked. When I finally came in her mouth, it was great! Jeannie thought so too, since she licked my cock clean.

We went back and joined everyone else. Soon the party really got going. Everybody got fucked up and ripped their clothes off. It was like an indoor nudist camp. Then Jeannie told me she was going to the bathroom.

About forty-five minutes went by. I started getting head from this one chick, so I didn't notice time slip by. Then someone called to me from one of the bedrooms. When I stepped into the bedroom, I got a real shock. There was my Jeannie, on the bed with legs stretched back so that her ankles were on her shoulders. She was fucking herself with a thick black dildo. When she realized how many guys were in the bedroom watching her, she told us to gather around the bed. She got on all fours, without removing the dildo, and started sucking and licking our cocks one at a time.

I don't think there was a limp cock in the house. Everybody wanted Jeannie. So without further delay, I reached down and pulled the dildo from her cunt. She moaned loudly. While one guy was getting his stick licked, I crawled up behind her and slid into a cunt that was so hot I thought my cock was going to burn off. I didn't want to come just then, so I pulled out and worked my cockhead up and down her slit to get her even hotter. I spit on my cock and slowly worked it back in. She was quite tight for a woman who seemed to enjoy fucking so much.

As I slowly stroked in and out of her, she pulled her lips away from the cock she was sucking. Her mouth was full of come, as the guy had orgasmed between her lips. After swallowing the guy's load, she turned her head and told me to take my time because she wanted me to last the entire ride.

She hung her head over the edge of the bed and resumed sucking cock as if she was born to it. While she was doing this, one of the other guys got on her and fucked her tits. She held them together to help him. All that time I was fucking her cunt like a battering ram. I must have been on the verge of coming about five different times, but each time I stopped and waited for the approaching orgasm to melt away.

So, there I was, fucking sweet Jeannie's pussy and watching the action happening around me. She had a cock in her mouth and one between her tits. When the guy fucking her mouth was about to explode, she yanked him out and jerked him off, adding his load onto her chest. It was a sight to see!

She finally took the last cock between her lips. It didn't take him more than five minutes to come. When she realized she'd finished them all, she told them to leave the room so she could be alone with me. I was pleasantly surprised, to say the least!

When they were all gone, she got on her hands and knees and told me to keep right on fucking her. While I did that, Jeannie grabbed the Wild Turkey and started licking the neck of the bottle. I reached around and played with her tits. I love nothing more than a set of large, firm tits. Her tits met all the requirements, with nipples as hard as rocks. It was then I realized why they called her Spike. It was because her nipples were like spikes.

I was reaching another orgasm. Jeannie started whimpering as

I shot my load. When I was spent, I pulled out. Jeannie took my cock in her mouth and sucked it back to life. When I finally got hard again, I told her to sit on my cock and ride me. She did so, riding me as if she were a jockey. At one point she leaped so high my wet cock flopped out. Then she leaned over and put her tits right in my face and told me to suck her nipples. She told me to let her know when I was going to come, because she wanted it in her mouth.

When we finished, it took us twenty minutes to clean up in the shower. I'm glad I met Jeannie. To this day she and I are happy together. She doesn't mess around as much as she used to, but when she wants to, I allow it. There is nothing like a big-titted woman to show a man what fucking is all about. Whoever said more than a mouthful is a waste didn't know what he was talking about.

MORE THAN A MOUTHFUL

I have always been excited by women with large breasts. My wife Angie keeps me more than happy in this department.

Angie's best friend is Julia. They shared a room back when they were in college. Julia has breasts of truly astounding proportions. She never dated much as far as I could tell. The thought of those tits not giving or receiving pleasure truly disappointed me.

Julia and I used to have fairly explicit discussions about sex and masturbation. I never thought I'd ever get to enjoy her delights.

About a year after we graduated from college, Julia came to town to see a play with us. To avoid the late-night drive home, she asked if she could spend the evening with us. We, of course, agreed.

After spending an enjoyable evening at the theater, we went

back to the house. My wife was working the night shift that week, so she changed clothes and left. Julia and I were alone as we prepared to retire.

I realized that this was my big chance. I got out the vibrator I'd given my wife last Christmas and went into the living room. Julia, clad in only a long flannel shirt, was lounging on the couch writing in her diary.

"Remember those discussions we had in college, when you were wondering whether it was okay to masturbate?" I asked her.

"Yes," she said.

"Do you masturbate?"

"Oh, yes. It's quite enjoyable, to say the least."

"Glad to hear you say that. May I ask what you've used?" As I said, our previous discussions were pretty straightforward, so even this frank question didn't faze her in the slightest.

"Not too much. I usually just use my fingers," she casually replied.

"Ever try a vibrator?"

Julia's eyebrows raised. I could see she was interested. Then she asked, "Why? Do you have one?"

"Funny you should ask . . ." I sat beside her on the couch and let her examine the toy for a little while. Then I showed her how to turn it on.

"It can be used on any part of the body," I remarked. I pressed it against the side of one of her breasts and gently ran it up and down. Even through the flannel shirt it stimulated her. She tensed and drew back. As calmly as I could, I told her to relax and allow the demonstration to give her the full effect. She thought a minute, then shrugged. She rested her head back on the couch and let me continue. Soon I was caressing her nipples with the vibrator's golden tip. I was dying to pull her shirt off so that I could finally see those huge white globes of quivering flesh.

Julia immensely enjoyed what I was doing to her. I put my hand on her knee and tried to pull her legs apart. She tensed up again. It took a little coaxing and reassuring, but I was finally able to convince her that there was nothing wrong with what we were doing, that it was simply good, clean fun between good friends. She spread her legs, and I ran the buzzing vibrator along her inner thighs. I worked my way upward and began to rub her pussy through her panties.

By now Julia was enjoying herself without reservation. She placed her hand over mine and helped guide the vibrator. I knew I had it made. I reached up with my free hand and squeezed her large, heaving breasts. I held the firm flesh through her shirt and bra and rolled her nipples between my fingers. When I suggested she get comfortable so we could do the job right, she raised her hips and pulled her panties off. I unbuttoned her shirt and helped her off with it. From behind her, I undid the hooks that held her bra tight, then slowly lifted the cups off the huge twin globes.

I watched in awe as her giant white tits flopped down onto her tummy, then rolled off to each side of her chest as she lay down on the couch. I picked up the vibrator again, wet it in my mouth and placed it on her bare pussy. She gasped and arched her back at the contact. I worked the vibrator around the opening of her pussy for a while, occasionally touching her clitoris. Finally pushed the tool inside her. She let out a soft, low moan, then placed her hand over mine and helped me bury it inside her to the hilt.

Then she took over, slowly moving the vibrator in and out of her hungry pussy. I stroked her thighs briefly, then concentrated on those huge, delicious breasts that had enchanted me for so many years.

Julia continued working on herself with the vibrator while buried my face between her tits, luxuriating in the feeling of having the soft, smooth flesh press against each side of my face.

All this time she continued to move the vibrator in and out of her pussy. She was working her way toward one monster of an orgasm. When her climax hit, she let out a scream and jammed the vibrator deep into her cunt. I pressed my fingers deep into the soft flesh of her hot tits. As her spasms subsided, I relaxed my grip and started tenderly kneading and stroking her tits. She turned the vibrator off and slowly pulled it out. She opened her eyes, looked at me and said, "Wow. What a kick. Thanks."

"I thought you'd like it. Now, while you're recovering, I have another question for you. Have you ever watched a man masturbate?"

My cock felt like it was about to burst. My balls felt swollen and heavy. I just had to get off somehow.

"No, but I've always wanted to watch a man jerk off," Julia said thoughtfully. "If you feel like demonstrating, go right ahead."

I quickly shed my pajamas and stretched out on the floor. I reached down, stroked my hard prick with one hand and rubbed my balls with the other. I kept my eyes on Julia's plump, naked body, explaining that I'd never jerked off in front of a woman before. My tempo gradually increased. Julia started fingering her clit and rubbing her big tits while intently watching me jerk off.

She sat down beside me. I moved my head onto her lap. While I continued my demonstration, I stroked, squeezed and nibbled her tits, which were hanging down onto my face. Julia pitched in by rubbing my chest and thighs while continuing to watch my hand pumping away.

As my orgasm approached, I slowed my tempo and warned Julia to watch. The closer I got, the slower I stroked. Soon I had the strongest orgasm I'd ever experienced. Big spurts of come shot three feet into the air, landing on my stomach and chest. A few drops even splattered Julia's breasts. She curiously lifted each breast and licked the drops. I couldn't tell from her expression whether or not she liked the taste.

I got up and started to pull my clothes on.

"It certainly has been an enjoyable, educational evening," she said. "Mind if I keep the vibrator?"

After what we'd just been through, how could I refuse? I invited her to spend the night with me.

I set the alarm to go off an hour before my wife returned from work. That would leave Julia plenty of time to return to the couch. We settled down to sleep. She lay with her back to me. I gently cupped her breasts.

I bought a new vibrator the next day, before my wife had a chance to notice her old one was missing. To this day, I wonder what Julia ended up writing in her diary that night.

THE WIDOW MAKER

*L*ast night a very strange yet touching thing happened to me. I boarded a flight at O'Hare Airport in Chicago on my way to a business trip in San Francisco. Next to me, in the window seat, was an attractive older woman who, I later learned, was sixty-one years old. I have always found women of all ages attractive. I enjoy checking out ladies in their fifties just as much as those who, like me, are in their twenties. I noticed that she had a trim figure, a well-endowed chest and wonderful legs—and she was dressed entirely in black. I started to read a book, but heard her crying. So I put my book down and asked what was wrong.

The woman apologized for distracting me and said she couldn't help crying. She introduced herself as Arlene and went on to explain that her husband had just died after a long bout with cancer. She was returning from burying him at his family's plot in New York. I encouraged her to talk, thinking that this might make her feel better, and by the time we began our descent into San Francisco, Arlene and I were chatting like old friends.

I noticed that she had slipped her shoes off. To someone with a foot fetish, such as me, it resulted in an instant erection. The sight of this widow's shapely feet and well-manicured toes encased in sheer, black hose was driving me wild.

By the time we landed I was quite heated up. Arlene and I deplaned with the rest of the passengers and picked up our luggage. She told me she couldn't bear to spend that first night at home without her husband, so I suggested she get a room in the hotel where I was staying. She thought it was a good idea, and we took a cab there together.

Unfortunately, upon arriving we learned that the hotel was booked up. The desk clerk called around, but all the area hotels were full due to a convention. I offered Arlene my room and told her I'd sleep in the lobby. She thanked me, but said she would only accept if I stayed in the room. I insisted that she take the bed, and I offered to sleep on the floor. She agreed to go upstairs and said, "We'll settle the sleeping arrangements later."

We took turns showering. I came out of the bathroom wrapped in a towel. Arlene was making up a bed for herself on the floor. My cock stiffened at the sight of her in a short robe, cut well above the knee. A vision of her lovely legs wrapped around my waist flashed through my mind.

Arlene and I haggled some more over who would sleep where, until I finally convinced her to take the bed. She did so, and I curled up on the floor. Once under the blanket, I pulled off my towel and tried to get comfortable. I watched Arlene walk to the bed and turn out the light. The drapes weren't fully closed, and thanks to the light coming into the room I caught a glimpse of Arlene as she untied her robe and let it drop to the floor. I was surprised to see that she, too, was naked! With wide eyes I watched her firm ass and legs as she pulled down the blankets. As she eased herself between the sheets, I got a good look at her full, mature breasts. I drifted off to sleep and was soon having erotic dreams involving the widow sleeping naked only a few feet from me.

Sometime during the night I awoke and stumbled to the bathroom to relieve myself. Still half asleep, I automatically went to the bed and started to pull back the sheets to get in. I saw Arlene's sleeping form in the bed and suddenly remembered the circumstances. I was about to drop the sheets and return to my bed on the floor when Arlene muttered in her sleep, "Ted, stop standing there and get into bed. You're making me cold." Ted, as I recalled from our conversation on the plane, was her deceased husband.

Arlene then reached out, grabbed me by the arm and pulled me into the bed. I settled down between the sheets, determined to slip out as soon as she was fully asleep again. However, Arlene prevented my escape by rolling into my arms with her head on my chest and one leg wrapped around mine.

I lay there, awake, for about twenty minutes. With each passing second my erection grew more insistent as I felt Arlene's breasts pressing into my side and chest. Her cunt hair tickled my thigh each time she shifted her position. My dick grew so stiff and tall that I soon felt it touch Arlene's hand. I was speechless when her hand slipped off her thigh and curled around my cock!

Arlene began to stroke my aching cock and muttered in a sleepy voice, "I see you brought me a present, Ted. I've missed it and boy, do I need it." I was convinced that Arlene was still asleep and thought I was her dead husband Ted. I was debating what to do, when she abruptly threw off the covers and rose to her hands and knees. Arlene raised her left leg, eased it over my hips and leaned forward to give me a passion-filled kiss. I felt her position my cock at the entrance to her pussy as she probed my tonsils with her tongue. I noted that throughout all of this, her eyes were still closed.

After several moments of kissing, the head of my cock began to pry her warm pussy lips apart. I watched as her eyelids slowly started to rise. The shock and surprise on her face was a sight I will always remember. She said, "You're not Ted!" but that didn't seem to change her mind about wanting to get fucked. She wiggled her hips from side to side, slowly working her way down my fat, hard rod. I still wasn't sure if she was really surprised to see me or if this was all just some fantasy she needed to act out, but it couldn't have mattered less. The fiery grip of Arlene's cunt took hold of my tool and sucked it all the way in.

And then nature took over. Arlene's hips moved instinctively and with the expertise of a woman who'd been riding cock all her life. My hips automatically began moving with hers. Arlene's mouthing of such words as "Yes, yes, it feels so good" soon gave way to animal grunts and cries of, "That's it, give me that dick. Give it hard!"

In between her groans and gasps, Arlene told me it had been two years since she'd had sex. Apparently her husband had been too sick to fuck her for a long time, and she'd been so busy looking after him she didn't have time to take care of her own sexual needs.

Arlene's hips were moving so fast they were a blur, and she soon climaxed in a series of orgasms that released two years of pent-up frustration. My cock, tormented for a mere six or seven hours by the presence of this shapely widow, soon demanded its own release. "Come inside me, honey," Arlene urged. "I want to feel your load." I was soon blasting a torrent of thick love-milk deep into her long-neglected pussy.

Arlene collapsed into my arms and cried tears of happiness and joy at her sexual release. If she felt any remorse at being in bed with a stranger only a few days after her husband's death, it soon passed, for in just a few minutes she was kissing her way down my chest and stomach to my cock.

Arlene licked up the juices that were still clinging to my cock, then took me into her mouth. Her bobbing head soon had me erect and ready for action once more. I rolled her over and eased my cock into her waiting snatch. This time she was wet and waiting for me.

My mouth found her breasts, and I sucked her big, erect nipples deep into my mouth. With her legs wrapped tightly around my waist, I rammed my cock deep into her cunt with all my strength. Arlene came several times, crying out for more as I hammered away. I kept changing the depth and pace of my strokes to maximize her pleasure and to prolong my own coming.

When I was close to orgasm again, I pulled out of Arlene's cunt and placed my throbbing cock between her breasts. I began to pump in and out between the two mounds of heavenly flesh. Arlene had raised her head and was licking the tip of my cock with each stroke. Knowing I was on the edge, I released Arlene's breasts and placed my cock in her mouth. It only took a couple of in-and-out thrusts for me to pump a load of semen into her hot mouth and down her throat.

We finally fell off to sleep. The next morning, before checking out, I screwed Arlene doggie-style on the floor and shot my come all over the bed. After I'd confided to her that I was a foot fetishist, Arlene put on her black nylons and jerked me off with her feet. I shot my final load all over those sheer stockings, which she then gave to me as a souvenir of our brief time together.